USA TODAY bestselling in London, England. SI
teenage sons—which gives her rather
an insight into the male psyche—and also works
as a film journalist. She adores her job, which
involves getting swept up in a world of high
emotion, sensual excitement, funny and feisty
women, sexy and tortured men and glamorous
locations where laundry doesn't exist. Once she
turns off her computer she often does chores—
usually involving laundry!

Millie Adams is the very dramatic pseudonym of
New York Times bestselling author Maisey Yates.
Happiest surrounded by yarn, her family and the
small woodland creatures she calls pets, she lives
in a small house on the edge of the woods, which
allows her to escape in the way she loves best—
in the pages of a book. She loves intense alpha
heroes and the women who dare to go toe-to-toe
with them.

Also by Heidi Rice

Revenge in Paradise

Hot Winter Escapes collection

Undoing His Innocent Enemy

Billion-Dollar Bet collection

After-Party Consequences

By Royal Arrangement miniseries

Queen's Winter Wedding Charade

Also by Millie Adams

Her Impossible Boss's Baby
Italian's Christmas Acquisition

The Diamond Club collection

Greek's Forbidden Temptation

Work Wives to Billionaires' Wives collection

Billionaire's Bride Bargain

Discover more at millsandboon.co.uk.

ROYALS & SCANDALS

HEIDI RICE

MILLIE ADAMS

MILLS & BOON

First published in Great Britain 2025
by Mills & Boon, an imprint of HarperCollins*Publishers* Ltd,
1 London Bridge Street, London, SE1 9GF

www.harpercollins.co.uk

HarperCollins*Publishers*, Macken House, 39/40 Mayor Street Upper, Dublin 1, D01 C9W8, Ireland

Royals & Scandals © 2025 Harlequin Enterprises ULC

Princess for the Headlines © 2025 Heidi Rice

His Highness's Diamond Decree © 2025 Millie Adams

ISBN: 978-0-263-34455-4

03/25

This book contains FSC™ certified paper
and other controlled sources to ensure responsible forest management.

For more information visit www.harpercollins.co.uk/green.

Printed and Bound in the UK using 100% Renewable Electricity
at CPI Group (UK) Ltd, Croydon, CR0 4YY

PRINCESS FOR THE HEADLINES

HEIDI RICE

MILLS & BOON

To Abby Green and Amanda Cinelli.

Great Modern authors
and even better Modern brainstormers!

CHAPTER ONE

Where the hell is she now? Is she trying to create an international incident? Because she's doing a spectacular job tonight of making me look like a complete ass.

Prince Rene Sven Conrad Gaultiere tuned out the excited chatter from his press secretary as he stood on the ornate marble balcony overlooking Gaultiere Castle's West Ballroom. He surveyed the centuries-old splendour, which was currently festooned in gold and silver décor, lasers streaming across the dancefloor as music throbbed and the clock edged closer to midnight. Like a raptor locating its prey, he found the woman in red satin he'd been looking for amongst the five hundred carefully selected guests, her blonde chignon glittering like a halo in the sparkle of light from a crystal chandelier.

That would be the woman who had been tasked with hosting the traditional New Year's Eve Ball by his side—to demonstrate the excellent union between their two neighbouring countries—but who had been avoiding him all evening.

The fury he'd been barely managing to keep a chokehold on ramped up another notch.

As if it wasn't bad enough that Melody Taylor had appeared only moments before the event started, then run off as soon as they had opened the Ball together, she was now busy flirting with Eli Carter.

Of course he wasn't remotely surprised Carter had sniffed her out, given the US hotel tycoon had an even more notorious reputation for seducing beautiful women than Rene himself—and the gown Mel was wearing plunged so low it turned her curvaceous figure into the Eighth Wonder of the World. But Carter's behaviour was not Rene's concern. Melody's, on the other hand...

She was here representing Androvia tonight—because she was Queen Isabelle's best friend as well as her personal assistant. This annual event was supposed to highlight the friendship between their two kingdoms—not how low an opinion the Queen of Androvia's PA had of Saltzaland's Prince, i.e. him.

As he watched, the woman who had entered the Ball on his arm tilted her head forward inquisitively, and Carter leaned closer to whisper something in her ear... Close enough to see right down the front of her gown.

Rene's fraying temper ignited.

Who the hell did Carter think he was? Coming on to *his* date for the evening, on *his* territory, at *his* event, in *his* castle? And what was Melody thinking? Carter was a wolf who would take pleasure in using her influence with Androvia's Queen for his own purposes.

Rene swore viciously under his breath.

Melody and he had always had a complicated relationship—which had only become more complicated when he'd made the mistake of sleeping with her, four years ago. But she was here to do a job on behalf of her Queen, and her decision to flirt with Carter, who had less ethics than an alley cat, by all accounts, was the final straw.

'As soon as the clock strikes midnight I'm out of here, Andre,' he said to his press secretary, interrupting the flow of information about what a spectacular success this year's Ball had been.

Not for me. Because my co-host has gone out of her way to make it abundantly clear she believes I am beneath contempt.

'But Your Majesty, we were hoping to get some photos for the press in...' Andre began.

'Forget it, you'll just have to make my excuses… And while you're at it, make Miss Taylor's excuses too,' he added.

Tonight, he was through ignoring—or attempting to laugh off—her antagonism towards him. He tugged his phone out of his tuxedo pocket. Midnight was less than a minute away.

About damn time.

Once the castle bell had tolled the hour, he was heading to his private suite. And Melody was going to accompany him—whether she liked it or not. He had no intention of allowing Carter to seduce her because she was *his* responsibility. Plus, it was past time he explained to her in words of one syllable that her rudeness towards him in public would no longer be tolerated.

Queen Isabelle had inadvertently presented him with the opportunity to clear the air with her PA when she had asked her friend to attend this event in her stead—while she was on her honeymoon in America.

Ironic to think he had once offered for Isabelle's hand himself. Not that theirs would ever have been a love match. But the Androvian Queen's hasty marriage to US sportswear entrepreneur Travis Lord had forced Rene to acknowledge something tonight which he had failed to address for four years. Melody Taylor needed to be taught some manners. He had been treating her with kid gloves, because she was Isabelle's best friend, and an integral part of the Queen's entourage—and she had only been eighteen years old that night.

Plus, she had captivated him, more than she should—which had made him determined to give her a wide berth ever since. Although why he found her so fascinating, he had no idea. She was a beautiful woman, but then, he knew a lot of beautiful women.

Perhaps it was her snotty attitude towards him, even before that night, right back to when they were children, which was so unlike every other woman he had ever encountered… Or maybe it was the way she had eventually succumbed to

their livewire chemistry—artlessly but without compromise…
After all, the memory of her shocked sobs of release, the tight
clasp of her massaging him to climax, still had the power to
wake him up late at night, hard and ready for her, far too often.

Even her animosity towards him had failed to kill their
chemistry completely, which would almost be funny if it
weren't so damned annoying.

But as the world-famous DJ the Castle's events planner had
flown in from Ibiza paused the music to count the seconds
down to midnight, Rene dumped his untouched champagne
flute on a passing tray.

Enough is enough. Tonight, she has pushed me too far.

He headed down the wide marble steps towards the ballroom
below, ignoring the many attempts to waylay him en route.

*No more kid gloves. No more avoidance. No more failing
to confront the elephant in the room.*

Melody had brought this on herself with her escalating
rudeness towards him over the past four years.

Tonight, she needed to learn the lesson he had learned
during the intervening years, that her hurt feelings were not
a good enough excuse to disrespect him and, more impor-
tantly, his office and his country, in front of their guests, the
international community and the world's press.

No one—not even that upstart Carter—was going to stop
Rene from getting that damn elephant off his chest once and
for all.

One thing was for sure. Melody Taylor would not be able
to ignore him—or give him the side-eye—a moment longer
once this never-ending event was finally over… In ten seconds and counting.

'Three! Two! One… Happy New Year, everyone!'

Mel clapped as the crowd erupted around her—relief flowing through her.

If only Isabelle had known how much spending the night in Gaultiere Castle would cost her. But the hours she had been forced to spend in Rene's home were nearly over.

Thanks to her carefully planned late arrival and all the demands on the Prince's time at an event like this, she had only had to spend five minutes by his side—which had kept the emotions he stirred under strict control.

Now all she had to do was make a swift and dignified exit.

The Castle's guest manager had assigned her a suite for the night in the East Wing, but she had no intention of waking up here tomorrow—the risk of seeing Rene again far too great. So she had arranged for an all-terrain vehicle to be made available to her in the Castle's garage. The five-hour drive through the mountains at night could be perilous, especially at this time of year, but the weather forecast was favourable, and the route had been clear when she and the rest of Isabelle's staff had arrived this afternoon.

All she had to do now was change out of the ball gown and flee. No one would even know she had left ahead of schedule until she got back to Androvia.

She edged her way through the packed crowd of revellers, who were busy planting impromptu kisses on each other. But before she got more than a couple of steps a soft tug on her elbow found her pulled against the chest of Eli Carter.

'Happy New Year, Ms Taylor,' he murmured in his deep American accent.

She pressed her palms against a solid wall of muscle to resist falling any further into his arms as the crowd surged around them.

Carter had been charming up to now, his interest in her flattering, and it had helped take her mind off her tumultuous reaction to being in Rene's home for the first time. But the hotel magnate's closeness now felt a lot more forward.

'How about a kiss to celebrate the New Year?' Carter said,

the arrogant amusement in his gaze almost as disconcerting as the abrupt switch from charming to flirtatious.

Tall, dark and hot, with an ego the size of the Castle itself, Eli Carter clearly had seducing women as one of his super-powers. And while he hadn't been remotely pushy up to now, she knew a womaniser when she saw one.

Thanks so much, Rene Gaultiere.

She couldn't quite shake the feeling that there was a cyni-cal edge to Carter's interest in her—which had nothing to do with her, and everything to do with Rene—because he'd asked her a lot of probing questions about Saltzaland's Prince during their discussion. But while she had very personal rea-sons for avoiding Rene, she had sensed Carter had reasons of his own for disliking the Prince.

She'd deflected Carter's questions easily enough, because the last person she wanted to talk about, let alone think about, was the man she had been determined to avoid all evening. And luckily, she was not the same naïve, insecure eighteen-year-old who'd once fallen for Rene's charms. But she didn't have time to deal with Carter now.

'Nice try, Carter, but I'll pass,' she said, forced to lean close to him as the noise levels in the ballroom reached deafening.

'Shame,' he shouted back, although he didn't look partic-ularly crestfallen, increasing her suspicions that he'd had a hidden agenda tonight she wanted no part of.

But just as he let her elbow go, the crowd parted behind him—and Rene appeared from nowhere.

Mel's heartbeat rammed her ribs—and plunged between her thighs.

The black tuxedo he wore was perfectly fitted to his tall, muscular physique, the shimmering lights from the antique chandelier above their heads casting his handsome face into stark relief.

She hated herself for noticing how magnificent he looked.

But, to her surprise, instead of saying something cutting or, worse, dismissive, Rene grabbed the billionaire's shoulder and yanked him away from her.

'Touch her again, Carter, and you'll regret it,' he announced, the low-grade fury shocking Mel, but not as much as the spurt of awareness. Or the horrifying shot of arousal as his broad shoulders flexed under the expertly tailored tux.

But then his furious glare landed on her. 'We're leaving.'

Her back stiffened with indignation—and hurt. She dismissed it. She didn't care what Rene thought of her. She had stopped caring a long time ago.

But how dare he look at her like that, as if *she* had done something wrong by talking to Carter, when he was the biggest libertine on the planet?

Carter threw up his hands in a defensive gesture, but the mocking tone was unmistakable when he shouted a reply above the chorus of 'Auld Lang Syne'.

'Perhaps we should let the lady decide who she wants to celebrate the New Year with, Your Majesty?' he all but sneered.

'The lady does not intend to celebrate it with either of you,' Mel interjected, her fury at Rene's high-handedness building. 'Because she's going home.'

She didn't wait to watch the pissing contest continue, turning to push through the crowd. Before she could reach the ballroom's service doors, though, a large hand grasped her wrist, forcing her to an abrupt stop. She knew whose hand it was when sensation sprinted up her arm.

'Not so damn fast.' Rene was so close she could smell him, that devastating aroma of cedarwood soap and man and expensive cologne.

The anger she wanted to feel tangled with the hole in her gut she had spent four years repairing. And the inappropriate yearning—as she recalled his touch, so sure and devastating, the feel of him, so overwhelming inside her… And the morning after, when he'd been gone and her heart had imploded.

'Release me.' She struggled against his hold.

'The hell I will. Where do you think you're going now?'

'None of your business.' She wasn't about to tell him of her plans, even though he couldn't possibly want her here, any more than she wished to be here.

She jerked her hand loose and shoved open the service doors, then lifted her skirts and ran past the line of waiters holding trays of champagne flutes aloft. But as the music faded behind her, she could hear running footsteps cutting through the noise coming from the kitchen.

She had barely made it through the kitchen doors before her pursuer snagged her wrist a second time. 'Stop, dammit. What are you running from, you little fool?'

She skidded to a stop, aware of the scene they were making in front of the kitchen staff, who were all watching with varying degrees of avid curiosity and shock.

She wondered what exactly was so shocking—that their Prince was behaving like an overbearing arse, or that his date for the evening was trying to get away from him?

'I'm running from *you*. Who else?' she snarled, breathless—it had been a long night already, and she was fast losing patience with his overbearing arse routine. 'Now, go away and leave me alone.'

'That does it. I've had enough of your nonsense tonight,' he said and then, to her utter shock, leant down, gathered her legs and scooped her up and over his shoulder.

Suddenly, she was upside down, staring at a pair of tight male buns clad in black serge, her belly bouncing in time with his purposeful strides.

It took her a full second to process what was happening. Mortification tightened her lungs, her breasts all but spilling out of her gown. But as soon as she had caught her breath, she began to kick and punch in earnest.

'Put me down, you oaf!' she shouted.

But he ignored her, even as her shoes flew off, and he marched her through the crowd of chefs and porters and serving staff—who were all gaping at them now in stunned silence.

'You want me to drop you on your head, then carry on struggling. Otherwise, be still,' Rene demanded.

She choked back a sob of outrage but stopped fighting, because hitting the deck in front of all these people would surely be worse.

After several eternities, they made it through the kitchens and into the bowels of the Castle. As the metal doors swung closed behind them and they were alone, she gave his back another almighty punch with the last of her strength. He didn't even flinch.

'Put me down right now, or I will scream my lungs out,' she threatened, impressed with the steadiness of her voice, given that her insides had turned to mush.

His shoulder hitched under her belly. 'Go ahead, no one will hear you.'

But after he had pushed through another set of doors, he finally deposited her on her feet in the ornate entrance hall of the East Wing.

Her bare toes sank into the embroidered silk carpet. She wrenched up the bodice of the far too revealing dress, which had dropped dangerously low during her ignominious exit through the kitchens, then lifted her head to glare at her kidnapper. Unfortunately, without the benefit of her heels, she had to look way, way up. The man was at least six foot two and she barely reached his collarbone.

It was just another humiliation to add to all the others he had heaped upon her over the years.

The cavernous hall—its twin mahogany staircases leading

to the gallery above them and the guest suites—was eerily quiet and dimly lit, the muted lighting from the wall sconces casting shadows over Rene's saturnine features.

He ripped off his bowtie and wrestled open the top two buttons of his dress shirt, then thrust the tie into his pocket, glaring at her as if *she* were the guilty party. Controlled fury rolled off him in waves. The spark of antagonism arced between them, ready to ignite the bristling tension like an accelerant in a sea of petrol, while making her brutally aware of how isolated they were.

The intimacy was as terrifying as the emotions making her breathing clog in her lungs. This was the first time she had been alone with Rene since that night. She should walk away. But her feet were rooted to the carpet, her accelerated breathing, her thundering pulse—the fallout from their wrestling match—making her annoyingly light-headed.

'What did you mean,' he demanded, his voice still rough with anger, 'about going home?'

Had she said that? Her dazed mind struggled to come up with an explanation, while also trying to understand why he cared.

'It was a figure of speech,' she managed. 'I'm going to my room.' At last, the strength returned to her legs and her feet began to cooperate.

But as she swung round his strong fingers grasped her upper arm and swung her back again.

'Wait a damn minute…' he said.

Sensation shot up her arm again. He hadn't touched her since that night, for four years, and now he couldn't seem to stop touching her. Her reaction was as volatile and all-consuming as it had been then—which would be humiliating if it weren't so pathetic.

'Don't touch me,' she said, but even so she was surprised when he released her. And lifted his hands, palms up.

'Okay, but dammit…' He thrust his fingers through his hair, raking the dark locks into haphazard rows, his frustration clear when he spoke again. 'Don't walk away from me again, Melody…'

The way he said her full name struck something deep inside her, that black hole of insecurity he had discovered once before and exploited so easily. She wrapped her arms around her waist to contain the panic threatening to overwhelm her.

But then he sighed and added, 'We need to talk about that night because it's…'

'No, we don't.' She cut him off with as much determination as she could muster, while being wrenched back in time to the biggest mistake of her life.

She'd been such a fool that night—such a naïve, eager, innocent, romantic fool. Why on earth had she trusted her virginity to him when she'd always known what a shallow bastard he was, especially where women were concerned? That her body still didn't seem to have learned that lesson only made her panic increase.

The only saving grace was that he would never know he had been her first…and her only lover. So far.

'I'm exhausted. It's past midnight and I want to go to bed,' she said, trying to keep her voice even when she was shaking inside.

Why was he bringing that night up now? Was he trying to destroy what was left of her composure?

'The last thing I need to talk about is ancient history,' she added, stepping away from him cautiously, as if he were an unexploded bomb. Because that was what this whole hideous standoff suddenly felt like. Explosive and terrifying.

She'd hated how easily he had forgotten her in the days afterwards, when she had tried to contact him… But his carelessness then, and the easy dismissal, was her insurance now against her body's idiotic reaction to him, *still*.

The fact that he had never referred to their night together had become a boon eventually instead of a cause for sadness and recriminations… It had given her a chance to repair the damage he'd done by discarding her so carelessly. And now he was trying to make her feel like nothing again… Well, no thanks.

'So, if you're finished with your caveman act…' she said, but before she could get away he snagged her arm again.

'You're not going anywhere,' he said.

'Let me go,' she demanded.

'Only if you promise not to run until we've got a few things settled.'

'Fine. I promise,' she blurted out.

She needed him to stop touching her. Because the feel of his fingers, after all these years, was playing havoc with what was left of her equilibrium.

He released her and slung his hand into his pocket. His gaze seared her skin. But she forced herself to stand tall and to ignore the riot of sensations and emotions—which were screaming at her to run again. She'd tried that already and it hadn't exactly worked in her favour.

'So, you're not planning on heading back to Androvia tonight?' he asked, his penetrating gaze astute and surprisingly lucid.

Why wasn't he drunk—when he had a reputation for over-indulging at parties?

She struggled to contain the guilty flush—and thanked God for the low lighting. 'Of course not. It's pitch-dark, it's probably snowing, I'm exhausted and it's a five-hour drive in daylight.'

He studied her for the longest time, clearly not convinced by her denial. But then the penetrating glare softened a fraction.

'Fine, you can go,' he said, as if she needed his permission. 'On the condition we have this out in the morning. No more avoidance tactics.'

Like hell we will.

What exactly did he think they had to talk about, anyway? She'd thrown herself at him that night, believing they'd made a connection of some sort, and he'd let her, then he'd left before she'd woken the next morning and ghosted her for weeks afterwards until she'd finally got the message: that she was just another notch on his bedpost who meant nothing.

On what planet would she want to revisit that humiliation? And to what end? So he could tell her again, in words instead of deeds, that she was a nobody? That he'd used her for a quick endorphin fix because she'd been willing and available? *No, thanks.*

'Your animosity towards me is starting to impact my work, and yours,' he continued in that authoritarian tone as if he were the boss of her. 'Tonight's little farce being a perfect example,' he continued. 'And with Isabelle now happily loved-up with her new husband we may have to deal with each other a lot more often.'

Her temper reignited at the patronising statement—the gall of the man, questioning *her* professionalism. She'd come here, she'd allowed herself to be dressed up like a courtesan and spent five never-ending minutes on his arm being treated like an accessory. And then four endless hours avoiding him so they wouldn't have a spat in public... And this was the thanks she got.

'I'll see you at breakfast, ten o'clock sharp, so we can discuss how to repair our working relationship,' he added. 'Or, rather, how you are going to start doing your job. And stop trying to screw up five hundred years of diplomacy between our two countries because of a few hurt feelings. You're not eighteen any more, Melody. And my patience with your childish attitude towards me is at an end.'

You bastard.

She bit into her lower lip, hard enough to taste blood, to stop herself from reacting to the carelessly cruel statement.

Her role in Androvia as Isabelle's trusted assistant was something she took incredibly seriously. It was the achievement she was most proud of, the one thing she excelled at. She made it her business to know and understand Isabelle's role and her responsibilities as Queen, to support her and counsel her, not just because she was paid a generous salary, but also because Isabelle had been her best friend since they were both ten years old.

She would never let Isabelle down… Not again, anyway.

That she had allowed Rene—or, rather, the incident between them four years ago—to compromise that closeness, that friendship, because she had never had the guts to confide in Isabelle what had happened that night, still upset her, and made her feel miserably guilty.

That he was digging at that sore spot by questioning her professionalism felt so unfair. But she sucked in a breath and refused to react. Because that would only prove his point. That she was an overemotional basket case who still wanted his approval, when nothing could be further from the truth.

And arguing with him had always been a pointless exercise. Rene knew all her weak spots and had none of his own—because he had always been more than happy to wear his arrogance and entitlement like a badge of honour.

The good news was, Rene was wrong about the impact of Isabelle's marriage to Travis Lord on their working relationship.

Because Mel knew that Isabelle's marriage was a sham. That her friend had only married the American sportswear entrepreneur to circumvent her father's will and facilitate a land deal. In fact, Isabelle's 'loved-up' new marriage was only due to last a year. After this debacle, Mel would simply impress upon Isabelle that asking her to act as a proxy in the Queen's dealings with Saltzaland's Prince was not a good idea, diplomatic-relations-wise.

Luckily, Isabelle knew that Mel and Rene had always been at loggerheads—ever since they were children and Rene had teased them both mercilessly whenever he visited Androvia's White Palace with his father. So Isabelle would not question her continued animosity towards him now. Or request she host any more balls on his arm.

'If you really wish to discuss our working relationship to-morrow morning, you can,' she managed, determined not to let him see how much his patronising accusations had hurt her. 'But FYI, my desire not to spend time with you has noth-ing to do with one night of poor judgement and everything to do with what an overbearing arse you have been ever since you were sixteen,' she finished with a flourish, glad when his eyes narrowed.

'I'll want your word on that,' he snapped, still behaving as if he were the boss of her.

'Go to hell, Rene,' she shot back. She was not about to give him her word because he didn't deserve it. Plus, she planned to be long gone by ten tomorrow morning—and *her* word actually *meant* something to her, unlike Rene.

'You can bully everyone else,' she added. 'But you can't bully me. Because I know exactly who you are. Now more than ever.'

She swung round—*finally*—and marched up the staircase in her bare feet, aware of him glaring at her. She kept her spine straight and refused to look back, but she could feel the prickle of awareness tangling with the anger and indignation in her gut every single step of the way.

But as she hurried to her guest room, she couldn't help be-rating herself again, for once being young and foolish enough to offer her heart to the Prince of Saltzaland on a platter. She should have known, even as a naïve eighteen-year-old, that an entitled bastard like him would trample all over it.

CHAPTER TWO

AN HOUR LATER, Mel's insides were still churning from her close encounter with Prince Overbearing Arse as she crept down the East Wing's service staircase in her winter gear, toting a bag packed hastily for the journey. It had taken an age to get out of the blasted dress and deconstruct the chignon a team of hairstylists had spent an hour constructing.

The bass beat of amplified music echoed dully in the concrete stairwell as she reached the entrance to the garage and keyed in the code given to her by Marco, the young mechanic she had charmed that afternoon.

She pushed the security door, which opened with a loud clang.

At least the New Year celebrations were still going strong in the ballroom several floors above—which meant she had no chance of being waylaid or manhandled by the Egomaniac again. Because Rene would have returned to the party—to find a willing woman to warm his bed for the night.

Twin tides of anxiety and temper were joined by the prickle of something that felt uncomfortably like envy—which she ruthlessly ignored. She had been one of Rene's conquests once, and while she now understood far too well why he was so irresistible to so many women, she had absolutely no desire to be one of his harem. The sex had been overwhelming, physically as well as emotionally, but being the centre of his attention for that one night—the focus of all that charm and charisma—had also been disturbing. Because she had managed to kid herself for weeks afterwards that they had shared something rare and precious—when she now knew they hadn't.

Sex was a game to Rene, one he played well, but it could never be a game to her.

His rejection had hurt, but what had hurt far more was how thoroughly she had allowed herself to fall into the trap of thinking there was a complicated man behind the mask of the dissolute Prince. Especially as she had known, even as a girl of ten, that Rene Gaultiere had no hidden depths.

When someone told you who they were, you needed to believe them. After all, her father had taught her that lesson before she had ever met Rene.

She pushed the unsettling thoughts to one side. This was all ancient history, which Rene had deliberately yanked out into the open with his caveman routine tonight. Maybe he enjoyed getting the better of her. It wouldn't be the first time, given their endless feud as kids, when he had taken great pleasure in teasing her and Isabelle. She had been the one to stand up to him because Isabelle had always been far too sweet. But he wasn't her problem any more, especially once she got out of here.

She scanned the cavernous, dimly lit garage in earnest, searching for the vehicle she had arranged with Marco to have fuelled and waiting for her, the keys in the ignition—ready for her to pick up first thing in the morning.

She walked along the rows of expensive luxury cars, gleaming in the half-light, then spotted an all-terrain vehicle at the far end, near the exit ramp. The huge silver car, its wheel arches almost as high as the low-slung sports car beside it, looked ready for anything... And like a lot more vehicle than she had ever handled before.

She swallowed the bubble of apprehension. Just because

she was more used to being chauffeur-driven these days didn't mean she couldn't handle the all-terrain monster.

She sighed with relief as the door opened with a satisfying click. The SUV was unlocked. Yup, this was definitely her ride. She slung her pack into the back seat, tugged off her ski jacket and clambered into the driver's seat.

The keys, though, weren't in the ignition. She frowned, then began to search for them, wondering where on earth Marco had left them instead.

'Looking for these, Melody?'

Her gaze shot up, and her heartbeat hit her chest wall.

The Prince of Saltzaland was standing leaning against a concrete pillar not five feet in front of the car, wearing dark jeans, boots, a black polo-neck and a shearling jacket—to ward off the chill in the cavernous space—and a cynical smile, while dangling a set of car keys from his index finger.

My car keys.

She gulped down the panic and glared. 'What are *you* doing here?' she asked, trying for indignation, and failing miserably, because her body was already responding to him as if it had just been plugged into an electric socket.

He levered himself off the pillar and strolled towards her, throwing the keys up and catching them in his fist.

He reached the car and wrenched open the driver's door.

'Get out,' he said, in the same he-who-shall-be-obeyed tone he'd used earlier, the cynical smile history.

'I will not.' She gripped the steering wheel. 'Just give me the keys.' She reached out to take them. 'Something came up and I have to get back to Androvia tonight,' she added nonchalantly. 'I'll have the car brought back first thing tomorrow, I swear.'

She hated to beg, hated even more that he had discovered her cowardly attempt to avoid him tomorrow morning, but the only option she had now was to lie her head off.

'I think not,' he said in the same forceful tone, which was starting to get on her last nerve. 'As I recall, you gave me your word once already tonight, which we now know is completely worthless, so it seems we are going to have to do this the hard way.'

She flushed, his humourless tone and the grim expression almost as disturbing as the adrenaline charging through her system.

She'd always hated cynical, jaded, don't-give-a-damn-about-anything Rene, but she was beginning to discover that cynical, jaded, scowling tyrant Rene was a whole lot worse. But where was this new Rene coming from? And why on earth was he suddenly so determined to rake over the coals of their one night together, four years after the damage had been done?

'I did not give you my word,' she replied, her grip tightening on the wheel.

'Precisely, because you knew you were going to break it,' he said, making her realise she had just waltzed into a trap of her own making. 'Which brings us back to your latest lie, that something came up in the past hour, when we both know you arranged to have this vehicle ready to leave tonight hours ago. Nice touch, by the way, charming Marco into not telling his manager.'

Her astonishment that he knew the young garage mechanic's first name had barely had a chance to register before he continued.

'At this point, I'm not sure what's more concerning, your tenuous relationship with the truth, how close you came to losing Marco his job—' his voice lowered, his scowl becoming catastrophic '—or your asinine decision to take your life into your hands by driving five hours alone at night through the mountains, just to avoid an adult conversation with me.'

The unfairness of his diatribe—which had left her with a

ton of unfounded accusations to unpick—left her speechless for about a nanosecond.

'Don't you dare sack Marco,' she said, swallowing the trickle of guilt at the thought she had put Marco's job in jeopardy because she had assumed Rene wouldn't even notice she was gone, let alone care.

'Don't worry, I don't intend to sack my best mechanic when you're the one who...'

'And I'm not scared of having an adult conversation with you, you egomaniac,' she interrupted him as her temper kicked in. 'I really do need to get back to Androvia.'

It wasn't a lie, she decided, because if she didn't leave now she might actually murder him—then where would the five-hundred-year-old diplomatic accord between Saltzaland and Androvia be, which he was suddenly so concerned about?

'Fine, then move over and I will drive you there myself,' he demanded, calling her bluff, the bastard.

'I will not,' she said, because that would defeat the whole purpose of leaving in the first place. And anyway, since when did she need to rely on any man, least of all him? 'I'm perfectly capable of driving home on my own.'

'Move over, or so help me I will move you myself. And I think we already know who will win that wrestling match.'

Damn and blast it.

She wanted to scream with frustration. But when he continued to glare at her she knew she'd lost this round. She did not need a repeat of their previous wrestling match. And if she continued to refuse it would only make it seem as if she really feared having a conversation with him. And she would actually rather die than let him know that.

Because, however horrified she was at the prospect of spending five hours in a car with him and being forced to listen to whatever asinine thing he had to say about that night, it would be far worse to let him know she gave a damn.

She bit into her lip for the second time that night and moved across the car's bench seat.

But when he leapt up into the cab and slammed the door his big brooding presence seemed to diminish the space, and her lung capacity again, despite the size of the vehicle.

He was so close she could smell him, and see the scar which ran across his forehead, just under the hairline.

A vivid memory assailed her—of tracing the raised scar with her fingertip while she lay in his arms and listened to his heart beating, the soreness in her sex dimmed by the heady blast of afterglow.

'How did you get this? I've never noticed it before.'

'It's not important.'

The yearning to know him, to understand the closed expression, the reason why he'd shut her out—and her certainty then that the scar, like so many others she had discovered that night, *was* important, despite his denial—pressed on her chest. And only made her feel angrier with herself now, as well as him.

She couldn't afford to romanticise his bad behaviour. The man had always been reckless and impulsive—and had partied to excess for years, ever since he'd first acceded to the throne at nineteen, in fact, after his father's death in a skiing accident. The gossip columns had been full of his crass exploits ever since. No wonder he had scars. Scars he richly deserved, no doubt.

Instead of initiating the conversation she dreaded, though, he shoved the keys into the ignition and switched on the engine. He leant across her to pop open the glove compartment, grabbed a small gizmo and clicked it, giving her another unwanted blast of his scent—cedarwood soap and the delicious aroma of his bergamot cologne—which her wayward pheromones really did not need right now.

Slinging the gizmo back inside, he slammed the compartment shut.

The heavy metal screen above the exit ramp began to crank upwards.

The Castle's forbidding Gothic facade was slowly revealed as he shifted into gear and peeled out of the parking space. Light swirls of snow fell onto the stone turrets as he drove up the ramp and into the courtyard, then accelerated through a gate at the end of the compound.

Fireworks exploded in the sky above them, to mark the end of the celebration. And the beginning of a brand-new year.

Funny, because she suddenly felt about a million years old.

She stared at the dazzle of coloured lights, thankful the popping noise and the powerful hum of the high-powered engine made talking impossible. But her relief was short-lived as they bounded onto the mountain road leading to the pass across the Alps and Androvia.

'Put your seatbelt on,' he shouted as the Castle—and the celebrations—disappeared in the Jeep's rear-view mirror.

Her heart sank into her toes, but luckily her fury at him, and this whole hideous situation, rose up to fill the gap. She could only hope it would fortify her for the road trip from hell in her immediate future.

CHAPTER THREE

'STOP BULLYING ME, you jerk.'

Rene ignored the caustic tone when Melody did what she was told—for once—and snapped the belt into place.

Her subtle rose scent filled the car, reminding him of all the sleepless nights he'd had over the past four years, the phantom scent pulling him back to that night—which was not helping with his temper one little bit.

He flipped the switch on the dash which turned on the searchlights on the SUV's roof. Twin beams illuminated the road ahead as they entered the forest.

'Relax.' He flicked a glance at her, strangely vindicated by her furious expression.

That makes two of us, then.

He'd known she was lying to him earlier—because Melody had always been a terrible liar, every single emotion she felt always visible on her face. But even so it had surprised him—after he'd had his garage staff woken up to question them—that she would risk her own safety just to avoid him.

He'd been waiting a good twenty minutes for her to put in an appearance, his fury and frustration, and that ache in his stomach—at the evidence of how much she despised him, which he hated even more—building by the second.

But right beside the fury was the kick of adrenaline. And awareness.

While Mel had always infuriated and antagonised him, he

also admired her refusal to back down from a fight. It was unfortunate, though, that her temper and that scent still had a marked effect on his libido. Especially as they were now going to be stuck together for five hours.

Then again, no woman had ever excited him the way she did.

Why else would he have taken what she offered that night, even though he'd known it would not end well? And why else would he have found it so impossible to get over her?

Clearly, they needed to confront the fallout from that night, after four years of denial, so they could both move on. But he'd be damned if he'd confront it before he was good and ready. And as they now had all the time in the world, way too much time, in fact, he would let her stew for a change— the way he'd had to all evening.

'Are you even legal to drive?' she murmured. 'How much have you had to drink tonight?'

He tensed at the accusation. How typical of her to poke at a wound which might never heal. But he'd be damned if he'd have her accuse him of endangering her life tonight, as well as his own, by driving under the influence when she had forced him to make this damn journey in the first place.

'For your information, I haven't had an alcoholic drink in four years,' he snapped, then wanted to kick himself.

He didn't need to defend his behaviour to anyone, and he didn't want her figuring out his decision to sober up for good had been made as he'd been tiptoeing out of her student digs in London—barefoot, dishevelled, hungover and racked with guilt.

It wasn't the increasingly brutal hangovers, though, which had messed with his head that morning after... It was the insane desire to wake her up and have her look at him again as she had the night before—as if he could hang the stars— which he had only narrowly managed to resist.

Fortunately, instead of figuring out the timing of his decision to stop drinking, she simply made a scoffing sound in her throat.

'Who's the liar now?' she murmured. 'If you haven't had a drink for four years, why were you hungover at Isabelle's wedding ten days ago?'

He hadn't been hungover, he'd been sleep-deprived—the familiar nightmares returning—at the prospect of spending hours sitting beside her at the banquet. Which had proved to be a titanic effort, just as he had expected it would be, because when she wasn't ignoring him, she had been giving him the evil eye.

One thing he intended to get across to her on this infernal drive was that her days of taking cheap potshots at him were over. She wasn't eighteen any more, she was a grown woman, and he was through putting up with her temper tantrums, when his decision to leave her sleeping that morning, and to ignore her texts and calls over the days that followed, had been one of the few unselfish things he had done in his entire life.

Not only that, but he was damned if he was going to keep taking all the blame for what had happened between them four years ago.

She had come on to him, not the other way around. Maybe he should have resisted her artless flirting. With a bit more maturity himself that night, and a bit less of the Napoleon brandy they'd both had too much of after she and her friends had come up to him at the West End nightclub, he might have been able to.

But what was past was past. And it was time she got over it.

'Believe what you like, but I am more than sober enough to drive,' he said, determined to put an end to the conversation.

He did not want her to know exactly how their one night had changed him or she might start getting delusions again.

Although, from the derisive glare she sent him, he doubted that would be a problem.

That she would always think the worst of him now made the ache in his gut twist, but he ignored it.

The harsh lesson he'd taught her, about not trusting him, not relying on him, not believing he was a good man, when he had always known he wasn't—nor did he particularly want to be—was a valuable one, which she ought to thank him for.

'I'd hazard a guess I also have a lot more experience driving this car on these roads than you do,' he added, shifting into first as the road began to climb along the ridge over-looking the Castle.

She shrugged and turned away from him to stare out of the Jeep's window. 'If you think I'm going to thank you for kidnapping me, you can think again, Rene.'

Kidnapping her?

He laughed. He couldn't help it. 'I see you're still as much of a drama queen as you were when I first met you,' he murmured, remembering that belligerent ten-year-old tomboy with an odd dose of nostalgia.

She'd challenged him at every turn even then—because she had been brave and loyal and prepared to defend her new best friend. So, of course, being a sixteen-year-old boy who had never had a friend he could trust, it had been all but impossible not to torment her and Isabelle even more.

'And I see you're still as much of an overbearing bastard,' she shot back.

'Touché,' he murmured, refusing to defend that troubled boy again.

He wasn't proud of the way he'd behaved as a teenager, but dealing with his father's volatile moods and violent outbursts over many years hadn't left that boy with much ability to process compassion or empathy. As a result, he didn't blame that boy too harshly for his antagonism towards other children—especially a girl like Mel, who he had been so jealous of at the time. Because she had a mother who loved her, a best friend who adored her, and she didn't appear to have a father at all, ready to discipline her for every infraction and punish her for any sign of weakness.

'Whatever it is you have to say about that night,' she said, the tone sharp enough to slice through steel, 'just…' She paused abruptly. He glanced her way to see her face break into a huge yawn. 'J-just say it,' she finished.

'Go to sleep. You're exhausted. We can talk later,' he said.

It was a cop-out, and he suspected she knew it from the way she stared back at him, her eyes narrowing.

But the truth was, now she'd put him on the spot, he wasn't ready yet to have this conversation. Her snotty attitude towards him, at Isabelle's wedding and last night's ball, had antagonised him beyond bearing, and he'd lost his temper, but now he finally had her at his mercy, he needed time to figure out an approach that wasn't going to make her even more difficult. Plus, her rose scent and the sight of her face, devoid of make-up, her wide blue eyes dazed with fatigue, wasn't helping to diminish the uncomfortable spike of awareness which had been tormenting him for four years.

'Seriously?' she hissed. 'You kidnap me so you can trap me into spending five never-ending hours in a car with you. And now you *don't* have anything to talk about?'

Talking isn't what we're good at.

The thought popped into his head and pulsed in his groin. He tensed—and forced his gaze back to the road.

Seriously, Gaultiere, what the hell is wrong with you?

Thankfully, the light snowfall gave him a way out. 'I need to concentrate on my driving until we get through the pass,' he said. 'Consider it a reprieve. But if you really *want* to explain to me why you are still behaving like a woman scorned four years after our hook-up, I'm all ears.'

She let out an outraged huff. 'A woman scorned?' she replied, the scorn in her voice unmistakable. 'You wish, Prince... Egomaniac.'

The insult might have had more heat if she hadn't broken off in the middle of it for another jaw-breaking yawn.

'Go to sleep,' he said again. 'Don't worry, this argument will still be here when you wake up.'

'You forget, I don't take orders from y-you,' she murmured, the fatigue slurring her speech when she yawned again.

'Consider it a suggestion then, not an order,' he offered.

She blinked slowly, her glassy eyes making the bright blue, lit by the searchlights reflecting off the dash, even more luminous than usual.

'Go to hell,' she muttered, but when she curled into the seat it took less than a second for her body to soften into sleep.

As the snow began to swirl and he concentrated on the road ahead, he was sure he could hear the murmur of her breathing above the rhythmic swish of the wiper blades. He took a steadying breath, only to inhale another lungful of her scent, the heady whisper of roses and female musk filling the car with too many memories...

And the heavy pulse in his groin got a whole lot more insistent.

Great!

CHAPTER FOUR

'*PLEASE TELL ME you're not a virgin, Melody.*'

'*No, of course not! I love sex, I have it all the time.*'

'*Are you sure? You're so tight. Am I hurting you?*'

'*No... Just... Maybe a little.*'

'*Shh... Here, let me touch you. Let me make it good.*'

The heat eddied through Mel's body, the strong sure touch easing the pain and bringing with it a devastating pleasure—enveloping her, surrounding her. It surged from her core to ripple over her skin and swell around her heart. Strong, vital, vivid...

'Melody! Wake up. We need to leave the vehicle...'

Strong fingers, *his* fingers, moved from her yearning sex to her shoulders, and dug into her biceps...

'Don't stop, it feels so good...' she murmured.

Why wasn't he touching her where she needed him the most? Why was he shaking her? When she was so close to something incredible? When it had been so long? Too long.

'Dammit, Mel, you need to wake up. We need to move.'

Her eyes fluttered open to find Rene staring at her, his expression fierce, his gaze wary, and concerned. Just as it had been that night.

'Melody, you're dreaming...' His gaze flashed with something hot and intense. But then his jaw flexed and his fingers dug into the muscles of her upper arms.

Cold lanced through her body. The roar of the storm,

and the vicious shivers beginning to make her teeth chatter, yanked her out of the dream.

'It's f-freezing…' she said, trying to dispel the last of the erotic fantasy featuring the man staring at her. What was she doing in a car in a snowstorm with Rene? Was this real, or just another of those recurring dreams which always turned to nightmares?

Not a dream. A far too intense memory.

If the brutal ache in her sex was anything to go by.

'The car has run out of petrol,' he said. 'The tank must have been ruptured when the undercarriage hit something about ten minutes ago.'

'What?' she asked, still groggy with sleep and yearning.

'Listen to me, Melody,' he demanded. 'The temperature's dropping fast. And we need to leave the vehicle before we freeze.'

He let her go to lean across the seat well and grab her bag. He unzipped it and began pulling out her clothes.

'W-w-what are you doing?' she asked, her teeth chattering harder, her breath fogging the air with his. 'What time is it? Where are we?' she managed, still trying to get her bearings.

The dark landscape outside looked eerily beautiful, lit by the car's headlights. Thick gusts of snow obscured the fir trees wrapped in white, which bent and swayed in the rattling wind.

'It's about three in the morning,' he said, his voice clear and strong and surprisingly calm. 'The road was blocked. I couldn't get a phone signal. But the GPS said there was a house, or at least a building, in this direction, so I headed towards it—which was when the undercarriage hit something—and we must have started leaking fuel. We need to find shelter because I haven't been able to call for help, so no one will know we're missing until the morning. And we're a distance from the road now.'

He shoved a couple of sweaters at her, then her coat and hat and gloves. 'Put these on.'

Definitely not a dream—he kidnapped me.

But even as the reality of where she was, and why, seeped into her brain, the grim expression on his face had the gravity of the situation dawning on her, too.

This was no time to argue with him. Or to be mortified about the fact he'd woken her in the middle of an erotic dream in which he was the star player. That could wait until they'd found somewhere warm and safe. She swallowed the lump of panic, but couldn't get her fingers to co-operate as she tried to pull on the jumper.

'Here, let me.' He brushed her numb fingers aside and dragged the jumper over her head, then fed her arms into the sleeves.

She wanted to take over, but as he continued to dress her like a child, adding extra layers then shoving her arms into her coat, putting on her hat and gloves, her hands were shaking too hard to resist—from fear or cold, she couldn't be sure.

Once he'd zipped up her jacket and tugged up the hood, he pulled her closer.

'I'm going to lead the way, okay?' he said, tugging his belt out of the loops in his jeans. 'It shouldn't be too far now.' Lifting her arm, he wrapped the belt around her wrist, then threaded the end through one of his belt hooks and fastened it. 'When we get out of the car, hold onto the belt with both hands,' he said above the whistling wind, and her chattering teeth. 'I'll be right in front of you. Don't let go, whatever happens.'

He grabbed a torch from the glove compartment and switched it on.

'Right. Let's go,' he said, his stark expression set with determination.

But when he swung around to open the door into the eerie, swirling darkness she grabbed his forearm.

'Wait!' she cried, her panic having downgraded enough to give way to a depth of emotion which almost scared her more.

He turned back, one quizzical eyebrow raised.

'What about you?' she said.

He was only wearing jeans and a thin sweater under the shearling jacket, his gloves looked like driving gloves and the beanie he'd put on couldn't be that warm either, while she had on four layers of winter clothing. 'You should take some of my sweaters,' she added, scared for him as much as herself.

What if they got lost in the whiteout? What if the house was further than he thought? What if it wasn't a house at all? How could he stay warm?

'I'll be okay,' he said with the same flippancy which had always annoyed her.

Why did he always do that? Pretend to be invulnerable, and immune to elements which could cripple lesser mortals. And make her feel as if her concern was insignificant and unnecessary.

'But I don't want you to die,' she pleaded, keeping a death grip on his sleeve.

He let out a low chuckle that would have annoyed her more if she wasn't so terrified.

'That's good, because neither do I,' he murmured, then he grasped her head and yanked her towards him to take her lips in a furious kiss.

She opened for him instantly, heat exploding with the giddy rush of yearning. His tongue delved—conquering, demanding, strong and unyielding.

She clung to him, never wanting the kiss to end. If they could just stay here and make love again, everything would be all right. Wouldn't it? Her fears dissolved until all that was left was the heat and the longing.

But he tore his mouth free with a tortured groan then pressed his forehead to hers, their breaths mingling in the chilly air.

'We're not going to die tonight, Melody,' he said, his strong hands massaging her stiff shoulders. 'Because we've still got a ton of arguments in our future.'

The foolish, flippant words were still echoing in her soul and wrapping around her heart as he launched himself into the frozen storm and dragged her out behind him.

CHAPTER FIVE

'YOU ARE WEAK, RENE. I tried to make you a man but, as always, you are a disappointment. Why don't you lie down, as you want to—the storm is stronger than you are...'

'No, it damn well isn't,' Rene hissed. But the reply to his father's caustic words was whisked away on the freezing wind.

He bent his head and kept going.

Every part of him hurt now, the parts he could still feel anyway. His cheeks were in a state of agony as he faced into the icy wind. But his father's voice, telling him what a failure he was—and had always been—galvanised his temper. And his determination to survive.

That and the thought of Melody huddled behind him as she clung on and kept going too.

This was his fault. He should have informed his staff he was leaving with Mel. Should have contacted the authorities while he still had a phone signal. Should never have taken that detour.

In fact, he should never have embarked on this damn drive in the first place. The mountain range here was mostly undeveloped and could be treacherous. The storm had come from nowhere, had not been forecast, but, even so, he knew the region well enough to know one's safety was never guaranteed.

But he'd been too mad with her, too determined to save her from herself to think clearly. And then he'd been too busy thinking about her, asleep beside him, to concentrate on anything else, until their situation had gone from bad to potentially catastrophic.

Maybe your father was right all along...

The words whispered on the wind, cruel, damning, but not necessarily incorrect, making him doubt himself once more.

But then Melody stumbled against his back. He stopped to drag her up with numb hands, and yanked her against his side. She looked up at him, her exhaustion clear even in the hazy torchlight.

'We have to keep going, Melody,' he shouted into her ear. 'Do you need me to carry you?'

She shook her head vigorously, forcing herself upright. Then pushed against his back, urging him onwards.

Pride and possessiveness swelled in his chest, the rush of adrenaline giving him the strength he needed to turn back into the wind and trudge on.

No way was he letting her die tonight. His lips cracked, still buzzing with the memory of their furious kiss in the car. He concentrated on the heat, the desperation to have her under him again.

They would get through this, and when they did, perhaps all they really needed to do was satisfy this incessant yearning, give in to the infernal chemistry once more... To burn it out for good.

He walked for what felt like hours, the pain lessening as numbness set in, the storm deafening, the exhaustion suffocating and so heavy it made each laboured step more torturous than the last.

The doubts grew back stronger. What if he'd set off in the wrong direction? Who the hell knew where they were at this point? The advice was always to stay with your vehicle.

'You are nothing but a spoilt child. To be a prince you need to be a man.'

His father's voice, so clear, so cutting, so disgusted with him, echoed again.

'Go away, you bastard. Leave me alone.' He lifted his head to shout into the wind…and spotted a shape through the trees. A solid shape.

Adrenaline surged, obliterating the old nightmares. A house? A chalet? Maybe. No lights. But shelter… Surely.

He grabbed Melody, but when she stumbled again he bent and slung her over his shoulder, the last of his strength pushing him through the pain, the numbness, the fear and the fury as he headed towards the structure which rose up through the trees.

He reached a two-storey building. Its ornate wooden balconies faced the valley below, which was obliterated by the raging storm. He climbed the steps to the porch to escape the icy wind at last.

'Put me down, Rene. I can walk.' Melody's cry had him lowering her to her feet.

Still, he gathered her close, scared to let her go. She softened against him, her body so small, so fragile, so weary.

He thumped the heavy wooden door. Pain ricocheted up his arm.

No answer. The closed shutters made it clear the place was empty. But it looked sturdy, well-kept, not derelict, simply deserted.

He tugged Melody up by her lapels to whisper in her ear. 'Wait here,' he said, his voice hoarse. 'Don't go to sleep. We have to get warm.'

But first he had to find a way inside.

Leaving her propped against the door, he stumbled the length of the porch, wrenched at the shutters. No luck. Then he spotted a door at the far end. Unlike the main entrance, there were panes of glass—and no shutters. Ripping off his hat, he wrapped it around his fist and punched the glass. It broke with a muffled crash. He shoved his hand through, the slice of pain dimmed by the burst of triumph.

Finding the bolt inside with clumsy fingers, he yanked it back. Then he shoved the door hard with his shoulder. But it only bent, still attached at the bottom of the frame.

He swore viciously, triumph giving way to panic. They couldn't stay out here any longer without freezing to death. He had to get the door open.

He stepped back and kicked it hard enough to crack the frame.

The door buckled and bent inward.

Racing back to Melody, he scooped her into his arms, carried her back along the porch then wedged them both through the broken door into the house. The scent of lavender polish and fresh, clean linen assailed his senses.

And then warmth enveloped him.

Euphoria surged. He found a series of switches. Flipped them. Nothing. But then an eerie glow illuminated what looked like a utility room.

Emergency lights, he realised as he heard the distant hum of a generator.

Staggering out of the small room, his numb fingers gripping Melody's, he slammed the connecting door shut behind them to contain the cold from outside.

The glow brightened, casting a blue light over the vast room they had entered—all dark wood and high beams and stone, with a mezzanine level above.

A luxury ski chalet...

Thank the Lord.

'It's beautiful... And it's heated. Hallelujah,' Melody murmured, her voice dull with fatigue but sharp enough to pierce through the mist fogging his brain.

His arm began to throb. He staggered, his balance shot, as he stared at the stone wall opposite, a huge unlit fireplace piled high with logs. The expensive furniture—sofas, coffee table, a white fur rug—levitated and began to dance.

Exhaustion wrapped around him like a blanket, taking away the pain. The fear.

'Rene, are you okay? Oh, my God, you're bleeding.'

He watched Melody, stumbling out of her layers of clothing.

He smiled. God, how he wanted to see her naked again. How he wanted to sink into that tight wet heat and have her hold him—and keep the nightmares at bay.

But as the disjointed thoughts collided in his head, the heat in his crotch built, becoming unbearable, and he couldn't seem to speak, couldn't tear off his clothing, because he was too busy waltzing with the furniture now—then floating, falling, crashing onto the soft white rug, which welcomed him with open arms.

'Oh, no...oh, no...oh, no... Rene, wake up. Please, wake up!' Mel dropped to her knees on the rug, gripped his arm to shake him. The panic rose like a wave. A tsunami of fear, coming from nowhere to bowl her over.

They were safe. Rene had saved them both. And now he was dead.

Terror clawed at her throat, threatening to choke off what was left of her air supply as she continued to shake his long, strong body, which was laid out on the rug where he'd slid—with surprising grace—to the floor.

But then he groaned. 'Stop. Shaking. Arm. Hurts,' he muttered, then seemed to lapse back into sleep.

Not dead. Alive. Thank you. Thank you, thank you, thank you.

She sat back on her heels, pushed the wave of panic back, to assess the damage and figure out a solution.

She'd been exhausted, wiped out, ready to sleep for ever

during their endless march through the storm, which had felt like a lifetime trek but could only have been about an hour.

He'd been there like a wall in front of her. Solid, unyielding, unstoppable, giving her the strength she needed not to let the fear overwhelm her.

Now you need to return the favour.

She had to get him warm first. Then get him out of the wet clothing. A new wave rose up, still fearful, but also focused, and determined.

The chalet was clearly some luxury holiday home—closed up for the season. But while it was a lot warmer in here than outside, it wasn't exactly balmy.

No way would she be able to figure out how to turn up the heating without leaving Rene, though, and she couldn't do that. Then her gaze landed on the lavish stone hearth, which was a signature feature of the living area.

The fire. Light a fire. Duh.

She kicked off her boots, wrenched off the heavy ski gloves, then scrambled over to the huge fireplace. Finding kindling, lighter fuel, matches, she sent up several more thank you prayers as she built the fire in record time, dredging up the knowledge from memories of staying in a small cottage in Wales the winter after her parents' divorce.

Good to know I learnt one useful skill during the worst Christmas of my life.

It took several attempts, but after figuring out how to work the flue she finally got the fire roaring.

She crawled back to Rene. He hadn't budged, but the frown on his face and the grimace flattening his lips suggested he wasn't in a coma, just trying to avoid the pain.

Grasping the edge of the rug, she used all her strength to drag him closer to the fire. The jacket, which had a rip in the arm, was soaked through. As was most of the rest of his clothing because, unlike hers, it wasn't made for an endless trek in a freezing snowstorm.

How on earth had he survived, she wondered, and stayed strong enough to break into the house and carry her in here?

She brushed his wet hair back from his brow.

'Rene, you idiot, why didn't you take some of my clothing?' she whispered, affection washing through her on another emotional tsunami. But then the thought of his lips branding hers before they'd thrown themselves into the storm turned the affection into something wilder and hotter and a lot more disturbing.

She pressed her fingers to her mouth, which, even numb from the cold, still held the imprint of that possessive kiss.

He groaned again and then began to shiver.

Stop daydreaming about a kiss that meant nothing...and get his wet clothes off.

She tugged off the leather gloves first, relieved to find his fingers chapped and red but with no signs of frostbite. It took her an age to undo the snarled laces of his boots and then pull off the wet jeans. Her own reserves of energy began to flag as she wrestled the soaked frozen denim over lean hips and the roped, hair-dusted muscles of his thighs. Again, the skin on his legs looked sore but not damaged. The jacket and sweater took even longer, but once she'd got them both off her gaze raked over him.

The firelight lit his muscular torso, the flickering flames turning the tanned skin to a burnished bronze and highlighting the sprinkle of dark hair which trailed through washboard abs. She flushed, remembering how she had reacted that night to seeing him naked. He was even more solid and overwhelming at twenty-eight than he had been at twenty-four—the scars she'd been so shocked by before somehow more pronounced. But then she noticed the blood seeping from a wound on his left arm.

And recalled the crunch of broken glass as he'd carried her into the house.

She shook her head, trying to snap out of the exhaustion. She had to stop the bleeding. She mopped the blood with his wet sweater, sighing with relief when she discovered it was a jagged wound but not too deep. The heat from the fire—and her juvenile reaction to seeing him virtually naked again— had sweat dripping into her eyes. She stripped off her under-shirt—leaving her in nothing but her underwear, because the room had become much warmer, positively toasty. She ripped the cotton into strips and gently wrapped his arm.

When she had finished he had stopped shivering and seemed peaceful at last. His breathing was deep and even, the grimace relaxing.

Dragging a throw from the couch with the last vestiges of her strength, she wrapped it around them both and snuggled against his right side, placing her hand on his belly.

But as woozy fatigue began to overwhelm her, the soft murmur of his breathing, the salty scent of sweat and the hints of bergamot and cedar drew her back into dreams of a night long ago.

'Shh… Here, let me touch you. Let me make it good.'

'Oh, yes, please do,' Mel had gasped as Rene's thumb found the place where their bodies joined, teasing, tempt-ing and tormenting her. 'I think you're missing the best bit,' she offered.

Rene chuckled, but all she heard was husky approval, in-stead of the disgust she had panicked she might hear when he'd asked her if she was a virgin.

Thank goodness she had kept that a secret—even though that thick thrust had hurt a bit. He certainly wasn't a small guy in any way, but the pain was fading fast now.

'How about this?' he murmured, and then his thumb swept across the perfect spot at last.

She bucked. 'Oh… Oh… Yes. Right there.'

The coil of pleasure tightened sharply, her body clamouring for a release which felt just out of reach as he caressed that perfect spot. The full stretched feeling—where he was lodged so deeply inside her—felt so good now too.

This feels so perfect. But how does he know just where to touch me?

'I can't… It's so much,' she gasped, suddenly scared by the intensity of her feelings. The perfection of his touch.

'Shh, Melody. I've got this… Just relax.' He cupped her cheek, his gaze fierce in the darkened room—and her heart contracted in her chest.

How could this be the boy she remembered? The boy who had once made her feel like nothing, but had made her feel so special tonight. The man who had flirted with her and flattered her all evening, ever since she had confronted him in the Mayfair club. He had made her feel cherished and witty and important in front of her friends, before they'd sneaked back to her place together.

He groaned heavily, the taste of brandy on his breath delicious as he kissed her with fury and purpose. Then he grasped her hips in both hands. 'I need to move.'

She lifted her knees, gripped his shoulders and nodded, giving him permission, eager to feel it all now.

He slid out of her, then thrust slowly, surely, but so carefully back in—filling her to bursting. But this time he nudged a spot so perfect her whole body quivered. She sobbed, the immense sensation rippling outwards.

He let out a harsh laugh. 'Good?' he asked.

She nodded furiously. 'Yes, do that again.'

'Your wish is my command,' he teased, but the deep

chuckle which followed felt even more validating, even more glorious, filling up all the inadequate places inside her.

The last of the discomfort disappeared as he held her firmly and stroked that perfect spot, over and over.

The pleasure swelled—soaring, bursting—until her sobs matched his grunts, their sweat slick bodies moving in furious unison.

Finally, she flew, the joy sweeping her body matched by the joy swooping into her heart. And as she sank into the bright, beautiful abyss he gathered her into his arms and kissed her forehead.

'That was incredible, Melody,' he murmured, his tone tinged with surprise as well as admiration.

And her heart whispered, *Yes, yes, it was. Surely this makes Rene Gaultiere mine now, for ever.*

CHAPTER SIX

MEL WOKE FROM a sleep infused with the scent of cedarwood and sweat, her body slick with longing, yearning for a connection, giddy with release…

It took a moment for her eyes to adjust to the half-light, for her ears to hear the storm battering the shutters outside… And to realise that Rene's scent wasn't a phantom memory any more from four years ago, and the warmth of his skin was real—her cheek pressed into the strong muscles of his back. For a moment she lay there, simply inhaling his distinctive scent and listening to the murmur of his breathing as she absorbed the shift from dreams to reality.

She wasn't that naïve girl any more, with delusions of love and for ever, but still it felt so good to be with him again—warm, safe, secure. He'd saved her. And that meant something. Although her exhausted brain couldn't quite figure out what.

But then he grunted and turned towards her. 'Melody?' he murmured, his voice gruff with sleep.

He wrapped his arms around her, drawing her close. Her heart jumped into her throat as she hugged him back, instinctively seeking the vivid connection they had once shared so briefly.

'I'm here.' She stroked his chest, the hair soft and springy against her palm, the beat of his heart solid and so reassuring. 'We're safe.'

He buried his face against her hair, his lips nuzzling her

neck. The burst of joy and validation was so sudden it felt like a continuation of the vivid dreams she'd had so often, reliving the pleasure, and the foolish infatuation, from that night. But the languid longing only became fiercer and more undeniable as the outline of his erection pressed against her belly through his shorts.

'Need you,' he moaned, his hands stroking, caressing.

But the longing didn't feel foolish or sentimental now. It felt elemental and life-affirming as she freed the thick length from his shorts—and found him hard and ready. For her.

'Yes, I need you as well,' she replied, heady with desperation as he delved into her panties to find her slick folds—touching, stroking, circling until the hunger became sharp and insistent.

He groaned, the sound rich with relief as he grasped her hips, angled her pelvis.

He levered up and over her, his urgency, his focus making her ache even more, her tired brain clinging to one thought: *I need him tonight, just to prove that I'm alive. That we've survived.*

He tore away the damp lace shielding her sex, but then found her core again with his fingers—using his thumb to drive her into a frenzy. She bucked beneath him, her sobs drowning out the sound of the storm which had nearly killed them both.

She groaned as the ache inside her turned to desperate pain, her body primed and needy.

'Don't wait,' she urged, knowing she wanted him to be inside her when she reached her release.

He dragged her knees up and plunged into her at last.

She welcomed the thick weight of him, driving deep, stretching her unbearably—joining them together again.

One thrust, two... The heady feeling of connection surged as exquisite pain turned to tortured pleasure and the glorious release exploded through her body, shattering her with stunning force. She heard his guttural shout, felt the slick heat inside her as he climaxed, too.

He collapsed next to her, then dragged her towards him. She snuggled into his arms and let herself tumble back into an exhausted sleep, safe and sated and secure again for the first time in four years.

Mel's eyelids fluttered open hours later, her body humming even as discomfort intruded too. Her mind drifted for a moment, still floating on a sea of sensation, and blissful ignorance. But, gradually, the anchor of reality drew her back to the surface. She became aware of the rush of wind, the rhythmic thump of the shutters rattling against the window frames, which had woken her in the night, the ambient blue, now joined by the muted daylight. And the subtle aches and pains—at her core, between her thighs and against her hip, where the floor was hard and unyielding.

She blinked and the shimmer of remembered pleasure dissolved in a rush, to be replaced by full consciousness as she became aware of Rene breathing heavily beside her.

Realisation struck. Of what she'd done. What *they'd* both done… Together, during the night.

She felt sore, used, still branded by the huge erection—which she'd begged him for. Not to mention the fierce rush of pleasure, followed by that foolish rush of validation.

Mel, you absolute idiot.

Emotions blindsided her—but in the cruel light of morning they were panicked and shaming, no longer visceral and life-affirming.

She shifted and stifled a groan.

The soreness, though, where Rene had taken her so comprehensively during the night, was nothing compared to the brutal regret making her ribs hurt. Because this was still Rene, the man she'd kidded herself cared for her once before.

Good grief, when would she ever learn? Yes, he'd been magnificent during the storm, protecting her, saving her, but giving in to the desire for a connection with him again, while they had both been barely awake, was madness.

She lay on her back, staring at the vaulted ceiling, scared to move, scared to look at the man beside her, slowly becoming aware too of the residue of his release, which had dried between her thighs during the night.

Wow, Mel, when you mess up you never do it by halves, do you?

The good news was she had just had a period, she reasoned frantically, so the chances of a pregnancy were slim... She would just have to hope for the best and take a test when she got back to the White Palace. *No biggie.*

She tried to gauge the intensity of the snowstorm outside, still battering their refuge. Was it morning yet? Surely it had to be... How long had they slept?

She eased herself out from under the throw, her skin warmed by the heated air in the room even though the fire was out. She slipped off the torn lace panties, which he'd ripped from her during their lovemaking session...

Not lovemaking, she told herself staunchly as she hunted for her clothes. More like no-holds-barred, dirty, sweaty, life-affirming and insanely dumb sex.

Which is, let's face it, what we have always specialised in.

She found her yoga pants and slipped them on.

The first time she'd had sex with Rene she had been high on vintage Napoleon brandy and the full glare of his undivided attention for an entire evening after their chance encounter in a London nightclub. This time she had been high on the erotic dreams which had never left her since that night, and the impact of waking up to discover she was wonderfully, gloriously alive, and he wanted her again.

Neither time had had any emotional significance. And that was what she needed to focus on now.

She found one of her discarded jumpers, which had dried by the fire, and tugged it on.

She needed a shower. But before leaving the room she risked a glance at Rene.

She let out a relieved sigh. He was still deeply asleep, his face flushed. Not all that surprising, seeing as he'd done the lion's share of the work to get them out of the storm—and during their late-night dumb-sex session.

Perhaps he wouldn't remember what had happened between them... All she could do was hope. And if he did, she'd just have to ensure he realised it was a one-off, never to be repeated.

Whatever happened, she needed to re-establish her boundaries now, and shore up her defences.

But as she continued to stare at him she frowned, noticing the reddened skin around the makeshift bandage on his arm. Then the harsh sound of his breathing registered too, above the noise from outside.

She knelt beside him to brush his hair away from his forehead, strangely drawn to the scar she remembered. But when her fingertips touched him, she gasped.

He's burning up.

She tugged the throw down to press her palm to his chest and felt his galloping heartbeat—as well as the shocking heat.

Rene was on fire. No wonder he'd seemed so deeply asleep. Was he even conscious?

She shook his shoulder as gently as she could. 'Rene, Rene, wake up.'

He let out a low groan. 'Stop. Arm...' he murmured, the words tortured.

She tugged off the makeshift bandage she'd applied when they'd arrived. But he flinched when she inspected the sore flesh around the jagged cut.

His lids snapped open, his dark chocolate eyes glassy with fever. '*Ouch!*'

'Rene, I think your arm is infected,' she said, becoming frantic when his lids closed again.

Guilt assailed her. She had been panicking about their night-time encounter, while he had developed a raging fever in the hours since...

Shivers began to rack his body. 'Cold,' he said, then reached for the throw she'd stripped off him.

'No, we need to get your temperature down,' she managed, wrestling with him for control of the blanket.

This time she won, far too easily. He sank back onto the rug, giving up.

Hastily, she stripped the throw off completely. A blush fired over her cheeks as she dragged his boxers up, to preserve what was left of his modesty, and hers, guilt consuming her now, as well as a rush of shame—and awareness.

'Don't move,' she said somewhat redundantly, as he seemed to have sunk into unconsciousness. 'I'm going to see if I can find water and some medicine,' she added to no one in particular.

Any medicine, she thought frantically. But first she should call for help.

No one knew where they were. From the dim strip of light coming through the shutters, it had to be daytime by now. And she felt as if she'd been sleeping for hours since she and Rene had...

The blush burned her cheeks.

Okay, maybe don't think about your ill-advised sex-fest while he could be dying.

She dived for her jacket, found her phone zipped into the pocket. Dead. Needless to say, she hadn't thought to pack her charger when they'd left the car. Next, she searched the pockets of Rene's coat, only to discover his phone was dead too.

She looked around the shadowy room. The furnishings were luxurious and expensive, the space beautifully designed. So, the lodge had to be in regular use.

She ignored the wrenching sensation as she left him lying on the floor in a pool of sweat, still shivering.

It took her less than two minutes to discover the chalet's mains power and phoneline had been knocked out by the storm. She searched the ground floor, which included a guest bedroom, a kitchen and a cold storage locker full of frozen food—well, at least they wouldn't starve—and then the master bedroom on the mezzanine level, but had no luck finding a phone charger.

Right, back to plan A, finding medicine and water. Because they were on their own, it seemed, until the storm cleared. She'd done first aid training a couple of years ago—what they needed was antibiotics or, failing that, some antiseptic and anti-inflammatories. And painkillers. Hopefully, it was only a localised infection.

She would need to clean the wound. Why hadn't she done that last night, before falling asleep in his arms? Or, better yet, when she'd woken up in the hours just before dawn, instead of deciding to have unprotected sex with him?

She pushed the renewed wave of recriminations to one side. *So not helpful, Mel.*

She rifled the cabinets in the guest bedroom's bathroom, becoming even more frantic when she found nothing, not even a stray toothbrush. The main bedroom's bathroom was equally bare, other than a sealed box of condoms.

Bit late for those. She pushed that thought to one side, too. *One catastrophe at a time, Mel.*

Then she remembered the utility room they'd walked through to get into the house.

She raced down the corridor and skidded to a stop in the doorway before she tore her feet to ribbons on the broken glass strewn all over the floor. After putting her boots on, she tiptoed through the glass to search the room. She hooted with joy when she found a brand-new first aid kit tucked next to the emergency generator.

Bingo! No antibiotics, but bandages, antiseptic, a thermometer and a ton of painkillers and anti-inflammatories.

After filling a glass from the kitchen with cold water and a bowl with gloriously hot water—the generator was a godsend and no mistake—she headed to the living area with the first aid kit under her arm.

Rene was still flat out on the rug, groaning—and not in a good way this time.

She set her cargo down beside him, then pressed the button to open the room's shutters. The storm cut out most of the daylight but added a pearly glow.

'Don't worry, Gaultiere,' she whispered as she plonked herself on the rug next to him. He didn't react. Day-old stubble darkened his jaw, making him look like even more of a reprobate than usual. But he also looked strangely fragile... The way he had seemed on their first night when she'd asked him about the scar and a look had flashed in his eyes—both vulnerable and defensive—before it had disappeared.

She blinked to control the rush of memory, and emotion.

Okay, maybe don't go getting delusional again. This is still Rene—the thoughtless, entitled egomaniac—he's just an injured, feverish, thoughtless, entitled egomaniac who saved your life, and can still *tempt you to make daft decisions.*

'You're not going to die on my watch,' she whispered, going on to repeat the words he'd said to her in the Jeep, what felt like a lifetime ago now. She found the thermometer and placed his head in her lap to tuck it under his tongue. 'Because we've still got a ton of arguments in our future.'

But as she brushed the sweaty hair back from his brow, her fingertips grazed the old scar and the disturbing emotions—which had driven so many foolish decisions, not just four years ago, but in the early hours of this morning, too—pushed against her chest once more.

CHAPTER SEVEN

'DON'T HURT ME. Not again… Please.' Pain lanced through Rene's head and seared his soul. Why did his father hate him so much? He'd tried so hard to be the son he wanted, a good prince. But, no matter what he did, the punishments, the rages, the tests he could only fail still came. Always.

The familiar fear consumed him, but then gentle fingertips brushed his forehead.

'It's okay, Rene. Just drink this. It'll help. I swear.'

The voice was so cool and strong it dragged him away from the searing heat, and the childish terror.

'Don't leave me again, not with him,' he whispered. The monster was still there, lingering on the edges of his consciousness, and only she could protect him.

'Shh, it's okay. I won't, I promise, but you must drink more water.'

Something touched his mouth. He opened dry sore lips, let the icy cold soothe his scorching throat. Was it her—the woman who had held him before, and kept the monster away with the fierce, furious rush of pleasure?

He clasped her wrist, forced his eyelids open despite the ten-ton weights attached to each one. She shimmered into view, her heart-shaped face so beautiful. The concerned expression calmed the emptiness inside him. He stared, captivated by the sight of those cornflower blue eyes—intent, determined, the full rosy lips so lush. Had he kissed them?

He must have, because he could remember her taste and knew he wanted to taste her again.

'He hates me,' he said, because he wanted someone, finally, to know the ugly truth which had been locked inside him for so long. 'And I can't make it stop.'

'Rene, it's okay, he can't hurt you any more,' she said, her voice strong with understanding and courage. A courage he had never possessed. 'I won't let him.'

He closed his eyes again as shame washed over him on another wave of searing heat.

Why had he told her? Would she hate him too now? For his weakness, his cowardice.

'If you complain, I will make sure you regret it. Do you understand?' his father's voice threatened again from the darkness.

He was too exhausted, too weak, to fight the fear, alone again…

'Sleep, Rene, you need sleep. You're safe. I think the fever's broken now…'

As he drifted into the darkness he could hear her voice, protecting him, and knew it was finally safe to let himself fall.

Rene jerked awake, then winced and cursed, before slamming his eyes shut again.

Had he been run over by a truck? Because he hurt, *everywhere*.

And who had turned on the searchlight? Because his retinas were on fire. He lifted his arm to cover his face and block out the light, but it took a while because the limb was a dead tree attached to his shoulder, unwieldy and not really his own.

He lay, taking deep shuddering breaths as he assessed the damage.

Thumping headache? Check. Aching bicep? Check. A

throat drier than the Gobi Desert? Check. Cheeks that feel as if someone has sandpapered them? Double check.

It was a technique he'd learned as a child, to cope with all those times he'd woken up in pain, with bruises in places no one could see, feeling broken inside.

He frowned.

Get a grip on the pity party, Gaultiere. That broken kid is long gone and good riddance.

After what felt like several eternities, he eased his arm down and reopened his eyes, with a lot more caution.

What the heck was he doing lying flat on his back on the floor? In a room he did not recognise. Because the décor—carved wood beams and dark stone, not to mention the floral throw covering his lower half—looked like something out of a luxury fever dream.

Fever? Dream? Melody?

He re-covered his eyes as the memories of the storm and—far too much more—came flooding back into his consciousness.

'Don't. Wait.'

Heat swelled as he recalled lodging himself deep. Thrusting hard.

But had that actually happened? Or was it just another wet dream? Everything was so hazy and confused, because the memory of kissing her neck, touching her swollen flesh, thrusting into her again, was all mixed up with other stuff. Like his father being an even bigger arse than usual. And her saying tender things while her eyes glowed with compassion.

Surely, he'd imagined that. How could it be true when she hated his guts? Almost as much as his father had.

He rolled to his side, then moaned, the pain in his arm exploding.

'Ouch. Dammit.'

Memories flashed back as he clocked the makeshift bandage on his arm. He'd cut himself during the frantic effort to get out of the storm... That much he remembered with clarity. Had Melody wrapped the wound for him? *Why?*

He levered himself into a sitting position.

Then took a moment to breathe through the dizziness while contemplating his surroundings. And attempting to decipher what was real and what wasn't from the mush in his brain. He gave up after a few minutes because it was making his head hurt more. And it already felt as if someone had hit him with a sledgehammer.

The outside was still an impregnable swirl of white through the open shutters, the muffled howl a sign the storm hadn't abated since last night.

A fire blazed in the hearth, and a pile of unfamiliar clothes had been folded neatly on the couch—which was helpful, because he couldn't see his jeans or sweater anywhere. All he had on was his shorts, and they weren't doing much to hide his reaction to the memories which he was fairly sure couldn't be real now.

He needed to find Melody and ask her what the hell had occurred during the rest of the night, though, to be sure... Shame washed over him. How he was going to broach the subject of possibly, maybe, having jumped her in his sleep he had no idea—but he wanted to be fully clothed when he had that potentially excruciating conversation.

After getting to his feet, it took another moment for the fresh wave of light-headedness to pass, before he could stagger over to the couch.

He selected a T-shirt and a pair of sweatpants from the pile. The T-shirt was too tight across his chest, and the pants too loose at the waist, hanging low on his hips, and were also way too short, finishing above his ankles. But at least the clothes were warm and dry and covered the essential bits.

Luckily, the thought of the conversation they now needed

to have—which promised to be even more difficult than the one they'd had to postpone, thanks to their journey into hell—quelled any lingering erotic dreams. Doubly good because the borrowed pants did not have a lot of spare room in the crotch either.

Maybe Melody was the one who had run him over with the truck.

His lips curved, making the chapped skin crack, as he remembered her snarky attitude from last night. And the battles they'd fought, and he'd won, first in the East Wing and then the garage. Why did those seem like several eons ago now, too? One thing was for sure. After their near-death experience, he wasn't angry with Melody Taylor any more. In fact, he felt weirdly okay about getting stuck here with her.

When it came to surviving a white-out in the Alpine wilderness in the middle of the night, he couldn't think of a better person to do it with than a badass like Melody. He certainly couldn't imagine any of the other women he'd dated over the years holding their own the way she had, without a single complaint, or 'I told you so'.

He headed across the living area, finally steady enough to go in search of her…

Surely, he couldn't have had sex with her again and not remembered it clearly? Because that would be a crime, in more ways than one.

He padded into a vast, brightly lit kitchen, drawn by the salty aroma of frying bacon. His empty stomach turned inside out, but he stood in the doorway, taking a moment to enjoy the view. And process the wave of affection which tightened his ribs.

Melody stood with her back to him, busy cooking at a stainless-steel kitchen range. She wore a baggy T-shirt which hung to mid-thigh, over a pair of yoga pants which clung to her generous curves. She'd piled her tawny blonde curls on top of her head in a careless knot, baring her neck. He could almost smell her there, just below her ear, the fresh scent another siren call to his senses.

The image of making love to her in the shadowy darkness as she begged him for release pulsed in his brain, and his groin.

Well, hell...

Surely that *had* to be a false memory, he decided, because it reminded him of all the others he'd had in dreams since that night in a cramped bed in her student flat in London. Even so, the sensory overload was so powerful the fabric at his crotch tightened again.

Damn, he wanted her still. Was that where these phantom memories came from? The urge, not the actual deed? Because that would be pretty lowering, but at least it meant he hadn't taken advantage of her again, like he had when she was a starry-eyed eighteen-year-old.

He cleared his throat.

She jumped, let out a cute squeak and then swung around, wielding a spatula.

'Rene, you're awake?' she said, her eyes widening as her cheeks ignited with colour.

Okay, interesting reaction.

In his experience, Mel only ever blushed in the throes of passion. Also, she didn't look as if she wanted to brain him with the spatula, which was her usual response these days to being confronted with his presence.

'How are you feeling?' she asked, her gaze slipping away, the blush going radioactive.

'Good... Mostly.' His voice rasped against his dry throat as his gaze zeroed in on the tell-tale burst of colour mottling her collarbone, revealed when the oversized T-shirt slid off one shoulder. Heat pounded into his crotch, but at the same time emotion wrapped around his torso. Guilt or tenderness, he couldn't be sure which, but neither could be good, given their history… And their current circumstances.

'I need to know,' he said, deciding to rip off the Band-Aid. 'Did we have sex again last night, or did I just imagine it?'

'Of…of course not!' Mel blurted out the knee-jerk denial, still struggling with the wave of relief at seeing Rene well again after thirty-six hours of extreme stress.

He had been delirious for hours yesterday, his fever not breaking until around midnight, in the grip of nightmares which had terrified Mel almost more than his spiking temperature. And he'd been virtually comatose ever since, every time she'd checked on him. But of course, Rene being Rene, the only thing the man could remember was the ill-advised sex they'd indulged in before he'd become feverish.

'Are you sure?' One dark brow winged up, his suspicion clear. 'Because you've gone an interesting shade of vermillion. And that's a colour I've only ever seen on your face once before…' he paused, his scrutiny intensifying '…four years ago.'

'I'm positive,' she snapped, trying for indignation but getting guilt instead. Because she'd always been a terrible liar.

His gaze zeroed in on her burning cheeks. She swung back to the stove and made a big production of turning off the heat then scooping the rashers onto a plate to add to the late breakfast she'd cooked—to give herself time to gather her wits.

Yesterday had exhausted her. And shocked her in many ways, when she'd watched Rene battle what appeared to be extremely vivid and terrifying nightmares. But when she'd woken up this morning and waited the whole day for him to wake up, she'd also had far too much time to think about where those nightmares could have come from.

He hadn't been lucid while in the grip of the fever, but his cries of pain, his confused ramblings, had seemed like those of a child, not the man she knew.

But the man was definitely back now, even though he still seemed a little shaky on his feet, was sporting a two-day beard and had dark circles under his eyes. Even in the borrowed clothes—which she'd found in the master bedroom she was sleeping in and had left out for him—he looked like a prince again—arrogant, overwhelming and untouchable.

'By the way, we didn't get here last night, Rene,' she began, attempting to steer the conversation in a different direction. 'We've been here for over two days now…'

The harsh curse interrupted her. 'How can that be right? Are you telling me I've been asleep for thirty-six hours?'

'Yes. When you weren't out of it with fever,' she murmured, deciding not to mention the other time he'd been awake. If he didn't remember that encounter clearly, it made sense not to enlighten him. Because it had been a mistake which neither of them needed to dwell on.

She heard his bare feet padding across the stone flooring.

'I guess that explains why I'm ravenous,' he said, the husky tone disturbing her even more.

She turned to find him standing too close, still staring at her with that sceptical expression on his face. Shouldn't he look ridiculous in those ill-fitting clothes, the pants too short and the T-shirt stretching tight across his pecs? Why was he still so hot? It really wasn't fair.

Her gaze dropped then shot back to his face, but her blush flared again, because the damn pants were tight in all the wrong places.

'Why don't you take a seat?' she said, plucking the toast from the grill and slathering it with butter, far too aware of the musty smell no longer masked by soap and the expensive cologne. Why did she find his scent even more compelling now?

'I've made more than enough for both of us,' she added,

desperate to fill the uncomfortable silence, and keep all the unnerving memories of the intimacies they'd shared, *accidentally*, under control. 'Luckily, this place has a cold storage full of enough food to survive a nuclear war.'

He took the hint and, after grunting his thanks, went to sit on one of the stools at the breakfast bar.

She took her time loading a couple of plates with eggs, bacon and toast, then placing them on the counter between them, along with glasses of orange juice and cutlery. But five minutes later, when she slid onto the stool opposite him, it still felt far too soon to face him again.

Why couldn't she get this reaction under control? The sex had been fast and frantic, nothing more than a basic, elemental reaction to surviving a life-threatening situation, obviously. She'd been half asleep and Rene had been barely lucid too. It hadn't meant anything. Maybe pretending it hadn't happened at all—lying to him when he'd asked her a direct question—was a little…unethical. But the fact he didn't really remember it only proved it hadn't meant anything to him either. Hardly surprising, given their first time had meant nothing to him as well!

But as she scooped up a forkful of eggs, determined to get through the awkwardness, and control the guilt, he grasped her wrist. Her gaze rose, his touch making her pulse spike. Could he feel it? Probably.

'What do you mean, I was out of it?' he asked, the wary expression calming her guilt—and panic—a little. Maybe he wasn't as confident as he appeared.

'You had a fever, which started yesterday. You were having nightmares, saying lots of weird stuff, begging me not to leave you with someone. Once it broke last night, though, you slept like the dead.'

Stark emotion flashed across his features, reminding her of

the expression on his face that night so long ago in London, when she had questioned him about the scar on his forehead.

In the years since, she had convinced herself she had imagined the guarded, almost panicked reaction. Now, as then, he masked it quickly, but this time she had seen it clearly. And knew what it was. Because she'd heard the same fear in his voice during the night terrors she had nursed him through for hours.

Flags of colour appeared on his cheeks, and he dropped her wrist. He dipped his head and dug into his eggs, clearly keen to end the conversation.

Curiosity consumed her all over again at the defensive reaction.

Who *was* the monster who had chased him in dreams? The one he'd begged her to protect him from… Was it possible the monster wasn't just a figment of his feverish imagination, but something more tangible, something real?

Was that why he'd been so surly and mean as a teenager? So cynical and reckless as a man. What if his life hadn't been as charmed and entitled as she'd always assumed?

Yeah, maybe don't drop down that rabbit hole again, or you'll only have yourself to blame if you get your heart broken.

She cut off the wayward direction of her thoughts—which could only be a carryover from the romantic eighteen-year-old who had wanted to find a connection with Rene, to justify the physical urge they'd both succumbed to that night… And in the early hours of yesterday morning.

She had always been drawn to him whenever he seemed vulnerable. But then, finding excuses for the selfish behaviour of men was a weakness she had always suffered from. After all, hadn't she succumbed to the same self-destructive naivete with her dad, determined to kid herself that he cared for her, that he loved her, that he wanted to have a relationship with her after the divorce, when he had made it abundantly clear to her in every way that he didn't?

Rene had done the same damn thing by sleeping with her then ghosting her, and yet she had *still* wanted to believe there was more to their lovemaking than a quick endorphin fix.

What on earth was the matter with her?

When someone tells you who they are, believe them, Mel, remember!

'I hope I didn't make a nuisance of myself,' he murmured, keeping his head down.

'No more than usual,' she said, determined to puncture the strange sense of intimacy, and get their relationship back to where it had been before their near-death experience.

After all, snarky had always been a much better defence against Rene's dark arts than curiosity and compassion.

He let out a weary laugh which didn't seem to have a lot of humour in it.

'*Touché*,' he murmured.

But as he began shovelling the bacon into his mouth like a starving man, she found herself dwelling again on those tortured cries. And her heart swelled against her ribs, as it had for hours while she had watched him struggle with those demons.

They finished the meal in silence, but when she got off her stool and reached for his empty plate he snagged her wrist again.

'Leave it,' he said. 'I'll wash up.'

She tugged her wrist free, far too aware that her pulse had started dancing a jig.

'No, thanks.' She tilted her head to one side. His colour was a bit better but he still looked washed out. 'I don't want you faceplanting in the kitchen this time,' she added. 'Because you're too heavy for me to carry anywhere and too big to step over.'

Her heartbeat accelerated alarmingly as a sensual smile curved his lips. She hadn't seen that smile for four years— the only time he'd ever bestowed it on her—but she could still remember its devastating effect. How annoying he could still use it like a lethal weapon to disarm all her defences.

'Fair point,' he murmured. The mocking light shimmering in the golden brown of his irises only added to his killer charm. 'I've discovered that sleeping for days on the floor is quite literally a pain in the arse.'

She collected the plates and headed to the sink, determined not to be charmed. Nothing had changed between them. He was still a prince, and she was still a PA—and she wasn't about to make the mistake again of thinking that he viewed her as more than just an easy lay.

Been there, done that and still have the inferiority complex to prove it.

Unfortunately, they were stuck here, alone together, until the storm broke or the phone line was restored. Or a search and rescue team came looking for them. Hopefully, that would be sooner rather than later, but until then she would just have to ensure she kept her wits about her—and didn't fall into the trap he had always represented.

After all, she'd already slept with him once without intending to—because he had a devastating effect on her libido as well as her common sense, even when they were practically comatose.

Rene had always been indiscriminate when it came to his sexual conquests—and he had a devastating personal charm when he chose to use it. But forewarned was forearmed.

She turned on the tap and began scrubbing the plates with more force than was probably necessary. She heard him get up from the stool and swear softly as he stumbled, but forced herself not to turn around.

'There's a guest bedroom on the ground floor you can use.

I've taken the master upstairs.' She threw the words over her shoulder, glad her voice remained unmoved.

She needed to make it clear that even though he was a prince they were equals here.

'I found a stash of toiletries in the laundry room under the sink,' she added, her nerves forcing her to fill the silence when he didn't respond.

'Are you saying I stink?' he asked.

She turned, then realised her mistake when she got another eyeful of his chest, temptingly displayed in the figure-hugging cotton. She folded her arms across her breasts, suddenly aware of the bra she had left drying in the laundry room when her nipples tightened under his amused gaze.

She gave him a deliberate once-over, then sniffed the air. 'I'm saying a shower certainly wouldn't hurt.'

But instead of reacting with indignation or anger as she'd hoped, he let out a gruff chuckle, his gaze still warm with appreciation.

'*Touché*. Again,' he said, the amusement in his tone not helping with the rabbit punches of her pulse, or her now painfully engorged nipples. 'Landing cheap shots is getting to be a bad habit, Melody.'

She took some satisfaction from the hit. And the thought that her provocative reply had set their relationship back on track. After all, their bickering had always been her safe space where Rene was concerned, a throwback to their childhood which she had clung to after that night to cover the hurt he'd caused. But the spurt of satisfaction was short-lived when his voice lowered even more—into a confidential rumble rich with innuendo—and his gaze drifted over her body with far too much entitlement.

'Be warned though,' he said, the intensity in his eyes as much of a surprise as the possessive tone, 'I'm starting to feel a lot better already, and once I'm back to full strength you won't find it as easy to best me.'

Gauntlet thrown down, he strolled from the room, the confident grace back in his stride. Her gaze drifted down to a muscular male backside displayed to perfection in too-tight sweats. And then jerked back up again.

For goodness' sake, Mel, stop checking out his butt.

But as she turned back to the sink and began scrubbing the plates hard enough to erase the design on them, heady desire shot through her overwrought body at warp speed. And it occurred to her that her safe space was now history. Because bickering with Rene was now almost as much of a turn-on as the light of approval in his golden gaze. And that mocking, devastatingly sensual smile. Not to mention the far too vivid memory of their latest X-rated faux pas. *Blast the man.*

CHAPTER EIGHT

'WHAT ARE YOU DOING?'

Rene turned from the stove—and the two ribeye steaks he was busy trying not to incinerate—to find Melody standing behind him, wearing a shocked expression. It was the first time he'd seen her since their shared meal the night before, so he guessed the shot of adrenaline at the sight of her in an outsize sweatshirt and the familiar yoga pants was to be expected. He'd never been a guy who preferred his own company, and he'd been stuck with himself for over twenty-four hours.

He'd slept like the dead again last night, after his shower. But when he'd woken this morning he'd found a plate of food left for him in the kitchen and a note on the counter which had been curt and to the point:

I'll be in my room. Don't disturb me unless rescuers arrive.

'I'm making us a meal—what does it look like?' he muttered, trying to ignore his frustration at her attitude, and the fierce joy at seeing her again, which seemed somewhat disproportionate, given the scowl on her face.

Apparently, she was not nearly as pleased to see him.

'Seriously? You know how to cook?' The blank shock was starting to get on his nerves.

'Don't look so surprised. I'm perfectly capable of cooking steak and potatoes.' He hoped. 'And I figured it was my turn.'

The truth was he'd been bored out of his skull. He had managed to use up some time since he'd woken that morning trying to figure out how to use a washing machine. Why did they make the controls so unnecessarily complicated? And after shrinking his sweater to a size no ten-year-old would be able to fit into, he'd managed to waste another couple of hours hooking the back door onto its hinge and cleaning up the broken glass.

But since then he'd had nothing to do.

The storm still hadn't broken, so he had eventually had to abandon his plan to venture out and locate their stranded vehicle so he could retrieve a phone charger.

Bored and far too aware of Melody, upstairs, in the master bedroom, ignoring him, he'd spent the afternoon lying on his empty bed being tortured by a ton of erotic images he couldn't seem to shake… Not unlike the dreams which had plagued him for years, which seemed to have morphed into brand-new phantom memories he couldn't shake either, not since their first night here.

All of which meant he was a lot more on edge than usual.

'*Really*?' she said. 'Now, I'm actually speechless,' she added, her astonishment joined by the glitter of derision in her gaze.

He switched off the gas, propped his butt against the counter and folded his arms over his chest, while trying to look less pissed off than he felt.

He knew she enjoyed mocking him, but frankly he'd had enough of her bad opinion and her snarky attitude to last him a lifetime already. And now they seemed to have an endless amount of time together—and she had made it clear she wasn't interested in entertaining themselves with mindless sex—he was more than ready to call out her attitude problem.

'What exactly is so damn surprising about me being able to cook a simple meal?' he snapped, aching for a fight. Because sparring with Melody was considerably more satisfying than spending hours alone with only phantom erotic dreams of her.

Go figure.

'It's not that,' she shot back, because they had always known how to antagonise each other. 'It's that you'd deign to cook one for *me*… Or be prepared to take turns here. After all, you're a prince, right, and I'm just staff—something you have always made abundantly clear to me.'

'*W-What?*' He was so surprised by the accusation, and the shadow of hurt in her eyes before she masked it, that he was actually speechless.

Okay, they'd always managed to touch each other's rawest nerves, but he had never been that much of an arse, had he? He was always courteous to his staff. He made a point of not expecting more than he was entitled to demand for the very generous salaries he paid them…because he had never wanted anyone to confuse him with the previous ruler of Saltzaland, a cruel and capricious despot who had a reputation for bullying his employees.

'When have I ever given you the impression I did not consider you—or anyone who works for myself or Isabelle, for that matter—my equal?' he finally managed.

Her eyebrows lifted as if she was surprised he was defending himself, which only aggravated him more.

'And surely the fact I have slept with you makes it blindingly obvious I never thought of *you* as an employee of *mine*…' he added. 'Because FYI, that is a line I would never cross. *Ever.* I do have some standards and one of them is not to be as much of a total bastard as my…' He stopped abruptly, realising he had said too much when her eyes widened and he saw the curiosity he remembered from the previous day, when she had mentioned the nightmares he'd had in her presence.

He raked his fingers through his hair. 'This is a pointless argument,' he offered, feeling brutally exposed. Why had he defended himself when what she thought of him didn't matter?

He'd done some crummy things in his time: thoughtless,

reckless, impulsive, arrogant and even entitled things. He would certainly never pretend to be a saint, and the way their one night together had ended proved that. But sleeping with women who might find it hard to say no to him was not one of those things.

He tensed as the phantom memory returned, which had come back to haunt him again last night—dreams of her, under him, on the rug in the living room, the tight clasp of her body massaging him to climax with staggering speed.

He shook his head to shake it loose, once and for all.

A dream, not a memory, dammit.

'Sit, so we can eat before this becomes a burnt offering.' He returned to the stove to dump the blackened steaks on the plates he'd laid out. He added the baked potatoes and split them open. Steam oozed out. The flesh looked too solid, but at least it wasn't raw.

He placed the plates on the breakfast counter, glad to see she had seated herself. Then he collected the butter and dumped it in front of her.

'Help yourself,' he said, hating the sharp note which he couldn't disguise.

Why exactly *did* he care about her low opinion of him when it was totally unfounded—on this score at least—and he had never cared about the low opinion of other women?

Then again, no other woman had ever been the thorn in his side that Melody Taylor had turned out to be.

To his surprise, she ate the meal he had cooked without making any more sarcastic remarks and didn't complain about the charred steak or the undercooked potato.

When he went to pick up their empty plates though, she touched his wrist. He glanced up and looked at her for the first time since they had sat down.

'Wait, I… I have something to say,' she said. She didn't exactly look contrite, but when she trapped her teeth beneath her bottom lip, the swift shot of lust felt less problematic than usual.

'Once, when we were kids…' she hesitated, her indecision strangely endearing because it was so unlike her '…you called me Isabelle's little beg-friend. And it upset me, a lot. Because I knew she was a queen, and I was essentially just the cook's daughter.'

He swore softly and sat back down. Damn, he'd forgotten about that insult. Probably because it was just one of the many he'd thrown at them both when he'd been left to his own devices in the White Palace while his father was visiting to speak to Androvia's Privy Councillors. He'd had so much anger back then, because of the fear he lived with daily. And taking it out on Isabelle and her feisty friend had been easier, and safer, than letting his father see how afraid he was.

He had assumed they would be easy targets because they had been smaller than he was, and girls, and they obviously adored each other. The truth was, he realised now in some twisted part of his brain, he had wanted to hurt them, to make himself hurt less.

In the years since, he'd absolved himself of those sins because he had believed, at least as far as Mel was concerned, he'd never hit his target. She had always been such a tough little cookie, had always given back as good as she got. Unlike Isabelle, who had often started crying, which had made her a lot less satisfying to provoke.

'I'm sorry,' he said, wondering why it had taken him so long to apologise when her head rose and he could see how astonished she was. 'I was a nasty bully back then and I'm not proud of the way I behaved towards both of you.' He shrugged. 'I suppose I should have apologised for that a lot sooner.'

The smile which edged her lips did strange things to his insides.

'Yes, you really should have,' she murmured, not willing to give an inch. But oddly, he wouldn't have it any other way.

'In my defence, I had no idea you'd taken that insult to heart. You always seemed so annoyingly bulletproof to all my attempts to patronise and belittle you.'

The slight curve widened into a genuine—and rather smug—smile. 'Of course you didn't. I would have died rather than let you know you'd scored a hit. And let's face it, you would have been even more insufferable if I had.'

'True.' He let out a rough chuckle. 'Damn, I think you've bested me again. This is getting to be an *extremely* annoying habit.'

She laughed, the smile brightening her face even more. And he wondered why on earth he had been so determined to upset her as a kid, when she had always looked so stunning when she smiled.

But then her expression sobered abruptly. 'Why *were* you so mean to us, when we never did anything to you?'

He tensed at the forthright question. How could he answer without exposing himself again?

She tilted her head, still watching him, the curious expression becoming far too astute.

'You know, I thought that you were just a naturally mean person back then. But I can't help thinking now, you were desperately unhappy for some reason.'

He let out a strained laugh—and forced himself to shrug—determined to cover the fact she had just scored another direct hit. Luckily, he was an expert at avoiding talking—or even thinking—about that sullen, insecure and messed-up boy.

'Back *then*?' he asked. 'And there I was thinking you have considered me a bastard ever since.' He let his gaze rake over her, determined to push this conversation onto another topic, one he was much more interested in. 'You've certainly given a very good impression of it… Except for one particular evening when we were too busy tearing each other's clothes off for you to remember how much you hated me.'

But instead of sparking the usual animosity, her gaze remained direct—and warm with compassion—which only disturbed him more.

'Honestly, I don't think I ever hated you, Rene,' Mel murmured, astonished not just to realise it was true, but that she'd said it out loud.

After all, she'd spent the whole day in her room, staring at the walls—and the terrible weather outside—simply to avoid having to talk to him about anything, let alone admit something so potentially explosive.

But somehow, she couldn't make herself regret it when his expression changed from cynical to guarded again.

'You kept that opinion well-hidden all these years,' he quipped, but he didn't sound so self-assured any more, which felt like another important win.

Maybe it was dangerous to want to see behind the wall he had always kept around his emotions. But she had always been curious about Rene, the boy as well as the man. If she hadn't, he never would have had the power to hurt her as a girl with those carelessly cruel barbs. Nor would she have fallen into bed with him so enthusiastically four years ago, as soon as he had shown an interest.

He'd been her first lover, was still her only lover, but she needed to stop beating herself up about that.

She'd tried to persuade herself for four years that he had never been that compelling, never that captivating and certainly not as complex as she'd wanted to make him. But she knew now that was always a lie she had told herself to stop herself from falling down that rabbit hole again.

Even when they were kids, he had fascinated her. How many afternoons had she spent bitching to Issy or to her mum about how awful he was, what a bully, what a meanie? When on some level she had enjoyed their sparring matches, even then. And had loved nothing more than to talk about him endlessly. Of course, at the time it had been on a kid-to-kid level, and a result of the fact that her father had paid her so little attention she'd had a self-destructive desire to get attention from anyone, however negative. But when she'd been eighteen and she'd spotted him in that nightclub, standing by the bar, and blurted out to her friends that she had grown up with the playboy prince, it really hadn't taken much persuasion from them for her to approach him and say hi.

Their sparring *that* night had quickly become flirting, and she had basked in the same approval he was showing her now. No wonder she had been intoxicated. Because while she felt a lot older and wiser now, and a lot less reckless, he intoxicated her still.

And then there were all the contradictions, which she saw so clearly now. He'd teased them mercilessly as a teenager, yes, but he'd also been dumbstruck when Isabelle had burst into tears. He'd treated her with care and attention in London too, making her first time memorable, even though he'd been gone the next day. And while he'd been a dictatorial jerk after the New Year's Eve Ball, he'd also nearly killed himself to get her to safety during the snowstorm. And then shown her heaven again in the early hours of the morning, however ill-advised it had been to succumb to their chemistry.

Her judgements of him and his behaviour towards her had never been objective. Because he excited and captivated her as much as he infuriated her... And he was right. As a boy, despite those hurtful nicknames, he had never treated her as the cook's daughter—but as a worthy opponent. And ever since, despite the huge difference in their status, she had always been able to be herself with him.

The revelation felt sobering but also strangely liberating.

She'd always considered him the villain and herself a fool for feeling anything for him at all, sure that the way she gravitated towards him had been down to nothing more than animal attraction—and some pathetic, unacknowledged desire to get approval from men. And, like so many women, she had confused sex with intimacy. But it was suddenly so clear there had always been more between them than just chemistry. A sort of prickly affection which saw each other's faults and enjoyed exploiting them. After all, fighting with him had always been as exhilarating as it was frustrating.

As he stared back at her, the expression on his face so wary, she found herself saying something she realised she wished she'd had the guts to say that night. And every time since when she'd used anger to cover her hurt.

'I wanted to hate you, Rene, after that night, because you were my first lover and I thought we'd made a connection, and then you ghosted me. And less than a month later you proposed to Isabelle. It hurt, knowing you could discard me so easily, but what hurt more was knowing I'd been stupid enough to invest so much emotionally in something so fleeting.'

His eyebrows launched up his forehead and he straightened. 'What do you mean, I was your first lover? Are you saying you *were* a virgin after all?' He swore under his breath. The shock on his face felt good—a vindication for that broken-hearted drama queen who had fallen asleep with dreams of spending the rest of her life in Rene's arms, only to wake up the next day and find the bed cold and empty beside her.

When Isabelle had told her of his proposal a few weeks later, it had devastated her... In her head, of course, she had understood his decision to ask the Queen of Androvia for her hand in marriage had been a political choice not an emotional one, but the hurt had still festered for years afterwards.

'You told me you'd had a ton of lovers when I asked,' he

said, his expression fierce with outrage and regret. 'Why the hell did you lie?'

She smiled, she couldn't help it, his volatile reaction to her virginity not just surprising but oddly flattering. Maybe that night had meant something to him, too.

She shrugged. 'Honestly, I think I was embarrassed about my inexperience.' Although if she had known his reaction would be this satisfying, she definitely would not have kept it a secret. 'And I was scared if you knew I was a virgin you might freak out and stop,' she added. 'And I definitely didn't want you to do that!'

He leapt up from the stool, then paced across the kitchen. He grasped his neck, massaged muscles which looked tight with tension. When he paced back again, his glare was full of accusation and more emotion than he had ever shown her before.

Another hit goes to Mel's virginity.

'You should have told me, dammit. I would have been more careful,' he said.

It was the last thing she had expected him to say, and it was her turn to feel the direct hit. Raw affection swelled against her ribs because he'd been more than careful enough. He'd made her first time spectacular, which she knew from the experiences she'd heard about from other girls at college was not the norm.

'You wouldn't have stopped then?' she asked, not ashamed any more to search for validation. She'd spent the last four years regretting that night bitterly, so it felt stupidly empowering to know he had been as blown away as she had—at least on a physical level.

His gaze jerked to hers. 'Not unless you had asked me to,' he said, sounding pained. 'But even that would have required a titanic effort as I was close to being past the point of no return as soon as I got you naked.' He slumped back down on the stool, tension bristling across those broad shoulders. That would be the same shoulders she'd clung to two nights ago.

Perhaps now would be a good time to admit what had happened the night of their arrival. Because her knee-jerk decision to lie again when he had asked her a direct question was beginning to look like a throwback to that misguided, insecure girl who had spent so much of her life hiding her needs and desires because she was scared they would never be reciprocated.

But then he lifted his hand to cup her cheek, and the naked emotion in his gaze derailed her train of thought completely.

'I'm sorry, Melody. I exploited our chemistry that night. And then I behaved like an insensitive arse. I wish I could go back and undo it all, but I can't. My only defence, and it's a pathetic one, is that I was in a bad place at the time.'

His hand slipped away but she caught his fingers and held on.

'I don't…' she swallowed, his surprised expression forcing her to say it all '… I don't wish you could undo it. Well, not all of it, anyway.'

A part of her would always be hurt by his decision to propose to Isabelle so soon after, even though she very much doubted the two things had been related. After all, he'd probably slept with a ton of women since that proposal had been rejected, and it wasn't as if he had loved Isabelle. 'You made my first time memorable, that's for sure,' she finished, which was the understatement of the century, but she didn't need to stroke his ego too much.

At least she could finally see that night for what it was—a livewire chemical connection—instead of what she had wanted it to be and it never could have been—a romantic one.

He rubbed his thumb across her lips, his gaze sharpening. 'You need to be careful, Melody. Because, in the interests of full disclosure, I still want you. A lot.'

Heat surged as the memories from that night—and two nights ago, when he had satisfied her again—pulsed along her nerve-endings.

'Do you really?' she said, unable to resist the urge to flirt.

He let out a gruff laugh, acknowledging the hit, then captured her wrist to tug her closer.

'I should also warn you,' he said, the husky words part threat, part promise, 'I have been bored out of my brain for the whole day.' He glanced out of the kitchen window. 'And it seems we may be trapped here...together...for at least another night. And now that we've declared a truce, and I'm not exhausted, I can think of all sorts of interesting ways to entertain ourselves.'

She took her time studying the weather, too. Adrenaline surged, because the vicious swirling snow outside no longer felt like a trap but an opportunity. The storm had cocooned them here in a place out of time. So why not take the chance to rewrite the mistakes of their past and enjoy this connection once more, before moving on? After all, they'd proved quite comprehensively a few nights ago they still had an exciting physical connection. And while she couldn't take back her white lie now without looking like a fool, a selfish part of her wanted him to acknowledge that when their time together here was over.

'Hmm, yes, you could be right about the weather,' she said, being deliberately coy, despite the fact that her pulse was battering all her erogenous zones now with even more fervour than the icy wind battering the glass.

His fingers gripped her chin and redirected her gaze to his. 'I have the perfect distraction to help us pass the time, Mel,' he murmured, his voice so husky she could feel it vibrating in her sex.

'Oh, do you, now?' she whispered back, although her own voice was so hoarse she wasn't fooling anyone any more, least of all him. 'And what distraction would that be?'

He stood up so suddenly his stool crashed to the floor. His gaze darkened with the intensity she had always found so intoxicating. 'You know damn well, you minx,' he said in the bossy tone she had found so aggravating on New Year's Eve.

She wasn't finding it aggravating any more. Quite the opposite, in fact.

He grasped her wrist and tugged her off her own stool, then banded his arm around her hips to drag her against him and cradle the growing ridge in his pants against her belly.

'Do you have any idea how much I want you right now?' he asked, the rough tone no longer amused. No longer smug.

'Actually, yes.' She ground herself against the delicious hardness, the feral urge to make him suffer almost as exciting as his lust-blown pupils.

Rene would always be a complex, fascinating and exciting man. But she didn't need or want him to be *her* man. Not any more. The pleasure he could give her, though—when he set his mind to it—had always been intoxicating and undeniable.

Giving in to that combustible chemistry wasn't dangerous any more. Because they were equals now. She wasn't a virgin, and she wasn't as naïve or as gullible as she had been four years ago. Nor was she as insecure. Because she had a job she adored and was good at, and she understood exactly now what sleeping with him meant... And what it never could.

Rene Gaultiere would never marry for love, or propose to a nobody like her. Nor did she want him to. Because she knew now what men like him—men who were closed-off emotionally and who would discard her, the way her father had once discarded her—could do to her confidence and self-respect if she became emotionally invested.

But Rene Gaultiere, the playboy prince, a man she knew could deliver when it came to no-holds-barred, dirty, sweaty sex was another matter.

He groaned, the loser again, then grasped her hips to hold

her steady. 'Okay, I surrender. Don't do that unless you are going to let me ravish you, or I may actually explode.'

She laughed, the joyous laugh of a woman who knew exactly what she wanted and how to get it.

She draped her arms over his broad shoulders, inhaling the intoxicating scent of soap and man and musk, and ran her fingernails across his nape, determined to be the hunter this time, as well as the willing prey. His vicious shiver emboldened her. She skimmed her thumb down the side of his face, the beard growth rasping against the pad, and imagined all the ways she wanted to ravish him, too.

'In the interests of full disclosure…' she teased, more than ready to exercise her newfound power, '…it just so happens I found an unopened box of condoms in my dresser drawer.'

His eyes flared with a feral passion which matched her own. 'I'm going to take that as a yes,' he said, then bent to scoop her over his shoulder.

She kicked and struggled, but it was all for show this time.

So when he slapped her backside and demanded, 'Keep still or I'll drop you,' as he marched out of the kitchen and headed upstairs to the master bedroom, she only laughed.

The adrenaline she had never been able to control charged through her system as he dropped her on the huge double bed. The snowstorm obscured the view of the forest through the glass wall at the far end of the room. But it didn't matter because all she could see was him.

'Get undressed,' he demanded as he tore his clothes off. 'The first time is going to have to be fast—to take the edge off,' he warned.

The thrill became turbo-charged as she struggled out of her own clothes, feeling truly alive, and empowered for the first time in her life.

She gulped down the wadge of desire as she gorged herself on the glorious sight of his body, gilded by the twilight which had managed to penetrate the storm. The dim light cast the planes and angles of his face into sharp relief, and highlighted the bulge of muscle and sinew. She found herself cataloguing all the scars and imperfections she had noticed once before, joined now by the healing scar on his arm.

She swallowed the burst of emotion, the memory of him carrying her through the storm suddenly a little too vivid.

Why was Rene the only man who had ever made her feel so bold, so seen, and yet also cherished?

The only thing you both cherish now is the sex.

Excitement built, obliterating the sentimental thought, as he grasped her ankle and dragged her to the end of the bed. Already naked, the thick jut of his erection made her sex soften and swell as she watched him scramble to find the box of condoms. He sheathed himself, his urgency as flattering as it was exciting.

But when he climbed over her and captured her lips at last in a mind-numbing kiss, she had to force the emotion back again.

Tonight was about sex, and pheromones, and indulging the spectacular chemistry they had denied for too long, and which they could indulge now without any messy emotional repercussions.

It has to be.

She grasped his head, sucked on his invading tongue and spread her knees to cradle his hips. The huge erection nudged her sex, but when he drew his fingers through the damp folds, to test her readiness and circle the swollen nub, she choked out a sob, her release already devastatingly close.

'Bad girl, Melody. You've been holding out on me,' he murmured, raw need belied by the mocking tone.

'Stop messing about and get on with it,' she demanded, desperate to feel that thick length inside her again. Determined to make it last longer this time than the last.

He chuckled, the sound rough. 'Your wish is my command,' he said, but just as her heart registered the echo from their first night, he grasped her hips and buried himself deep.

She cried out as the huge erection impaled her.

He stopped, giving her a moment to adjust, and swore against her neck, all trace of the mocking amusement gone when he murmured, 'You feel so good. So tight, just like that first time.'

Because you're the only man who has ever been inside me...

She pushed the revealing thought to one side and tugged his head back to gasp in his ear, 'Stop talking, you lummox, and move.'

His raw chuckle pushed at a place deep inside her, joining them, uniting them in their shared pursuit of desperate pleasure for pleasure's sake.

'Patience, Melody,' he mocked, but then established a punishing, undulating rhythm, touching every part of her, and stroking the spot deep inside which only he had ever found.

She rose to meet him, frantically reaching for the glorious oblivion, so close and yet still too far—which he was deliberately denying her.

The rat.

Slowly and surely, though, the pleasure built like a wave. Gathering and rising inside her, it became a tsunami, his grunts of effort matching her sobs of need.

'Yes, *yes*!' she cried. 'Don't stop.'

'No way,' he grunted, his fingers digging into her hips, forcing her to take more, to take all, to take everything.

The wave blasted through her, thrusting her into that beautiful, terrifying abyss, before she heard him shout out—from a million miles away, through the storm—and crash over behind her.

CHAPTER NINE

THE WOMAN HAS destroyed me again.

Rene pressed his face into Melody's hair, inhaling the sweet scent of sex and woman and roses in greedy gulps of air. Then groaned, aware of the vicious heat still pulsing in his groin, despite the titanic climax.

How the hell could he want her so much?

He dislodged himself and then flopped onto his back beside her before he collapsed on top of her—or worse, got hard again.

He needed to pace himself.

They had all night. And by the end of it he wanted to have this wild hunger for her sated, so they could make good on their truce and part, if not friends, at least not enemies.

He rolled his head towards her, to find her staring back at him, her eyes as dazed as he felt.

He grinned. She looked as shattered as he did.

Finally, I've bested her, too.

He lifted a heavy hand to brush one unruly curl back from her face and hook it behind her ear.

'Now we've taken the edge off, we should probably take a break before round two.'

Her brow arched speculatively, and a wave of affection for her blindsided him. Why had he never realised her snarky attitude was one of the things which had attracted him to her in the first place?

'Round two?' she asked. 'Who said there's going to be a round two?'

'Isn't there?' he asked lazily, not rising to the bait for once, the afterglow like a drug.

Her complexion went the same interesting shade of vermillion he had noticed the day before. 'I'm really not sure…'

'Hey…' He skimmed his thumb across her lips to silence the refusal he thought might be coming—and really did not want to hear. 'Surely, we owe it to ourselves to take one night? To explore this…' his gaze drifted down to the pert nipples he had every intention of feasting on next—once he'd got his breath back '…connection,' he murmured. 'We were too drunk to do it more than once four years ago. And after surviving that storm… We deserve it.'

He propped himself onto his elbow to stare down at her— the surge of longing unprecedented. But then, he had always been supremely confident about his ability to seduce any and every woman he desired… Except Melody Taylor, apparently. And after that first time he had lost the urge to seduce any woman but her.

Was that why he found her so tempting? So compelling. So irresistible. So unique. Because she had always presented a challenge he couldn't be sure of winning. Had always made him work for her approval.

He frowned. Wow, that would make him incredibly shallow, wouldn't it? That he could be so captivated by the thrill of the chase. But so be it. Now he'd finally caught her, he didn't plan to let her go too easily.

'We nearly died, Melody,' he said, laying it on a little thick.

'Don't you think you're being a bit of a drama queen?' she offered, throwing his own words back at him.

'Maybe.' He kissed the tip of her breast, rewarded when she gasped, and the rosy peak tightened. 'But I still think we'd be nuts not to enjoy each other for the rest of the time we're stuck here together. Before we go our separate ways.'

No point in pretending this could be more than a port in a storm... A very hot port in a surprisingly fortuitous storm, as it turned out.

They had been heading here all along, he realised. The bitching and bickering and endless arguments hadn't just been about the way their one night had ended, but also about this insane spark that had tormented them both for four years.

He'd hurt her by running out on her that morning like a damn coward. But thankfully she would never know how much of a coward he'd really been. That his decision to propose to Isabelle a few weeks later had been a direct result of his inability to forget Isabelle's best friend the way he'd wanted to.

It occurred to him she was no longer that innocent girl—the thought of other men enjoying her sent an uncomfortable spike of jealousy into his chest.

He forced himself to ignore it when she snorted.

'Prince Egomaniac strikes again.' She wiggled out from under his arm and scooted across the bed, then dragged the sheet up to cover all those delectable curves.

Shame. The vague feeling of regret sharpened—that he'd been her first lover but all he'd really taught her was how to be cynical about sex.

'Are you saying you *don't* want to have your way with me again?' he teased to cover the surge of longing—and the spurt of jealousy and regret.

If she knew how much he wanted her, she would use it against him—she had always been contrary. But, to his surprise, her gaze skated over him, the naked longing unmistakable—and undisguised.

She pushed her hand into her hair, which was a glorious mess of curls. 'I'm saying I need to use the bathroom.'

He chuckled at her pragmatism, relief flowing through him. Mel might enjoy mocking him, but she had never been coy. It was one of the things he had always adored about her…

He rolled onto his back and stacked his hands behind his head, aware his erection was already perking up again, but not bothered any more by the insistent need. Or the fact she could see it.

'Fine. I'll be waiting to seduce you when you get back then,' he said.

The lazy feeling of satisfaction and arousal was a heady combination which had to explain the constant yearning. And the unfamiliar desire to go back and correct the mistakes of that night.

Just a physical urge. That was all. Which they could now indulge with one hot night of wild, adventurous and unapologetic sex. He yawned and watched her shuffle to the master bathroom in her sheet, feeling utterly content for the first time in…a very long time.

'Hurry back,' he called after her. 'You don't want to leave your prince waiting.'

She stuck a middle finger up at him, over her shoulder. 'Go to hell, Gaultiere,' she said, but the familiar insult only made the brutal hunger surge. And perked the erection up even more.

He barked out another laugh.

Down, boy.

'Please, Rene… Stop torturing me. I need… More…' Mel groaned, the vicious heat pummelling her from all sides as his devious mouth worked her into a frenzy.

'I do love the way you beg,' he answered, glancing up from his position between her thighs.

'You bastard,' she moaned.

Then she arched up, tortured, as his finger thrust into

her—first one, then two, stretching her, caressing her—while his tongue continued to tantalise and torment her clitoris.

They'd done hard and fast first last night, then slow and devastating, before she'd fallen asleep in his arms.

She'd been in the grip of dreams, of him, *always* him, when he'd woken her, and asked if she could take him again…

A part of her had wanted to say no, her mind still hazy with sleep, a weird pressure on her chest. But then she'd seen the morning light peeking through the storm clouds and the urge to make the night last just a little longer had made it impossible to do anything but drape her arms around him and offer him everything.

But she'd been trapped in this maelstrom for what felt like hours, his lips, his mouth, his teeth nipping and licking every part of her. And tearing down all her defences. She felt raw, exposed and so needy it hurt.

She'd gone over not once but twice, each orgasm more brutal, more searing than the last. But now he was just toying with her, and she couldn't stand it any longer.

She fisted her fingers in his hair, yanked hard. His sharp grunt of protest was satisfying. Almost.

His head rose and he stared up at her, his eyes bright with the fierce desire that matched her own.

'Try that again, Melody…and you'll get no satisfaction at all,' he murmured, but then he buried his head between her legs again and, holding her hips, captured the tight nub of her clitoris between his lips and suckled harder at last.

She cried out, the orgasm tantalisingly close, but then he retreated again, leaving her wanting.

She opened her mouth to protest, but he scooped her up and flipped her over onto her stomach before lifting her hips.

He impaled her to the hilt in one devastating thrust. The orgasm barrelled towards her, shocking in its intensity. His hands captured her breasts to thrust harder, to take more. The cries choked off in her lungs, the moans vibrating through her chest, the raw pleasure too much as the thick length lodged so deep it felt as if he were a part of her now.

The wave hit at last, sweeping her over the edge into glorious oblivion, his thrusts becoming harder and more frantic.

The delirious afterglow washed over her as he grew even larger then shouted out his own release.

They both collapsed onto the bed, his big body covering hers. His ragged pants shuddered out against her ear, the huge erection still *there* inside her.

Did he feel it too? This all-consuming pleasure. This brutal connection.

But then he whispered against her ear, his voice husky with desire, 'You see how much better it is if you wait… Miss Impatient.'

She choked out a laugh, trying to dismiss the frantic beating of her heart, the emotion like a boulder on her chest now.

'You always have to have the last word, don't you, Prince Egomaniac,' she murmured, her voice muffled by the pillow.

Rolling off her, he gathered her in his arms. She could hear the thundering beat of his heart as she laid her head against his shoulder. He stroked the sweaty hair back from her brow and tucked a finger under her chin to lift her gaze to his.

With the three-day beard he looked more like a pirate now than a prince, but so gorgeous it made her heart skip several beats. And the doubts returned.

Had she made a terrible mistake agreeing to spend the night with him? Because their first night together—and the snatched sex of their first night here—paled in comparison to what they'd shared in the last twelve hours…

For all his faults, Rene was—and always had been—a generous and inventive lover. Why was she even surprised that being the focus of his skills for a whole night was even more addictive now than it had been four years ago?

'Teasing you has always been irresistible,' he murmured, the approval in his gaze making her heart hurt even more. He cupped her cheek, then leant down to press a kiss to her lips, which felt more intimate than the mind-blowing climax they had just shared.

What would it be like to be the focus of his attention for ever?

The question whispered across her consciousness, foolish and desperate and reminiscent of that insecure girl, the yearning terrifying in its intensity.

She blinked, struggling to contain the idiotic emotion, the desperate longing to be his for more than one night, which she knew was an impossible dream.

He would never commit to one woman, and she had no desire to waste any more of her precious confidence on hoping he would commit to her.

This is about sex, and chemistry. You don't love him, Mel. You just want him. And he wants you. There's a difference.

She sat up, trying to create distance, and control the endorphin rush caused by spending a night in his arms. His gaze drifted down to her nipples as the sheet slipped to her waist.

'Those breasts really are a work of art,' he said, running his thumb under one tender peak. 'I could actually feast on them for hours.'

'You already have,' she said and forced herself to smile, even as the thought that their time was nearly up made her heart stutter in her chest.

She turned to discover the spectacular view of the gorge below them, which the chalet perched on the edge of, was ow clearly visible through the floor-to-ceiling glass.

The storm had passed. Their time was up.

'We should get out of bed and see if the phone lines are working,' she said, trying to be firm and practical. And ignore the massive weight now threatening to crush her ribs—at the thought of never being with him like this again.

This too shall pass, Mel. You've just reanimated an old crush, that's all.

But as she sat up, suddenly desperate for some alone time to sort out her wayward emotions, he grabbed her arm.

'Wait...' he said, his gaze directed past her shoulder, his eyes narrowing. 'What the hell is that?'

She turned and saw it, too. A small flying object, hovering above the gorge about ten feet from the picture window.

'I have no idea...' she began.

She stared at it, confused, as a red light blinked and then a white light flashed.

He swore viciously and dragged her back, flinging the sheet up to cover her bare breasts.

'It's a drone,' he said, his eyes dark with fury. 'And it's taking pictures.'

Leaning past her, he slammed his fist on the button next to the bed to lower the shutter. But as the metal shield came down, protecting them from the drone, she could hear banging on the main entrance downstairs—and a muffled voice booming from a speaker.

'Your Majesty, are you in there? Are you safe? This is the mountain rescue team.'

Rene framed her face. 'It seems we've been found.' Was that regret she could hear in his voice, or just another figment of her crush? 'Stay here while I get dressed and let them in.'

She nodded, the emotion so thick in her throat she couldn't speak.

He left her sitting in the darkness. She heard the search-and-rescue team entering the house, could hear the muffled voices and the crackle of radios as they informed the outside world that the two of them had been found safe and well.

But as she showered, washing away his scent, then got

dressed, she became far too aware of all the tender spots, the soreness, where her body had been well used during the night, and yet still yearned for his touch.

When she ventured downstairs half an hour later, the house, *their* house, was full of people, including the commander of the mountain rescue team, the rest of whom were outside with a parade of snowmobiles, a couple of paramedics—who insisted on giving her a thorough medical check—a police chief, three officers and several Palace officials from Androvia, who explained that as soon as she was cleared, Isabelle was frantic to speak to her.

But she couldn't find Rene anyway. When she finally worked up the courage to ask where he was, one of the police officers told her he was already on his way back to Saltzaland.

But he didn't say goodbye.

The foolish thought pierced the daze of unreality gripping her as she was bundled into a large black SUV. She got another jolt when they passed the Jeep they had abandoned four nights ago, now being hooked up to a snowmobile to be towed back to Gaultiere Castle.

As soon as the SUV hit the mountain road to Androvia, the Palace official handed her a satellite phone and Isabelle's voice came over the line, clearly distraught and trying not to show it. Mel reassured her friend she was well and gave her a heavily edited version of events, then had to repeat the same story to her mother, who had arrived in Androvia from London two days before to wait for news.

The relief when the calls were over was short-lived though, because as the car travelled through a phalanx of people and reporters and photographers camped out at the gates of the White Palace she realised how selfish she had been in the past four days. She hadn't given a thought to Isabelle or her mum or all the other people who had been drawn into the frantic search to find them. All she had really thought about was Rene and herself and what it had meant to be with him again.

The White Palace staff welcomed her back as soon as the car stopped in the courtyard and she climbed out. Then Isabelle appeared on the Palace steps and rushed down them to wrap her in a fierce hug, tears of relief streaming down her face. She held her friend, aware of the Queen's new fake husband Travis Lord standing behind Isabelle and looking surprisingly concerned and relieved for someone who wasn't supposed to have any real skin in this game.

Mel tried to be happy, tried to smile, tried to feel comfortable with the outpouring of love and concern from Isabelle and then her mum and her work colleagues and friends and even Travis Lord, as the day wore on.

But the truth was, she didn't feel found. She felt lost again. The way she had when Rene had disappeared once before without a word.

But as she lay in her own bed again that night, and tried to fall asleep without him beside her, she knew she only had herself to blame—for her aching empty heart and the cruel feeling of rejection, of loneliness, of never being good enough, that reminded her of her childhood.

Because she'd let herself fall down the rabbit hole again. Despite all her best intentions.

This isn't love, it's infatuation. Don't be melodramatic, she told herself staunchly.

But if that was true, a small voice whispered from the darkness, why did it hurt even more this time?

CHAPTER TEN

'Issy, hi...' Mel murmured, disorientated to see her friend by her bedside. She blinked, trying to clear the fog from her brain. She'd fallen asleep in the early hours, all the reasons why she had been an utter fool to sleep with Rene again finally quieting enough for her to drop into exhaustion.

'Good morning, Mel. How are you feeling?' her friend asked gently, the concern from yesterday still thick in her voice.

'I... Good. Better,' she said, which wasn't entirely the truth, but she was determined to make it so. 'By the way, I should contact the cabin owner and thank them and pay for the damage,' she said. It was something which had occurred to her yesterday, while she was trying to divert her brain to the practical, instead of mooning over Rene or getting upset about his abrupt departure.

Isabelle smiled. 'It's already been done.'

Mel frowned. 'But I should pay, not you.'

'I didn't pay, Rene did,' she said gently. 'He also sent an official message of thanks to the rescue team.'

'Oh...' Mel murmured, hating that the mention of his name only made the aching pain in her chest return. 'That's good.'

Apparently, he'd thought of everyone yesterday. Except her.

She stretched and rubbed her eyes, trying to cover her reaction, aware of the dull headache pounding at her temples when Isabelle crossed the bedroom and opened the curtains.

Bright sunlight flooded the room. She sat up abruptly, a dart of shame clearing the last fog from her brain, even as the dull headache became razor-sharp. 'What time is it?'

No wonder Isabelle had come to wake her. It had to be past noon already.

'I need to get dressed,' Mel added, becoming frantic. She needed to find her safe space again, which had always been her career, and her place as Isabelle's trusted companion and adviser. 'I'm so sorry. I should have been at work hours ago.'

She'd already missed almost a week while being stuck in the cabin with Rene. And there was a lot of work to do now Isabelle had unlocked Androvia's future with her fake marriage to Travis Lord.

But when Mel went to whip back the sheet, Isabelle sat back on the bed and grasped her wrist to prevent her getting up, a strange expression on her face.

'Mel, it's okay. You don't need to go to work today. That's not why I'm here...' she began, her gaze softening with sympathy.

'But...of course I do,' Mel began, confused now as well as wary. Why was Issy looking at her like that? As if she were fragile and needed protecting, when their relationship had always been the other way round. 'There's so much to do. Now you're married to Lord we can finally get started on all the infrastructure projects prevented by the conditions of your father's will.'

Isabelle had come up with the scheme to marry the US champion snowboarder-cum-billionaire businessman in desperation, so she could circumvent the conditions her father had insisted on. That when he died, his daughter—who had only been eight at the time of her parents' death—must be married before she could make commercial decisions about the huge tracts of land owned by Androvia's royal family.

Mel had never been convinced that pretending to be madly in love with a total stranger was a good idea.

Added to that, Lord was a self-made billionaire who had come from nothing, had no respect for monarchy and exuded the kind of animal magnetism which would burn most women to a crisp at fifty paces. Even women who hadn't been impossibly sheltered, as Issy had been her whole life. But Mel had been unable to refute the fact that Isabelle had to marry someone to get control of the land, and as Issy had insisted that someone definitely was *not* going to be Rene she had eventually been forced to support Issy's wild scheme.

'Now you're finally free to develop the land and stimulate some much-needed economic growth in Androvia, we need to figure out which projects to prioritise, not to mention getting the negotiations for Lord's resort on the White Ridge finalised, and the press release issued,' Mel rattled off. The leasing of the land for Lord's resort was the lure Issy had used to get him to agree to the marriage, so that needed to be a priority. 'And we've only got a year before the divorce, so time is…' She trailed off though when her friend laughed and she noticed the sparkle turning Isabelle's green eyes to a bright emerald.

'It's okay, Mel,' her friend murmured, the colour on her cheeks surprising Mel even more. Isabelle was a serious person—she always kept her emotions controlled because she'd had to, becoming Queen while still a child—but right now she looked… Well, not serious at all. 'There's not going to be a divorce,' Isabelle said.

Mel simply stared back at her. 'There's… There's *not*? But… Why not?' she managed, hopelessly confused now. 'Wasn't that the deal you made with Lord?'

Issy took Mel's hands in hers and squeezed, then shook her head. 'Not any more.' The secretive smile that curved her lips grew until it brightened her whole face—and made her look happier than Mel had ever seen her, as if she were lit from within. 'I've fallen hopelessly, completely in love with him, Mel.' She laughed, the sound so full of joy it was almost a giggle. 'And, unbelievably, Travis has fallen in love with me, too.'

'Why is that unbelievable?' Mel replied instinctively, because she had always been the Queen's biggest ally, her greatest supporter, her closest friend… Although maybe she wasn't that person any more. Was that Travis Lord now? After only a few weeks? Mel tried to force a smile to her lips and dismiss the panicked thought. Not to mention the jolt of panic at the thought of being replaced in Isabelle's affections.

Isabelle deserved to be happy after dedicating so much of her life to her country and her people. And if her friend had genuinely found love with her fake husband, and if the man deserved her, that would be amazing. But what if Travis Lord wasn't that man? What if he was simply exploiting Issy's sweet nature and her inexperience with men? Wasn't it Mel's job to make sure?

'You're incredibly lovable, Issy. I've loved you ever since I met you,' Mel said, wishing she could believe her friend's revelation. 'But are you sure? It seems awfully fast. You've only known him for a couple of weeks…'

She didn't want to burst Isabelle's bubble. But her own experience of hot, charismatic men was that you should never make the mistake of relying on them. Or being blind to their faults. And you certainly shouldn't risk falling in love with them, because that would tend to make you do both.

Oddly, the thought reassured her. She couldn't possibly have fallen in love with Rene because she was still very aware of his faults. Most notably, his ability to seduce her into thinking she was special to him, when she knew she wasn't. And walking away without saying goodbye!

The sparkle remained in Issy's eyes, though, even as her

expression became astute and considering. 'Actually, I got to know him during our stunt date and the months afterwards, while we were planning the wedding on different continents. We...' she looked down at their joined hands, a sure sign she was nervous '...we were texting each other—a lot—during that time.'

'Really? But why didn't you tell me?' Mel asked, then wanted to grab the words back. How needy did she sound? And how jealous and insecure.

But how could she help it, when she suddenly felt as if everything was changing too fast, and not for the better.

Isabelle shrugged, the blush brightening. 'Honestly, I think I was embarrassed at how excited I was about those texts.' The uncomplicated grin returned. 'Perhaps I should have realised I was already falling in love with him.' She chuckled. The light, effervescent sound was one Mel had *never* heard come out of her friend's mouth—it *was* a giggle. Should she be charmed by it, though, or even more disturbed?

'Travis called it sexting!' Issy added. 'Which might explain why, as soon as we were alone together on our wedding night, well...' the blush deepened '...we discovered we had a *lot* of chemistry.'

'Okay...' Mel nodded. 'That's...exciting,' she said carefully, trying to get a handle on this sudden change in her usually serious friend—and control the panic. Because these revelations signalled a fundamental change in their relationship, too. Isabelle had *never* kept secrets from her. But then, Mel thought miserably, she had kept several from Issy. Not just her night with Rene four years ago, but also what had really happened between them in the cabin.

'Yes, it was, *very* exciting,' Issy said with considerable fervour. 'I had no idea I even had a sex drive. But listen...' Her expression sobered. 'I actually didn't wake you to talk about me…and Travis.' She sighed. 'Even though he is one of my favourite topics. LOL.'

Whoa. What the heck?

Mel's surprise was turning to astonishment. Had the Queen of Androvia just made a joke about her husband and said *'LOL'*, like the teenager she had never been allowed to be?

Before Mel could process her astonishment, though, at this novel new playful side of her friend, the Queen squeezed her fingers again.

'But seriously, that's enough about me. We need to talk about you…' Issy swallowed heavily, her gaze softening again '…and Rene,' she continued. 'Because a situation has arisen, and Travis and I think you should take a break for a couple of weeks in his house in Colorado until it all blows over.'

'What…? What about me and Rene?' Mel managed as guilt consumed her.

Did Issy know, somehow, about what they'd been doing in that cabin?

'Mel, there are pictures,' Issy said gently, her expression becoming pained but her tone losing none of the sympathy and concern.

'What p-pictures?' she whispered, the bottom dropping out of her stomach.

'Of the two of you, together,' Isabelle added carefully. 'The morning you were both rescued.'

Mel yanked her hands free, panic and shame clawing at her throat.

The drone? Oh, God. No.

Her stomach twisted, and nausea rose up her throat.

She'd been naked, clearly having spent a torrid night in Rene's bed. Good grief, she'd probably still had the sheen of afterglow in her eyes from the titanic orgasm he'd just given her. And the press had *pictures*…

She covered her mouth, scared she might throw up.

While it was doubtful that salacious photos of them would have a detrimental effect on Rene's reputation, because he was a man, and a prince, and was already known as a playboy, it would be devastating for hers. But far worse—it would be devastating for Isabelle's reputation, too. Mel was the Queen's trusted adviser, a loyal member of her team, and she'd been caught *in flagrante* with the neighbouring Prince.

The press wouldn't just shame *her*. A scandal of this magnitude would make a mockery of *everything* Isabelle had tried to achieve over the last fourteen years to prove herself a worthy and dignified Queen. It could even put in jeopardy the integrity of all the projects they had been working so hard towards in the last few years.

'Issy, I'm so, *so* sorry. I've ruined everything,' Mel began, not sure how she could make amends. 'I should never have…'

'Mel, don't apologise. This is *not* your fault,' Isabelle interrupted, her voice firm and determined, the tone a combination of the loyal friend and the regal Queen.

'How can it not be my fault when I'm the one who slept with him?' Mel cried, sickened now not just by her thoughtless, reckless behaviour but by the fact she had managed to trash everything—her reputation, and Isabelle's and Androvia's—and all the achievements she was most proud of in her life, for one night of pleasure.

But Isabelle simply grabbed her hands and held onto them, her gaze direct and devoid of judgement.

'Listen to me, Mel. Don't you *dare* blame yourself for the unconscionable behaviour of the person using that drone. They had no right to take intrusive photos of you two. And no right to sell them. And the press had no right to print them and post them online. Or to be camped outside the Palace now, but that's what they do… And it's what we have lawyers and security teams for.'

Mel's heart sank into her imploding stomach, the shame overwhelming.

The photos were on the internet. Naked, explicit photos… And the press were outside the Palace.

She tugged her hands free and leapt up from the bed, frantic and feeling sicker by the second but aware of one thing. She had to minimise the Queen's involvement in this catastrophe.

'I need to leave. You and Travis are right. I should resign… to limit the damage…' She crossed the room, flung open the doors of her armoire and pulled out a suitcase.

She would have to give up her job, the work she loved, and leave Androvia and the Palace, which had been the only real home she had known since she was ten. But all of that served her right for being a fool and bringing this mess to her best friend's doorstep.

But as she began to frantically fill the suitcase, her mind whirred. What would she do? And where could she go?

Her mother had returned to London the night before, after she had been assured Mel was okay. She had a full schedule of catering jobs, several of which she had already had to cancel to come to Androvia, worried about her daughter, while said daughter had been busy indulging in an insane fling.

But as Mel hauled her clothes off the rail and threw them in the suitcase, Isabelle appeared by her side and took her arm again.

'Mel, stop.' The quiet command cut through Mel's panic, enough to have the clothes sliding out of her fingers and falling to the floor. Her knees began to shake.

'I refuse to accept your resignation,' Issy said, 'as you have done nothing wrong. And Travis and I are *not* suggesting you leave for good, just for a couple of weeks until this dies down and we can get the Crown's lawyers working on getting the photos deleted and Travis and my PR teams have worked out a story you're comfortable with to feed to the press,' her friend continued. 'This is your home and will always be your home.' Isabelle grasped her other arm and gave her a gentle shake. 'You're my family, Mel. The *only* family I had for a very long time. And no way am I letting you deal with this mess alone.' She gave a hefty sigh. 'A mess which is absolutely and unequivocally *not* your fault.'

She tugged Mel towards her and wrapped her arms around her. 'Do you understand?' she whispered against her ear.

Mel shuddered as a wave of emotion welled up inside her, the panic and shame joined by the unbearable weight of gratitude and love.

'But I've made such a mess of things,' she offered, her voice shaking.

She didn't deserve Isabelle's support. But having it meant everything.

'Do you understand me?' Isabelle repeated, her voice softer but still firm, like the hug.

Mel nodded, tears stinging her eyes, the emotion jammed in her throat. She choked out the first sob, then couldn't seem to stop as Isabelle held her and soothed, her voice calm and measured and reassuring.

The great gulping sobs were hopelessly self-indulgent and melodramatic, but she couldn't seem to stop. Isabelle held her and comforted her until the storm finally passed.

Eventually, she managed to persuade Isabelle to leave her to get dressed, but only after she had promised to come to Isabelle's study in the East Wing as soon as she was ready. Apparently, Travis Lord had already assembled a team of lawyers and hired a 'crisis management' guru to discuss next steps.

But as Mel showered and dressed the headache continued to pound at her temples, and the nausea lay like a sleeping dragon in the pit of her stomach.

Isabelle was wrong.

She *had* messed up. And while she wasn't responsible for the behaviour of the press, this situation *was* her fault in many ways. She had been impossibly selfish and, worst of all, naïve, thinking she could sleep with Rene and there would be no consequences. And she had also been dishonest. Isabelle trusted her and she had destroyed that trust. Because she hadn't told Isabelle or her mother the truth when she had arrived the day before, and now she was dragging Isabelle and her new husband—not to mention the rest of the Palace staff and the Androvian monarchy—into this mess with her.

And why had it come to this? Because she had been determined to indulge some idiotic fantasy that she and Rene had *more* than chemistry?

An hour later, as she made her way to Isabelle's study, dreading having to face her friend and her new husband—and all the other people who had no doubt seen those pictures too, and discuss ways to handle the fallout—her mind drifted to Rene.

The tears threatened again, because all she could see was the way he'd looked the last time she'd seen him—dishevelled and intense, naked and hot, with the beard, the scars and the healing wound on his arm making him dangerous and impossibly handsome and, for a fleeting moment, almost hers.

She swallowed the tears down ruthlessly.

You need to hold it together now and forget Rene for good. Because all your childish obsession with him has ever meant for you is trouble.

But as she walked into Isabelle's study and saw the array of people assembled there, ready to stand by her and to help her out of this mess, all she really felt was even more alone.

CHAPTER ELEVEN

'I DON'T WANT to be a burden,' Mel said for what seemed the five hundredth time in the past hour as she sat amidst the team of lawyers and advisers while everyone carried on talking around her, discussing outcomes and strategies to deal with the PR nightmare that her life had become. 'And I definitely don't think I should stay in His Majesty's home in Colorado…' she added, the thought of going into hiding in North America for the next two weeks, in the home of Isabelle's consort whom she barely knew, only making the situation seem more surreal. And depressing.

It already felt surreal enough being in Isabelle's library office, surrounded by leather books and the scent of lemon polish and old paper, with Travis Lord now seated behind the desk co-ordinating the team he had assembled. This place had always been so familiar because it was where she and Isabelle conducted their morning briefings, to discuss schedule commitments for that day and any other important business. But it had always been just the two of them and she had been the one supporting the Queen, not the other way around.

'Mel, please stop saying you're a burden when you're not.' Isabelle sat beside her on the leather sofa and covered the hands Mel had clasped in her lap to stop them trembling.

'Yeah, and please stop calling me His Majesty. It freaks me out,' her new husband added with a theatrical shudder, his smile encouraging Mel to share the joke. 'Travis works, seeing as we're family now, right, Belle?'

'Yes, of course, Vis,' Issy joked back.

Mel forced a wan smile to her lips. Her heart lifted, though, at least a little, at the latest evidence that her concerns for her friend and her newfound love were unfounded.

Mel had never seen Issy so confident and relaxed in anyone's company before, except maybe her own. And certainly not when her courtiers or advisers were in attendance. But it was clear she and Travis Lord really were mad about each other, the intimate looks, the shared jokes and the casual touches—not to mention the nicknames—a testament to how much they not only supported each other but enjoyed each other's company.

Mel had decided in the past hour she liked Lord, a lot. And she trusted him. He not only appeared to adore her best friend, but his irreverence and playfulness was something Issy had always needed more of in her overly structured life.

At least that was one less thing Mel needed to worry about, she thought miserably.

'How about we wrap this up now?' Travis said, giving her a watchful look before nodding to Arne, the Queen's chief courtier, and the six other people in the room, who Mel had been introduced to but whose names she had instantly forgotten in the blur of stress and embarrassment. 'Miss Taylor is clearly exhausted, and we have a plan of action now to handle this situation,' Travis continued with more confidence than Mel felt. 'Belle and I can talk in private with Miss Taylor about travel arrangements.'

Arne ushered the team of lawyers and the Hollywood crisis management consultant and his assistant out of the library.

'Thank you,' she said, stupidly grateful for all the work these people were willing to do on her behalf, once the room was cleared, and the door closed behind Arne.

'Listen, Mel, my place in Colorado is the best option as your bolthole...' Travis began.

Mel opened her mouth to suggest again she find her own refuge for the next few weeks—because surely Travis and Isabelle had already both done more than enough—when Arne burst back into the room.

'Mr Lord, Your Majesty, Miss Taylor—' he addressed them all, looking flustered, which for Arne was unheard of, because he was the most unflappable man on the planet '—I have just been informed that Prince Rene's helicopter has landed at the Palace helipad.'

'Rene's *here*?' Mel gasped, the foolish bubble of hope swiftly quashed by a surge of panic and distress.

Why on earth would she be happy to see him, when his arrival would only exacerbate the crisis they'd spent the last hour trying to solve? And anyway, what was he doing here when he'd made no attempt to contact her for twenty-four hours?

'I see,' said Isabelle, looking grave, because she had to know all the reasons why Rene showing up unannounced was not good.

At the exact same time Travis snarled, 'Oh, yeah? It's about time that entitled bastard showed up.'

'Travis, did you ask Rene to come here?' Isabelle said as she stood, the concern in her tone making the emotions in Mel's stomach twist into a tight knot.

'Of course not, Belle. The last damn thing I want is that guy making this even worse,' he said. He cradled his wife's cheek, the tenderness in his eyes so vivid Mel's stomach rebelled more. 'But don't you think he ought to take some of the flak?' he added, casting a fierce look at Mel that made her feel both grateful for his support but also ashamed. It felt wrong, not just to need Travis Lord's protection but also to accept it, considering she'd doubted his integrity only a few hours ago.

'Because, let's face it,' Travis continued, 'if that bastard hadn't taken advantage of your best friend—and had made more of an effort to protect her in the twenty-four hours since those photos were taken—she wouldn't be in the press's cross-hairs in the first place.'

Taken advantage of?

Mel was still struggling to process that assertion when Rene strode into the room and her emotions went into freef-all again, for the second time in a single day.

He's shaved off the beard that made him mine.

The idiotic thought popped into her aching head as she struggled to contain the inappropriate thrill at seeing him again.

He looked commanding and unapproachable, like the Prince he was—the autocrat who had insisted he drive her into the storm—instead of the man she had discovered, or thought she had discovered, in their cabin.

'Leave us, Arne,' he demanded, then marched across the room, straight towards her, unaware of Isabelle's tentative greeting and Travis Lord's furious scowl.

'You need to pack,' he said without any greeting. 'I have a plane fuelled and waiting at the airport in Saltzaland to take us to the Caribbean,' he went on, the clear, calm tone mak-ing it hard for her to process the command, or even what he was asking.

'What?' she murmured, wondering if she had somehow leapt into an alternative reality and this was all an insane dream that she would wake up from… Hopefully very soon. Because the pain in her stomach was getting worse, the knots of tension and panic and hurt now tangling with a surge of longing which made no sense.

They were over. In fact they had never even begun. He'd made that very clear by disappearing yesterday.

He took her arm to haul her off the couch.

'I'm taking you to a private island my father owned near the US Virgin Islands. But we need to go now.'

Everything was happening so fast she couldn't even formulate a question before he was marching her out of the room, his grip firm on her upper arm.

'Rene, what are you doing?' Isabelle began, her voice rising. 'You can't just...'

But then Travis laid his hand on his wife's shoulder and stepped into Rene's path.

'Back the hell off, buddy, and let the lady go, right now,' he demanded, the sharp tone finally snapping Mel out of the weird dream state she seemed to have lapsed into.

'The hell I will...' Rene shouted back.

Mel wrenched her arm free.

'What are you even doing here?' she managed, her voice surprisingly lucid considering her insides were in turmoil. Seeing him again, which had triggered the inevitable physical response, had been humiliating and shocking enough, but having him drag her out of Isabelle's study as if she were a piece of baggage was even worse.

She concentrated on her anger to control the new wave of pain and panic.

Why had he appeared now? Was he concerned about her reputation or his own? He hadn't even said goodbye at the cabin and now he felt he had the right to order her about.

And why on earth would she want to go anywhere with him when she knew he didn't care for her, not really?

'We need to talk,' he said, his voice grave and his eyes dark with something she couldn't even begin to process, because it looked weirdly like possessiveness and concern. 'But we're not doing it here. A press release is going out today, and I want to be on that plane before it happens, so we don't have to deal with the fallout.'

Mel's mind was still reeling, her heart galloping full tilt into her throat, when Travis stepped between them and grabbed Rene by the lapel of his suit jacket.

'You seem to forget, pal, the lady gets to decide where she goes and who she goes with. Not you.'

'Take your hands off me, pal,' Rene roared back, his eyes wild as he slapped Travis's hands away, 'or I will knock you flat. The lady is *my* concern, not yours.'

'The hell she…' Travis began.

But then Isabelle flattened a palm on her husband's chest to stop him from retaliating. 'Travis, back off,' she demanded like the Queen she was.

Her husband cursed loudly but did as his wife demanded, and stepped back.

Isabelle turned to Rene, her voice still firm. 'What on earth is wrong with you, Rene? You're behaving like a barbarian. You're scaring Mel. You're scaring *me*, and I won't stand for it.'

It was Rene's turn to swear profusely.

Mel realised she wasn't scared, just hopelessly confused and very wary, because the feelings inside her didn't make any sense. And she needed them to make sense if she was going to deal with the situation.

She had a right to be furious with him for turning up here unannounced and making a scene after leaving her high and dry twenty-four hours ago. But when his gaze landed on her again, something else joined the tangle of raw emotions in her gut… Guilt.

Because she realised that, along with his fury and the possessiveness, she could also see hurt in his golden gaze.

'I apologise, Isabelle,' he said tightly.

'Lord,' Rene added, giving Travis, who was standing next

to his wife but still looked as if he was spoiling for a fight, a curt nod. 'I appreciate you think you have to protect Melody,' he added, his voice still tight with anger, 'but you don't. Because I'm here to do that.'

'What makes you think you have the right to…' Travis began, before Mel finally found her voice.

'Melody happens to be standing right here, and she can protect herself,' she cut in.

Everyone stared at her, but she didn't care. Because she suddenly felt a little less panicked, a little less fragile and pathetic. She'd been behaving like a complete wet blanket ever since she'd found out about those photos. Heck, ever since she'd discovered that Rene had left her again. But that was not who she was.

She didn't let other people stand for her because she stood for herself. And she didn't let other people fix her problems because she fixed her own problems. And she didn't let other people protect her because she protected herself—and that also meant protecting her heart from reckless, careless men like Rene Gaultiere. Because she had learnt that lesson as a little girl, when her father had walked away without a backwards glance.

Maybe she'd forgotten that in the last week, after having to rely on Rene to save her from the storm, but she wasn't about to forget it again.

'What press release are you talking about, Rene?' Isabelle asked quietly, breaking the silence with a question that hadn't even occurred to Mel. 'What does it say? Perhaps we could combine it with the one we've worked out with our crisis management team,' she added, ever the diplomat.

But Rene simply shook his head, his gaze still fixed on Mel as he dropped another bombshell. 'It's a press release announcing my engagement to Melody Taylor.'

Isabelle gasped. Travis swore again.

'But we're not engaged,' Mel said, hating the jump in her pulse and the burst of adrenaline which she had to quash.

Was this some kind of trick? Or simply a sick joke? She couldn't marry Rene and, even if she could, he hadn't asked her.

'It's the best way to protect your reputation,' he said. 'Until the press are off our backs.'

'So, it's a fake engagement?' she said, hating that brief spurt of excitement even more.

'I'm not sure how faking an engagement is going to improve this situation,' Isabelle mused.

'Me either,' Travis concurred, looking as if he was ready to punch Rene again.

But Rene simply ignored them both to stare at Mel.

'We need time to talk, Melody.' His eyes narrowed, the accusation clear in his expression—as well as the vicious blast of heat which made her nipples tighten and throb. 'Because I remember *everything* that happened now, including our first night in the cabin.'

Guilt yanked at the knot in her abdomen.

He *knew*? About the sex they'd had, which she'd denied and then completely forgotten about until this precise moment, thanks to the tumultuous events of the past two days.

She barely had a chance to process how she felt about the revelation, though, when he added, 'And now I know *exactly* what happened, we need to discuss the possible repercussions and how we are going to deal with them.'

What possible repercussions?

For a split second she had no clue what he was talking about, but then his gaze dipped pointedly to her belly.

And suddenly she understood. He hadn't come here to rescue her reputation, and he wasn't issuing a press release stating they were engaged because he wanted to marry her, but because he thought there was a slim chance she might be carrying the Saltzaland heir.

Instinctively, she placed her hand on her midriff, even though she was sure she couldn't be pregnant. But she hadn't had the chance to take a test yet. She hadn't even thought about it, because she had been too busy dealing with the emotional repercussions of his latest desertion.

'We can have that conversation here, in front of the Queen and her husband, or we can have it in Mermaid Cay in private. Up to you.'

Both Isabelle and Travis protested, but Mel knew that Rene wasn't giving her a choice. She couldn't talk about the intimate details of their misguided relationship in front of her friend, and she didn't want to involve the couple any more—because this was her problem to solve.

She would have to accept Rene's invitation. And his protection. Even go along with his lie about an engagement and travel with him to a private island on the other side of the world, where she would be completely at the mercy of desires and passions she had never been able to control around him...

All because she'd made a stupid mistake, and then compounded it by lying.

It took her a good ten minutes to cut through Travis's protests and Isabelle's concern, while Rene remained silent. Eventually, though, she managed to persuade them to let her go with him.

Half an hour later, with a hastily packed bag at her feet and Rene, who had barely exchanged a word with her once she'd agreed to accompany him, sitting stiffly beside her as the noisy helicopter lifted off, Mel stared down at the crowd of photographers and reporters still parked outside the Palace gates. She brushed away an errant tear with her fist, feeling trapped but determined not to let him see how vulnerable she felt.

The helicopter journey across the Alps to Saltzaland took over an hour, but mercifully the noise in the cabin was too loud to have a conversation, which gave Mel some precious time to gather her shattered emotions. And think.

By the time the chopper settled in the courtyard at the back of Gaultiere Castle she had managed to get enough of a grip to formulate a plan of sorts.

A sleek black limousine was parked on the other side of the helipad, dwarfed by the Castle's imposing three-hundred-foot façade. As Rene spoke to one of his advisers in hushed tones and a parade of footmen arrived to take her one bag to the vehicle, which was transporting them to the airport, Mel stared, transfixed by Rene's home. Even in the daylight, the dark brickwork and grandiose mix of Gothic and Byzantine architecture made Gaultiere Castle look much less welcoming than the White Palace where she had spent so much of her childhood. Isabelle's home had a similar six-hundred-year-old history, but the white limestone and fanciful turrets made Androvia's Palace seem like a fairytale in comparison to this, which was more like the castle of an evil king straight out of childhood nightmares.

The forbidding architecture fitted her mood, though—and Rene's, it seemed, from the scowl on his face—when he took her arm again, as he had done in Isabelle's study, to escort her to the limousine like an errant child.

She allowed herself to be led, determined not to speak too soon or lose her temper. She needed privacy for what she had to say.

As soon as they were cocooned in the back seat of the luxury car, though, and the door had been closed by one of his many footmen, a tinted screen shielding their conversation from the driver, she broke her silence.

'Rene, this is unnecessary. We don't need to fly all the

way to the Caribbean to have a private conversation,' she said, trying for reasonable.

He barely glanced her way. 'Put your belt on.'

The echo of the dictatorial way he had treated her the last time they'd been in a car together made her temper spike. She forced herself not to react, though, and snapped on the belt.

She hated having to appease him, but she couldn't gauge his mood. He'd always been a forceful man but the emotions swirling in his eyes now seemed more volatile than any she had ever seen before. Plus, she had put herself in this situation by lying to him about their first night in the cabin, so she did have some explaining to do.

'How long is the drive to the airport?' she asked.

'Thirty minutes,' he said, all his attention on the view through the window of snow-covered pines.

He's sulking. Just say sorry and make him see reason.

She took a careful breath and tried to remain calm, despite the lungful of his scent—bergamot and cedarwood and man—which triggered memories she did not need.

The good news was that half an hour should be more than enough time to apologise for her white lie and then put his mind at rest about any lingering 'repercussions'. The bad news was that she needed to find a way to defuse his temper first, which had never been her forte. Especially when her own temper was threatening to erupt.

She cleared her throat, struggling to find the right words, the right tone, which would allow her to keep her pride while also de-escalating the tension making her stomach hurt.

'Look, I'm sorry I lied when you asked me about that night...' she began.

His head swung around, but what she saw in his eyes shocked her. Not anger but raw emotion, reminding her of the look in his eyes when she'd asked him about his nightmares.

'Why did you?' he demanded, his tone hollow as his gaze raked over her.

She shrugged, trying not to overreact. But why did he look so upset...in the grip of emotions she didn't understand? If she didn't know better, she could have sworn she'd seen fear in his eyes.

'I guess... I don't really know,' she said, struggling to re-member exactly why she'd been so determined to cover up that brief misguided interlude. 'It just seemed like a mistake that we shouldn't dwell on. And talking about it would give it more significance than it deserved.'

Instead of placating him, her clumsy explanation only seemed to upset him more.

He leant across the car and cradled her cheek in his palm. She jolted, the sudden touch, the tender, tortured look in his eyes as he searched her expression like a lightning strike to all those emotions she was trying to keep under strict control.

'Damn it,' he said, his tone raw. 'Don't lie to me again. Just tell me... Did I...' She saw his Adam's apple bob as he swallowed. 'Did I have your full consent?'

His tone was so low with self-loathing it took a moment to register what he was asking her. But when it did, her heart rammed her throat and guilt blindsided her.

Had he thought...?

'Yes, Rene. *Of course,*' she whispered, feeling sick that her white lie had ever made him think... 'That's not what happened.' She covered his hand with hers and held on, her gaze locked on his, desperate to reassure him.

He pulled his hand out from under hers, his gaze still fierce, still searching as he framed her now burning cheeks. 'You're sure? I didn't take advantage of you?'

'No, you didn't, Rene. I helped you out of your boxers. I wanted you inside me, desperately. It had been four years since the last time, and I guess the adrenaline rush from surviving a near-death experience made resisting the hunger impossible.'

At last, she seemed to get through to him. He released her cheeks and slumped back in the car seat. Relief washed over his features.

She placed her hand on his knee. When his gaze connected with hers he looked hollowed out, vulnerable still, but the fear was gone.

'I'm sorry, Rene. I didn't... It didn't even occur to me you would think something like that...' she finally managed.

He nodded, then scrubbed his hands down his face. But when he met her gaze again his expression had changed. The shutters had returned, and the frown. He didn't look vulnerable any more, he looked determined.

'Thanks for clarifying that,' he said, but there wasn't a lot of gratitude in his voice. 'So, my next question is, when was your last period?'

Her cheeks flared with heat of a very different kind. 'Why do you need to know that?'

'You know why,' he said curtly. 'I didn't use protection and I happen to know you weren't taking the contraceptive pill while we were there.'

'How do you know that?'

'Because we didn't bring any toiletries from the car,' he said flatly, the implacable, frankly condescending tone only disturbing her more. His gaze dropped to her abdomen. 'You could be pregnant.'

'Well, I'm not,' she said, her indignation building. 'How do you know I wasn't taking the pill before that?' she began, trying desperately to regain ground. She realised her mistake though when his gaze narrowed.

'Were you?'

'Well, I...' she faltered.

'Don't you dare lie to me again,' he said.

'I'm not going to lie,' she protested.

His angry scowl deepened. 'Given your track record…'

'Okay, I'm not on the pill,' she murmured.

'So, when was your last period?' he asked again.

Her face burned. But then she remembered her plan had always involved divulging this information. So, what exactly was she getting embarrassed about?

'Actually, that's precisely the point I was going to make,' she said, trying to sound confident and in control. 'I'd literally only just finished my last period when we…' she stumbled, his gaze still locked on her face '…well, you know. So, it's extremely unlikely I'll be pregnant.' She paused, ready to deliver her coup de grace. 'But I'm more than happy to take a pregnancy test today to put both our minds at rest. So, there's absolutely no need for me to travel to the Caribbean with you.'

'When *exactly* did your last period finish? I want a date,' he said, not sounding impressed with her coup de grace.

'Why does that matter? The point is I can take a test. And then we'll both know I'm not pregnant.'

'The date,' he demanded again.

She threw up her hands. 'Fine, the twenty-eighth. Okay, satisfied?'

'Not at all. Because male sperm can live inside the womb for up to five days,' he said.

'So what?' she countered, getting mightily sick of that patronising look, and the third degree, while also having absolutely no clue what he was getting at.

'So if you finished your period on the twenty-eighth, and we had sex on the first of January, you would have been over a week into your cycle when my sperm died.'

'But a pregnancy is still extremely unlikely…' she countered, scrambling to rescue her reasoning while her head was starting to explode. 'And the test will prove that…'

'No, it won't.' He cut her off again, the patient tone deliberately condescending. 'Because if you do a pregnancy test less than nine days before your *next* period is due you have at least a thirty percent chance of a false negative...'

'When exactly did you become an expert on the female reproductive cycle?' she snapped, even as her heart began to clatter against her ribs as she could see her foolproof plan to avoid this trip—and guard against all the ways he could hurt her again—going up in flames.

'When I woke up this morning and realised my memory of that night wasn't some weird erotic fantasy, the way you'd made me believe,' he snarled, the patient tone gone. 'You should have told me the truth about what happened. If not after that first night, then when we spent that last night together, *all night*. You had *hours* when you could have said something. Why the hell didn't you?'

She turned away from him to stare out of the car window, bitter tears stinging her eyes again and blurring the sight of the airport sign, telling her she still had at least another ten miles of this torturous conversation to get through. She tried to swallow past the lump in her throat, terrified that he would see her break.

He was suggesting they spend well over a week together before they could take a reliable pregnancy test. She did not want to spend another week with him, given her aptitude for doing delusional, self-destructive things when she was with him.

She folded her arms around her midriff, desperately trying to hold the panic at bay.

'Talk to me, Melody,' he said, his voice low with frustration, but lacking that accusatory edge.

She scrubbed the tears from her cheeks, then turned to him, and the truth spewed out.

'You left me there, Rene, alone, without even bothering to tell me you were leaving. I had to find out from one of the police officers.' She pressed a hand to her chest, could feel the thundering beat. And forced the anger to the fore, to cover the turmoil of other emotions. Why should she be ashamed of the fact the sex had meant something to her? 'I know what we shared wasn't supposed to mean anything. But it still made me feel like nothing. That you didn't even think I was worthy of a goodbye. *Again*. You're the only man I've ever slept with...' she blurted out. He'd asked for the truth. And now he'd got it.

But, instead of looking surprised, he simply nodded. 'I know,' he said.

'You... You *know*?' she gasped, shocked by the flare of something fierce...and possessive in his eyes.

What the hell was that about, given that he had discarded her so easily less than two days ago?

He sent her a wry smile that only confused her more. 'If it helps, I haven't been able to take another woman to bed since the first time we made love either.'

Her heart gave a giddy leap. But then she got a clue.

'Now who's lying?' she said bitterly. 'Don't forget your amorous exploits have been all over the media for the past four years.'

'Been keeping tabs on me?' he murmured, but his fierce expression did not look amused.

The pulse throbbed in her sex, almost as if her traitorous body was preparing itself to take him. And she hated herself even more.

'This isn't a joke,' she fired back, determined not to give in to the yearning this time.

'Dammit, Melody.' He reached over and brushed his thumb across her cheek. 'Don't cry.'

'Then don't lie to *me*,' she said, pushing his hand away.

'The press doesn't know everything,' he replied, his tone surprisingly gentle. 'I didn't say I hadn't dated other women.

I said I hadn't slept with any.' He pushed out an unsteady breath, looking strangely unsettled. She knew how he felt. 'I wanted to forget you. I tried. It's why I proposed to Isabelle. It drove me nuts that I couldn't think about anyone but you when I was with other women. It still does, in fact, because, let's face it, we're not exactly good together anywhere *but* in bed,' he said, sounding exasperated as well as frustrated.

How flattering.

'Telling me you haven't been able to get over sleeping with me for four years, but you really wish you had, isn't quite the compliment you think it is,' she said, determined not to be swayed by the deep-seated longing for his attention which had tripped her up too many times before.

He wasn't saying he cared about her, he was saying he wanted to have sex with her. One thing which had never been in doubt was their chemistry. But, frankly, what had that insane chemistry ever really got her? A few mind-blowing orgasms. And the same fear of abandonment, that hideous feeling of not being enough but never knowing why, which had dogged so much of her childhood.

'You know, my father walked out on me and my mum when I was eight years old—' she forced the words out '—and I never saw him again.'

Why not tell him all of it? Make him realise this wasn't her first rodeo when it came to having men treat her like nothing. She'd once blamed herself for her father's departure, and she'd done the same thing, subconsciously, with Rene. Because she had always been so ashamed of being hurt by his thoughtless behaviour, but why should she be ashamed when she wasn't the one who had been callous and careless?

'One day my father was there,' she continued, because he hadn't replied, his expression carefully blank, 'and the next he wasn't. My mum tried to make it okay. She kept insisting the divorce wasn't about me, it was about them. I guess they must have argued before he left. But I don't remember that. All I remember is birthdays and Christmases going by for years afterwards with no cards, no gifts, nothing. Not even a phone call from him.'

She took another deep breath.

Rene was staring at her now, his reaction unreadable, the only sign what she had confided had affected him at all the muscle in his cheek which kept clenching and releasing. Maybe he was embarrassed with her oversharing, maybe he was bored, but even if he didn't need or want to hear this, she needed and wanted to tell him.

'So yes, I lied about that night,' she said. 'And I'm sorry I made you think, even for a moment, you might have done something terrible…' Although she couldn't help wondering now why he would have gone there, assumed he would even be capable of something so unconscionable. Perhaps that overreaction was a clue to all the things he had never been prepared to talk about to her. The monsters he had fought in those nightmares but refused to admit were real.

She was too weary now, though, and too scared—at the thought of having to spend days with him on some private island, knowing the yearning was still there—to think about any of that.

'I was protecting myself, Rene. I didn't *want* to get in too deep. To rely on you at all. And I was right. So, if you think I'm going to go to this island with you—on the *outside* chance that I *might* be pregnant, after the crappy way you've treated me…then I'm telling you now. I won't. Not until you at least give me an explanation as to why you thought it was okay to abandon me again without a word.'

CHAPTER TWELVE

RENE STARED AT the woman in front of him, not sure what to say in his own defence. Her honesty had floored him, but the sadness in her eyes was crucifying him.

He'd been livid this morning when he'd seen the photographs—which he'd spent twenty-four hours using every resource and legal avenue at his disposal trying to have destroyed—plastered all over the internet. The more reputable sources had at least blurred out Mel's nudity, but many others had not. The headlines, though, had been predictable and salacious. And all of them far more critical of Melody's behaviour than his: *The Prince and the PA's Secret Snowbound Love Shack! The Queen's Ambitious PA Snares a Prince! Rescued at Last...but Did She Want to Be?*

He didn't really care about the hit to his own reputation. It wasn't as if the press or the usual keyboard warriors on social media had ever taken him seriously—and, in truth, given his past behaviour, he had brought most of that negative attention on himself. But Melody's vilification—a woman whose status and lack of experience of this kind of exposure made her much more vulnerable than him—had made him feel sick. The sight of those intrusive photos had also triggered vivid memories of Melody not just in his bed yesterday morning, but under him on the white rug that first night, cradling him as he thrust heavily inside her...

And suddenly the impotence and shame and fury had increased tenfold. And he'd known he could not stay away from her a moment longer.

The fury though had not just come from her lie about that first night in the chalet, but the growing fear that he might have done something unforgivable. A fear which had morphed into anger during the frantic arrangements to figure out a way to protect Mel, deal with the repercussions of that night and get them both as far away as possible from the viral storm.

The decision to whisk her away to Mermaid Cay—because it was the only place he could think of where they could be alone until the publicity blitz blew over—had been a kneejerk one. But he could see now that decision and the possibility of a pregnancy had also been a convenient excuse to insist on privacy and seclusion.

But as she stared back at him now, with the sheen of tears in her eyes, the last of the excoriating anger deflated, until all he had left was the fear.

He needed to protect her. And if she was pregnant they would have to figure out what to do about it. But his intentions had not been entirely altruistic, or unselfish. Because he still wanted her.

Something had happened in that cabin which had blindsided him. And it hadn't just been the sex, however much he might want to believe that.

When she had announced with that crack of pain in her voice that he was the only man she had ever slept with, it had delighted him on one level while also adding to his fear. Because he could see all her vulnerabilities—after she had laid them bare with honesty and openness and the kind of genuine, unsullied emotion which he had never possessed. Never *could* possess.

Her tale of the bastard who had fathered her and then deserted her was far too reminiscent of the thoughtless way he had treated her—by walking away four years ago, while protecting himself, and two days ago, while persuading himself he was trying to protect her.

A part of him knew that the decent thing to do now would be to let her go. Free her from the toxic legacy not just of her own father's callous behaviour but also his own. But he had never been a decent man… And, frankly, how could he do that when she might be pregnant with his heir?

Stop lying to yourself. This isn't about a possible pregnancy. It isn't even about your guilt over those photos and your failure to stop them. This is about your inability to put her needs above your own.

He sucked in a breath and forced himself to face the truth.

He didn't *want* to let her go. Not yet. He'd tried to do that over the last twenty-four hours, and it had only made her situation worse—and the yearning more intense. If nothing else, they needed this break to finally deal with the obsession they had fallen into with each other.

If she was pregnant he would demand marriage—and make the engagement real. But he would never be whole, never be able to offer her more than physical pleasure and financial support, would never have the courage to be honest and unafraid, not to mention dependent on another human being. Because his father had beaten those sensibilities out of him a long time ago.

But he owed her at least some of the truth if he was going to persuade her to get on the damn plane, because he could see the usual stubbornness in her eyes, as well as the hurt he had caused.

'Melody, I left that morning because the police confirmed my suspicions about the drone. I was desperate to have the photos destroyed, if possible, before anyone could publish them—so getting back here as soon as I could was important.' He ran his thumb down the side of her neck, felt her delicious shudder. 'I'm only sorry I failed to find the bastard before he sold those photos to the highest bidder.'

She tugged away from his touch, the hurt and confusion on her face still there. 'Why couldn't you come and tell me that, before you left?'

At least this question was simple to answer.

'Because I didn't want that bastard getting a chance to take any more photos of us together,' he said.

'But you could have contacted me, told me what was going on, this morning?' she said, but she didn't sound quite so sure any more. Or so upset.

Progress.

'Did you want me to?' he replied.

She simply stared at him, the vulnerability in her eyes crucifying him all over again.

'After the photos went viral,' he continued, because he could see she was struggling to understand her own reactions at this point, 'I figured the last person you would want to talk to was me, given that I was the one who had made you a target in the first place.'

Instead of agreeing with him, though, as he had expected, she frowned, then stared down at her hands, which were clasped so tightly in her lap the knuckles had whitened.

She huffed out an unsteady breath. 'This mess isn't your fault, Rene,' she said so softly he almost didn't hear her. 'I may want to blame you for a lot of things, but you're not responsible for what unconscionable people choose to do for a living.'

He thought of all the times he had been caught in compromising positions before that night four years ago—the excessive drinking and partying once his father was gone, and the endless round of beautiful women he'd had on his arm in the years since, to try and force Mel from his mind. And he knew she was being naïve about his role in this debacle, and far too forgiving.

He tucked a knuckle under her chin, tipped her gaze up to his. 'I've been a target my whole life, Melody. I knew the score. I should have protected you from them and I didn't.'

She blinked slowly, her expression unsettled and even more unsure. 'That's not your job,' she said softly.

Yeah, it is, he thought but didn't say, because he knew it would only exacerbate her stubborn streak.

The soft rap on the window had them both tensing, before he realised the car had stopped moving.

'Your Majesty, we have arrived at the hangar,' his flight attendant said, who stood by the car. 'Are you ready to board?'

'Just a minute,' he said.

He turned to Mel, who looked flustered now, and still hopelessly confused. Time to push his advantage.

'Come with me, Mel,' he said, determined to use the carrot first, and at least make it *sound* like a question, before he made any more demands. After all, he already knew Mel did not respond well to the stick. 'We can't do a reliable test for at least ten days, according to the obstetrician I contacted. By which time my legal team will have hopefully had some luck having the photos taken down.'

She took another deep breath, her indecision clear. But at least it wasn't an immediate no.

'Can you stop the press release saying we're engaged? It's not true and it feels dishonest to pretend it is,' she said. 'And I'm perfectly capable of protecting my own reputation.'

Frustration and even hurt twisted in his gut.

'No, I'm afraid not,' he said smoothly. He'd be damned if he would take her away now, only to leave her even more exposed to prurient speculation when they returned. Plus, there was a chance she *could* be pregnant, in which case he had every intention of making the engagement a real one. 'A select number of journalists have already been briefed.'

She sighed. 'I really wish you hadn't done that...' she managed, and he found his temper kicking in. Why was she so damned determined *not* to announce an engagement? If she was carrying his child, marriage would be a *fait accompli*. Surely she knew enough about royalty and how it worked to understand that.

'Isn't it going to make things even more complicated when we return and we have to announce the engagement's off?' she offered.

'We'll deal with that situation when we know you're not pregnant,' he said curtly.

Her frown deepened, but she didn't reply. At least she wasn't going to argue the point right now.

More progress.

'What exactly are we supposed to do on this island for ten days?' she asked.

He laughed, he couldn't help it, the tension in his gut releasing, while the familiar heat spiked. 'The place is an island paradise. Fully staffed, with perfect weather at this time of year. There's swimming and snorkelling, sailing and some great hiking trails... And if none of that appeals to you—' he paused, going in for the kill '—I'm sure we can think of something else to amuse ourselves.'

He wasn't about to pressure her into having sex with him. But denying their chemistry had already got them into a world of trouble over the last four years... And he saw no reason not to take the opportunity this break offered to finally deal with this insane physical attraction. After all, they'd both been without sex for four years, which was precisely why they'd been unable to keep their hands off each other in the cabin. At least now they would be fully conscious and not under stress, so they could make informed decisions about how to proceed—while preventing any other unforeseen mishaps if they chose to indulge themselves. And didn't they deserve the release good sex could bring, after the emotional roller-coaster they'd both been on in the past week? Not to mention denying themselves for four years!

Cupping her cheek, he ran his thumb over her lips, rewarded when she didn't pull away, and awareness darkened her eyes.

Her breath caught on a sensual sob.

'I need an answer, Melody,' he pressed. 'Are you coming with me or not? Or do you want to continue arguing? Because we both know how that is likely to end,' he finished, his voice becoming huskier by the second.

She eased away from his touch, but he could already see the answer in her eyes. And heat pulsed in his groin.

'Okay, I'll come,' she said, still frowning. 'But only because I really don't have a lot of alternatives—and I don't want to put the people I love in the firing line.'

He let out another husky laugh, knowing he had won, despite the adorably belligerent expression on her face—which he would take any day over hurt and vulnerability.

Grasping her neck again, he dragged her back for a swift kiss. 'Good,' he said, releasing her to get out of the car and announce their departure to the flight attendant.

As he escorted her across the tarmac to the private jet, he placed his palm on the small of her back and felt another delicious shudder. The triumphant feeling surged. Leaning close, he whispered in her ear, 'And please don't feel you have to spare my ego,' he teased, 'by implying my company isn't enough to persuade you.'

She scoffed, the tart sound a balm to his soul. 'Don't worry, Your Majesty' she said, throwing the words over her shoulder as she mounted the plane's stairs ahead of him, 'I won't.'

CHAPTER THIRTEEN

MEL FLOPPED ONTO the lounger by the pool. She sighed and stretched, letting the sun relax tired muscles, and breathed in the sea air, scented with the fragrance of the nearby Ginger Thomas tree, its bright yellow blossoms out in force today.

It had been three days since they'd arrived at Rene's estate on Mermaid Cay—a private island of rocky hills and mangrove swamps and a shoreline of secret coves and stretches of soft white sand gently lapped by the translucent blue of the Caribbean Sea.

The five-bedroom main house—which, according to the estate's manager Marcia, had been constructed by Rene's grandfather in the nineteen-fifties, not long after he'd purchased the uninhabited island—perched on a rocky ledge with an infinity pool and was surrounded by several equally well-appointed guest cottages. The villa's commanding position overlooked a wide sandy beach edged by rock pools and the verdant beauty of the island's interior, which included an abundance of frangipani, bay rum, tamarind and mango trees as well as the ubiquitous Ginger Thomas and a host of other flora and fauna which Marcia had identified.

The clean, elegant style of all the buildings was a mix of Colonial and European design made up of wide stone verandas, wooden walkways and bright airy rooms featuring all the mod cons while also having the ability to blend seamlessly into the landscape. Mel's guest bedroom suite featured an outdoor rainfall shower, a luxury bathroom, a four-poster bed and an open terrace with a view of the pool.

No wonder she felt so relaxed after three days in this paradise.

Most of the journey here—which had included twenty hours of flying with a brief stopover in New York's JFK to refuel and a forty-minute speedboat ride from St Thomas—had gone by in a blur of snatched sleep and panic after being swept up in their desperate attempt to escape the press storm. But in the days since, her anxiety over the photos and the future of her career—because how exactly was she supposed to be a benefit to Isabelle's monarchy if she was now notorious as Rene's 'snowbound lover'—had settled. Surely, given enough time, the furore would die down and the press—and public opinion—would move on.

Isabelle had been in touch and Mel had even managed to do some remote working yesterday from the house's study, negotiating an itinerary for the Queen's upcoming trade tour in the US with her new husband.

She'd slept like the dead over the last two nights too, recovering after their snowbound ordeal, not to mention the long night in Rene's arms when neither of them had done much sleeping.

The tranquillity of her surroundings and the easy-going way of life, far away from the publicity storm, had all helped her to relax and get things into perspective. That and the fact she hadn't seen Rene since they had arrived.

Not once.

But what had been a welcome relief at first—because panicking about her response to him and their complicated, often antagonistic relationship had never been good for her stress levels—was becoming less welcome as each day passed.

When she'd woken up yesterday morning to another breakfast alone, she'd realised she missed him. If nothing else, his company had always been exhilarating. But she hadn't been able to track him down all day, nor could she figure out what he was spending his time doing.

According to Marcia—and Fred, the villa's gardener—the Prince was 'busy working'. But because she hadn't seen him yesterday evening either—when the resident chef had laid out another incredible meal for her on the table overlooking the beach—she had no idea what exactly he had been 'busy working' on. After all, Rene was famous, or rather infamous, for not taking his work as Saltzaland's Prince that seriously, far too interested in his own pursuit of pleasure and beautiful women...

Except...

'If it helps, I haven't been able to take another woman to bed since the first time we made love either.'

She squinted into the sun, the bombshell he'd dropped en route to the airport four days ago making her heart clench and release—and the butterflies in her belly do backflips. She hadn't wanted to believe him, had tried to convince herself in the days since that he had to have been lying.

But the more she thought about it—and she had thought about it *a lot*—the more she couldn't figure out why he would lie.

Of course, he'd tried to qualify his abstinence as some kind of physical aberration, an inconvenient side-effect of their sexual chemistry and, by implication therefore, definitely not evidence of any kind of emotional connection. An emotional connection she'd spent four years trying to convince herself too couldn't exist.

But what if it could?

What if she really *was* the first woman to ever have made a lasting impression on him? Because something else—another throwaway comment he'd made during their drive into the storm—had come back to her too during the last forty-eight hours while she'd had far too much time to overthink every aspect of their relationship.

'I haven't had an alcoholic drink in four years.'

She hadn't registered the possible significance of that timing either when he'd said it.

But now she couldn't stop obsessing about that, too. And tying herself in knots about what it might mean.

What if Rene wasn't the man she had always dismissed him as—reckless, shallow, entitled, and impulsive—but someone else?

She'd spent the last three days trying not to dwell on that disturbing possibility—and how much she was starting to miss his company—doing everything from going for long hikes to learning how to cook conch fritters with their chef Jevon, or jogging to the next cove for a swim. But it was becoming harder and harder for her to keep her desire to discover the *real* Rene while she was here on hold. Or to stop all the questions piling up in her head which had always remained unanswered.

And then there were those nightmares. The awful fear in his voice that night, the scars he wouldn't talk about. What did that signify too? She'd considered him a bully when she was a child, and he'd confirmed as much. But she couldn't shake the feeling there was more to discover about that boy. She knew his mother had died suddenly of a brain aneurysm when he was still a baby, and that his father had been rigid and autocratic—according to Isabelle, who had met him several times—but why had Mel never considered that might have had some bearing on how Rene had behaved? Or the way he had gone totally off the rails as an nineteen-year-old, as soon as his father had died.

She grabbed the sunscreen she had left by the lounger before her morning snorkel and began to rub it on. The weather had been as idyllic as everything else here—a perfect twenty-six degrees, the sea breezes as invigorating as the tropical showers every afternoon—but her skin was still adapting to the sun after an Androvian winter.

It wasn't the sun, though, that made her flesh prickle and hum, and her heart skip, when she spotted a lone figure running along the beach.

Rene.

Her heart did another clench and release, while her nipples tightened into peaks beneath the fabric of her bikini.

In running shoes, a loose vest and shorts, his hair damp and his muscles glistening with sweat in the morning sunshine he looked typically gorgeous. And overwhelming.

A hot rush of yearning pulsed in her abdomen, but instead of letting it scare her again she leapt to her feet and waved to attract his attention.

'Rene!'

He glanced round and sent a brief wave back. But instead of running up the stone steps from the beach to join her on the pool terrace, as she had hoped, he continued running around the point, no doubt to one of the guest houses—because she knew from Marcia he hadn't been sleeping in the main house.

Another big red flag which she had missed.

Rene was *definitely* avoiding her.

She grabbed the silk kimono on her lounger, found her sandals, then headed down the beach steps to follow him.

Time's up, Rene.

They had seven more days at least before they could take a reliable pregnancy test. And, if nothing else, she wanted to finally know…*everything.* About the man as well as the boy. All the things she'd let ride or dismissed or allowed him to avoid answering. Didn't she deserve that? Didn't they both?

He had always fascinated her, but she'd stopped herself from looking deeper because of her own vulnerabilities—and the incessant yearning she had always struggled to control.

But it was way past time to stop hiding.

She was an adult now, they both were. And what if there had always been more to this relationship than just a physical craving? Things had shifted between them in the cabin. The connection they shared had deepened. But did that mean there could be more to their relationship than just sex?

It still terrified her to hope, to know she might be reading more into recent events—his decision not to sleep with another woman for four years, to stop drinking, to save her from the storm, then protect her from the fallout from those photos and the cruel headlines with the extreme decision to announce their engagement—than was actually there.

But she refused to be a coward any longer. If he didn't care for her, could never love her, she wanted to know that so she could stop torturing herself with all the 'what ifs'...

Once she arrived on the beach, though, he had disappeared. Luckily, the wet sand held the imprint of his tracks, past the rocks, towards the guest house at the furthest end of the estate. She followed his footprints, her determination to confront him building, along with that vague feeling of insecurity.

What if he'd been avoiding her because he was already bored with her?

What if he was angry about the possibility of a pregnancy, however slim?

It wasn't until she got to the guest villa, artfully nestled in a grove of frangipani and hibiscus, the buds already giving off a sweet subtle fragrance, that the sound of running water hitting stone covered the lapping of the waves against the house's private beach.

She stepped onto the veranda and followed the splashing sound to the back of the house, her heart stampeding into her throat. And all her erogenous zones.

Was he washing in the outdoor rainfall shower?

Her heart rammed into her larynx, making speech impossible, when she passed the corner of the house and spotted him, standing not ten feet away, with his back to her—his naked body glistening in the sunlight as water cascaded over the sculpted muscles and sinews.

Her gaze devoured the sight—tight glutes, strong back, impossibly broad shoulders, long legs roped with muscle and dusted with dark hair—as arousal barrelled through her system like a runaway train.

She couldn't breathe. He was so incredibly beautiful, but as he stepped back, out of the water, to squeeze shampoo from the dispenser and began soaping his hair, the rivulets of water drained away from his skin and she noticed the scars, illuminated for the first time in the daylight.

Her heart throbbed painfully, threatening to block off her air supply, as the compassion she had worked so hard to suppress swelled.

The scars were all small—a nick here, a graze there, a mark that might be a burn—and would have seemed insignificant, but why were there so many of them? And why were they all in places where they would be unlikely to be seen? Across his buttocks, on the small of his back, under one shoulder blade.

She stood, unable to take her eyes from him, realising that whatever—or whoever—had caused these injuries, Rene had never led a charmed life as she had always assumed.

Perhaps they had been accidental, caused by the reckless life he had led in his late teens and early twenties, but whatever had caused those scars, he had kept the extent of the damage hidden from everyone, including her.

Suddenly, she felt sick with guilt, for judging him and never questioning the validity of all the things said about him in the press over the years. He was still frequently referred to as the 'playboy prince'—but how could he be that man when he hadn't slept with another woman, hadn't even had an alcoholic drink in four years?

He finished rinsing his hair, then slapped one palm against the quartz tiles, while his other hand disappeared in front of him.

The fog of guilt and recriminations cleared in a rush, though, when his arm began to jerk in furious motion, and he groaned.

The wave of arousal slammed back into her at the realisation that he was pleasuring himself. And she gasped.

He glanced over his shoulder and his hot gaze fixed on her face.

'Melody?' he murmured, his eyes glazed with desire, his hand still wrapped around the turgid erection when he turned towards her.

Trapped, exposed and so in need of him, she stared back, a furious burst of compassion tangling with desperate yearning.

He straightened away from the wall, stroking the thick length, but his gaze remained locked on hers. Raw need drew tight in her abdomen and made her nipples swell and harden beneath the damp bikini.

He dipped his head. 'Take it off,' he said, his tone thick with desire, the command unmistakable…and undeniable. 'I want to see you, too.'

She obeyed without question—in thrall not just to his need now but also her own.

The kimono slid off her shoulders and dropped to the deck, the silk rough against her oversensitive skin. But her fingers were shaking too hard to unhook the bikini bra. She heard his gruff chuckle, and embarrassment scorched her cheeks as she gave up trying.

Who was she kidding? She'd never been a seductress, had never even attempted to do a striptease for a man before now.

He crooked a finger. 'Come here.'

She hesitated.

'*Now*, Melody, before I come get you,' he said.

She did as he demanded, compelled to obey the urgent command. As he switched off the water and faced her, she couldn't take her eyes from that thrusting erection, mesmerised by the length, the hardness, the girth, and the thought of having it lodged deep inside her again—branding her as his.

He tucked a knuckle under her chin when she reached him, his gaze aflame with heat when it met hers. 'Turn around.'

She did as she was told. The bikini top snapped off and fell to the stone tiles. She covered her breasts instinctively, the weight swollen and heavy in her hands.

His arm wrapped around her waist to hold her steady as her knees weakened. The thick erection prodded her back as he devoured her neck with his mouth and his other hand delved into her bikini panties.

She sobbed, bucking against his hold, the touch too much, so much, as he found her clitoris and worked it ruthlessly.

She shot to peak, the orgasm brutal in its speed and intensity.

Hollowed out, floating in afterglow, she found herself scooped into his arms, her heart dangerously close to shattering too.

The guest bedroom, like hers in the main house, opened out onto the beach, the daylight dazzlingly bright. But when he dropped her onto the huge bed, then reached into the dresser, found a condom and ripped open the foil packet, it wasn't the sunlight which left her dazed as the wave of afterglow cleared but the vicious yearning, not just for sex but for so much more.

'Lose the panties,' he demanded while rolling on the condom, his eyes fixed on her face.

She scrambled out of the bikini bottoms, everything inside her clenching and releasing, tensing and twisting with need, her heart most of all.

He cradled her hips, pulled up her knees to position her, then plunged deep in one ruthless, all-consuming thrust. Her body struggled to adjust—the too-stretched feeling overwhelming. But the frantic, furious strokes soon sent her soaring to another peak.

She clung to his shoulders, trying to control the rush of painful pleasure, the shattering weight of her heart pummelling her chest wall, even as her fingers slipped over damp flesh and touched the small scars.

He worked the spot he knew would trigger her orgasm with ruthless efficiency, the ragged pants of their breathing the only sound.

The pleasure built, twisting, torturing, tormenting, dragging her up, and forcing her over.

She cried out, flying free at last, but as he sank into her arms, his big body shuddering through his own vicious climax, weighing her down into the mattress, she held onto him and struggled to stop her heart from shattering too.

CHAPTER FOURTEEN

SO MUCH FOR staying the hell away from her.

Rene gritted his teeth and eased out of Melody's body, his senses reeling from the violent climax. And the rush of arousal when he had turned in the shower, while trying to masturbate away his obsession with her, only to find her staring at him with the same fierce desire darkening her eyes.

'You're rather bossy when you're aroused, aren't you?' she murmured.

He choked out a laugh at the sanguine tone.

She lay beside him looking adorable and sated. But not exhausted, the way she had on the long plane ride to get here. The bruised shadows under her eyes the night they had arrived had disturbed him so much he'd decided to leave her alone. The intent expression on her face now, though, was equally unsettling.

He shouldn't have jumped her—after promising himself he wouldn't—but staying away from her had only increased the hunger. So maybe it made sense to keep her in his bed for the next seven days. It might help them both take their minds off everything else, because one thing was for sure— sex with Melody tended to make him forget everything, including his own name.

'And you're rather bossy the rest of the time, so I figure we're even,' he said easily. 'Now, where were we...?' He cradled her cheek and ran his thumb down the side of her neck, determined to keep things light and about the sex now. He swept her collarbone, before trailing a finger between her breasts and circling the plump nipple which had been begging for his touch ever since he'd got her naked.

She shuddered deliciously, already primed for another round, but as he leaned to capture the stiff peak in his lips, her hand covered herself, stopping him mid seduction.

He glanced up. 'Problem?' he asked, then wished he hadn't when he registered the astute, searching look—and the sheen of emotion turning her eyes a misty blue.

'I have a question…' she said, her expression shadowed with something which looked weirdly like sympathy. 'How did you get all those scars, Rene?'

'What scars?' he replied, as panic had the afterglow fading.

She'd asked about his scars once before, and he'd had no problem deflecting the question. But that was four years ago, when his defences had been bulletproof. Those defences weren't bulletproof any more, the knowledge and determination in her face reminding him of the woman who had survived a snowstorm and nursed him through a fever. Who had stood up to him and the press and had refused to crumble even when she'd been exhausted.

How the hell did he defend himself against someone who he suspected had always been so much stronger than he was?

She touched his forehead, lifting the hair still damp from his aborted shower and traced the line very few people even knew was there.

'You know which scars, Rene,' she said carefully, the gentle tone making his panic increase.

How could she see so clearly the boy he had kept hidden for so long?

He drew away from her touch to stare down at her.

Heat pounded in his groin.

She was so artlessly seductive, the unruly mess of tawny

blonde hair cascading over the pillows, her sun-burnished skin flushed with pleasure, her plump curves something he would happily have feasted on for hours. But he couldn't do emotional intimacy, especially with a woman like her, who had always been able to see through the ploys he used to shield that boy from discovery.

'I hope you realise you're killing the vibe,' he said, hating the defensiveness in his voice.

'I just want to understand you better, that's all,' she said, the hurt in her eyes making him hate himself more.

'What makes you think there's anything more to understand?' he replied, frustrated now, as well as wary.

This was why he didn't do deep. Why he couldn't let any woman mean too much to him. But when she reached for the sheet to wrap it round her breasts, as if she were protecting herself from the sharp tone, the yearning flared. And he knew it was too late. Because she already meant too much.

Why else would he have been so willing to announce an engagement? So determined to protect her from the fallout from those photos. So desperate to make her accompany him to Mermaid Cay. Why would he have woken up in a pool of sweat this morning, his body hard and ready for her, after dreaming about her round with his child? Especially when he had never even thought of becoming a father—and certainly never considered he would ever want to father a child, before now.

And why would he have been unable to touch another woman since her?

It should be funny—that someone so artless and frankly innocent had managed to ruin him for other women—but he had never felt less like laughing in his entire life.

'I should go back to the main house,' she said, the hollow tone making his chest contract.

She stood, clearly intending to walk away, and he lurched across the bed without thinking and grasped her wrist.

'Don't...' He swallowed past the blockage in his throat. 'Don't go... I still want you.'

He could feel her pulse pummelling her wrist, could see her arousal, and knew she wanted him too. But instead of melting back into his arms—so they could forget about everything, together—she tugged her hand free, her gaze shadowed with regret.

'I know you do, Rene, but sex is not enough. Not for me. Not any more,' she said.

'Why the hell not?' he snapped, his frustration—and panic—getting the better of him. 'It's what we're good at, dammit. And there can't be anything else, not with me. You know that even better than I do.'

He didn't want to show her more, didn't want her to know about the dark things in his past which had formed him and the fear which would always be there inside him. Because if she ever found out the truth about that broken boy, masquerading as a man, as a prince, she would be appalled.

But instead of the snarky comeback he had expected, she sat back on the bed and a smile curved her lips which didn't reach her eyes.

'Why do you always do that?' she asked, the gentle tone only disturbing him more.

'Do what?' he replied, genuinely confused now, as well as wary.

'Try so hard to make everyone believe you're shallow and selfish, when you're not?'

He frowned, shocked by her response and the way it made him feel—desperately needy and even more terrified.

Why was she looking at him like that? With tenderness and understanding? Panic clawed at his throat. He thrust his fingers through his hair, the rigid tension making his stomach hurt.

He was going to have to tell her, at least some of it. To give her some insight into the man he was, instead of the man she wanted him to be.

'I never figured you for the sentimental sort,' he managed in a last-ditch attempt to put them back on track, but she only laughed, the sound tinged with sadness.

'Me either, but here we are.'

Her fingers skimmed down his back and he tensed. The swift shot of arousal was almost as torturous as the surge of need, which had nothing to do with the heat pooling in his lap when she circled the scar on his hip.

'I understand if you don't want to talk about them…' she said, far too perceptively. 'I know how hard it is to let anyone see your vulnerabilities,' she added. 'But I just want you to know you can talk to me, and I won't judge. Not any more.'

He looked over his shoulder to find her watching him, the soft, coaxing tone matched by the affection in her eyes.

Turning, he captured her hand in his, tugged her closer and framed her face.

How could he still want her—so much? When she was scaring him half to death with this conversation. But when he saw the desire in her eyes he saw his way out.

The *only* way out now. He'd let her see too much, and for that he would have to pay a penance. But once she knew enough, she wouldn't mistake him for a good man ever again.

'If you really want to know, you can,' he said, resigned but also determined.

Melody Taylor had convinced herself she was falling in love with him. He could see it, even if she couldn't. She wasn't the first woman to make that mistake—but she was the only one he had ever felt a responsibility to protect. And the only one he had ever needed in his bed.

He couldn't let her go. Not yet. Maybe not ever. Which meant they would have to set parameters. And the only way to do that was to tell her some of the ugly truth.

His gaze glided down to where her nipples peeked over the clutched sheet. He skimmed his thumb over the swollen tip and felt her jolt of response.

He let out a harsh laugh. 'But I think we'd better get dressed first and do this somewhere neutral or we're liable to get sidetracked.'

She nodded and scrambled off the bed. She pressed her hand to her bed hair, looking even more adorable. And vulnerable. 'I should go back to my room. Will you... Will you come over for lunch?'

'I've got work to do...' he said. It wasn't entirely true. The state business he had been handling online could be postponed and he could reschedule the meetings he'd lined up with his advisers and the legal team too—as they worked to turn around the media backlash from those photos. But he needed some time to figure out exactly what to say to her, to extinguish that sheen of emotion in her eyes, without destroying the desire.

If she was pregnant—in fact, even if she wasn't—he might have to marry her, because he wasn't convinced now that he would ever be able to let her go. But she needed to know how much he could give her and how much he couldn't. Because the man she wanted him to be had died inside him a long time ago. And there would be no resurrecting that boy, not even for her.

'I'll come to the main house for dinner and we can discuss...' He released a careful breath. 'Where we go from here.'

She nodded again, but the smile which brightened her whole face made guilt press against his throat. Because the hopeful, happy smile made her look like the girl who had always intoxicated him but he had refused to see. The smart, savvy, brave kid who had once stood up to him, and the artless teenager who had seduced him so effortlessly, and the woman who would always challenge and excite him, but whose tough exterior hid someone far too sweet and idealistic.

'That would be... I really want that,' she said, the enthusiasm in her voice making his throat tighten even more. 'I think we need to be honest with each other. That's all.'

'Sure,' he said, but as she rushed from the room in her sheet and he heard her gathering up her clothing to head back to the main house, he knew honesty wasn't something he could ever give her. Because the whole truth would leave him far too exposed.

CHAPTER FIFTEEN

MEL STEPPED OUT onto the pool terrace. The sea breeze flattened her simple summer dress against her body, tantalising all the places still buzzing from the morning's lovemaking.

She shivered even though the temperature was warm. The outdoor dining table had been set with fine china and crystal stemwear for two, the surrounding trees and scrub lit by sparkling fairy lights. The scent of salt and tropical blooms and the soft lapping of the sea below completed the scene, making it magical and impossibly romantic.

But it wasn't until she spotted Rene standing in the shadows with his back to her, staring at the beach below, that she could release the breath which felt as if it had been clogged in her lungs all day.

He was here. Just as he'd promised.

He looked typically gorgeous, his tall, broad-shouldered physique imposing in the loose linen shirt and faded jeans.

'Rene, you came,' she said, then felt foolish when he swung round.

'Of course. I said I would,' he murmured.

But then he swept his hair back from his forehead—and she wondered if he could be as nervous as she was.

He hadn't shaved since that morning, but somehow the rugged look suited him as he crossed the terrace towards her. The lights draped in the Ginger Thomas tree sparkled in his dark eyes as his gaze swept over her figure.

The butterflies in her belly dive-bombed into her abdomen.

Why hadn't she brought a more suitable dress with her? Something stylish and sophisticated. She'd packed so quickly—and she and Rene had never done romance in their relationship—so it hadn't even occurred to her to include a dress in her luggage appropriate for what suddenly felt like their first ever date.

But then she didn't really have anything appropriate in Androvia either. She dug her teeth into her bottom lip, aware that the pant suits and fitted blouses and skirts she wore in her role as Isabelle's assistant were no more seductive than the summer frock she had on.

The truth was she didn't have anything in her wardrobe which would put her on equal terms with a prince.

Inferiority complex much?

'Melody,' he said softly, then brushed his knuckle across her cheek. 'What's wrong?'

'Nothing.' She blinked, touched by the concern in his gaze.

How come she had never noticed how perceptive he was, how easily he had always been able to read her—while she had felt shut out from his moods, his emotions.

Don't panic, that's what this evening is supposed to solve, Mel.

She forced herself to smile, trying to recapture the bolshy woman who had always been able to hold her own, instead of the fascinated—and far too easily swayed—girl.

'I guess it feels odd for us to be together and not arguing,' she said.

His brows lifted, but then he laughed. The husky sound and the approval in his expression made the butterflies in her belly dance.

'Or tearing each other's clothes off…' he added.

It was her turn to laugh, even as her cheeks heated, the memory of that morning still so vivid. 'That too.'

'Come on, let's sit, so the staff can serve the food and head back to the mainland,' he said, nodding past her to indicate the young waiter who had arrived.

She steeled herself against the familiar shudder of reaction when he placed his palm on the small of her back to direct her to her chair.

Once they were seated, the server placed a platter on the table filled with the conch fritters she loved.

'This looks delicious, thank you,' she said.

'Jevon said they're your favourite.' The boy beamed, then addressed Rene. 'I've left the rest of the meal on the serving trolley, Mr Gaultiere, as you requested,' he said. 'And Jevon says you're all set for the rest of the week—he's left an assortment of meals in the freezer and the fridge is fully stocked. If there's anything you need, Marcia said to contact her. She wanted me to let you know a cleaning crew will be here for an hour each morning, but otherwise you've got the island to yourself.'

Rene nodded. 'That's great, Jerome. Tell everyone I appreciate their hard work and to enjoy the break.'

The boy smiled. 'Yes, sir.'

He left swiftly, leaving them alone in the moonlight.

'You dismissed the staff for the rest of the week?' Mel asked, trying not to overthink his motives. She guessed it must have been a titanic effort to prepare for their arrival at such short notice, and they certainly deserved the time off.

Leaning back in his chair, Rene's intense gaze roamed over her. 'Yeah.'

'Why?' she asked, the butterflies doing somersaults.

Was it possible he craved the chance to spend some time alone with her? That his feelings might have deepened, too?

He shrugged, before lifting the carafe of hibiscus lemonade. 'They've earned some paid vacation after the shifts they all put in getting this place ready,' he said as he poured them both a glass. 'And we don't need to be waited on, we proved that in the cabin.'

'True.' She forced a wry smile to her lips as the butterflies relaxed.

She scooped up a bite of Jevon's delicately spiced fritters, then swallowed it down with a mouthful of the fragrant lemonade.

She'd got way ahead of herself again but, even so, the chance to spend the rest of the week—until they could take the test—alone with him here was filled with possibilities.

'Plus, I don't want to risk anyone seeing you naked in the rainfall shower, or anywhere else for that matter.' The low tone made the pulse of awareness at her core pound. 'Anyone but me, that is.'

'That sounds rather presumptuous,' she said, trying to get the butterflies to behave again. 'And possessive.'

But her half laugh came out on a raw breath when his eyes narrowed.

'Presumptuous? I don't think so.' His lips curved, the sensual smile as provocative as his gaze when it dipped to her breasts—the nipples poked against the light cotton like missiles ready to launch. 'But possessive?' He let out a strained laugh, the sound arrogant and amused. 'Definitely.' He leaned forward, to trace a finger over the pulse point punching her collarbone. 'If you haven't figured it out yet, Melody, you're mine. And I suspect you always will be.' The kick of fierce joy was swiftly followed by apprehension though when he added, 'Your body knows it, even if you don't.'

His finger trailed down to brush the tight peak. She jolted back as savage yearning swept through her body.

'I thought we agreed this isn't just about sex?' she managed as the cutlery she'd barely used clattered onto her plate. 'That I need more than that.'

'I'm not sure there is more,' he said, but the muscle in his cheek tensed, and she wondered if he was really as confident and in control as he appeared.

She hoped not, because that would put her at even more of a disadvantage.

'I know you want everyone to think that, Rene, but I don't believe you,' she offered, determined not to let him use his usual avoidance tactics.

He cocked his head to one side, but the shuttered expression wasn't fooling her this time, because the muscle in his jaw was working overtime again.

'You think because I have a few unexplained scars I'm a good guy, is that it?' he said, the curt tone another giveaway. 'We have an incredibly strong physical connection, Mel. Unlike you, I know exactly how rare that is, because I've never shared anything like it with another woman. But don't make the mistake of confusing the endorphin rush of great sex with something more.'

She stiffened, absorbing the deliberately patronising tone—and the well-aimed hit to her confidence and belief, not just in herself but also in him and what they could have, if he would only let her in.

'It's not just the scars, Rene, it's other stuff.'

He swore softly. 'Like what, dammit?' He sounded angry now, but somehow it felt like progress, the mask he had worn for so long starting to slip.

'The nightmares… They seemed so real. You sounded so terrified, like an animal caught in a trap they couldn't escape.' She took a steadying breath, sympathy and compassion overwhelming her again as she recalled his broken, desperate pleading. 'Or a child being punished for something they didn't understand.'

His eyes narrowed, the frown becoming catastrophic, but he didn't deny it.

'The monster you were so afraid of… It was your father,

wasn't it?' she said, wondering why she had never seen the answer before now. Fear could drive so many conflicting emotions, she knew that, because her fear of rejection—after her dad had just disappeared—had made her terrified of trusting her own heart for so long. Was it any surprise that Rene had chosen to hide that terrified child behind the façade of a reckless playboy prince?

His gaze darkened, his voice when he spoke, though, was tight.

'Okay, yes, my father was obsessed with appearances. He also suffered from violent mood swings and could not control his temper whenever he considered my behaviour to be unacceptable.'

'But if he was hurting you, why didn't anyone stop him?' she asked, disturbed not just by the words but also the pragmatic tone.

'Don't be naïve, Mel.' He sighed, suddenly looking weary. 'The palace officials were forced to cover it up because he was their prince and their employer.'

She reached across the table to cover the hand he had fisted on the cloth, disturbed not by the patronising words—which she understood now were just another of his many defences against feeling too much—but by the flat acceptance in his eyes.

'He hurt you, Rene,' she said. 'And they didn't protect you when they should have.'

He shrugged, then tugged his hand free, to rake it through his hair. 'He needed help. In retrospect, I believe my mother's sudden death had a catastrophic effect on his mental health—and I became the focus of his rage and pain. But because of who he was, they didn't give him the help he needed.'

A tear slipped over her lid. Why was he still protecting that man? And punishing the boy for something that had never been his fault?

'But you needed help, too,' she said, a gulping sob queuing up in her throat.

He swore again, then brushed the tear from her cheek.

'Don't you dare cry for that little bastard, Melody,' he murmured, the horrified expression on his face part shame, part shock. 'It was never that bad.' She knew he was lying. She had seen the scars, and those were just the injuries which had left a mark. What about all the others—not just to his body, but also to his confidence and self-esteem?

He got up from the table, his agitation clear as he crossed the terrace to stare out at the sea again, his back rigid with tension.

'And let's not forget,' he continued, 'I have got my own back on him by being the worst prince Saltzaland has ever seen.'

The rueful tone only made her heart hurt more for that little boy who had had no one to protect him. Getting up from the table, she scrubbed the tears from her cheeks, knowing they weren't helpful, and crossed to him.

'Except that's not true either, is it?' she said softly, refusing to let the flippant remark pass. 'Saltzaland has a well-run monarchy. You work much harder than you let on.' She had seen the shift he'd put in at the New Year Ball, being effortlessly charming, and always diplomatic. And still remembered his fury at her unprofessionalism that evening. She had also seen the way all his staff responded to him, not out of duty or deference to his title but out of genuine warmth and respect. 'You stopped drinking and carousing years ago.'

He turned to stare at her, his gaze wary—as if he couldn't bear for anyone to see there was much more to him than the reckless playboy.

'Just because you let the press print whatever they like about you,' she added, annoyed she'd believed those exploitative stories and unfounded criticisms for so long, too. 'It doesn't make it true.'

He blinked slowly, then shook his head. 'Who knew?' he said as he cradled her cheek. 'Beneath the kickass Valkyrie is a hopeless romantic.'

The cynical tone made her sad.

'I'm allowed to be angry for that boy,' she said, refusing to apologise for her feelings. 'He deserved so much better.'

She swallowed down the urge to say more, though. He wasn't ready yet, to hear how much her feelings had grown, how strongly she felt, not just for the boy but also the man. She could wait for that. The approval and awareness in his gaze was enough. For now.

'Maybe.' He lifted her chin and lowered his mouth to hers, to whisper across her lips, 'But how about we stop wasting time now and get back to what we do best?'

She pushed down the regret—that he was still determined to sidetrack her with sex.

'What about our meal?' she asked.

The question came out on a shuddering sob as his hands delved beneath her panties to cup her bottom—and pull her against him.

'We'll have to take a raincheck,' he groaned as he devoured her neck and ground the growing ridge in his jeans against her yearning body. 'It's you I want right now, not conch fritters.'

The desire rose—fast and furious and, as always, unstoppable.

He found one stiff peak and suckled it greedily through her dress. She barely managed to choke out a 'Yes,' as the heat built to an inferno.

Lifting her into his arms, he headed across the terrace towards her bedroom. She dropped her head back and let the passion sweep away her doubts—and the fear of rejection which had made her a coward for so long.

She plunged her fingers into his hair and worshipped him with her lips, peppering kisses across his cheek, his chin, and the cruel scar on his forehead.

All they needed was quality time together, for him to see what she saw, for him to believe in what they could have together. And surely there couldn't be a better way to pass that time than exploring and exploiting the wild rush which had brought them together in the first place?

Much, much later, she sat on his lap, naked but for the silk kimono as the sea breeze rippled over beard-roughened skin and he fed her titbits from their dinner table in the moonlight.

This is enough for now, her heart whispered, even as the burst of afterglow turned into the bright, scary bloom of intense emotion.

CHAPTER SIXTEEN

'WHEN EXACTLY ARE you two planning to do the test, Rene? Because we want to make sure we're still ahead of the story if Miss Taylor turns out to be carrying your heir.'

Rene frowned at the computer screen, and the pragmatic look on his PR manager's face on Teams. He'd known Jack Kendall since college, so they didn't tend to stand on ceremony. But right now, he wished the guy wasn't quite so damn blunt.

Rene shrugged. 'I guess we can do it tomorrow morning,' he offered, 'without risking a false negative result.'

He'd been prevaricating for days now. Because he knew, whatever the result, once they had done the test, their time in Mermaid Cay would be over. They couldn't stay here indefinitely, however much he might want to.

But he'd also been holding off because Melody hadn't pushed. And somehow that bothered him more.

He'd set the parameters he'd needed to set a week ago and she'd seemed happy with that. But as each day passed— while they spent the hours snorkelling, swimming, taking lazy lunches by the pool and sitting out each night on the terrace to devour another of Jevon's meals in between bouts of devouring each other—he could sense how dependent he was becoming on having her not just in his bed but also in his life.

Her forthright, open nature and her sharp wit had made it impossible for him to fob her off with the irresponsible playboy persona he had cultivated over the years for everyone else, even with Jack on occasion. She took him and his work seriously. And had figured out exactly how much he wanted his country to succeed, and that he cared deeply about his subjects and his responsibilities. She'd even taken to giving him advice on how to handle the official duties he had always considered himself so unsuitable for, thanks to his father's bullying. In fact, her emotional intelligence and her astute understanding of the pressures and duty of monarchy had finally made him realise why Isabelle had hired her in the first place.

Like an arrogant, entitled ass he'd always assumed the Androvian Queen had simply wanted a companion, and had generously given her best friend the job. But he understood now, Melody had always had the sort of skills which would make her a major asset to Isabelle and her monarchy. And also, he thought now, as a consort to Saltzaland's ruling Prince.

Of course, they hadn't spoken about the possibility of marriage—because Melody seemed convinced that she wasn't pregnant. The problem was, he was becoming certain, after spending the last week with her, that he would want to marry her now even if she wasn't carrying his child.

He'd spent so much of his life hiding all his flaws and weaknesses, and the ugly truth about his relationship with his father, behind a mask of cynicism and indifference. But he hadn't realised how lonely his life had been until this week. Until he had someone who understood him, who could see all those flaws and weaknesses, who knew about the darkness in his past and still had faith in his abilities.

But how the hell did he tell Mel he wanted to marry her, without exposing himself more? Or worse, exploiting the soft light he saw in her eyes now every time she looked at him? He knew enough about Mel—her strength of character, her courage and empathy—to know she would want him to love her before she would agree to marry him, whether she was pregnant or not.

But to him, love had always been just a word that people used to compel obedience or to expose vulnerabilities—after all, hadn't his father pretended to love him while 'disciplining' him so harshly for every minor infraction?

He admired Melody, he enjoyed her company—she excited him and challenged him and delighted him, in bed as well as out—and he wanted to be able to protect her, but he could never love her. Not the way she probably wanted to be loved—fully and without compromise.

He was already in too deep to pull out. Enough that marriage seemed like a good compromise when it never would have before. But how did he get her to let go of all her romantic dreams without destroying her spirit and her confidence, the way he had several times before?

'That's great. Get in touch with the result as soon as you have it.' Jack perked up. 'Let me know how you want to proceed, then we can figure out how best to spin the result either way,' he continued, making Rene's head start to hurt. Jack had always been a shark when it came to creating narratives that would ensure Rene's screw-ups—and his steadfast refusal to engage with the press—didn't rebound on Saltzaland. That was why he'd hired the guy when they'd both graduated. But he was beginning to see the drawback with Jack's methods now, because he was talking about Melody like a commodity instead of a person, the cold calculation in his expression repulsive.

'The engagement announcement was a stroke of genius, by the way,' Jack added. 'You were right about that, and I was wrong. It's worked a treat to switch the public perception of those photos from sleazy to romantic,' he continued, his crude reasoning threatening Rene's gag reflex.

The engagement announcement had been made on the

spur of the moment to protect Melody from the fallout from those photos—and because he'd felt hideously guilty about the events of that first night when he had finally remembered all the details.

It had never been intended as a ploy, though, to push a favourable narrative for the Saltzaland monarchy.

'All the press can talk about now is your whirlwind snow-bound romance, and where the hell you are. FYI, looks like the press may have guessed you're in the Caribbean, so probably best to clear out of the love shack in the next couple of days and return to Europe.'

Rene tensed. 'Jack, I'm not enjoying the sarcasm,' he said stiffly.

Jack simply laughed, not used to Rene taking exception to his caustic comments about his personal life. Probably because Rene had never taken his personal life that seriously either until now.

'The point is, we don't want an accidental pregnancy messing with the "true lurve" narrative,' Jack said, doing sarcastic air quotes. 'So, if you did hit the jackpot we should probably hold off on the news until we've set a wedding date. And got lots of shots of you two looking cute together. We don't want the press thinking this is a shotgun wedding, 'cos that would be bad.'

Rene's temper kicked in. What the hell? Did Jack think he intended to turn his own marriage into a publicity stunt?

'Whatever,' he snarled, needing to end the conversation before he lost what was left of his cool with the guy. 'I'll speak to you tomorrow,' he said and clicked the 'leave meeting' button.

The only thing he'd be telling Jack tomorrow was that he was fired.

He'd give the man a generous severance package and good references, because they'd been friends for a long time. And

Jack had been a useful buffer back in the bad old days, when Rene had been drinking to excess and trying to fill the empty spaces inside him with meaningless sex. Jack had been a necessary evil who had once stopped him from having to deal with the consequences of his own dumb decisions—but he was a part of his past now.

The Playboy Prince had been dead for four years—and Melody had shown him he did not need to hide his ambitions for his monarchy behind that façade a moment longer.

Shutting the laptop with a snap, he took several deep breaths to calm his temper. The morning sunlight glimmered on the translucent blue and the thought of Melody—waiting for him in the master bedroom—helped to untangle the knots in his gut.

He'd left her fast asleep, her pert bottom peeking out from under the sheet. Because he'd exhausted her during the night. *Again*.

Thank God, he hadn't woken her when the nightmares—which had begun to chase him again after their heart-to-heart a week ago—had jerked him awake just before dawn, the sweat cooling on his body and making him feel clammy and unclean.

He tugged open the desk drawer and lifted out the box one of his assistants had handed him before he'd left Saltzaland. It felt heavy in his palm, which was ridiculous because it couldn't weigh more than a few ounces.

They should probably do the test tomorrow, so he could start getting Melody on board with what needed to happen next. He had always known that eventually he would have to take a wife. But there had never been anyone he'd considered right for the role, until now. Melody was perfect in so many ways. Not only was she a modern working woman who understood the business of monarchy, she was also smart and beautiful and he found her endlessly fascinating and exciting. So there was no chance of him getting bored.

But, despite the pragmatic assessment, regret pushed against his chest. Because, for once in his life, he had no desire to return to the real world.

He wanted one more day, so he could see the fierce joy in her eyes one more time before he told her the whole truth: that he couldn't offer her the happy ever after he suspected she wanted—but that they would make a strong team, if he could pry her away from Isabelle.

As he went to place the box back into the drawer, a throat cleared behind him.

He swung around to find Melody standing in the study doorway, her hair damp from a shower, her delicious curves covered by the silk kimono he'd tugged off her in the past week more times than he could count.

Disappointment engulfed him, his plan to wake her up—by caressing her in all the places he knew would make her beg—ruined.

'You're awake?' he said inanely, but then he noticed the strange look in her eyes—part sadness, part confusion—and his disappointment became sharp and jagged.

How much had she overheard? Because he didn't want Jack's callous assessment of their situation freaking her out.

'What's wrong?' he asked.

'I just… I wondered where you were,' she said.

Relief rushed through him, even though she still seemed wary and unsure. She couldn't have overheard his conversation with Jack, or she would have had words with him about it. One thing Melody never did was back down from an argument. Or shy away from tough conversations, unlike him.

'Sorry,' she said, her face flushing with colour. 'That sounded clingy.'

Huh?

He frowned, unsettled by the defensive tone. Since when had Mel ever considered herself less than his equal? But then he found himself smiling at her wary expression. No wonder she had captivated him so comprehensively. Her reactions were as unpredictable as they were unique.

'Not a problem. I love it when you cling,' he teased, determined to lighten the mood. And maybe seduce her back into bed.

But, instead of taking the bait, her expression remained serious as she dipped her head. 'I think we should be safe to do that now, and not risk an incorrect result.'

It was only then he realised he still had the pregnancy test kit in his hand. He stared down at it, wishing he could shove it back in the drawer and forget about it for another day.

But how could he do that without giving away the fact he didn't want their time alone here to end? Then an odd bubble of hope expanded under his breastbone.

He hadn't given a lot of thought to the result, but if she *was* pregnant he would have a much stronger case for insisting on marriage. So there was that.

Standing, he lobbed the box to her.

'Good idea,' he said, as she caught it one-handed.

'Why don't you do it while I figure out breakfast?' He glanced at his watch, trying for a nonchalance he didn't remotely feel. 'How about we eat at the guest house round the point? The cleaning crew will be finishing up there now and then they can do this place.'

She nodded. 'Of course,' she said.

But, as she tucked the box under her arm, the strange formality in her tone had him reaching for her arm.

'Hey,' he said, stopping her in mid-stride.

She turned towards him, her eyes shadowed. Something wasn't right and it was starting to bother him.

He tucked a knuckle under her chin. 'You know the result doesn't matter, right?' he said, forced to expose himself. After all, the chances of a positive result were slim. And he probably couldn't rely on it to get him what he wanted, even if she was carrying his child.

'I'll still want you. Whether you're pregnant or not.' He pressed a kiss to her lips.

Her shudder of reaction was like a gunshot to his gut, triggering the familiar arousal, but also making the knot in his stomach return. He forced himself to draw back—not to take more. Not yet, anyway.

'We make a good team,' he added, deciding it was time he started laying the groundwork for the proposal he planned to make to her when they returned to Saltzaland.

She nodded. 'Yes, we do.'

'I think we should consider making our engagement real, whatever the result,' he blurted out.

Her brows rose, her face flushing with colour. 'But… *Really*?'

She sounded so astonished he was a little taken aback. Surely, she must have realised this was where they had been heading all along? But then he noticed the naked hope in her eyes, that flash of vulnerability and fierce tenderness, and the knot in his gut cinched tighter.

'Rene, I need to tell you something…' she began, the emotion in her voice so thick that the fear—she was about to say something she would soon regret—blindsided him.

'Don't… Not yet,' he said, swiftly cutting off whatever she had been about to say as his panic increased. He cradled her cheek, brushed her damp hair behind her ear, the well of affection for her terrifying, too. 'Let's discuss the practicalities over breakfast.' He had to start managing her expectations now if he was going to make this a commitment he was comfortable with. 'The truth is, though, marriage is the logical next step for me,' he continued. 'I need an heir, although not necessarily right away,' he continued, starting to babble as he watched the joy in her eyes fade and the hope dim. 'And you have all the assets I want in a wife. Professionally as well as personally. Frankly, it's a win-win.'

The last of the joy in her eyes died.

He steeled himself against the impulse to pull her into his arms, to apologise for hurting her again. He had to be cruel now, to be kind. He didn't want to give her false hope—and he didn't want to lie to her again.

She nodded. But as she walked away from him the empty, uneasy feeling in his gut refused to settle.

He headed over to the guest cottage, to rustle up something for breakfast from the supplies Jevon had left them. But once he got there his hands started to shake—as the uneasy feeling grew.

Because he couldn't forget the blank look in her eyes, or rationalise the thought that he had just destroyed something infinitely precious without intending to.

Mel stared down at the one pink line on the pregnancy test kit. And waited, and waited… But no other line appeared. The result was negative.

Her stomach plummeted the rest of the way into her toes.

This was a good thing, and what she had always expected. So why did she feel even more gutted now than she had twenty minutes ago when she'd been about to tell Rene how much she loved him, and he'd stopped her?

She dropped the plastic stick in the bathroom bin, then washed her hands. But as the crater in her stomach grew, she knew why. Somehow or other, without ever consciously admitting it to herself, she had hoped desperately that she might be pregnant with Rene's baby. So she would have an excuse not to confront the regret—and fear—in his eyes, not to have to interpret what that pragmatic proposal really meant.

'You idiot,' she murmured to her reflection, the heartache in her expression only confirming her worst suspicions.

That she had wanted to find a reason to justify allowing herself to fall hopelessly and completely in love with him.

She pressed a shaky hand to her belly. Her empty, unpregnant belly.

To be fair, though, falling in love with Rene had never been a conscious decision so much as an organic development. How could she not fall in love with him, when in some corner of her heart she had always known her feelings for him had never been rational, never been safe or pragmatic, and had always been about so much more than physical attraction.

In the past week, riding on the crest of a wave of his approval and attention, the fierce joy had always been tempered by the knowledge that he didn't love her in return. She'd told herself that didn't matter, that it didn't have to be immediate, that love could always grow, and from the things he'd told her about his traumatic relationship with his father it was no wonder he was so cautious.

But every time they made love—the passion between them only becoming more incendiary and unquenchable—every time she saw his spontaneous smile when she said something he considered witty, every time he challenged and provoked her, every time he asked her advice and listened to her answer intently, she had fallen deeper and deeper into the delusion that somehow she would be the one to break down all those barriers he had been forced to put around his heart long ago.

'...we don't want an accidental pregnancy messing with the "true lurve" narrative... We don't want the press thinking this is a shotgun wedding, 'cos that would be bad...'

The conversation she'd overheard echoed in her head.

She knew Rene wasn't planning to use her to create a 'lurve narrative' for the media, the way his PR guy had implied. She'd heard the sharp disgust in his voice when he'd ended the conversation. And she knew him well enough now to know he did care about her because of the affection in his eyes when he smiled at her, because of the fierce passion when they made love, because of all those moments when he made her feel cherished and important. She also knew he didn't care enough about his media image to ever propose marriage simply to sell a false narrative to the press.

But the cynicism of the discussion had made her realise how delusional she had allowed herself to become. And how naïve she had always been without ever realising it. Because she had believed with increasing conviction over the past week—every time she lay in his arms sated with afterglow, every time they laughed or joked together, every time he respected her advice and considered her opinions so carefully— that if she told him how she felt he would welcome the news. And even if he couldn't love her yet, he would be more than willing to give love a chance to grow.

But instead, he had guessed what she was about to say and shut her down.

He was a much better man than he believed himself to be. And an exceptionally good prince. But she knew now that an offer of marriage from him would always have been based on pragmatism and practicalities. However much he enjoyed her company, however much he wanted her sexually, for him marriage would always have been a business proposition.

The foolish wish for an unplanned pregnancy had been her subconscious longing to provide her with a reason to accept such an offer. To drop even further down the rabbit hole of believing theirs could be some kind of fairy tale romance— when Rene had never been allowed the luxury of that innocence and hope, even as a boy.

She could end up spending the rest of her life hoping for something that was never going to happen. And she couldn't bear to risk that, because it would remind her far too forcefully of that little girl who had kidded herself for so long that her father would return one day, would welcome her with open arms, would tell her the divorce had never been her fault and that he loved her unconditionally.

Waiting, hoping and eventually discovering she wasn't enough had nearly broken her then. But she had eventually survived and prospered—thanks to her mum's support, and Isabelle's, and because she'd discovered a purpose and a job she loved.

Until Rene.

Until those days in the cabin, when she'd finally admitted to herself how obsessed she had always been with him—and this week, when she had come to realise he was a much more complex man than she had ever believed.

Discovering that man had been wonderful, but also terrifying. Because while she had made herself so vulnerable to love, he had been careful to keep a large portion of himself back.

He had offered her scraps—delicious, beautiful, wonderful insights into the man he might have been if his childhood had not been so broken, and he hadn't been forced to protect himself. But she could see now that was all he would ever have to offer her.

She dressed hastily and packed the small bag she had arrived with, what felt like several lifetimes ago. She wrote a goodbye note for Rene, folded it into an envelope and placed it carefully on the dresser with trembling fingers, then walked quickly along the wooden walkway in the opposite direction from the guest cottage where Rene was making breakfast for them both—probably badly, she thought, the choking sensation in her throat becoming painful.

When she arrived at the island's small dock the cleaning crew were busy loading up the speedboat they had arrived in, which was docked next to the power catamaran she and Rene had used to head out for a snorkel safari on the reef only the day before.

Grief and sadness pushed against her chest, but her flight instinct spurred her on.

The boat's captain agreed to give her a lift back to St Thomas, looking nonplussed. Thankfully, though, he didn't question her further as she sat on the small bench seat beside the cleaners.

The boat puttered away from the quay, then reared in the water to speed towards the horizon. She forced her gaze forward and refused to look back.

The last week had been a heartbreakingly beautiful dream full of so many possibilities, but she had to face a future without Rene in it. She could have made him a good wife, because he was right, they did make a great team… But she would always want so much more than that. And he had made it clear, in all the ways that counted, that he didn't.

CHAPTER SEVENTEEN

'MEL, HONEY, WHEN exactly are you planning to head back to Androvia?' Elise Taylor's voice was concerned but firm at the other end of the phone line.

Mel gazed out of the kitchen window of the small cottage in Wales, where she had been staying for over a week.

Not staying. Hiding, she thought miserably.

The drystone walls at the back of the property framed the view over the still waters of Llyn Dinas towards the dramatic rocky peaks of Dinas Emrys where, according to local legend, the white dragon of the Saxons and the red dragon of Wales had fought each other.

'Soon,' Mel replied to her mother, hating the halting note in her voice. She'd got a flight to London from St Thomas but had only been at her mother's house in Paddington for twenty-four hours before a press photographer had appeared. So she'd fled to this off-grid bolthole in Wales, owned by one of her mum's friends. Ironically, it was the same bolthole they'd used once before, during that soul-destroying Christmas after her parents' divorce. She never would have thought she could feel more adrift, more unsure, more unhappy than she had that winter. She'd been wrong.

She let out a heavy sigh. What she needed was to get back to work, back to her life in Androvia. But she didn't want to bring more negative media attention on Isabelle and Travis. Or rather, that was what she'd been telling herself religiously each day, while reading all the books on her e-reader which she hadn't had time for in years, or trekking through the forests of the Snowdonia National Park to the picturesque mountain village of Beddgelert to buy supplies and catch up with as much of her workload as she could in a café with an internet connection, while avoiding going on any of the news or gossip sites.

'How soon?' her mother said gently. 'Because Her Majesty phoned me again this afternoon. She's worried about you, Mel, and so am I.'

'You didn't tell her where I am, did you?' she asked, hating the panic in her voice and the echo of cowardice. What was wrong with her? She needed to contact Isabelle properly, instead of sending her daily texts and then switching off her phone before her friend could reply.

'You asked me not to, so I didn't,' her mother said carefully, as if she were talking to the little girl Mel had once been, who had always needed so much reassurance that she was worthy and important, after her father's desertion, instead of the strong, determined woman she had become. But then that woman would not still be hiding out in Wales, nursing her completely self-inflicted heartbreak, instead of dealing with the fallout from the end of her fake engagement.

'This isn't like you, Mel,' her mother added, sighing. 'What happened in the Caribbean?' she asked, finally addressing the subject Mel had been busy avoiding. 'Because Prince Rene hasn't issued any statement about the engagement being off, sweetheart.'

What? Why not?

She frowned as she watched the mist roll off Dinas Emrys and the clouds darken.

'Are you sure?' she asked. She hadn't wanted to read any of the stories, because it would just make coping with the massive hole in her heart even harder.

But why hadn't he issued a press release announcing their breakup a week ago?

She'd been clear in her note. That she wasn't pregnant and he didn't have to feel bound by the promises he'd made to protect her, because she could protect herself.

But it had been over a week… And how could she return to Androvia until the whole story had been given a chance to settle? Which couldn't happen until the story broke in the first place. What on earth was he waiting for?

'Yes, of course I'm sure. I've been doorstepped by paparazzi for the last seven days, darling, asking where you are and where he is and why you're not together,' her mother added, the rueful, patient note making guilt snake into Mel's stomach.

Where Rene was? What the…?

'I'm so sorry, Mum…' she began, then jumped and almost dropped the phone at loud rapping on the front door of the cottage. Who on earth could that be?

'Listen Mum, I'll ring you back. I think someone must be lost.' It wasn't the first time in the past week that a stranded hiker had needed directions.

'Call Her Majesty first, before you call me back,' Elise instructed, her no-nonsense tone reminding Mel of how her mother had spoken to that fragile child instead of the woman she was now. 'She's your friend as well as your employer, Mel, and she wants to know what the hell is going on. As do I.'

'Right,' she said, then managed to say her goodbyes before her mum went into lecture mode, which she totally deserved but wasn't sure she was strong enough to deal with yet.

Wow, Mel. Pathetic much?

She walked through the cottage kitchen to the front door, the banging getting louder and more insistent. Whoever this hiker was, they were pretty entitled.

But then she spotted a mud-splattered Jeep parked in the

front yard. Not a hiker. Was that the forest ranger's vehicle? Maybe there was a wildfire, although it seemed unlikely, given the persistent rain.

Pulling the old-fashioned dead bolt, she wrenched the heavy oak door open. 'Hold onto your…'

Then heat flushed through her whole body and her heart stopped dead, before careering into her throat to cut off her air supply.

'*Rene?*' she whispered, so shocked to see him standing in a field in Wales, wearing jeans, boots and a sheepskin jacket and checked shirt, the collar turned up against the cold, his dark hair glittering with raindrops, she wondered if she was hallucinating.

Her fingers lost their grip on the door. He slapped his palm against the wood to shove the door open and stepped into the cramped hallway. He slammed the door shut behind him with a loud bang.

'Correct,' he said, his voice low with what she could already see darkening his eyes.

Fury.

'W-what are you d-doing here?' she stuttered, although the quiver in her voice was nothing compared to the trembling starting to make her body shake as she retreated down the hallway.

Why was it so good to see him again, even though he looked so angry with her?

'You little coward… You ran out on me.' He grasped her upper arm and marched her through into the kitchen.

'Let go of me!' she said, trying to tug her arm free. A losing battle as it turned out, because his fingers only tightened on her arm like a manacle—and sent sensation shooting through her body right beside the shivers of shock and yearning.

He yanked her around to face him, then cupped her head

to pull her towards him, forcing her to inhale a lungful of that stunning scent of cedarwood and man.

His forehead dropped to hers, and suddenly she could feel the shivers racking his body as well as hers.

'Dammit, you little fool,' he murmured, caressing her neck, the words choked out on ragged pants. 'I didn't know where the hell you'd gone, Melody.' The snap of anger was replaced by something else—something hollow and broken and scared... 'I've been searching for you like a madman. Don't you *ever* do that to me again, or I swear you will not be able to sit down for a week.'

She wanted to be indignant at the dictatorial tone, to cover the aching pain in her heart at seeing him again, at feeling his body pressed against hers, inhaling his scent, his sadness. But she knew his threat was an empty one because she could hear the fear and panic in his voice, feel it in the fury of his kiss when he captured her mouth with his.

She should tell him no, should push him away, should stand her ground, but instead her lips opened instinctively to let him in.

He claimed her, branded her with the furious kiss, devouring her breathy sobs, thrusting his tongue inside to reach all the empty recesses of her heart, her soul.

His hands grappled with her sweatshirt, tugging it over her head, then he scrambled to release her bra. Her head dropped back, her moan of desperation broken and yearning as his mouth found the aching tips of her bared breasts. He suckled strongly, drawing arrows of sensation down to her throbbing sex.

She thrust greedy fingers into his hair to drag him closer, arched her back to give him better access, her sobs becoming heady pleas of desperation.

He lifted his head suddenly, to search her face, his eyes

wild, his need transparent, his desire fierce and elemental and untamed.

'I need to be inside you...' he croaked, part plea, part demand.

She nodded, unable to speak, not knowing what was happening but knowing it was everything she had ever wanted because the same urgency, the same desperation she had felt for days, weeks, months, maybe even years—ever since that first time—was reflected now in his face.

Not just the physical need but also emotional, the intimate connection between them so vivid, so clear, so undeniable.

He grasped her waist, lifted her onto the kitchen table, then set about tugging off her sweatpants, yanking down her panties. Suddenly she was naked, vulnerable, her emotions like her body, laid bare.

But as she banded an arm over her aching breasts he ripped open his fly, tugged down his shorts and the heavy erection burst free—hard, long and thrusting upwards.

He cupped her buttocks, dragged her towards him, adjusting her hips, lifting her knees to leave her fully exposed, her core already slick and swollen with her juices.

But then she slapped her hand against his chest, which heaved beneath the soft cotton.

'We need a condom,' she managed.

He stared at her. 'Do we?' he asked as his eyes searched hers. 'Because there's nothing I want more in this world right now than to get you pregnant. So you can never leave me like that again.'

She shuddered, the raw longing in his gaze and the husky truth in his voice shattering her heart all over again.

The thick ridge pressed against her centre—hard, huge, insistent—but as her body yearned for the heavy thrust which would lodge him to the hilt and make her his again, he stood, holding her gaze, waiting for her answer.

She swallowed the boulder of emotion which had derailed her before and barely shrunk at all in the past week, and clasped his face in unsteady hands.

She took a torturous breath and forced herself to finally say what she had wanted to say a week ago.

'You need to know first, Rene, that I love you.' Tears stung her eyes, the vulnerability overwhelming, when he swore softly. But she didn't see fear any more, she saw acceptance.

Her whole body began to shiver, despite the warmth from the iron stove behind them. She needed an answer from him—something, *anything* to give her some hope—because having him want her, having him need her wasn't enough.

'I think I've always loved you,' she managed, the hiccup of breath threatening more tears. 'I understand if you don't love me back now. If you're not there yet. But I can't live without the chance that there will be more one day. I just can't.'

He pressed his forehead to hers, the thick erection sliding up to brush the bundle of nerves at her core and making her jolt. But instead of thrusting inside her, he held her close and breathed into her ear.

'I know, and I'm sorry. I'm so sorry I wouldn't let you say it.'

She reared back, terrified of what he was going to say next. What was he sorry for? Was he going to tell her what she had suspected a week ago? Was he going to confirm that she had been right to run after all?

'I was terrified, I admit it,' he murmured, the tone tortured. 'I didn't want you to say it because I thought I would never be able to say it back and mean it. But when I found that note...' He cursed and let out a shuddering sigh, his arms wrapping so tightly around her he nudged that molten spot again, melting the last of her resistance. But it was the desperate conviction in his voice, in his eyes, which melted her heart. 'So polite, so reasonable, and so unlike you. And all I could think about was how I couldn't lose you. That I couldn't *ever* be without you by my side…' he pressed his palm to her cheek, the sheen of longing in his eyes so vivid, so vulnerable and yet also no longer afraid '…as my princess, my partner, my lover, my everything. To be perfectly honest, the strength of what I feel for you right now seems more like insanity than love. But is that enough?'

She nodded, covering her mouth, the tears scalding her cheeks. 'Yes, yes, it is,' she said.

She threw her arms around his shoulders and adjusted her hips to press against the huge head of his erection. 'Now, for Pete's sake put us both out of our misery,' she demanded.

He choked out a raw laugh. 'Have I told you I even love how damn bossy you are?'

But, before she could reply, he grasped her hips and slid hard and deep, impaling her to the hilt in one all-consuming thrust.

She let out a broken sob, the feeling immense and as overwhelming as always, but as he began to rock his hips out and back, forcing her to take all of him, driving them both towards that glorious oblivion with dizzying, devastating purpose, she clung to his shoulders and moved with him.

Agonising bliss charged towards her—hard and fast—cresting and crashing as her sobs of release matched his harsh grunts of pleasure.

His hot seed burst inside her—finally branding her for ever as his.

As her heart shattered with love and hope, she stroked his neck, tumbling into the sweet, stunning rush of afterglow, and pressed her lips to the scar beneath his hairline, branding him for ever as hers, too.

A while later he finally let her go, to gather his clothing. She stepped off the table, but when her knees wobbled he scooped her into his arms, dropping a kiss to one thrusting nipple.

'I want to protect you, always,' he said, his gaze fierce.

It was an expression she had seen many times before on his face, but why had she allowed her own insecurities to misinterpret it?

Of course he loved her. He just didn't know how to say it, how to talk about it, how to show it or even understand it, because he'd spent his childhood with a man who had made him feel unlovable.

'So don't ever run out on me again, okay?' he demanded.

She nodded, humbled by the passion in his voice, and the determination.

'Okay, but you've got to let me protect you too, Rene,' she said, brushing his hair back to stroke the scar. 'Don't shut me out again. Will you promise?'

'It's a deal,' he said, hugging her close, his breathing harsh. 'Now, show me where the damn bedroom is, so I can get naked too and we can seal this damn deal properly.'

She let out a raw laugh and pointed to the staircase.

But as he marched up the stairs, holding her securely in his arms, she knew, as much as she would love to have his child, it really didn't matter if he got her pregnant. Because he would always be hers now. And she would always be his.

EPILOGUE

One year later

'I BAPTIZE YOU, Mia Isabelle Elise Gaultiere, in the name of the…'

Rene grinned as the Archbishop drew a wet cross on his three-month-old daughter's forehead and she let out an indignant yell, drowning out the rest of the prayer.

As the poor man went to hand the squalling baby back to her mother, Rene reached in to take her.

'Hey there, Princess, don't worry,' he murmured to his child. 'Daddy won't let the bad man do that again.'

He smiled as she continued to show off her lung capacity to the small collection of invited guests he'd insisted on for the private christening, after a lot of back and forth with his advisers and the palace press officer. His little princess kicked and bawled, her face screwed up in outrage, but began to quieten when Rene gathered her against his chest and pressed her to her favourite spot, on her daddy's shoulder.

'Well, that went well,' Melody whispered to him, the tone wry despite the sparkle of humour in her eyes—the incandescent blue which his daughter had inherited.

God, how could he love this woman more? Not only had she given him a daughter he adored exactly nine months after that rainy day in Wales, but she made a magnificent Princess, ready not just to take on the responsibilities of monarchy but to improve every aspect of his life and work.

'Yeah, no one messes with Princess Mia,' he whispered back as the officiant struggled to finish the ceremony above their daughter's still surly protests. 'Not even the Archbishop of Saltzaland.'

He chuckled as he leant down to kiss his wife. But then he inhaled her scent above the talcum scent of their baby—and the familiar need shot straight to his groin.

He forced himself to draw back, determined to put a choke-hold on his desire.

As the small congregation came up to congratulate them both he patted his daughter's back, while rocking her from side to side and crooning words of encouragement. It was a move he'd perfected in the early hours of the morning over the past three months—every time he raced into the nursery to pick her up whenever she cried. And, as always, because Mia was already a daddy's girl, it did the trick.

Travis Lord—who, with the Queen of Androvia, had just been appointed as Mia's godparent—joined him and Mia as the guests made their way through the Palace to the state-room where the rest of the ceremony to celebrate Mia's naming day was being held.

Travis's heavily pregnant wife and Melody walked ahead of them, chatting away as if they hadn't seen each other in months, when Rene knew for a fact Melody had visited the couple only a week ago to introduce them formally to Saltzaland's new Princess. He'd missed his wife and child horribly during those twenty-four hours. But the strong friendship between the two women had been a godsend as Melody had settled into her role as Saltzaland's new Princess, so Rene couldn't complain too much.

'You're a pro already with her, man,' Travis murmured, impressed.

'It's easier than it looks,' Rene replied as his daughter let out one last hiccup of outrage, then sighed and snuggled against his neck.

Her slight weight made his heart feel so full with love he sighed, too.

'I sure hope so,' Travis replied. 'We're gonna have to hit the ground running. Belle's having twins, we just got the confirmation,' he added, sounding shellshocked.

Rene let out a gruff laugh, surprised all over again at how much he'd come to like Lord. They had been forced to spend a lot of time together by default in the early days of his marriage to Melody—a rushed affair after Mel and he had discovered they had hit the jackpot in Wales—because their wives were inseparable.

But somehow the animosity and antagonism which had driven his early association with Lord had turned to an unlikely friendship. He'd come to enjoy Travis' healthy irreverence for monarchy but also to respect his deep, abiding love for Isabelle, a woman Rene had always had a great deal of respect for too. But new fatherhood had added an additional bond between them, because Travis had looked to him for advice ever since Isabelle had become pregnant—completely by accident, according to Melody—six months ago.

'Two heirs for the price of one,' Rene said, unable to resist ribbing the guy just a little. 'Your Privy Council must be overjoyed.'

'Yeah, don't even get me started on that...' Travis groaned. 'Belle's already freaking out about what we're going to do if the first twin is a girl and the second a boy. She figures it's not fair for the male heir to inherit the throne, but apparently Androvia's rules of succession are strict on male primogeniture...'

'Tell her to change the rules then. We did,' he said simply.

Travis stopped dead. 'Seriously? You did that?'

'Yup. I signed the decree two days before Mia was born,' he said. 'Because Satlzaland's rules of succession have never been subject to an act of parliament, the sovereign can adjust them by decree. I'm pretty sure the same is true for Androvia.' It had required some work on his part and they hadn't informed the press yet—because they'd already had enough press scrutiny to last them a lifetime. But, even so, the decision that his monarchy would be one where the line of succession was no longer determined by sex had been the easiest he'd ever made. It also had the added benefit of being a decision which would have infuriated his father.

The act of signing that decree had finally confirmed to him that he was no longer bound by that man's anger or his lack of trust in his abilities any longer. After a course of therapy—encouraged by his wife—Rene had come to understand that his father had always blamed him, a tiny baby at the time, for his mother's death, and punished him accordingly. He wasn't sure if he would ever be able to forgive his father for allowing his grief to become so toxic, but at least he knew now that he had never been responsible, as a child or a man, for the dark legacy of his father's pain.

'Cool,' Travis replied. 'I'll let Belle know—it'll be one less thing for her to stress about,' he finished, sounding relieved. 'To be honest, the whole unplanned pregnancy thing already threw her for a loop, and now the news that we're having two babies has been a double whammy.' It was Travis's turn to grin. 'Not gonna lie, though, it's kind of hot, seeing her panic about becoming a mother when I already know she'll be awesome. But then her superpower has always been overthinking stuff.'

Rene laughed. 'While yours is going with the flow.'

Travis nodded and grinned. 'We're opposites for sure. It's what makes us such a great team, kind of like you guys.'

'True,' Rene agreed.

Mel's courage and positivity and work ethic had turned out to be a productive and passionate counterpoint to his cynicism. They were both hard-headed though, and they'd had more than a few disagreements over the past year—not least about Melody's dedication to her role as his consort. He didn't want her working too hard and while she'd been pregnant he'd had to lay down the law a few times—and when that hadn't worked, because she was still as stubborn and contrary as ever, he'd seduced her into a puddle of need.

As they strolled into the salon his gaze tracked to his wife, now deep in conversation with her mother and Isabelle. Her head lifted and her gaze met his, almost as if she could sense him watching her. The awareness in her expression made his pulse spike and need swell again.

The doctor had said they were good to go now and had been for weeks. But he'd been holding off. He'd chosen to sleep in an adjoining bedroom after the birth, not wanting to intrude on her while they were both snatching sleep in between dealing with Mia, because they'd made the decision not to employ a nanny just yet. But Mia was sleeping much better now. And he was struggling to sleep himself without Mel beside him.

Tonight, perhaps it was time he took the initiative. If she wasn't ready for sex, he would just have to channel the memory of those twelve terrifying hours of labour and deal with it, but he wasn't sure he could survive much longer without being able to touch her, to hold her.

As she stared at him now, the hot look in her eyes made the heat—and yearning—in his gut grow. But how did he know he was interpreting that look correctly and it wasn't just wishful thinking on his part?

He broke eye contact first, then patted Travis on the back. 'You need any tips, Travis,' he said, feeling for the guy, having two babies to deal with in a few months' time, 'I'll be happy to help. But all you really have to do is love them un-conditionally.' He stroked his daughter's back and inhaled the baby scent he'd become addicted to. 'And they make that easy for you.'

'Yeah, kind of like their moms, I guess,' Travis replied with a wry smile. 'Thanks, man. But don't be surprised if I'm calling you at two a.m. asking you how to change a diaper.'

They both laughed. But as they went to join their wives, Rene knew, whatever happened tonight, everything would work out. Because he loved Melody unconditionally. And always would.

Mel stood silently at the door of their daughter's nursery and watched Rene gently stroke their baby's back. Love pressed against her heart, even as the heat—which had been driving her to distraction for weeks now—made her core soften and ache. In nothing but a pair of pyjama bottoms, which hung low on his hips, even from the back, her husband looked good enough to eat. Her nipples peaked painfully against sheer silk as she imagined kissing his skin, inhaling the scent of ber-gamot and cedar she adored, and feeling him hot and heavy inside her again. She had been fully healed for weeks now, and taking contraception for over a month, but while she'd seen flashes of the fierce hunger she remembered in his eyes, he hadn't touched her since Mia's birth.

It was driving her insane but also feeding insecurities she thought she had buried when they'd conceived Mia a year ago now.

But at least now she had a plan—one she and Isabelle had been hatching together for over a week, after Mel had finally got the guts up to confide in her best friend.

She'd changed into the see-through negligee Isabelle had loaned her that afternoon five minutes ago, as soon as Rene had collected the baby after Mia's final feed to put her down for the night. A nervous smile curved her lips as she remembered Isabelle's whispered words as she'd handed over the garment before Travis had escorted her to their helicopter.

'This never fails to get Travis going—but it's no good to me at the moment. In fact, I doubt I'll ever be able to fit into it again.'

But Mel's smile at the memory of Isabelle's disgruntled expression faded as the nerves returned while she watched Rene press his hand to their child's back as she settled, clearly unaware of Mel's presence.

What would she do if he didn't want her any more? She'd read how that could happen to some men once they'd witnessed their partner giving birth—and Rene had been nothing if not frantic during those hours.

That said, he'd been so loving and supportive and attentive—with her and Mia—ever since their daughter had been born.

Mel frowned. In fact, at times he'd been a little too attentive. She suspected they were going to have trouble with Mia when she got older because her daddy doted on her so much. And they'd had more than a few cross words because Rene had shown his dictatorial side, demanding she not 'overtax' herself since before the birth, even though she was perfectly healthy, had a staff of people ready to help if she needed it and she adored her job.

'You're my best girl, aren't you, princess?' he whispered to their child, who was already fast asleep.

Mel felt a tiny spike of jealousy, followed by a wave of embarrassment—and consternation.

Seriously? She was becoming jealous of her own daughter now? This situation was getting ridiculous.

Time to stop worrying and take charge, Mel.

Pushing the doubts to one side, she cleared her throat. 'I certainly hope she's not your *only* best girl,' she said.

188 PRINCESS FOR THE HEADLINES

Rene straightened and swung round, giving her a full frontal of that magnificent chest—which she had been reduced to ogling every night when he came in to get his daughter.

'Melody?' he said, startled.

But then his face flushed and his gaze swept down, flaring with fierce passion. And suddenly she didn't feel ridiculous any more.

She could feel his hunger and need raking over her skin like a physical caress, even as the front of his pyjama bottoms swelled.

Her heart rejoiced. Along with her clitoris.

She'd been an idiot. Of course he still wanted her. Of course he still needed her. His reluctance to touch her had probably all been part of the 'not overtaxing her' agenda that she intended to have words with him about... *Later*.

He swore softly as he strode towards her. He clasped her hips, grasping fistfuls of the sheer fabric.

'Where the hell did you get this?' he hissed, clearly trying not to wake their sleeping baby despite the extreme provocation. 'Are you trying to kill me?' he finished, but he didn't sound mad, he sounded desperate, his voice so husky it made her whole body throb.

She grinned, delighted with them both.

'Isabelle. It's a freebie from a new designer,' she explained. 'But fair warning, I may very well have to kill *you* myself if you don't make love to me right this instant.'

'Are you sure?' he asked, his eyes wild but his tone cautious.

'Absolutely.'

He groaned as he dragged her into his arms, the already huge erection prodding her belly.

'I'm going to have to thank Isabelle,' he muttered before devouring the pulse point in her neck.

'Thank her later,' she said, boosting herself into his arms—

so needy and desperate already herself she was scared she would explode before he even got inside her.

But as he carried her into their bedroom—and proceeded to show her exactly how much he still wanted her with a force and fury that excited her beyond measure—it occurred to her she was going to have to buy Isabelle a new negligee, because this one was already toast.

Hours later, as Mel lay, sweaty, sated and deliciously sore, and gazed at the winter moon shining through the mullioned windows, she felt the slow, steady beat of her husband's heart against her back. He slept peacefully, his face pressed to her hair, his strong arms holding her securely.

Their baby girl would wake them both up in a couple of hours. Her breasts already felt full of milk, even if her nipples were pleasantly tender now from her husband's lips instead of their daughter's.

But as she fell into a deep sleep she knew she would dream of him holding her, loving her, fiercely and without regret. And—while she suspected that she and Rene would always butt heads, because they were both such strong-willed people—she made herself a solemn promise never to doubt him, or herself, or the strength and constancy of their love ever again.

* * * * *

HIS HIGHNESS'S DIAMOND DECREE

MILLIE ADAMS

MILLS & BOON

For Flo,
who lets me go where my imagination takes me.

Love forever.

CHAPTER ONE

PRINCE ADONIS ANDREADIS had always known that his wedding would be a magnificent spectacle. A man of his wealth and stature could have nothing other than a glorious and singular occasion to mark his nuptials. Even if those nuptials existed only to secure the bloodline, and therefore access to the throne of his country.

It was just he hadn't expected to feel anything about it.

His father was dying. There was no denying the reality.

His father had told him that he had done enough damage to the crown and the family reputation that he owed him a marriage minted in perfection.

Adonis couldn't disagree.

What Adonis knew was that he had done a fair job of exercising his demons in the form of debauchery, all around the globe.

And while he had not intended to besmirch the crown, it was likely he had.

Well. Besmirched in the eyes of citizens his father's age. The younger generation was…decidedly fond of his exploits. He was a meme.

Knowing his time as king was on the horizon, he'd agreed to his father's demand. That he marry a suitable woman. His father had provided him with a folio of acceptable women.

He had spent years being a terrible playboy but even he had never chosen women off of a menu.

He couldn't say he felt like he owed his father, so much as he owed his country. His years of debauchery had never been intended to cause strife for the citizens of Olympus. No, his target had been much more personal.

The end result, however, was his infamy.

Adored by the youths, decried by the elder generation.

He had to find a way to unite the two schools of thought, however. And marrying seemed the way to do that.

He'd chosen Drusilla Stalworth not because of any blinding attraction to her, or her profile in the folio provided by his father, but because she was American royalty. The granddaughter of a former president, the daughter of a billionaire business mogul.

He had decided to reform, to forge an appropriate alliance and to marry as quickly as possible. His decisions had been clear, concise and quick.

He couldn't recall deciding to get married in a cathedral by the sea, however. But it seemed as if that's what he was doing.

The building was glass; glorious light shone through the windows.

It was warm. Odd. He'd expected it to be cold.

He looked out into the pews of the church. There was no audience. And for a moment he felt outside of himself. But he continued walking up to the front. And there he stood, waiting for his bride. The doors opened, and there she was. A halo of glorious gold. White.

Her hair was piled on top of her head, and a veil concealed her face.

She was like a floating confection. An angel.

Spun sugar and sweetness. So strange that he should have a visceral reaction to her, because he could not recall ever having a reaction like this to Drusilla in the past.

No. He had always been decidedly neutral on his intended, which had been fine with him.

She was beneficial. She didn't need to be anything else.

But now, the sight of her held him suspended.

It was like being reborn.

And then, he was certain he felt something bite his leg.
He looked around the room, and was struck yet again by
the fact that it was empty, except for himself and Drusilla.

He reached down and gripped his thigh. And there was
warmth there.

He was confused.

Groggy.

Why?

Suddenly, the doors to the church blew open, and the
wind was as an icy blast. All the warmth from before faded
away. And Drusilla kept on walking toward him. But then
her veil blew off. And he looked into the eyes of a stranger.

As snow began to fall inside the chapel.

The chapel?

No. There was no chapel.

He wasn't in Cape Cod having a wedding. He wasn't…

Suddenly, everything around him fell away. And the wedding dress transformed itself to a parka. While the chapel
became a vast wilderness.

And then, his vision went black.

And he tried to cast his mind back, to figure out exactly
how he had gotten here…

CHAPTER TWO

Two hours earlier

STEVIE PARKER WAS cold and annoyed. The longer her take-off was delayed, the more money she was losing. She needed to get this cargo over to the East Coast. If she didn't, she wasn't going to get paid, and if she didn't get paid then it was going to be another very long winter.

When storms disrupted things half the time, and there was no way for her to get paid if she wasn't actually making her deliveries, it was a recipe for disaster.

Her dad couldn't work anymore. His liver was shot, and he was barely hanging on.

Things weren't getting any cheaper. Inflation was making it impossible to feed her family.

She sighed heavily.

She loved her sisters. Every last one of them. All six of them.

But their household was an expensive one, and everybody else was still in school.

And Stevie wanted them to finish school. She didn't want them to end up like her. Not that she didn't enjoy her life. She loved piloting. Flying planes was the closest thing to being free as far as she was concerned. And she really valued that freedom.

But taking over her father's shipping company had been

a necessity rather than a dream, and while it was something she loved, if she'd had the whole world of choices in front of her...who knew what she'd have done?

It didn't matter. She did love to fly.

For a few blessed hours at a time, she was flying above her problems. Flying above everything. Stevie might never be a powerful or important person in the world, but she had the ability to escape in a way most people didn't.

She valued that. She appreciated that ability in herself.

She thought that she was pretty amazing actually. Though, with her flight grounded, she wasn't feeling particularly amazing.

It was freezing in Bozeman, and only getting colder.

Her only hope was that there was a small break in the wind so that she could take off. And as soon as she got the all clear, she was going. She meandered into the bar, and took off her puffer jacket. Her ponytail snagged in the hood, and she wrinkled her nose. She tried to fix her hair as she walked up to the bar.

"Hey, Stevie," said Frank, the bartender.

"Hey. Can I get a coffee?"

"You think you're going to fly out?"

"As soon as the wind breaks. If they let me take off I'm going to. I've got a get this cargo to Boston."

She was pretty sure that the final destination for the gear she was carting was Martha's Vineyard. Very fancy. Some royal wedding.

"Well, be safe. It's nasty out there."

"Nasty doesn't worry me. Not making my deliveries worries me."

And that was when she saw him. Sitting in the back of the bar, in a corner booth, black hair pushed back off of his forehead, a large hand wrapped around a glass of whiskey.

He was looking at her. Right at her. His gaze was intense, and it made her want to turn away from him.

But she found she was unable to. All she could do was stare.

She swallowed hard.

The bartender looked at her, and then raised his eyebrows. "He's been here for hours," he said. "Not the usual clientele."

"No." She sighed. "He wouldn't be."

"Wonder what his story is."

She tore her gaze away from the stranger. "I don't have time to wonder about things like that."

Her phone buzzed. A notification letting her know that the blanket grounding all flights had been lifted for now.

"I gotta go."

She knocked her coffee back and turned away from the stranger. She slipped her coat back on as she walked through the terminal, headed toward the corridor that would take her outside to where her plane was parked.

"Stop."

The voice was commanding. Deep. And she found herself agreeing, even if she couldn't figure out why. She turned slowly. It was him.

"I'm in a hurry," she said.

"And so am I. You said that you were headed to Boston?"

His words were faintly accented, but she couldn't quite place what the accent might be. He was... He was stunningly handsome. She'd never seen a man like him.

His skin was olive, his hair black. His eyes a crystalline blue. His jaw was square, and his nose a straight blade. His lips were... She couldn't recall ever looking at a man's lips before but she was captivated by his. He looked familiar. Vaguely. But she couldn't quite place him. It wouldn't surprise her to learn that he was famous. The black suit that he wore fit him exquisitely. And it looked like it cost more money than she had ever made her life.

"Yes. I'm going to Boston. I have a cargo plane."

"I need to get to Boston."

"Sorry, but don't you have a private jet?"

"I do," he said. "Did you think that I might fly commercial?"

"I don't know. But I have a very short window to get out of here, and I need to take it."

"And I will go with you."

She stared at him. "You won't."

"Yes, I will. I will pay you handsomely." He named a figure that just about knocked her back. She wouldn't have to worry about money for a year if he paid her that much. It was… It was ridiculous. Obscene.

"You have to be kidding."

"I'm not kidding."

"How do I know?"

"What's the worst that could happen? You have an extra passenger on your flight."

"You might assault me."

"Midair? That would turn out badly for me, I think."

"Unless you're a hijacker, and you know how to fly the plane."

"If I could fly my own plane, then believe me when I tell you I would be flying a very different plane out of here."

"Why do you need to get there so badly?"

"Trying to get to a wedding. It would be a bad look to miss it."

He was certainly dressed smart enough to be attending a wedding. He could go in the back with her actual wedding delivery, and her other cargo.

"All right. Come with me. But I doubt you're going to find the seating arrangements to your liking."

"Well, sleeping rough is definitely not my first choice, but things happen. And I have lived a life filled with un-predictable turns of events. I think this will hardly feel like a singular event."

"Not to me it won't," she said. "This is my day-to-day. You don't have a parka?"

"No. Why?"

"You better brace yourself."

She couldn't help but laugh as she opened the door to the walkway, where it was already bitingly cold.

The glass corridor shielded them from the wind, and the other more aggressive part of the elements, but not from ev-erything else. And when they stepped through the entry-way that would take them out to the plane, the wind was like knives.

Though he did not react. Did not buckle.

Strange. Because it was freezing.

"Come on," she shouted over the roar of the wind. She got into the cockpit, and then walked over the seats and into the main part of the plane. She opened the door there, and yelled down below. "Climb on in. You're getting added to my cargo."

He got into the plane, and looked around. It was sparse. There was a chair that faced sideways next to all the cargo. And then there was her seat up in the cockpit. There was a copilot seat, but she would not be inviting a stranger to sit up there with her.

"Have a seat."

She did her preflight checks, including looking at her report from the mechanic and making sure everything checked out as being in good order. She signed off on the report, and passed it out of the cockpit to the bundled-up man standing on the tarmac.

"What are you transporting?" her passenger asked.

"A few things." She did a physical check of the instruments and waited for her all clear from the tower.

"Your box says wedding."

"Yeah. Some royal shindig out at Martha's Vineyard? I don't know. I've got flowers I think. On ice. Not that we're short on ice."

"True," he said. "You don't recognize me?"

"Do you recognize *me*?"

He lifted a brow. "Should I?"

"Not any more than I should recognize you, I reckon. Unless we met and I don't remember. I do meet a lot of people in my line of work."

"We haven't met."

"All right, then."

"What's your name?"

"Stevie," she said. "Buckle up. I gotta get going. We've only got a small break in the weather here, and I gotta get up above these mountains."

"All right."

He sat down.

Right then, she got the go-ahead from the tower.

"Buckle," she ordered.

"As you wish."

He did.

She engaged the engines, and the propellers began to turn.

"I'm not going to lie to you," she said. "Going to be rough."

"Thanks for the heads-up."

The casual vernacular sounded strange with his accent.

"I don't want a lawsuit on my hands or anything." The plane began to trundle down the runway, and Stevie felt a kick of adrenaline. She flew almost every day, but the rush of knowing that she was going to make it out of here, the triumph of having defeated the storm, gave her a slightly spicy feeling at the moment.

"Here we go." They picked up speed, the wind pushing them along, turning them into an icy bullet as they shot down the runway, and began to achieve liftoff.

And then, they were airborne.

And it was as bumpy as she had feared.

They jostled around like they were on a road filled with potholes, as she pulled back and increased the altitude. The snowy mountains around them were majestic. Glorious.

She loved to fly.

She checked her radar and frowned. There was some rough weather up ahead as they headed east. But it seemed like once they cleared the mountains it settled down.

They were still climbing toward altitude, still getting jostled. She looked back at her fancy passenger. He had a sort of grim, stoic look on his handsome face.

She bet that this was a whole different way to travel than he was used to.

She snorted, and carried right on.

When they made altitude, things settled down a little bit.

She checked her instruments, and began to relax. Settled in for the flight. It was so loud in this tin can there was no making conversation. But she wasn't regretful about that.

Picking up the passenger while she was flying cargo was one of the weirder things that had ever happened to her. But it really hadn't made any sense to leave him behind. He had a wedding to get to.

She blinked. That was odd. A wedding. She was transporting goods for a wedding. Maybe he was attending that wedding. Of course it would attract very rich guests.

But then, he hadn't said anything when she had commented. But she could definitely tell he was kind of a whole thing.

She didn't have time to think about that. Or worry about it.

She just had to keep on flying.

But then suddenly, her instruments dipped, revived and dipped again.

She'd never seen that happen before. She'd heard about it, in training, of course, but she hadn't actually experienced it. She tried to keep her cool. She looked out at the horizon, and could see nothing but white. They were socked in. She needed her instruments to tell her where she was. She couldn't rely on sight, not in weather like this.

She swallowed hard, and tried to get a gauge for what was going on. Her altimeter was still working, and she wondered if she could navigate to a different airfield…

But then, the altimeter went out too.

"Oh, no."

She started flipping switches. It was a catastrophic electrical failure.

And she couldn't panic. Because she was the one in charge.

It hit her then, quite bitterly, that *that* was the story of her life.

She supposed she could have emotions when she was dead.

Her heart hammered as she tried to clear her mind and focus on the task at hand.

She had a backup engine, but she did not have backup instruments. And the power source that was supposed to engage in case of any problems wasn't working.

She looked down below, and her heart started to pound. There was one vaguely clear spot that she could see coming up ahead. And if she used her knowledge, and general take of the area, it was possible that she could land.

But she was afraid that if she kept on flying eventually they were going to come into regrettable contact with the mountainside. If she died, her family was doomed. Her chest locked tight, and she began to tremble. But she couldn't lose her cool. She could not afford to. Panic filled her but she didn't let it win. Slowly, she began to push down, maneuvering them down, steadily. She kept her eyes out the windshield, her vision their only hope, her experience their only guide.

She was twenty-five. She'd been flying planes for four years. But it was always something she felt like had been in her blood. Something innate. Her dad had done it. Before he had been deemed unfit.

Her dad.

Her chest clenched tight. She had to do this.

She had to.

She gripped the yoke hard and pushed down, bringing them lower and lower, and she turned around just briefly to take a look at her passenger, who was beginning to undo his buckle, his expression one of concern. "Stay buckled," she shouted. And then, she lost control. A thermal shot up, and rocked the plane, and suddenly, she found herself disoriented. And the descent became bumpy.

She wanted to close her eyes. She wanted to shield herself from the reality of what was happening. She had to keep them open. She was the one in charge.

She was the one that was going to keep them alive.

An echo of her life these last few years.

And all she could think was that it really would've been

nice at one point to have somebody who took care of her. Instead, she was going down in a blaze of pointlessness.

Leaving behind seven people who counted on her for their care.

Her dad had always thought it was dumb her mom had died of an illness when he flew cargo planes for a living.

He had always thought it should've been him. Flying around in his rattly old contraption that somehow she'd convinced herself was safer now that she was flying it and making sure to dot every i and cross every t before taking off.

But no. Apparently not.

She didn't even have time to say a prayer, before she realized they were in the tops of the trees. Before the wing clipped a pine, and they went hurtling toward the earth. After that, she didn't remember a thing.

CHAPTER THREE

HE WAS HERE because he had decided to take a cargo plane to his wedding. It all came back to him in a flash of light. The bar. The terrible scotch. The tiny little woman in a very large coat with a round, earnest face and freckles on her cheeks who was supposedly a pilot, but didn't look old enough to be a high school graduate.

She'd crashed.

Suddenly, Adonis sat upright.

The full-scale force of the cold hit him then. The wind slapping him in the face.

"What happened?"

"Stay calm."

Stevie. That was the girl's name. The pilot.

"What the hell have you done?"

"The instruments went out on the plane. I didn't *do* anything." She paused for a moment. "Other than save your ass, that is."

The plane.

He looked around, slowly taking in more details.

They were *in* the plane, sort of. But the outside had come inside, because the back end was broken off, and he supposed they had been saved only by the fact that somehow the front of the aircraft had remained intact. "It really is a good thing you kept your seat belt buckled," she said. "Otherwise…" She looked meaningfully back at the open end of the plane. And he could see the cargo strewn all over the ground. Spreading out for a good distance behind them.

He wasn't given to fear, and he could confidently say that his behavior in the past had been self-destructive at best. But that hit. Hard. A very real echo of the reality of mortality.

It was an inglorious end. Or would've been.

He frowned. And he put his hand back on his leg.

The pain suddenly cut through his delirium, and it was like the world had split apart. The pain was excruciating and the cold was unbearable. Her face was too sharp and too clear, and too pretty to bear and he had to fight to keep from being torn into pieces by the competing feelings.

Shock.

Pain.

Cold.

Her.

He pulled his hand away and found it sticky and hot with blood. "What happened?" he gritted.

"I've been trying to stop the bleeding," she said. "I know you didn't hit an artery or you'd be gone by now."

He looked down and felt a shameful wave of nausea. His leg was… It was *damaged* was a kind word for it. He could see through to the muscle and bone.

"That isn't good," he said.

She looked at him like he was an alien life-form.

"No," she agreed. "It's not."

He realized then that he had a belt around his upper thigh.

"I had to get the bleeding stopped," Stevie said. "It was a lot of blood."

He nodded. "Are you hurt?"

She shook her head. "Banged up. But miraculously…

Okay. I suspect I don't feel some of the pain because of adrenaline."

"I guess this is what I get for taking a ride from a stranger." He tried to laugh.

"I'm sorry. You're probably gonna miss that wedding."

"All right." He didn't know what else to say. After all, nothing seemed that important.

Not in the face of all this.

"What did you think about?" she asked, her voice muted.

"When?"

"When the plane went down."

She looked as small and young as he'd first thought. But he hadn't been worried at all. He hadn't even given a thought about the plane going down, to the inclement weather being a problem. That his pilot who had been right when he'd landed the private jet, saying he didn't think smaller aircraft should fly in the weather.

No, he hadn't worried. He'd seen her, seen an opportunity and thought it was more evidence of everything going his way. As always.

Until the plane had gone down.

"You first," he said.

She sniffed, and he realized it was from the cold. Not tears. She moved around, opening up boxes, uncovering some blankets, some coats. Part of the cargo that she had.

What brand of woman was this? Hell, what brand of *human* was she?

There was no self-pity. No weeping or wailing. She seemed as together, as poised as she had when piloting the plane, and he could not fathom why that was.

"This wasn't for the wedding," she said. "It was for a small outdoor outfitter. Thank God that was part of the cargo." She wrapped herself in a sleeping bag, and then put one over the top of him. "Though it does make me want to ask God why he didn't just keep us in the sky, since he's out here providing miracles." She sighed. "Maybe when you can move a little bit we can get you into the sleeping bag."

He nodded. "Maybe."

She sniffed again. "I thought about my father. And how there was no way he was going to be able to take care of my six sisters on disability. And then I thought how he's probably going to die in six months, and then there will be nobody to take care of them at all. Nobody left to run the business."

"You support your family?"

"Yes. I don't mind. I love them. But realizing that I'm the only one keeping them from the streets… That's terrifying."

"Not your own death?"

"Well. If I'm dead, I suppose we don't have to worry about me."

"Perhaps."

"What did you think about?" she pressed.

He had thought of his father. How there was no spare. How for all his exploits he was going to die actually trying to do the thing his father had asked him to do. And about how he would never be able to redeem the family name in the way his father had wanted.

He would never be able to redeem himself.

He'd never thought much about it, since his life had been a pantomime and not really his own. Now, perhaps, it never would be.

Maybe either way, it never would be.

"I thought about my home," he said. It was true.

"Where is that?"

"It's a small island in the Mediterranean. Beautiful. The water there is like crystal. The island itself has white sand.

Palm trees. But also olive and cyprus. It is not flat. It's mountainous. Volcanic. Like Olympus."

"Are you Greek?"

"Adjacent," he said. "I speak Greek. But also Italian, French, Mandarin."

"English?"

He tried to smile, the sort of charming smile he often treated women to. "I thought that was obvious."

"I've never even been outside the country."

"Well, now that you didn't die, you can if you would like."

She screwed up her face. "Maybe. Assuming we don't die of exposure before somebody finds us. I don't know where we went off radar. We won't arrive at our destination. But it's going to depend heavily on how able they are to pick up our coordinates. I'm afraid to walk too far from the plane, but…"

"You can't leave me here," he said. "I'm liable to become a meal of one of your North American wildcats."

"Well. That is true," she said. "A cougar would probably enjoy chewing on you."

"They have in the past."

She blinked. "What?"

He smiled again, at her naïveté this time. "Never mind."

She was… A country bumpkin. He had never met anyone like her.

He wasn't sure he would've chosen to if the option had been presented. Well, not knowing that it would end up like this.

"I didn't get your name," she said.

"Does it matter?"

"I told you mine."

"Yes," he said. "Stevie. Like a small boy, or a witchy rock star?"

"I prefer the witchy rock star. I suspect my mother meant it in the slightly more tomboyish fashion."

"My condolences."

"Well, I'm pretty resilient."

"Clearly."

"Tell me about where you live," she said. She had let his name go easily enough. It wasn't that he was opposed to telling her. But Adonis was a particular sort of name. And if somebody recognized it, then they would know exactly who he was.

Again, not that it mattered. His being a prince hadn't stopped the plane from going down. And perhaps therein lay a real look at his arrogance.

He had functionally believed himself to be bulletproof because he was... Important.

He didn't even have a spare. His father needed him.

Was he truly so ridiculous?

Was he so hollow that he had never truly considered these things? He had thought he would gallivant around the world and prove to his mother that she'd made a mistake in leaving him all those years ago, after which he'd ascend the throne.

What it seemed like now was perhaps a mix of his father's rigidity and his mother's selfishness and he did not care for that at all.

Any more than he liked having those arrogant plans derailed.

He thought instead of the warmth of home. The air, the water. The food.

"We have some of the best food in the world. Fresh ingredients. Fish, lemon. Olive oil."

"I'm hungry," she said.

"You have any food in here?"

"I might," she said brightly, suddenly scampering from

the wreckage and going out into the snow. She examined some of her crates, a couple of which were intact.

Then she pushed one of them back into the ship, her eyes alight with determination.

"I'm going to look in here. This was for a specialty shop…"

She opened it up, and the contents were revealed as cured meats and cheeses.

"Oh," she said, her expression rapturous. "We're going to be okay. What we need to do is try to get the back part of the plane sealed up."

"We?" he asked, gesturing toward his leg.

"Well. I will. And then we have food. It would be great if I could start a fire, and melt the snow. You don't want to just eat it, because then… Well, hypothermia."

"Where did you learn all of this?"

"A lot of it is just knowing. From living in Montana all my life. You had to know how to be safe in the wilderness. What we don't want is to attract the attention of animals, though. This food is a boon, but it's going to smell incredible to a bear."

"We don't want that," he said.

"We don't."

"What we really want is to be rescued."

"Agreed."

She sighed. "I have flares and a flare gun. But I'm going to have to time it. It depends on if anyone's out looking for us. I've got to take inventory and see what we have."

"Is there anything I can do?"

He realized that his default was that he was quite comfortable being served. Such was the life of a prince. But this was a survival situation, and this small woman must be horrendously exhausted after what had just happened.

"Probably not," she said. "Appreciated though. If you move too much that wound could start bleeding again. I'm just grateful that it's a pretty clean gash. I think some metal from the plane got you. But… It just could've been worse."

"I'm sure."

As it was, he knew that he was facing physical therapy. Among other indignities. There was no way something like this was simply going to heal.

He had never been betrayed by his own body before. Though, he supposed it wasn't his body's fault that flesh was soft enough to be cut by razor-sharp metal.

He watched as the girl scrambled around.

And then came back with their food.

"Let's get something to eat, Clem," she said.

"Pardon me?"

"You haven't told me your name. I decided to give you one."

"Clem?"

She sniffed. "Short for Clemuel."

"That is ridiculous," he said.

"The entire situation is ridiculous, if you haven't noticed."

He snorted. "Believe me. I have."

"Good. That means at least some of your faculties are working."

"You seem more cheerful."

"The prospect of food, and the fact that we have a way to keep warm can have that effect."

"Yes." Something gnawed at the back of his mind. And just like that, it appeared fully formed. "It is likely that I can be traced."

"What?"

"My phone is able to be tracked."

"Does anybody know that you're with me? I mean, I have

that find my thing on my phone too, but I don't think it's going to work out here."

She didn't understand. There was, of course, a sophisticated tracking system on his phone. But not just his phone, there was also something in his watch. In the soles of his shoes. He was a prince who preferred to live his life as independently as possible. The heir to the throne of his country. Nobody took chances on his whereabouts. If he didn't appear when he was meant to, it would be noted.

Whether or not it would work in the wilderness, he did not know.

"Nobody has to know that I'm with you," he said. "They just have to know where I'm not."

"All right," she said. "You were going to go to a wedding."

"I was."

He was trying to think if he had ever talked to a person like this. One who had no idea who he was. Of course, he had never talked to a person while his leg was flayed open either. So there was that.

It was for that reason he didn't really want her to know who he was. It was weird. Because if he were to die out here, he would have never given his name to the last person who ever saw him alive. But also, it might be…

The one chance for him to be with someone who actually saw him as a person. That wasn't something he had ever wanted before.

He could honestly say he wasn't concerned over his authenticity or anything like that.

But it was quiet out here. And there was none of the revelry that he liked to surround himself with. None of the distraction. He couldn't even move. And so for him in that moment, it seemed like maybe being with a person who saw him as simply that—a person—might be the best way forward.

"Well. Then we can hope that actually works," she said. "I know that at some point my sister Daisy will track my phone. I just don't think..." She scrambled over all of the debris, to the cockpit. She opened up a box at the center of the plane. She took out her intact phone. And held it up. "I don't have any service."

"You only just thought to check that?"

"Yeah. I'm kind of in shock. Also, I think on some level I figured we wouldn't have any service."

"Does it have that GPS on it that lets you make a call even without service?"

"It's blank. But I can check." She entered in 911, and he could see the phone screen go black. "It's not calling out," she said.

"I can try mine."

"Where is yours?"

He looked around. "I... I actually have no idea."

She went back to where he was, and searched around.

"I don't see it."

"Great. It might have flown out with the other debris. It wasn't in a safe box. The box exists so that no one is playing on their phone while they're trying to fly," she said.

"Wow. Is that a risk?"

"Not with me. I always pay attention. I can't stress to you enough that the fact that you aren't dead right now is because I'm actually a great pilot."

He laughed. "You have to forgive me for not fully being able to internalize that."

"Hey. I get it. It feels like more of a disaster than a rescue. It was a rescue. Believe me."

She was very earnest. And he decided he would believe

her. Because again, if they were to die, or him specifically, since he was the one with the open wound, then there was no point in being suspicious. No point in being hostile to the last person he would ever see.

This pretty little enigma who reached him even through the blinding pain he felt now.

It really was a shame his leg was destroyed. Because one last round of sex might've been nice. Of course, she could always be on top.

"How old are you?"

She wrinkled her nose. "Random."

"Is it?"

"Yes."

"It was related to my train of thought."

"Okay. I'm twenty-five."

"Excellent."

She simply looked at him like he was infinitely baffling. She looked like something that might be native to the snow and mountains. Like a small rock-climbing mammal. Or a particularly hardy goat. Cute, but perfectly capable of surviving in a harsh environment.

He was descended from warriors. So many nations were founded on conflict, and his was no different. The strongest had risen to the top, but in all the generations since, there had been peace. Peace, affluence. He considered himself a man in control. He invested in many industries, building his personal wealth portfolio beyond that which a mere monarch could easily obtain unless he was criminally exploiting his people. And while he possessed confidence in his ability to do what needed to be done, he had never had to worry about his physical survival.

She seemed to wear a certain amount of acceptance of things with the same practicality she wore that parka.

It was freezing inside of the airplane, but he knew it was shielding them from the harsh elements.

She unwrapped the package of the meat, which was sliced thankfully, and cured. And then did the same with the cheese, which was not sliced, but she began to peel great hunks of it off with her hands, and he couldn't afford to feel anything but gratitude over that.

"Probably not the fanciest dinner you've ever had," she said.

"Maybe not. And you?"

"Possibly. This is pretty high quality. If I were at home I would put some bacon and onions in a big pot, put a lot of butter with it. I fill the pot up with broth, add a bunch of red beans and some ham hocks. Simmer it for a bunch of hours. Serve it on some rice. That sounds good," she said.

She looked dreamy just then. He didn't think he had ever had such a simple meal as the one she was talking about. And yet, he couldn't deny that it sounded comforting and warm.

"You have sisters," he said.

"Yes," she said. "Six of them. Two sets of twins."

"Two sets of twins?"

"Yes. So it's me, Daisy, Rose and Lilac, Bristol, Topaz and Opal."

"Interesting names."

"Yes. They are. All around. My mom was in her flower era when the three after me were born. Then she decided to be unique again, and Bristol stands alone thematically, like I do. Then she decided to go with precious gems for the youngest twins. She died when they were two. They don't even remember her. But they'll always be her gems."

"Sorry. I know it's difficult to grow up without your mother."

"Did you lose your mother?"

"Yes. But she didn't die. She just left."

"That's worse," Stevie said confidently.

"Is it?"

"Well. Not for her I guess. But for you. Your siblings."

"I'm an only child."

"I should've known that," she said smiling. "You have only-child energy, Clem."

"What does that mean?" He found himself offended in advance.

"I don't know. You just seem singular. One in the world. I don't think I seem like that at all. I have siblings to take care of. A dad to take care of. I'm one of many."

"I can honestly say I have never met a twenty-five-year-old woman who pilots cargo planes and scrambles around the wilderness like an expert. And I've known a lot of women."

Those eyes widened, and then her cheeks turned pink. She cleared her throat. "I'm sure you have."

He felt almost guilty. He hadn't meant to embarrass her. It hadn't occurred to him that such a mild innuendo could cause embarrassment.

But clearly for her it did.

She was so… Innocent seeming. And yet, not at all. The way she talked about cooking, large hearty practical meals, the way she had said she had to take care of everybody. Yes, she was innocent, but not. A strange sort of creature.

When they finished eating, silence settled around them. It was beginning to grow dark.

They were covered by the sleeping bags that she had found, but it was still cold.

"Come here," he said.

She looked at him from her position across the cargo space. She said nothing.

And he felt…a burst of heat and recklessness, an odd feeling of gratitude he'd never experienced before. Perhaps that was survivor's giddy joy racing through his veins. Or maybe it was just her.

"There's good body warmth between us," he said. "Why not use it?"

"Oh," she responded. "No good reason, I guess."

He wished that he could maneuver enough to get a blanket underneath him, but he was feeling weak. Not a word he would have ever used to describe himself in the past. He didn't like it. He would take any added warmth he could.

She looked very hesitant as she got down beside him.

"Don't look at me like that," he said. "I'm hardly going to ravish you in my present state."

She blinked. "And if you were in a different state?"

"Well, Stevie, if the two of us are going to die, then it would be a terrible shame to practice chastity in the face of our inevitable demise."

"Oh," she said, her voice strangled.

"You are twenty-five," he said.

"Is that why you asked how old I was?"

"It was a passing thought."

"I don't know that I want to sleep next to you now."

"Don't worry. My leg is far too maimed."

She moved slightly closer to him, and even with her keeping a bit of space between them, there was warmth.

So perhaps, he thought, as he began to drift off to sleep, they wouldn't die after all.

He supposed he would find out in the morning.

Or not. If they didn't wake up.

CHAPTER FOUR

STEVIE FELT COCOONED in warmth. She was so comfortable. The pillow beneath her cheek was firm, but she didn't
mind it. She shifted, and she felt someone's arms tighten
around her.

She froze. That was a completely unfamiliar feeling.

And suddenly, she remembered everything.

And realized just then that she was not resting her head
on a pillow, but her mysterious stranger's chest. Her hand
was also on his chest, his beating heart right beneath her
palm.

She was torn between being mortified that she had ended
up like this in her sleep, and being grateful that he was still
alive.

She sat up, and looked around the plane. Her heart was
pounding double time.

She had never slept with a man in her life. Not that this
was sleeping with him, sleeping with him. But she had never
done that either. She had never done either thing, thanks.

She was quite typically pure as the driven snow.

Well. Right now the snow wasn't so much pure as punishing.

Of course, purity could also feel punishing, she knew that
for a fact. She wasn't a virgin because of her convictions,
but rather her circumstances.

She was too busy for men.

It would be a shame for us to die without sampling another of life's vices...

She closed her mind off to that. They weren't going to die. She was annoyed though, that she…somewhat agreed with him.

"Good morning," she said loudly.

He stirred. And opened his eyes slowly. He looked rumpled, and yet somehow magnificent. A plane crash and loss of blood hadn't done anything to diminish the intensity of how… How sexy he was. And he really was very sexy. He was…quite beyond anything she had ever experienced before. Granted, her experience was very limited. But she had seen men. She lived in the world. She didn't have to be a great seductress to know what was out there.

He was spectacular.

She had been ridiculous when she had decided to call him Clem. In truth, she was trying to do something to diminish the impact of him. Her chest hurt.

Just suddenly.

She had been very afraid that he was going to die. When she'd had to put the tourniquet around his leg…

It had been a truly terrifying experience. She had taken a fair amount of first-aid training, but it really hadn't prepared her for this. It hadn't prepared her for the reality of somebody bleeding while she tried to stop it…

But there he was. Okay.

Gorgeous.

And they were still stuck.

"Good morning."

"Sorry. We aren't rescued yet. But you didn't die in the night."

She tried to present that as optimistically and cheerfully as possible.

"I appreciate that," he said.

"It would've been a tragedy."

"You don't know that for sure."

"Are you an evil warlord?"

"No," he said.

"Then I'm pretty sure it would be a tragedy if you died."

"Some of my past lovers would undoubtedly disagree with that take."

"Oh," she said, feeling unaccountably disappointed. "Why? Are you not accomplished?"

It had been a bold question, and she was not inherently bold when it came to topics like that. But she was otherwise bold, and maybe that was why it seemed reasonable to say out loud.

"Oh," he said. "I'm very accomplished. It is only that I am temporary."

"And that upsets them?"

"It has been said."

"I see."

"Have you been out foraging for acorns this morning?"

"No. Because it's cold. And I'm not a squirrel."

"You have a slight squirrel energy."

"Do I?" She wrinkled her nose. And then immediately stopped wrinkling her nose.

"Yes."

"Great. Well, another thing to add to my résumé."

"If we get out of this," he said. "I'll make sure that you're rewarded."

The way that he looked at her was suddenly so serious. It struck her in a strange place in the chest. She had no idea who this man was. And he didn't seem to want to tell her. That did make her wonder if he was a warlord. Or something. Because why not just give her his name?

He must be famous.

She cursed the lack of access to the internet out here. She cursed her own attention span when it came to popular culture. Well, it wasn't really her attention span. It was what she had time for. If she wasn't flying cargo, then she was taking care of her family. She was busy. She was mending clothes, knitting, making dinner. She was working outside in the garden, feeling the earth between her hands. She liked it all. She liked her life, in truth. She didn't find it difficult or confronting in any way. She just found it to be…life.

But money. Money was a worry.

And he was promising to reward her.

She believed that he was rich. He definitely looked like he was. Not that it was a certain indicator of anything. A man could definitely put on some nice clothes and pretend to be above himself. Con men existed for a reason.

But she didn't think that he was one. Well. She thought about what he had said about his past lovers. Maybe he was… A grifter in other ways, but she really did believe that he was rich.

The way that he had approached her, with all that confidence, like she would bend over backward to do exactly what he wanted, spoke of a man who was so innately used to being deferred to. She had never met anyone quite like him. She knew a lot of men who were demanding and commanding. Knew a lot of men who thought that they should be listened to simply because they were men. But that wasn't the way that he behaved. It was difficult to parse. Difficult to explain. And yet, she did.

"What do you mean by that?"

"I'm a man with a great many resources. And you saved my life. I won't forget it."

"I… I wish that I was in a position where I can tell you that I didn't want your money. But I'm not."

She suddenly felt very small, very aware of the fact that there was a vast wilderness out there, on the outside of the wrecked plane.

Her plane was wrecked.

Which meant the business was effectively halted. Even if there were insurance claims she could file, there would be delays, and there could be issues.

And if there was any interruption of service, pay, she was in huge trouble.

All of her clients were going to have to use other people. And if that happened, then how was she going to get them again?

This was a disaster of epic proportions. He had offered her all that money to take him to Boston, and she could definitely use that money. But now she was infinitely in need of more.

"Yes, I gather that."

"I'm sorry. It must seem very…crass to you. Being with somebody like me. Who needs to beg you for money."

"You haven't begged. And there is nothing crass about you. Indeed, you have conducted yourself with extreme bravery these past few hours. What you have done actually deserves a reward beyond money, but I'm a man with money. And that means it is the manner with which I can reward you."

"Well. I could hardly just let you die."

"Again, some of my ex-lovers might have."

"That's very concerning."

"It is," he agreed. "But I have had some time to reflect, as I lay here incapacitated. Perhaps my life needs to change."

"Really?"

"Isn't that what a near-death experience is for? Reformation? Transformation?"

"I don't know about that. I'm going to go back to my life the way that it was. I have responsibilities. I have people to take care of. I can't afford to transform. I mean, if you give me money… I guess there will be something of a transformation. But I'm going to go right back to work. I'm going to get another plane, I'm going to make sure that I'm operational as quickly as possible. That's all I want. Stability."

"Stability?"

"Yes. Do you have any idea what it's like? Watching your bank account, watching the money evaporate from it. Watching the price of eggs go up, and knowing that there's nothing you can do, because God knows you need eggs. I mean, I have chickens for that very reason. So the eggs didn't hit me that hard. But I don't have a cow. The milk really is a burden."

"No," he said. "I don't know what any of that's like."

"I feel like I work so hard, and it just… Never seems to be enough. It's disheartening. Because you would think… I do an honest day's work. I have a family home, and that makes me one of the lucky ones. My dad is still alive, and that's lucky too. But he has medical issues, and they aren't all covered under his Medicaid. Sometimes there are really expensive bills. And then there's my sisters. They all need things. All the time. Everybody always needs things."

"And what about you?"

She shook her head. "I'm the one earning the money. If I needed things too, that would just be irritating. I don't work for me. I work for them."

"That hardly seems fair."

"Fair isn't a thing. Didn't anyone ever tell you that?"

"No."

"Well. I'm here to tell you, life isn't fair. So consider that your first time."

He stared at her for a long moment. "What would you do if you had all the money in the world?"

"I would make sure my family was taken care of. For a start. Then I would try to fix some of the things that are broken. Some of the things that make it so people like me have to work so hard. Work so hard and never dig out. It's like spinning on a hamster wheel. I don't think it should be that way."

"I see. And do you have ideas as to how to fix it?"

"If I had all the money in the world I would consult with the smartest people. I would invest the resources that I had—the money—and I would educate myself. And then I would listen to those people. There are a lot of experts who talk to world leaders, and I assume they get money for consulting. It's big business. I also think it's big business to keep the problems, rather than fix them. Because if people need their problems to be fixed, then they're more likely to care about what this candidate or that candidate is doing."

"American politics," he said. "I am blessedly unfamiliar."

"All right. You're not American. Well. I have a dim view. I'm out here working hard trying my best to make a living, and it's never gotten me much."

"I will fix that," he said. "I swear to you."

"Well. I appreciate it. And I'll hold you to it. If we get out of here."

She couldn't even worry that much about the reward. They had to get to safety first. All of it was theoretical if this man died.

"I'm going to go outside and try to see if I can find what we need to start a fire."

She looked at him one last time and found she had a hard

time catching her breath. Then she turned and moved to the plane's makeshift exit.

She blinked against the harsh light and let her eyes adjust.

It was beautiful out here, even though it was austere. Even though they were trapped.

It was quiet. In some ways, more restful than her life usually was.

But she had to make sure they had water. And it would be best if she could figure out how to get a fire going outside too.

She tramped into the woods, trying to shake off any of the fear that she felt. Any concern about wild animals. She was hell-bent on finding something to help her clear away some snow, and get some dry wood.

She was going to try to call on the supplies that they had in those boxes, and her years in Girl Scouts to get a fire going.

She started to gather sticks, and bring them back toward the plane.

"Stevie."

She heard her name coming through the curtain of blankets that she had draped over the opening of the plane.

She scurried inside. "I need to be able to stand up," he said.

"No you don't," she said. "You need to stay right there."

"I can't stay right here."

"Clem, you gotta take care of yourself," she said, forgetting for a second that his name was a game she was playing with herself.

"Stevie, I have very little modesty to my name, and the call of nature and the answering of it is not something that concerns me any, but this is a shared space."

"Oh." It took her a second, but then she realized he was…

Well. Practicalities, of course. "I just collected some... Some sticks. I can see if one of them will work as a crutch. I'll help you up, though."

She was worried his leg might be more than just cut. If it was broken, then it was going to be very difficult for him to stand up. Though she knew that sometimes shock could provide a little bit of insulation against pain. She didn't wish that for them.

"I'll help you up, just a second."

She went outside, and examined the sticks that she had gotten. One of them seemed like it was a very competent walking stick. She went back to the edge of the woods, and searched around until she found another. He could use them as trekking poles in the snow. And hopefully that would keep him upright. Because if not, and he fell, then they were going to be in a hell of a situation trying to get him back up.

"Okay," she said. "I'm going to help you. But you also have to help, or you're not getting very far."

"All right," he said, seeming irritated now.

He was clearly not a man used to needing help. And why would he be? He was so tall and strong. He was probably used to being able to do whatever he wanted. Whatever he needed.

Forget all the rest.

She bent down next to him, and urged him to drape his arm over her shoulder. He still smelled good, somehow. Like whatever expensive cologne he was wearing, and the night air of the forest sank down into his skin. She didn't know how he managed that.

He shouldn't be so devastating still. And yet.

She handed him one of the makeshift poles. "Okay, lean on me with part of your body, and that with the other half.

And let's try to get you up. If you start bleeding again, you're going right back down. Practicalities be damned."

She looked at him, and her heart rate sped up. There was sweat beading on his forehead, and his teeth were clenched. "Let's go," he said.

She began to help lift, as he pushed his own self up, his incredibly impressive upper-body strength making the feat much easier than she had imagined it might be. "Hand me the other pole," he said, leaning heavily over her.

"I don't want to drop you," she said.

"I'm fine," he said.

He released his hold on her and grabbed hold of the first stick with both hands, supporting himself on that, and his good leg.

Then she grabbed the other pole. "Okay," she said, "use those to help support you. I can stand on the outside of the plane and try to help you get down. The snow is deep in places, it's going to make it tricky."

"Stevie, I have traveled the world. Traversed it over so many times there are few places left unexplored. This is one of them. I consider it an opportunity, not a detriment to have this moment, and I will seize it as I have every other adventure. Firmly about the throat with both hands."

She had no idea why his words should create an erotic shiver inside of her.

She had no idea how she so readily identified it as an erotic shiver, given that her life had been void of those.

But the minute that she had met him, it had been like colliding with the inevitability of all that she had been missing out on.

She was, frankly, trapped with a man who exuded the kind of sexual temptation that she had never once been exposed to.

Like being tossed into the sea to learn how to swim, rather than being able to slowly get her feet wet in the kiddie pool.

It would be a terrible shame to practice chastity in the face of our inevitable demise...

She shut that off. The man was...injured. She had no call objectifying him so. Though, he had sort of objectified himself, in truth.

Angrily, she stepped out of the plane, and watched as he leaned forward, planting one pole down in the snow, and then another, before using the entirety of his upper-body strength to vault himself out of the plane, and land on one foot.

"Thank you," he said. "This works."

"Don't stab yourself through with one," she called, as he disappeared into the woods. His movements might be slow, but they were deliberate, his coordination unquestionable.

She would've said that he was a man who had never done a day's worth of labor in his life, and yet he seemed at ease with the physicality of what was asked of him now.

He was an enigma.

She decided that she would worry about him in five minutes. And until then, she would focus on the fire.

She went back into the plane and began to scrabble around the different boxes. Inside, she found a lighter. There weren't even any Girl Scout shenanigans required.

She laughed as she took hold of a flat piece of bark and began to clear snow away to create a bare patch of earth. There, she began to lay out the necessary tinder to get a fire started.

In the plane she found a pot in the cargo, and though she wasn't entirely sure how she was going to suspend it in the fire, she knew she would figure it out. At this point, things were going shockingly well.

Thankfully, she didn't have to go looking for him, because he reappeared just as she was trying to decide whether to pause and go after him, or continue on in her fire starting.

"You've been busy," he said.

"I'm never anything but busy."

"It seems so."

"Well, what's the alternative? Sitting around feeling sorry for ourselves."

"I feel like I would be quite good at that."

He grinned.

Everything about him just then absolutely made a mockery of that. He was standing out there in the snow in what still looked like a very nice suit, cut open, looking quite at ease.

"You are… You are the strangest man that I have ever met."

"It's fair, then. Because you're the strangest woman that I've ever met."

"How am I strange?"

"For a start, I've never met a female cargo pilot before."

"Well. What do you do for work?"

"I invest."

She snorted. "Don't even get me started on the stock market. It's an unnecessary game that we don't have to play that creates poverty and financial crisis."

"Really?"

"Yes. And then every corporation has a primary job to their stockholders, it isn't to their customers or their employees." She snorted. "Shameful."

"You're a very opinionated woman," he said.

"Show me somebody without opinions and I'll show you somebody who doesn't have enough thoughts in their head."

"Well. Perhaps that's my problem." She didn't believe that either. Whatever he was, it wasn't honest.

She wasn't sure why she was so certain of that, but she was.

The man was entirely full of it.

"I'm going to melt some snow. We can't go eating the snow, or that's a one-way ticket to hypothermia. I don't know that this fire is going to be warm enough to sit around to actually…counteract being outside, but… Well, we have it."

"I'm not going to chance sitting down in the snow," he said. "I may not get back up. But I would like to stand for a while."

"The bleeding didn't continue on?"

"No. The tourniquet and the bandage seem to have helped. But I imagine I should keep my movements to a minimum."

"Very likely."

"You look worried."

"Well, the prospect of infection worries me quite a bit. Not trying to be grim, just…"

"Practical."

"Practicality is sort of the linchpin of survival, I would say."

He nodded slowly. "And you don't find the stock market to be practical."

"I surely don't."

She put some snow into the pot, and held it over the fire. She switched hands back and forth, trying not to scald herself, but the snow melted quickly.

Then she set the pan aside, in the snow, hoping it would cool enough for them to drink quickly.

She lifted the pan to her lips, and drank. "Thankfully,"

she said, handing the pan to him, "this will be a renewable resource. For a while."

"A good thing."

She looked around. "I'm going to make a way for us to sit around the fire. At least until the wind conditions pick up again. Right now it's not any cooler out here than it is in the plane."

She went back inside, and continued to dig through the boxes. There was a camping chair, and then another. More sleeping bags. She went outside and set them up as close to the fire as possible, and he managed to get himself sat down in one. She got sleeping bags, and wrapped one around his shoulders. His mouth turned up into a half smile, and he looked up at her. She was immobilized for a moment by those mesmerizing blue eyes.

"Thank you," he said. "I can't recall ever having been cared for quite so nicely. Maybe there was a nanny that I'm struggling to place."

She felt an unexpected pang of sympathy for him. And also, recognition. It had been a long time since anyone had cared for her, and she missed it. Very much.

She went back inside, and grabbed the meat and cheese they had eaten last night. She speared some of the meat slices on a stick, and held it out over the fire. It might not need to be cooked, but they would both enjoy something warm.

He reached out. "Let me," he said. She handed him the stick with the meat slices, and he turned his attention to roasting them.

"Do you cook?"

"Not often. I'm busy. And typically have someone do it for me. I make a decent breakfast." He looked up at her, and grinned.

"Was that supposed to make me think of something?"

"Yes. That I have many women I make breakfast for after entertaining them in my bed." Her stomach went tense. And then he tilted his head to the side and frowned. "That would be a lie, though. They don't stay the night. Though I have been known to make an omelet late at night before a woman goes back on her way."

"You're not close to anyone in your family, are you?"

His shoulders tensed. "Why?"

"I don't know. You seem to be suggesting that you have a lot of…liaisons. And I don't have time for that kind of carry-on. I have a job, I have my sisters, I have my dad. You told me that you have a job. You also told me that your mother left. So…"

"I have my father."

"Are you…close to him?"

His expression went austere. "We have and always been. We don't see eye to eye about a great many things. But my father is a good man. He is…unaffected."

"What do you mean?"

"When my mother left, I was sent into a great and terrible spiral. I was a terribly unpleasant little boy. No one could deal with me. My father, no one on the staff. He would offer increasingly higher amounts of money for people to come and tame me, but nobody could. Eventually, he hired Greta. And Greta was Norwegian, and thought it best to raise children outdoors. She took me to Norway for a while, had me run around among the pines. This is not wholly unfamiliar to me." He looked up, and around. "Only Greta was able to tame me. And it was by… Not trying to. She was perhaps the last person to truly take care of me. Though she was not a soft touch. Don't get me wrong. It was not an indulgent sort of care. She denied me, for the first time. I had otherwise never experienced denial. Other than the removal of my mother's love, of course. Though, I'm not entirely certain that I ever had that."

"Oh," she said.

The kind of childhood he spoke of was one filled with the sort of privilege she could only ever imagine. But it was… also sad sounding. It didn't put her in the mind of happy memories, or ease. She would've said that she couldn't feel sympathy for somebody who was as apparently rich as he was. But in that moment, she did. They ate the roasted meat, and cold cheese. They drank more water, and sat outside until the sky began to darken. There was nothing to do in a situation like this but try to conserve energy. In many ways, they were lucky. They had food. They had a way to make fire. They had supplies, unexpectedly.

"I guess you missed that wedding," she said, looking up at the stars.

He nodded slowly. "I guess I did."

"I'm sorry," she said.

"No matter. Though, I suppose had I made it, I would be dancing there now. Rather than…" He gestured to his leg.

"You certainly can't dance now."

"Have you not learned yet the dangers of challenging me?"

A hint of amusement crept into his face.

He gripped the makeshift trekking poles, and propelled himself up out of the chair. Then he let one drop, and extended his hand.

"You have to be joking," she said.

"No, I am always deadly serious about dancing."

She was stuck in the middle of the wilderness with the most beautiful man she had ever seen, and he was asking her to dance. She had never been held in a man's arms before.

It made her feel so many things she hadn't even considered feeling before, not like this. Not so close, and personal and real. He lit her up inside. Made her feel like a woman in ways she never had before.

What if they did die out here? And when they found them, they were nothing but frozen bones. She would've wished that she had danced. She would have wished that she had…

So many things.

So she went to him. In her parka, with him leaning on that pole, and he wrapped his arm around her waist, and held her close. He was still leaning heavily on the pole on his bad side. But his hold was firm, and she found herself shocked yet again by his strength.

She looked up at him, and his eyes were burning now. Or maybe it was just a trick of the firelight.

Her heart beat heavily, a surge of excitement winding through her.

This was ridiculous. And ten kinds of wrong. There was no way that she should be… Caught up in the moment like this. In circumstances.

This wasn't her. And it wasn't her life.

And you may never get back to your life.

Eventually they were going to have to make a choice. She was going to have to decide if she wanted to try and hike out of here, or if they should wait where there were supplies. She might die.

It was a very real risk.

And suddenly, who she was seemed so distant. It felt much more real to be this woman. One who didn't have all these people depending on her. One who was held, warm and secure in a man's arms.

This was like a dream she had never had before.

One she had never allowed herself. She had let herself believe that her life had to be stark. Spartan.

But it was all a girl like her could have. All she could aspire to. Because she had to work, and work was the most important thing. Because... Because.

And yet right now, she felt alive with possibility. And it almost felt like... She was being given a chance to live. Out here under the clear sky. Out here, where her life might just end.

"I don't understand what's happening," she said.

"The same thing that's been happening since the moment I set eyes on you," he said.

"And that is?"

"When two reactionary elements meet. Chemistry."

"But that doesn't happen to me," she said.

"Why not, Stevie?"

"Because I am a cargo pilot. With six sisters and a sick father. Because I am not special. And I never have been."

"I cannot believe that. That you, standing here, brilliantly alive in the face of all of this, could ever believe that you weren't special. You are. You are extraordinary. I have said it, and therefore it is true."

"You're very arrogant," she said.

"Yes. A well-documented part of my charm."

They were odd words. She frowned. "Documented by who?"

"One never really knows." He brushed past that, and then, brushed her cheek with the back of his knuckles, and that made her forget the words even better than his quick redirect. His hands were warm somehow, in spite of everything. "You don't have time for liaisons?"

She shook her head. "No."

"Out here we have nothing but time."

She had never been saving herself for somebody special. But it was pretty miraculous to think she might've been saving herself for somebody this hacking gorgeous. Because he was. And yes, he was injured. Yes, they were out in the wilderness. But he was right. If this was it, what was the point? What was the point of restraint?

What had it ever gotten her, in fact?

She was an adventurous spirit. It was why she was a pilot. Well, that and it was an inherited legacy. But she loved it because she liked to take that leap. She liked that moment when she was suspended in the air, and climbing.

That was this. Suspended. In awe of the moment. Of the beauty. That was everything.

He hadn't even done anything overly intimate, and yet she felt on fire.

She had never been this close to a man.

She didn't really want to tell him that. She didn't want to do anything to impact the power of the moment.

He wasn't taking advantage of her. She was the one taking advantage of this. This moment out of time. This moment where she got to be whoever and whatever she wanted.

This moment where she got to…be free.

Utterly and completely.

She stretched up on her toes, and before her nerve could desert her, she leaned in, and pressed her mouth to his.

CHAPTER FIVE

ADONIS HAD BEEN on the receiving end of any number of kisses. Passionate, cruel, expert. But none like this. There was an innocence to Stevie's kiss. It was fresh, like the air. Like the snow.

Unspoiled like all the landscape around them.

It made him forget about the pain in his leg. It made him forget that they were stuck in an unforgiving wilderness. Or perhaps it made it seem like it was a good thing.

Like this was what they had both needed in their lives in that moment. Though he couldn't explain it.

He had lived the last thirty-five years with little feeling. Especially since his mother's departure.

And in all the years since, he had sought external pleasures to give him the feelings that his own heart could not.

But now he felt like he was being warmed from the inside out. And that was all Stevie.

He had told her the truth when he'd said he had never met a woman like her before. Indeed, he had not met another person like her, regardless of gender.

And so he kissed her, like he was starving. Which he was. Like they were dying—which they might be.

It might well and truly be his last meal, he realized.

They were freezing, of course. And it would be cold if

he stripped her bare. But they had sleeping bags. And he was grateful for that at least.

He was irritated that he didn't have a full range of motion, but they managed to get back into the plane together. They didn't have to worry about the fire. It would burn itself out with all the moisture around.

Stevie took a sleeping bag, and laid it down, then put another unzipped sleeping bag wide over the top of it, grabbing the ends of both, and zipping them together into a larger cocoon.

"That is a brilliant trick."

"Pretty basic camping skills," she said. "But perhaps necessary."

"Believe me when I tell you, I would like for all of this to have much more finesse. But I am…hampered."

"I'm worried," she said, her eyes wide, "that I'm going to do you harm."

"If you do, it will be worth it."

He began the process of lowering himself down, and getting into the sleeping bag, while Stevie did the same. She was much more nimble and agile than he was. She unzipped her coat, and took it off, setting it beside the bag. She looked at him, her eyes wide.

"Take your clothes off, please," he said.

He was not one to say *please* usually. But there was something so earnest about her that it compelled him to be softer than he normally would be.

He beckoned her to him, and kissed her mouth. She was warm and soft against him, and he parted her lips and tasted her deep. She was so sweet.

This strange little pilot, who had saved his life, and kept him alive here in this vast wilderness. And this wasn't what he had joked that it would be earlier when he had first talked about the two of them making the most of their situation. This wasn't about her being the last woman he might ever see, may ever taste, though, of course, he couldn't help but think about that. It was about her. Because if he didn't have her, he would not be able to die a happy man, whether that was now or forty years from now.

She whimpered, and gasped as he bit her lower lip, kissed her chin, down her neck.

Then he gripped the hem of her top, and pulled it up over her head.

"Not too cold?"

She looked at him and shook her head.

"Good."

He unhooked her bra, and revealed small, perfect breasts. They were beautiful, just as she was.

He moved his thumb over one of the tightened buds, and watched as her face contorted with pleasure. There was something so fascinating about the way she was experiencing this.

She looked amazed. Filled with wonder, and he couldn't help but allow the same feeling to echo inside of him.

Such a strange thing, when he could not recall sex filling him with wonder in the years since he had first lost his virginity.

And yet now, he felt it.

Perhaps that was the glory and miracle of their survival. Perhaps it was all the everything.

"Take the rest off," he said. She complied, her eyes never leaving his as she wiggled out of her jeans, and he assumed all else beneath the sleeping bag.

She began to attack his shirt, undoing the buttons, and once she had exposed his chest to her gaze, she moved her hands over him reverently.

He let his head fall back, the pleasure doing so much to blot out the discomfort in his leg.

He helped her shrug his jacket and shirt off his shoulders, leaving his chest bare, and she leaned over him, kissing him on the mouth, and then scattering kisses over his chest, his stomach.

When she looked back up at him, her cheeks were flushed, her eyes bright with excitement.

"Yes?" he asked, feeling a strange surge of amusement at her enthusiasm.

"You're just beautiful," she said. "And I want to make the most of it. The most of this."

"As do I."

He hauled her upward, up, so that she was seated on his mouth, where he began to devour the heart of her.

If this was going to be his last meal… So be it.

She gasped, her hands going to his hair, as he held her fast and pleasured her.

She made a sound that might've been one of protest, but it shifted quickly enough, to one of need. He devoured her. Until she cried out his name. The name she didn't even know. The one she had given him.

Until she was shaking and sobbing.

She didn't even know his name. And yet for some reason, that made it all feel real. It made it all feel…that much more powerful.

Undeniable.

He moved her back down his body when her cries had subsided, and kissed her, her naked body crushed to his. He undid his belt, the closure on his pants and freed himself.

"Take me inside you," he said, his voice hoarse.

She looked at him with an unknowable expression on

her face, but moved, and he felt the head of him go against her hot, slick channel.

For all that he had thought he would die of pain just yesterday, he thought now he might die of pleasure.

She began to sink down onto him, and paused for a moment, then resolutely brought herself down over him, a cry on her lips as she did.

He reached up, and grabbed hold of her head, brought her mouth down to his and kissed her savagely, as he moved, as he claimed her even as he lay prone.

They would survive this. He was determined of that. Because a world that contained pleasure like this was too beautiful to leave.

He whispered those words against her mouth. How glorious she was. How miraculous. She began to whimper, and he felt her body begin to ripple with pleasure. Felt as she grew closer and closer to another release.

And when she did, when she drew her head back and called out his name, he let go. Her name on his lips. And he did know her.

And she knew him in the only way that mattered.

This was real.

He couldn't explain it.

It was primal. Two people who had survived something that should've taken them. And yet they lived.

The evidence of it was in every cry, every sigh, every torrential wave of pleasure.

And when it subsided, she curled up against his chest, and went to sleep. But he didn't sleep for a very long time.

When she woke the next morning, flashbacks of the night before held her immobilized. Just as he held her firmly. It wasn't like waking up that first morning with him. Where she had been confused as to how they held each other so closely. She knew how now.

She had given herself to him. Completely. Every part.

She hadn't known… She hadn't known that existed inside of her. It was…stunning. Wondrous in a way.

A brilliant discovery, really.

She was passionate. She had taken something she never had before, and it had been… It had been glorious.

She blinked back tears. If they did get out of this, their worlds would never mesh. He had promised her an award for this, and now it felt… Wrong almost to take it.

She would have to, though. Because she would have to go back to her life.

Or they would never make it out.

There were only two options. Right now, both of them made her feel sad.

She moved away from him, and began to dress.

She looked down at him, and felt her whole body catch fire.

She could never regret that. It had been wonderful. He had shown her pleasure. He had shown her sensations her body was capable of that she hadn't even known. Now she was going to have to make some more time for that kind of thing. Because now she knew.

Even as she thought it, she knew she was lying to herself. Even as she thought it, she knew she was being…foolish. Because of course there would never be anybody else. Of course. Of course it would be him, always. Who was first and best.

Well, that was just sad. She wasn't going to let herself think that. She wasn't going to let herself think that anything was going to end here. Not their lives, and not her sexuality.

She steeled herself, and put on her layers. Then she went outside to get the fire going.

Her legs were still shaking. From all his kisses. From everything she'd discovered with him.

She'd had no idea.

It was like he'd wrenched open a portal inside of herself that had previously been firmly shut. She'd never had time to think about things like this. She'd never had time to wonder what sex would really be like, or what she would be like with a lover or…any of that.

He'd taken her to a class all about herself. He'd shown her new things, new feelings.

When she'd set out on this flight she'd had no idea they would crash. No idea she would get lost. No idea…what she would find.

It felt dramatic, really. But her experience with him had been…altering. In a way that nothing else ever had been. Ever could be.

And she wanted to keep it for herself. Part of her wanted to keep this for herself. Even though it was foolish. The man needed a hospital. She needed to get back to her life.

But this had been…well, nicer than a plane crash had any right to be.

She moved about their campsite, reinvigorating the fire and getting some snow back on to melt.

Then she heard a sound. Like helicopter rotors in the distance.

"Oh, please be what I think you are."

The helicopter sound came closer. And closer.

She knew a moment of fear, then one of regret. And then…then she sprang into action.

She ran back into the plane. "Clem. I think they're coming. I think it's search and rescue."

"Perhaps," he said, his expression stoic.

She chose not to look at him too closely.

She ran back outside, and started waving her hands at the clear sky. There was nothing there yet. But they were coming.

Then she saw one black helicopter. Followed by another. And another.

It was a fleet of helicopters, not military, but shiny and expensive looking.

As one began to descend, she moved, hugging the side of the plane wreckage to stay clear.

The fleet began to lower itself down into the snow.

Her heart was pounding, the relief that was rioting through her so intense she could scarcely stand it.

A man got out of one of the helicopters, wearing a stark, black suit. He had an earpiece in his ear, and something on his lapel. He looked like... Secret Service.

"You there," he said. "The Prince. Where is he?"

"The... The Prince?"

"Yes. The Prince. Prince Adonis Andreadis. We tracked him to this location. Is he alive?"

Her heart was thundering hard, and she was dizzy. "Yes he's... Well, he's inside the plane."

Stevie Parker had crashed her plane with a *prince* on board.

Stevie Parker had lost her virginity, grandly, to a *prince*.

And that was when it hit her.

Prince Adonis.

Of course.

He was... He was famous. A legendary playboy prince. How had she not recognized him? Of course, she didn't pour over magazines with his pictures in them, but of course she had seen his face before. It was just that she would've never thought...

She had been carrying cargo for a royal wedding.

Adonis hadn't just been trying to get to a wedding, he had been trying to get to *his* wedding.

The realization made Stevie wish they'd just leave her to die in the snow.

CHAPTER SIX

IN TRUTH, Adonis could remember very little about the rescue. Once he had been taken to the nearest medical facility approved of by his father's team, they had determined that he was significantly more unwell than he had originally imagined. He had thought that because he was conscious, able to eat and able to communicate that he was more or less fine. He had lost a significant amount of blood, and the wound had been dangerously close to going septic.

And all the while, he wondered about Stevie. What had happened to her? If she was well.

Stevie…

She hadn't just kept him alive.

Their night together had been extraordinary. If anything had given him the will to live it had been that.

But he'd had no contact with her since and he didn't like it. The media had been in a frenzy. For two days he'd been missing, without a trace, and while there had been rumors he was off on a bender before his wedding, there had also been some concern for his safety.

And in the time since…

The media had been frenzied.

He'd been stranded in the woods with a female pilot who had saved his life. Stevie's name had been printed, along with a photo that had clearly been taken of her from across a street in some Montana town. Which meant she wasn't in the hospital but it also meant she was wandering around unprotected.

He felt protective. Angry.

And outraged at his inability to do anything because his body was choosing to be so…mortal about it all.

He came to the end of his tether two weeks into his recovery.

He wrenched out his IVs, disconnected every monitor and stormed into his father's office in the palace with the aid of his shiny black cane.

"I need to get out of here."

"Do you?" his father asked, not raising his head.

"I promised Stevie a reward."

"Ah yes," said the old man, looking quite spry for someone supposedly knocking at death's door. "Stevie Parker. Twenty-five, of Bozeman, Montana, pilot. A poor pilot, at that."

"You've done your research."

The King nodded. "Of course I have, Adonis, you were alone with her for days and I needed to know who she was. Especially with the media so enraptured by the story."

"Have you offered her protection?"

"Protection?" his father asked, sounding incredulous. "It's you who might need protecting. She's going to be able to sell her story."

"What makes you think there's a story?" His father stared at him. Hard. "Father, I am injured," he said, gesturing to his leg.

"So you're saying you did not have sexual relations with the girl?"

He cleared his throat. "I didn't say that."

Damn his father for knowing him. Damn *himself* for being so predictable.

"You know the media has decided there is a potential romance between you."

"Yes. But doesn't the media always?"

"Hmm. But not always when you have a fiancée."

Drusilla.

He had chosen her because she was the best option. The most expedient.

He was no longer certain that was the case.

Stevie had saved his life.

Stevie was the last woman to set him on fire.

Stevie was the woman the press couldn't stop talking about.

Stevie might be the answer to everything.

The truth was, whatever his father thought, his time with Stevie had not been about a playboy reverting to type. What had passed between them had been singular, and he'd thought continually of her since they'd been rescued.

Yes, he'd wanted to protect her, and that had been his driving focus as he remained trapped in the hospital bed, but he also...

Wanted her.

And the truth was the backlash over the wedding was something he didn't feel was fixable. Drusilla was already unhappy with him over the scandal surrounding everything, and he suspected she would rather they called it off altogether.

He knew he wanted to.

He knew what his solution was.

"I think previous plans might need changing," he said slowly.

"Which previous plans?" his father asked.

"The future Queen of Olympus must be smart, brave and resourceful, do you not agree?"

His father looked at him through narrowed eyes. "Yes."

"She must be popular with the people, and of course there must be chemistry between us else she leave me for the bright lights of Hollywood."

His father scowled. "My own mistakes are not on trial here."

"Well, we can litigate those another time." He lifted a brow. "A princess who is down-to-earth, who has spent her life working. Who knows how to engage with the majority of the populace...because she is like them."

"Of course those things would be good, but I am hard-pressed to believe you could find such a woman who is also suitable."

He smiled. Slowly. "Oh, I have already. I think that Stevie Parker is a much better solution to the problem you've been trying to solve."

Stevie was... Well, she was furious. She'd been back at her home in Montana for two weeks, she had no reward, no contact with Adonis, *His Royal Highness*, at all. She was being hounded by reporters. Because now it was a global news story. That the Playboy Prince had crashed in the wilderness, and had been saved by a female pilot, and everybody wanted to know what was happening.

And on a personal note... She'd been worried about pregnancy. Weirdly sad when her period had come and oddly bereft even in her fury over everything.

In the two weeks since the accident had occurred, her entire life had been turned upside down. Not only did she not have the means to work, she didn't have her anonymity, her privacy, anymore. And she was still poor as a duck.

It was not a conundrum that she had ever expected to find herself in.

One time, when her sisters were very small, a news crew had come to the school to do a feature on the solar panels that had been installed, making the school the first in the state to run off of alternative energy.

And Topaz had said, quite seriously, *I avoided getting on camera. I don't want to accidentally become famous.*

They had all laughed at that. Stevie most of all.

I don't think that you're in danger of accidentally becoming famous.

People worked tirelessly to become famous. She didn't think it was going to happen to someone accidentally.

And yet, here she was. Embroiled in accidental fame while coping with… She wasn't going to call it *heartbreak*. That was dumb. She'd had sex with the guy one time. She was…thwarted because he'd made promises he hadn't kept. That was all.

To say she didn't care for it was an understatement.

And yet it was becoming an issue everywhere she went. Even in the grocery store in her tiny town. Normally she would've said the citizens of the little Montana hamlet couldn't have cared less about celebrity. But her saving a prince had made waves.

She growled in a fury, and went over to the stove to look at her dinner. Red beans with bacon and onion and ham hocks.

That just made her think of Adonis all over again. And she got even more furious.

Then she heard a knock on the door.

Her sisters clambered from down the hall, from their shared bedroom, hollering and fighting over who was going to answer the door.

"We don't know who it is," she shouted, wiping her hands on a dishcloth as she made her way to the front.

But she could tell that the girls had already opened the door. And then there was a chorus of screams.

"If it's an ax murderer, I swear to God…"

But then she saw. Her sisters were frozen, staring at the man standing there. And she couldn't blame them. Because there he was in all his state. And he was still in a *state*.

He had on black gloves, and one hand was clutching the silver handle of a shiny black cane. He looked imposing and severe. There was no question that he was a man used to being in charge.

Of course.

How had she not realized? Really, how had she not *realized* who he was?

Because his bearing was something beyond. It was *royal*.

And he was here. *Prince Adonis*.

"Stevie," he said, her name so exotic on his lips.

And it made her…

Oh no, she wanted to swoon. She was so, so angry at him and he was still so gorgeous he sent her whole body into a fine fiery frenzy.

She'd come back home and had tried to be the girl who took care of her sisters, the one who handled paperwork and practicalities. The one who fought with insurance companies and lost sleep over the mortgage and paying for health insurance.

But he immediately reminded her she was more than that now.

That she was a woman who'd taken a lover and the impression of his hands on her body still left her burned.

Her sisters turned to look at her, like a chorus of baby owls swiveling their heads, eyes wide.

She was worried, for a moment, that the truth of it all shone brightly on her skin. That what the press was writing about them was true. That they'd had a…liaison out there in the wilderness with nothing but the stars as witness. That she had fallen prey to his charms like every other woman to ever cross his path because she was absolutely the opposite of special.

She was just like all of them.

And for her he'd been…singular.

"Your Majesty," she said. Because she couldn't bring herself to say his name. Not out of respect. For her own…sanity.

"Not Clem?"

"Well, it turns out that's not your name. Though, you didn't tell me that. Maybe because when you promised the reward you were intending to welsh on it, and you didn't want me to track you down."

"Believe me," he said. "I'm not worried about being tracked down."

Of course not. His people could track him down if they needed to, and mere peasants would never be allowed entry past his threshold. And yet there he was at hers.

He stepped inside without being invited.

"Stevie, I have come to make amends. I'm sorry it's been two weeks without contact and without protection from the press. I have been undergoing *forced recovery*." He said it like it had been torture. "But I recently decided my recovery was over."

"You mean you… You just left your sickbed?"

"Yes."

"Well. They probably frown on that."

"Undoubtedly. But many things that I do are quite frowned upon. Somehow I persevere."

She squinted. "It helps when you are insulated by money and power."

"Undoubtedly. Is there a place where we can speak?" He looked at her sisters. "Privately?"

She bit the inside of her cheek. "No," she said. "Not in this house. There are eight people living under this roof."

"I see."

"Girls, let him in."

Her sisters parted like the sea and he came in on his cane, looking at ease and practiced as if he had used it all his life.

He looked around the place, and she knew a moment of shame. Which was silly. One thing she had never been was ashamed. Because they had worked for all this. And it might not look like much to somebody else, to a prince, but it was hers. The little ramshackle house with its thread-bare rugs, and charming yellow kitchen. It had kept them. Sustained them.

And she gritted her teeth against any rising embarrass-ment.

"I'm here to speak to you about your reward."

"Oh." Her heart rate picked up.

"I've been thinking. And I believe that I have thought of just the perfect way to thank you for what you've done for me. And to give you a role that I know you will excel at."

"Do you?"

"Yes. You quite literally saved my life. And that is not something I will ever forget. But beyond that, listening to you speak about your life was…inspiring."

He lifted his chin, his expression arrogant. "I would do this properly, but the crutches prevent it. However, I have not come empty-handed." He reached into his suit jacket, and took out a diamond ring. She could scarcely believe what she was seeing.

It was the most spectacular piece of jewelry she had ever

seen in her entire life. Beyond anything she could have even imagined. Beyond…everything.

"Stevie Parker, you saved my life. And so I have decided, that when it comes to the matter of who is the most suitable woman to become my princess, it is you. You are going to marry me."

CHAPTER SEVEN

WHATEVER TRAJECTORY HIS life had been on when he had boarded that cargo plane two weeks ago, it was *not* that now.

And as he stood there in the small, humble house at the top of a mountain in rural Montana, having just proposed to the most unlikely woman on earth, he felt for the first time that his life was not entirely in his control.

Yes, there had always been the crown, the inevitability of it. But he had vowed to himself as his father had aged that he would do what needed to be done to preserve the integrity of Olympus, and when his father had gotten ill he'd realized the time for change had come.

He had sown his wild oats until it was time to reap responsibility, and then he had agreed to marry a woman who was suitable to the position as princess.

But two weeks ago, it hadn't been Stevie.

And now, Stevie was the only choice.

Seeing her was a gut punch he hadn't anticipated. She was more beautiful than he remembered, even here in this tiny little house, with bare feet.

Perhaps she was even more beautiful.

But that wasn't why he had chosen her.

The media frenzy surrounding the plane crash was incredible. It was a storm. Speculation and sensationalized headlines. There were endless fan edits of pictures with him and… Women who were mainly not Stevie, but photographs that had been taken from stock photography sites of female pilots, with love songs playing in the background, and it made absolutely no sense to him, but they were going around the internet with alacrity.

But there wasn't much to be done about that.

Still, the action that he had to take in response to it had become abundantly clear.

Stevie was, for lack of a better way of thinking of it, the people's choice.

She had saved his life. And the world was entranced by the idea that this scrappy American girl had been all that separated a prince from his untimely doom.

Yes, he could've gone on and married Drusilla. But there was no point to it. It would never accomplish what marrying Stevie would. And, his marriage to Stevie would end all of her problems. He had enjoyed listening to her talk. About how she would change the world. He had decided that she would be good for his country.

Good for him.

"I… Was that a proposal?"

"Yes."

"It came across as more of a demand," she said.

"Stevie, I think you and I know there is no question."

While he could not allow his attraction to her to be the driving force behind his decision, surely she must feel it now? Surely she must…

He was offering her a life of luxury and there was no shortage of chemistry between them. Why would she refuse him?

"Well, there is," she said, crossing her arms and looking up at him, her expression filled with mutiny. "Because

I am not a yes-woman. And I'm not a plaything. I have a life. Here. In this house. I have a garden. I have a business."

"Currently your garden is under a foot of snow, and I imagine your business is not operational considering you don't have a functional plane."

"That's just a season," she said. "All around. Time changes things."

"This could change things more than just seasonally."

It was then he realized that her sisters were standing there. Staring.

"Stevie," one of them said, her voice a breathless rush.

"I think your sister thinks you should marry me," he said.

"Don't speak for me," she said.

"My apologies."

"I'm Daisy," she said.

She looked to be about five years younger than Stevie.

The other girls were...girls still. And he imagined that Daisy was doing a lot of the day-to-day caregiving.

"My apologies," he said, again. "But, I do think that you can agree becoming a princess would dramatically improve your sister's life." He looked at the girls. "And yours."

"Money is just money," said Stevie. "And if I didn't earn it, I don't know how I feel about it."

"You were willing to take a reward from me."

"That I had *earned*," she said.

"You've earned this. Surely you've seen the media reports."

"Yes. All the speculation that we... That we somehow had a torrid affair in the snow when you had a massive cut in your leg."

"Yes. Those rumors."

"I've been being hounded by the press. And I refused to tell them anything."

"Another thing that makes you perfect. You haven't played into their hands, and it is extremely refreshing. Most people would have tried to profit off the nature of the stories, but you did not. Further proving your worthiness."

"I'm not a hunk of beef that you can try to evaluate. Or grade. I'm a woman. And I am not a prize in the bottom of your cereal box."

"I'm not certain what the context of that is."

"You've probably never had a box of cereal, have you?"

"No."

She simply stared at him. "I like my life."

He didn't know what to do with this. It had not occurred to him that Stevie might resist his demand.

"You might like your life, but your life is also a struggle. If you could simply…exclude yourself from the struggle, why wouldn't you?"

"Because life doesn't work that way," she said. "If you go cutting corners it's always at the expense of somebody else."

"I'm not asking you to cut corners. I *need* a wife."

"Two weeks ago you were about to have a different one, which you did not tell me about, by the way and had you…" She looked at her sisters, then cut off her sentence. "What did you do, stash her in your attic?"

Ah. So this was the issue. She was stressed about being seen as the other woman.

"I told her very regretfully that she is no longer the ideal choice to be princess of Olympus."

"That poor woman. Also, how murderous is she? Is she going to kill me in my sleep?"

"Drusilla is fine. Believe me when I tell you, she will have already found another prospect for a rich husband. We were not in love. My marriage was always going to be a dynastic choice. You know who I am now, Stevie, and you understand that my reputation has not always been the best."

"That would be because your actions haven't always been the best."

"Granted," he agreed. "But, I have a certain amount of popularity with the youth in my country. It is the older generation I have trouble with. But everyone is captivated by you. Everyone is captivated by the mere thought of you. And that is something that I wish to make the most of."

"It's something you want to exploit," she said. "And I'm not sure if I'm comfortable with that. It's…craven at best."

"Perhaps it is. But the world is craven. As you said, when corners are cut, someone pays. But you have an innate sense of justice, and a desire to see things change. Not only will you have money, Stevie, but you will have power. Not only will your family want for nothing, you will be responsible for making decisions that have an impact on a nation of people."

"But I didn't even go to college."

"And what difference does that make? College doesn't speak to intelligence, but privilege. Just as my position as Prince speaks to the very same. You have something. Something different. You are who I want by my side."

"It's not a very romantic proposal."

He turned and looked at one of the younger girls, who was probably about twelve. He was not an expert on children. "It was not meant to be. I did not get the impression that Stevie is a romantic."

"She's not," one of the other girls said. "But maybe if you treated her like she was, she would soften up a little bit."

"Hush, Opal," said Stevie. "I don't want romance. *Especially* not from him."

But her cheeks went pink. And he wondered if that was

strictly true. They were no longer stuck on the side of a mountain in a hollowed-out plane.

Perhaps then she did see things a bit differently between them.

Of course, they would have to have children. They had already proved there was fire between them in the bedroom. The idea of taking her in a soft bed, without worry of frostbite or potentially bleeding to death, was an appealing one.

That was something he was very much looking forward to.

She was as beautiful as ever. This beacon of glory unlike any other and he craved her touch again. He wanted to feel what he had that first time.

"I am offering you the greatest promotion you will ever receive," he said.

And then, Stevie did something he did not expect at all. She bent over at the waist, and was silent for a moment, before she reared back and revealed that she was gasping, choking on her laughter. "Oh. My promotion from *nobody* to your *wife* is simply the greatest thing that will ever happen to me. How can I ever refuse you, Your Royal Highness?"

"It is not funny. It is simply true."

She hiccupped. In a rather unladylike fashion. "Your ego is astonishing," she said.

"My name is Adonis. I have done my level best to live up to the name. Many would say I have done so indisputably."

"I can't believe you. You are… You deserve to be told no. That's what you want to get. You're used to people simpering and falling down at your feet. I can tell. Women especially. But not me. I'm not simply going to give you whatever you want after you lied to me then vanished for two weeks, and then showed up like I haven't been navigating this insanity by myself."

"I thought you wanted your reward," he said.

"I'll live without it. I've been managing just fine this whole time, and I'll keep on managing."

"Stevie!" Her sisters were grumbling. And it was clear why. Of course they wanted her to marry him. It would be a key to a much easier life for them. Everything would be different. They would be happier. They would be well-fed. They would live in luxury.

They would not be eating beans and sharing a bedroom in a dilapidated cabin.

"I will be here for one more night. Should you change your mind, come and find me."

He gave her the card of the hotel that he was staying at, pressing it into her palm. She looked at it, and him, and then cast it onto the ground. "Don't wait around."

He turned around, and walked toward the door, maneuvering it open while hanging on to his cane. And then he stepped outside into the freezing cold, as the door slammed shut behind him.

He had been refused. By a peasant.

It was nearly as shocking as the plane crash.

CHAPTER EIGHT

STEVIE WAS FILLED with adrenaline. And rage. So much rage.

She couldn't decide what she hated most. That he had been willing to exploit her vulnerabilities, her poverty, so that he could get what he wanted or…

That she had been tempted to say yes.

He was offering her a life she'd never imagined. Not when she couldn't see past the day-to-day. The next paycheck, the next therapy her father would need.

He was offering her…children. To be her husband.

She'd never really seen herself with those things.

She hadn't imagined a wedding or a marriage or a life away from her family. She'd never been able to afford it.

That he was the most beautiful man she had ever set eyes on, and he was proposing marriage.

Because he was the only lover she'd ever had and she dreamed of his hands on her skin at night when she tried to sleep. But he'd lied to her about who he was—even if by omission—and he'd been engaged and…

He was offering her the chance to become a princess and she wasn't immune to such a fantasy.

She really didn't know what she hated most.

It was difficult to say.

"Stevie."

Her father's weak voice came back from his bedroom.

She tried to gather herself, and walked back there.

"Is it true?" he asked.

Her poor father. He was so gray. So gaunt.

He was nothing like the man he'd been even five years ago. He had been vibrant then. And even though he had been grieving, he possessed physical strength.

But he had been hiding the bulk of his pain. His drinking. And then when his liver had begun to fail him...

Everything had fallen apart.

Everything was falling apart.

"Is what true, Dad?" For a horrifying moment, she thought he might be asking if the rumors that she'd had a torrid affair with Adonis were true.

"He asked you to marry him."

"Oh... I... There's no way that it could've been really serious."

"Daisy said that it was."

She had tried to downplay the whole event with her dad. The plane crash, everything. But, of course, once it made its way to the media in truly sensationalized fashion, he had gotten a version of it that was out of her control.

"Well, I can't take it seriously," she said. "I can't take it seriously because... Because it's impossible. Improbable."

He reached out; his touch was weak. And there were tears in his pale blue eyes. "Stevie, I failed you as a father. I fell to pieces when your mother died. And I drank myself into this state. I'll never forgive myself for it. But don't make the same mistakes I did."

"I'm not going to develop a drinking problem," she said, and then felt guilty about it. "I'm sorry..."

"That isn't what I mean. Don't fall into the belief that you need life to be hard. That you have to cling to the struggle, rather than accepting a solution. So many people have wealth and riches, Stevie, why shouldn't you? Why shouldn't the rest of the girls? You did a brilliant thing saving that man. I'm your father, and I love you. I could never have made you a princess, but I should've treated you more like one." A tear slid down his cheek. Stevie felt her insides tighten. "I want you to take this. Take this thing that I couldn't give you. So that when I'm gone I'll know that you're living a beautiful, easy life. So that I know your sisters are. They are somewhere in Europe wearing beautiful clothes, instead of working yourself into an early grave."

"Dad…"

"I mean it, Stevie. You believe… You believe what I did. Which is that at some point your hard work is going to get you somewhere. But this is as far as it ever got me. And this is as far as it's ever going to get you. Unless you take this big hand up. You saved his life. You deserve every inch of what you're being given now, and more."

She didn't want to say yes to Adonis. Not after the scene earlier.

But she could see the truth in what her father was saying. And she could see his very real worry.

"I don't want your legacy to be a struggle."

Her heart broke definitively. And right then, she determined that however long her father had left, she wanted his life to be easier too. She wanted him to have something for all his work. Because for all that he felt he had failed her…

"You haven't failed me, Dad. You had it really difficult. I know that losing Mom was hard."

"It was hard for you too," he said.

Well, maybe that was true. She had been a young woman who hadn't had much chance to grieve, but she wasn't bitter about it. There was no point being bitter.

But perhaps there's no point in stubbornly insisting you keep on struggling either.

"Okay," she said. "I'll accept."

She felt like she was free-falling. But her dad was right. What was the point of all this sacrifice when it would only take her so far?

What was the point of sacrificing at all if she wouldn't do this one thing that would change their lives forever?

She didn't need to find the card he had given her. She knew the name of the hotel.

It was the nicest one in Bozeman.

She got in her old truck and drove down to town, bundled up in a parka and heavy mittens. Thick boots.

She looked and felt nothing like a princess.

She couldn't even…

There were too many aspects to this to even fully…take it all on board.

It wasn't just that he was asking her to marry him, it was that he was asking her to be a princess. It wasn't just that he was asking her to be a princess, it was that he was asking her to move to a country she had barely even heard of, much less been to.

She parked her truck against the curb and walked across the street to the grand, stately building.

She went to the front desk. "I'm here to see… I'm here to see Prince Adonis. You can tell him that it's Stevie."

"Well, hot damn," said the man who was tending the counter. "Stevie Parker. You're the woman who saved his life."

"I feel that details of my bravery have been greatly exaggerated."

"Spoken like a true hero. He's in Room 340. Go on up."

Stevie felt that it was a shocking lack of security for an

actual prince, but she wasn't going to reject the ease. Because she still felt like she was utterly and completely turned sideways, and she didn't know how she was going to find her balance. She got into the old, slow-moving elevator, and pushed one of the gold buttons, wincing as it groaned its way to the top floor. It was a beautiful building, but it was old.

The elevator reached its destination and the doors opened, and she wandered out into the hallway. The carpet was a jade green, and the scrollwork on the crown molding really was very nice. She had never been in this place, because it was too rich for her blood.

Maybe not now.

She let out a long, slow breath, approached the room number where he was staying, the one at the farthest end of the hall, and knocked.

The door opened a moment later. And she was slightly dizzy, slung into a sense of déjà vu, since their positions were reversed from earlier, but of course she was entering his glorious hotel suite.

A hotel suite.

Her heart started to beat a little bit faster.

And then there was him.

His impact was not lessened. Not from having already seen him today, not from having seen him nearly bleed out… He was an undeniable presence. No matter what.

"I…" She swallowed hard. "I need to speak to you."

"Come in," he said.

With her most grumpy and determined face firmly in place, she stomped into the room. She crossed her arms and looked up at him. If only her crossed arms were the shield she was trying to use them as. "I spoke to my father."

"I didn't even realize your father was there."

"He's ill. Too ill to simply pop up when there are visitors

over. He's mostly confined to his room. But I… I talked to him. He wants me to accept your proposal. And I'm not going to argue with him. I see it the way that he does. He doesn't want to worry about his daughters. When he's gone. And he is going to be gone. Maybe in the next year. And I just… I want to give him peace of mind. And I do want my sisters to be taken care of."

"There's nothing wrong with you wanting to be taken care of as well," he said.

"I'm not certain that marrying a stranger is me taking care of me. Regardless of how rich you are."

"But I'm not a stranger. You put a tourniquet around my leg, and stopped me from bleeding out. We made love."

She gritted her teeth. "Don't call it that. I've done enough reading about you to know that you sleeping with a woman doesn't make her less a stranger."

"Historically, maybe. But you saved my life, Stevie. Allow me to change yours."

His words were spoken gravely, and she had the sensation that this was a real, true vow that he was making.

"What is it exactly that you want from me?"

"I require what any man in my position does. A woman who can be beloved by his people. And children."

Stevie had never really considered having children. Mostly because she had her sisters. The idea of children had actually always been a terrible burden. But if her sisters were taken care of… Did that mean that she could want children of her own?

"Well, I… I can't say that I am in a rush to have a physical relationship." She tried to meet his gaze. But everything inside of her went hot. Molten.

She could remember what he had said to her when they had been out there in the wilderness. When he had… Said that perhaps they should partake in case they were going to die.

When he had touched her and…

"That's all," she said.

"A fine statement, Stevie, but we will have to look like a couple for all the world."

"That's fine."

"A physical relationship is inevitable, so why not simply… Begin it."

"It's that easy for you?"

"No. I think it's that potent between us."

"Oh."

She felt then a thousand years younger than him and incredibly gauche.

"We've already had sex," he said.

"It's different now, though," she said. "And you know it. You didn't tell me who you were. You lied to me."

"Ah. So now we have recriminations?"

"I was hardly going to give them in front of my sisters. I didn't want them to know that I… That I was so weak."

"Is it a weakness to take even one moment of pleasure in your life when you think you're going to die, Stevie?"

"Yes. It is. Life isn't about pleasing yourself. You obviously don't know that. Because you are the notoriously debauched Prince of Olympus. You might as well be Zeus himself."

"I require my encounters to be consensual. And I am never a swan."

"I don't even… I don't even know how to respond to that. It is outrageous. I will marry you. Because it is the best thing for my family. But… I just wish you had told me who you were."

"You can see why I couldn't."

"Because you thought that I would instantly turn into a gold digger?"

"You may be pregnant now," he said.

She went still. "Is that why you asked me to marry you?"

"It is a concern."

"I'm not," she said. "I started my cycle right after I got back. So. No pregnancy."

"I see. Well. That was not a contingency of marriage."

"It just would've been convenient for you? Because you wouldn't have had to sleep with me again?"

"Perhaps I wasn't clear. We have chemistry. That is yet another reason that it is incredibly practical for the two of us to marry. It was one reason it seemed prudent to break off my arrangement with Drusilla."

"How nice for both Drusilla and me. That you possess such a scant moral compass."

"Better than my mother's. But no, it is not as good as my father's. And I can admit that. I can."

"And where does that leave me?"

"I need a moral compass, Stevie. I won't lie to you. That is a significant reason that I think you will be good for me as well. I need somebody to help me stay…correct. You have proven to me that you are a woman with great fortitude. You are a woman who knows what she stands for. That matters."

"Am I supposed to be flattered by that? That you want me to…be your Jiminy Cricket?"

"I'm not asking you to be flattered by anything. I'm simply asking that you make the reasonable choice."

And of course he felt that marrying him was the only reasonable thing. It had nothing to do with what had passed between them in the wilderness.

Not for him.

But maybe that was the issue. Maybe people weren't really romantic. Her father wanted her taken care of, but he'd never said he wanted her to be loved. But in his position, he couldn't afford ridiculous frills. Maybe it wasn't any different when you were a future king.

You just had to be like wham bam be my wife, ma'am, or something.

She'd never been a romantic.

Not before.

It was petulant to be wounded by a lack of romance she'd never fantasized about.

She found she was anyway.

"Now what?" she asked, her voice small.

"You and I will leave directly. On my private jet. I will send people to help your family pack, and we will bring them to Olympus as soon as it is practical for them to go. I know that we will have to prepare a place for your father that is medically sound."

Yes. That was why she was doing this. Her family was going to be taken care of.

"I don't want to leave them."

"They will be fine," he said.

"So you say. But they're used to having me around."

"And instead, they will have resources."

"My sisters are young. I'm not going to wholly abandon—"

"No one is suggesting that you do. But I am suggesting perhaps that your family can survive without using you entirely as a crutch."

"I… All right. I will agree because…" Her throat tightened. Because she had a choice. But opposing him wouldn't get her much of anything. So why?

Because she was Stevie Parker. Really no one extraordinary. And he was Adonis Andreadis. He was offering to make her a princess. What could she do in the face of that?

Nothing. Nothing at all but…comply. That was the beginning and end of everything.

And that was how she found herself whisked off to the airfield. Going into a part of the airport not even she had ever been into. She knew what it was. It was where the private planes flew out of.

And when they got on the plane, her heart nearly gave out.

"This is the most beautiful machine I've ever seen," she said.

"I find that I'm a bit cool on airplanes at the moment."

"Oh, I'm not. I never could be. That was a freak accident. And even then, we didn't die."

"Twice would be pushing it, don't you think?"

"Who knows," she said, looking around at the shiny, glorious space. "Can I see the cockpit?"

CHAPTER NINE

THIS WAS THE woman who would become his queen. This woman who was more interested in the cockpit of the plane than the private bedroom.

"I… Yes," he said, looking at her as if she had grown another head.

"What?"

"I've brought other women on this plane, and they are not usually interested in the cockpit."

"Don't talk to me about other women," she said, looking annoyed. "You show me the cockpit."

"All right," he said. Declining to make the joke about how they usually wanted to see half of that word anyway.

It occurred to him as he brought her in to view the state-of-the-art instruments and plush chair that she really was irked that he had mentioned other women. She wasn't just being funny, or playing up again. She was less experienced than the other women he had been with, and he had to be a little bit more careful. He wasn't used to that. He was used to people like him, who saw sex as a game.

But Stevie clearly didn't. Which meant…

He had never imagined a marriage where he was…monogamous. Many people thought that it was an outdated concept, which really was a return to the way people had often conducted themselves in the air of dynastic marriages.

Monogamy was, in his opinion, the bastion of the middle class.

But his future wife was middle-class.

He was suddenly agog at that.

"Can I sit for a moment?"

"Go right ahead," he said.

She sat in the captain's chair, stroking the yoke lovingly, and he thought she had only just looked this excited when they made love.

"The royal advisors will probably have issues with a princess who wishes to fly," he said.

She looked at him fiercely. "Flying is part of who I am."

"I understand that. Though, they may not wish you to fly me."

"Oh, why? Because I crashed with you just the once?"

"Maybe."

They went back to the seating area of the plane, and settled in. And he thought now might be the correct time to broach the topic of fidelity.

"I do not mind if you take other lovers," he said.

She went visibly red. "Well, I mind," she said. "And I wouldn't want you to."

"I see."

"What?"

"I had thought that might be the case."

"That I would have an issue with my… My husband sleeping with other women? That seems pretty par for the course."

"Not for people like me."

"Well, I'm people like me. I want… I don't want you going around being with other people. I don't want you to lie to me. Or trick me."

"A marriage is very long," he said. "Who knows what you want in the future. Perhaps you will crave some adventure."

"Then I'll go fly a plane in an ice storm in Montana. I'm not especially amped for adventure at the moment."

"You have had a lot of it lately."

"I never really saw flying as an adventure before," she said. "My dad was a pilot. Before everything went wrong."

"Before your mother died?"

"Yes," she said.

He wondered what that was like. To have experienced a loss like that, but not to be haunted by the specter of the person.

Not to know whether or not she could come back. It was a whole different situation from what had happened with him, and objectively a bigger tragedy. And yet in some ways he did think she might be right. It might be easier to reconcile. Because at least then nobody chose to leave you.

And they couldn't come back when they felt like it.

Couldn't reinjure you, reopen the wound.

You'd have no one to flaunt your lifestyle at, no one to fight with even when they weren't there.

"Your father didn't recover from that?"

"No."

"In many ways, I don't think my father recovered from my mother's betrayal."

"Did he develop a debilitating drinking habit?"

"No," he said. "My father became more of what he was. Ruthless. Firm and controlled. Not cruel, not in any regard. When I say he's ruthless, I mean with himself. If there have ever been other women since my mother, I have not borne witness to it. Neither has the nation. My father took all the transgressions of my mother inside of himself, and turned them into honor."

"Like he was doing his best to neutralize them. To counter them."

"And what is your father going to think of me?"

"He was not best pleased with my decision," he said. "But I'm never going to be the King that my father is. And what I need in a wife is different than what he seems to think I need. Because I need differently than what he does."

"Of course I actually know who you are," she said. "I didn't ever follow tabloid stories about you, but I know of you. By reputation. It seems to me that you would want a wife who is as worldly as you are. Sophisticated. Well-traveled."

"You're a pilot. You aren't well-traveled?"

"I fly one route across the country, and anyway, I meant that as a euphemism for *sex*. Because I've only ever had sex with you."

He felt that like a gut punch. He had never considered that she had been a virgin when he had taken her so roughly in the plane. And now he felt… He felt something that was strangely like guilt, and guilt wasn't something that he was accustomed to.

"You… You had never had a lover before?"

"When would I have had the time? I was busy. Taking care of my family, working, I… You know, I never especially wanted to be in a relationship. Not after what I saw happen with my father. I don't ever want to love somebody so much that losing them makes me lose all of myself. My father was never a cruel drunk, Adonis." She wrinkled her nose. "I don't know how I feel about that name."

"Nobody does. But it grows on you."

"Does it?"

"No," he said.

"Anyway, my dad was just sad. He was sad, and he couldn't ever find himself again. I never want that. It's hard enough to lose somebody. Hard enough to go through grief let alone when it's…your person. The one that holds you up.

I never wanted to be dependent on someone else to hold me up. It's impractical."

"I don't disagree. Though I come at it from a slightly different direction. Human beings are liars. And whatever they say, it is to accomplish their immediate goals. I don't see myself ever having enough faith in another person to feel the way my father once did about my mother."

"It's all the same, really. Love is just too expensive."

"Indeed," he said. He looked at her proud profile. She was a strange little creature. She seemed to be soft skin stretched over bones of steel. She had supported so much, carried so much for so long, and it was apparent in the way she held herself now. The way she vowed with her words to never depend on another person. It was a good thing. Because he needed her to be strong. And because no other person had ever depended on him, and he would hate for her to be the first one.

"You probably know most especially that I shouldn't be counted on."

"You're going to lead a whole country. Is that what you're going to tell your people?"

He smiled. "No. But I think we can both agree that perhaps being depended on to be a symbol, and being depended on as a spouse are two different things."

"Well, you don't have to worry about me."

"I've been through a plane crash with you, Stevie. I'm not especially worried."

As they took off, she looked out the window, her expression resolute. "I love flying," she said. "Because it's about freedom."

"Is it?" he asked.

"For me it is."

"And you need freedom, don't you? From the burden of family?"

She looked at him, her expression fierce. "I would never call my family a burden."

"Love can be a burden," he said.

Unfortunately he knew that from experience. If he didn't love his mother, then there wouldn't be a problem that she had left.

The scorched earth left behind by love was something he was all too familiar with.

"The crown is a burden. Having to marry and produce children is a burden. And I do it. It's even something that I want to do, in some ways."

"What's your point?"

"It doesn't mean it isn't heavy."

"Family isn't heavy."

"That just isn't true. How long has it been since you've done anything for yourself?"

"A life spent serving your own self is an empty life. Surely you must feel that."

"I don't. What I feel is that life can be brutal and short. And if you can obtain pleasure, then you ought to."

"Is that what I was? Your response to the short brutality of life?"

"Yes. But I was the same for you."

Her cheeks went pink. "I didn't want to die a virgin. Who does?"

"Nuns, I would think. If you don't die a virgin, you kind of lost the game."

"Very funny. I'm not a nun, anyway. And I wanted a little something nice. But that was different."

"Different for you than for me?"

"A little bit," she said. "I wanted something I hadn't experienced before. You just wanted a little bit more."

"What if I told you that it was different?"

"I am off to see to some business," Adonis said. "Miriam will look after you."

Which was how she found herself being whisked through gleaming halls with the other woman just in front of her.

"I can't wait for you to see your room," she said cheerfully. "It's stunning. Adonis had it outfitted in a way he thought you would like."

How would Adonis even know what she would like?

It didn't make any sense to her. Miriam opened gilded double doors, to reveal a bedroom that was so airy, so light, so soft, she could scarcely breathe. It was all shades of blue. The colors of the sky.

Soft layered fabrics on the bed, around the bed, acting as a canopy.

Simply glorious. Everything was soft and indulgent, and nothing like the cabin. And yet, somehow, it was her. Entirely.

She didn't know how he had figured that out. Or maybe it was a lie. Maybe he hadn't been the one to decorate the room at all, but it was…wonderful.

"I will draw you a bath," Miriam said. "You must be tired after the journey. There will be a dinner tonight in your honor."

"Oh," she said.

"And I know your family is due to arrive tomorrow."

"Are they? That's the first I've heard about it."

"Yes. Everything is being prepared for them. Your sisters will all have their own rooms."

She felt…stunned by that. And whatever the reasoning behind her agreeing to this, she knew resolutely that she had made the right choice. Because all of her sisters would be getting something so wonderful out of it. And her dad would be getting peace of mind.

"Your father will have medical staff on hand to see to his needs. And he will have a room with everything he could possibly want."

"I'm... I'm still quite stunned about all this."

"I think it's wonderful," said Miriam. "That the Prince has chosen to marry someone who's more like... More like all of us. Someone who knows what it means to work and to struggle."

She nodded. "I do. And when I am princess, I promise you, I won't forget about it. I promise that I will advocate for all of you."

"We're lucky. We have good leaders. But... How can royalty ever really know what it's like for normal people?"

She shook her head. "They can't."

And she made a vow then and there that she would never forget what it was to be a normal person. Even amid all the silk, and all the finery.

The bath that was drawn for her was amazing. The water was scented, the tub itself sunken into the floor, and placed next to a window, which offered incredible views of the sea. She loved Montana. But of course... It wasn't by the ocean. And this was extraordinary.

When she got out of the bath, there was a beautiful dress laid out on the bed waiting for her. And once she had put it on, she was... She was ambushed by a team of people who did her hair and makeup.

When she was done, she didn't recognize the stranger in the mirror. Her eyes looked brighter, her skin perfection. Her hair was tamed in a way she was certainly never able to manage on her own.

And when she was ushered into the dining room, she didn't know what she expected, but it hadn't been...him.

Resplendent in a suit, the table set just for the two of them.

"I thought that it was meant to be a welcome dinner," she said.

"It is," he said. "But I felt as if it wouldn't be fair to spring my father on you just yet. Or indeed, a significant crowd."

She was quite tired. Though she felt like she was in a dream, which made it difficult to really say how she felt.

"I hope that the menu is to your liking," he said.

And as if on command, the doors opened. Servers came in with trays heavily laden with plates. And the food that was set before them was a culinary adventure like she had never seen before. Yet again, she felt…a sense of deep happiness. Excitement over this life that she found herself thrust into. She hadn't expected this. And on the heels of that excitement came guilt yet again.

Because she had fancied herself more stalwart than this. She had not imagined that she would be a person who would be so easily impressed by the soft and finer things in life. And yet here she was, simpering over soft fabrics and lovely food.

And just for a moment she decided to let herself enjoy it. Because she was here. Because the decision was already made. Because he was glorious, and because the meal looked good.

And why should she fight it? Why should she fight it when she had already decided?

"You look like you're waging a war inside your head," he said.

"I'm not continuing to," she said. "I promise. I might even relax and enjoy this."

"Have you ever relaxed and enjoyed anything?"

"Not as a matter of course."

He chuckled. "Oh, Stevie."

"Hard work is the most valued thing in my family. It's the

thing that keeps us all going. My dad built his cargo transport business from the ground up. My mom… She raised animals for food at the homestead, she planted a garden, she made bread, she was… She was everything. Everything to everybody."

"And somehow you ended up doing both her job and his job."

"Well, I let the farm animals go. Frankly, that wasn't my calling."

"Yes," he said.

"But yes. I did. I did end up doing all of that."

"And so perhaps you should not be filled with so much consternation over a change in fortune."

"I don't trust it," she said. "Respectfully."

"I guess you have no reason to trust me. Though, as you pointed out, I was your first lover."

She looked up at him, trying to keep from blushing. "Yes. Though, you shouldn't be quite so full of yourself about that. It's really because I never had the opportunity before."

"You do know how to make a man feel special."

"Well, why does it need to be special for you? I'm certain that you deflowered half a dozen virgins in the last week alone."

"There has been no one since you, Stevie. And no virgins ever. I'm a rake. We don't go after virgins. It's kind of antithetical to the whole rake code."

"I didn't realize that a rake had a code," she said.

"I do," he said. "And it's one I take quite seriously. Because… You know who my mother is?"

She scrunched up her face, and tried to remember what she had read about Adonis's mother. "She's an actress, isn't she?"

"You really are charmingly unconcerned with popular culture."

"You really are quite full of yourself that you define yourself as popular culture."

He laughed. "Perhaps not me, but definitely my mother. She's Lana Andrews."

"Oh," she said. "She was quite famous in the nineties."

"She would throw herself at a window if she heard you say that. I would like to be there to watch."

"Well, it's true. I mean she was on posters and the like."

"Yes. After she left my father. She was somewhat famous beforehand, but of course becoming a princess raised her cachet. She gave birth to me, and she decided that sitting around in Olympus was not what brought her joy. So she decided to return to Hollywood. And my father said she could not be the Queen and an actress."

"Like you don't want me to be a princess and a pilot."

"No," he said. "I can't say I especially do."

"But your mother wasn't happy. Losing her identity, I mean."

"Her identity?"

"She was an actress. And perhaps she thought she could give it up, but maybe she couldn't."

"You are giving an awful lot of credit to a woman who typically plays the part of villain in my backstory," he said.

"I mean I can understand why. A mother who leaves her child is difficult for anyone to root for. But… I know what it's like to love something. A job. To have it be part of you." She looked at him. "You don't know what that's like, do you?"

He frowned. "I perhaps know what that's like more than anyone. I am going to be king of Olympus one day. My job is born into my blood. There is no argument to be made or had about it. It simply is. I simply am."

"Well, don't you suppose that can be true for an actress, or a pilot?"

"Perhaps. But then, she made a choice. You made a choice to become my wife."

"True."

"You would never abandon our children."

"Of course not," she said. Then she looked down. "Though I hope that if I am extraordinarily miserable with the work that I'm doing here you will help me figure out a way to be less miserable rather than being rigid."

"It just wasn't befitting of a queen that she continue working in Hollywood."

"Who decides those things? It seems to me that we often make our own snares."

She was familiar with that. She had, after all, stepped into this one willingly.

But if his father wanted his mother quite so badly, then why hadn't he been able to find a compromise?

Of course, if she had wanted to marry the King, and have his child, why hadn't she figured out some compromise work-around?

It seemed to her like they had both willingly taken the most damaging option and gone at it.

She wasn't an expert in that kind of thing, but she had a mother who hadn't chosen to leave, and a father who would've done anything to keep her with him.

"My father would have given my mother the moon if it would've kept her with him," she said, not entirely meaning to say it out loud.

"But my father is not just a man. He is a king."

"What does he think about you? And the way that you live."

"He despises it. But it is not so simple for him to remove me from my position. There is no spare."

"So he can make compromises."

"I quite like your honesty, Stevie," he said. "Your forthrightness was one of the things I enjoyed about you when we were stuck in the mountains. But if you say things like that when you meet my father, you may find yourself at odds."

"And will he tell you that you can't marry me?"

"I cannot be told."

"Ah. I see."

He scowled. And she couldn't help but be amused by how boyish he looked then.

She took a bite of the steak in front of her, and nearly melted beneath the table. It was so glorious.

"This is wonderful."

This was so strange. It wasn't like a plane crashed into a remote mountainside was her domain, but it was certainly more hers than his.

He had always been a man in possession of power, it was unquestionable. She had seen it from the first. But here, in this vast place where she felt small, not in the way the wilderness made her feel small, he seemed to expand.

There was nothing here he wasn't in command of. Different, she thought, than when they had been at the mercy of the elements.

He was at the mercy of nothing.

She didn't know why but it made her feel sad. Because it was as if he was an entirely different man from the one that she had first kissed. From the one that she had made love to. But this was the man that she had agreed to marry, in this place that was so wholly foreign to her, foreign in a way that had nothing to do with language or food or location.

She felt disoriented for a moment. It was impossible to figure out exactly how she had gotten here.

How she was on the verge of becoming a wife, which was big and difficult to try and wrap her head around all on its own. But it was more than that. It was being a wife. Being a princess. Princesses might as well have been unicorns to her growing up in Montana. The stuff of myth and legend, and entirely not real.

She swallowed hard. "When is that… When exactly are we…"

"Next month. We will announce the engagement shortly, and we will keep it brief. It's for the best. I was prepared to marry Drusilla after all, only two weeks ago, and it is time for me to fulfill that obligation. My father will not live much longer."

She felt like she had been punched. "Oh. I'm sorry. I didn't… I didn't realize."

"I didn't tell you. Why should you realize?"

"I am very sorry. I didn't realize he was not well."

"He has been. For some time. It doesn't matter how much money you have sometimes. If disease is going to ravage you, then it will."

"I suppose," she said. "Although, I only know it from the other side. Where medical bills make living hard for everyone else too. But I guess in the end… It's all the same."

"I suppose in the end we are all the same," he said. "That's a bleak thought."

She shrugged. "Is it bleak? Or is it just one of those immutable truths? The kind that actually makes people feel a little bit closer, rather than like we are completely different species. I would rather know that we're made of the same stuff. Flesh and blood and bone."

"And I would rather be immortal. But… I had to face the fact that I was not, only recently."

"Yeah. I felt that one too."

For a moment, they smiled at each other, and it felt familiar. She wanted to call him Clem.

Yeah. She had spent a few days in the snow with a prince. And they had felt the same.

And now she was in his palace, and she really didn't. She was sorry, though, about his father.

"So we're both losing our dads, then."

He nodded. "Another thing that serves as a reminder that we perhaps have more in common than we don't."

"Well, I wish we didn't have that in common."

"Tomorrow," he said, his body language signaling an abrupt change of subject, "you will begin etiquette lessons."

"Is my family arriving?"

He shrugged. "Yes. But you lived with them until only recently, it isn't as though you have been long separated. And believe me, they will settle in just fine. In fact, your sisters will probably stay holed up in their rooms for weeks. What they have prepared for them is incredible."

She frowned. "Don't speak like you know my sisters."

"They are about to become mine," he said.

"Is that how you will see them? As your family?"

"Whether or not you believe it, I did choose you for a reason. And it wasn't just PR."

"But it is a lot PR. Because you like the way that we will look to your citizens."

"Yes. I do. But I also think you're going to add something of value to me. As you said, people, humans, we are all the same. But we have very different experiences that often make us feel as if we don't. As if we aren't. I am hoping that you will help me with my blind spots."

That made her feel…better. She wondered if he knew that it would.

Because that made her feel as if she had earned the position. It was the work she had done before that made her valuable now. The life that she had lived was what made her valuable.

"Well. I hope I can do that."

"You must be exhausted," he said abruptly.

"I am."

"Why don't you go to sleep. I will have some cake and tea sent to your room, if you would like something sweet before you turn in."

She wasn't sure if he was being kind, or if he was dismissing her directly. She decided it didn't matter.

"Thank you."

And when she lay down in that bed, and actually went to sleep, she didn't feel any more like she was dreaming than she had been when she was awake.

CHAPTER TEN

THE NEXT DAY, Adonis was up in a fury of determination. There was something about Stevie that tested him in ways he could not allow. He had things to accomplish. All of that was bearing down on him as he grappled with the reality of his father's health. He wasn't afraid of responsibility. He wasn't afraid of much of anything, but the enormity of it was not lost on him.

And the need to be invulnerable.

One thing he knew for certain, that while his father had been a good king, and would be until the very last day he lived on earth, he had been affected by the loss of Adonis's mother. And Adonis would not allow himself to be similarly affected. His father was a hard man, one that was difficult for people to connect with. Adonis wanted to give the people warmth. Adonis wanted to fill in the gaps that had been left behind by his father's rather austere ruling.

It was an art form, one that he had been perfecting these many years. Because while somebody might look at him and see nothing but mindless indulgence, what he saw was a facade that was not easily cracked. Whatever he felt, he could always look like he was at ease. Whatever he wanted, he could always look as if he was wanting more of it.

His father was conscious of honor, of appeasing the more conservative members of the country, and Adonis acknowledged that had to happen, but, then he also knew that the country was in bad need of some levity. Of plans for the future that felt bright.

A feeling he understood. His father was every inch a Royal. In that untouchable, implacable way.

Stevie would be the people's princess. There would be no doubt.

She would appeal to them in a way that the royal family simply didn't. She would seem like someone who understood, and indeed she would.

But that meant controlling his response to her. Especially because…he trusted nothing. And why would he? He could not allow any feelings that he had for Stevie to have dominion over him.

And so he vowed to himself then and there that he would not touch her until after they were married. A chance for him to practice a bit of restraint. Because he was going to have to find that middle ground. And he was determined to do it.

Both for his own sense of control, and for her…

For her. She'd asked and he wanted to give her what she wanted, even when it wasn't what he wanted.

Though, it might be what he needed.

Her family arrived early, and Stevie was already in classes, so Adonis made sure to greet them.

The sisters came tumbling in, bright and wide-eyed, small excitable versions of their older sister. And he wondered if that was who she might have been had she not had to take on so much responsibility at such a young age.

The girls went excitedly off to their various rooms, led by their different attendants. But Stevie's father stayed behind. Adonis had yet to meet him, and the older man was walking with assistance from a cane, much like Adonis.

He stuck his hand out, his intent to aggressively shake Adonis's hand apparent. Adonis responded in kind.

"Nice to meet you," he said. "I'm Roger."

"Adonis," he responded.

"I know that you're a prince," he said. "Soon to become a king. But you know, Stevie is one of the things I love very most in this world. All those girls, they're treasures. If you do anything to hurt them, I will come back and haunt you. And if there is still breath in me, I swear, I'll exhaust the last of it taking you down a peg."

Adonis couldn't help but feel an immense amount of respect for this man, who was weak and ill, and societally lower than Adonis in every way, and yet not above being a protective father when the moment warranted it.

"I will take care of them," he said. "Stevie told me that she did this in part because you encouraged her to. And I will not dishonor that gesture. I swear to you, I will care for all your daughters as if they were my own family for all their lives. They will never want for anything."

"I believe you," he said. "And I'm a pretty good judge of character. So I'd like it if you didn't disappoint me."

"I'll do my very best."

At lunchtime, there was a large spread put out for Stevie's family, and Stevie joined them, looking as bright-eyed with excitement as her sisters had. And he understood then, that no matter that caring for them was a very real burden, Stevie loved them with everything she was.

She really was doing this for them.

There was something about that recognition that made his heart twist slightly, that made him feel a slight sliver of guilt. She had accused him of taking advantage of her desperation. In some ways, he supposed that he had.

In that moment, he wondered if he was just a little bit more like his mother than he had ever thought he might be. Because he had always thought that she had taken advantage of his father. Yes, he was a king, but he had been lonely. He had not wanted one of those dynastic marriages where the couple did not know one another. Once upon a time, his father had been warm. Once upon a time, he had been a different man, a different king altogether. And her ambition had destroyed that.

Had he done the same to Stevie? Had his own aims blinded him to the fact that he was using her abominably? He certainly wanted to give back more than he was taking. Or at least equal of it.

She didn't want love. That was the thing.

But she did want to fly, and he had been quite hard-line about that. He supposed he was going to have to think of it differently. Because that conversation had made her sympathize with his mother, and now that he thought about it, it made him sympathize with her too.

After they were done eating, everybody piled out of the room, and he grabbed hold of Stevie before she could leave, the two of them by themselves in the dining room.

"What?" she asked.

"Why are you cross with me now?"

"I'm not," she said. "It's just… They're very happy. And I'm happy. But it definitely underscores the enormity of all of this."

"Yes. Well. There is quite a bit of enormity to the situation."

She rolled her eyes. "I wasn't speaking of that, and I think you know it."

"I know nothing of the kind." He tried to force a smile. It wasn't usually this difficult. "If you wish to leave, you know you can."

She looked shocked. "Is this some kind of a joke? After my family has come you're offering me the chance to leave?"

"It's only that I now appreciate what you said to me before. But I am manipulating a vulnerability that you have."

"Well. You are. But that doesn't mean that there aren't enough good things that go with it for me to weigh out that decision and decide to take the manipulation. I'm strong, Adonis. If I didn't want to be here, I wouldn't be."

"That I do believe."

"So I'm just going to have to get used to it. And stop sulking."

"Were you sulking?"

She lifted a shoulder. "A little bit."

He found that he wanted to dig in deeper. Who she was. What made her, her. And it was that impulse that made him pull away.

"Tomorrow," he said. "We will be getting into the ballroom etiquette portion of your training. I will be participating in that."

"Ballroom?"

"Dancing," he said, grinning.

"Dancing… I didn't agree to any dancing."

"We did once," he said, thinking of when they'd been just Clem and Stevie, out under the stars.

"I suppose we did," she said, looking away.

"I said that you could back out now," he said. "If you're afraid."

She looked back at him again, the challenge making sparks shoot from her eyes. "I'm not afraid of anything."

The next day, she showed up at the dancing lessons in a glorious, golden ball gown. And he smiled to himself as she entered the room.

She was only here because she was challenging him, he knew that. He respected that.

Stevie was nothing if not… Well, everything she had been when he had first met her. Putting her in a palace, promising her a title, none of it had changed her. She was resolutely stubborn and strong. And he was thankful for that. Because if not for her tenacity, he would've bled to death on the side of a mountain.

"You look every inch a princess," he said.

She looked around the room. "There's no instructor?"

"No. I've no need of a teacher to show you how to dance. I personally have taken dancing lessons since I was a child."

"I thought that you were untamable as a child."

He smiled. "Yes. Quite. But I never minded a dancing lesson. Typically, it involved being in a woman's arms. I quite took a liking to it, especially around the age of fourteen."

"Shameless."

"Yes."

"Why?"

"Why what? Why be shameless? I think the greater question is why do people choose shame?"

"No. That's not what I mean. I mean… Your mother, she created a big scandal when she left your father. Yes, I googled all that. And she hurt you. I know she did. So why are you…"

He gritted his teeth. "Why am I like her?"

"You're not," she said. "I know you're not because you care so much about the future of your country. But on the outside, to other people, you look like you might be. I guess what I don't get is why it didn't make you like your father."

"Because I still wanted her attention. Isn't that a terrible thing, Stevie?"

He felt scraped raw to say it, but he couldn't hold back with her. She'd nearly watched him bleed out in a wrecked plane. Why not tell her about the things that made him bleed inside?

Stevie frowned. "I don't know that it's a terrible thing. I think it's quite a relatable thing."

"By keeping myself in the headlines, I made it so that my mother couldn't ignore me. Also, I made myself more famous than she is. I know that bothers her. And I'm also quite certain it's why my father never really reined me in. I did what he couldn't. I made sure she couldn't run away from this reality. From what she had left behind. I made sure that we followed her."

"Were you... Were you aware of that when you were a teenager causing all these...dramas?"

"Oh, yes. Because every time I did something I knew there would be a headline, I imagine her face when she read it. And I imagined my headline being bigger than hers."

"I understand that. I've never much had occasion to be petty or vindictive, but I feel that I would be."

"Yes," he said, regarding her closely. "I have a feeling you are not one who would take a slight lying down. Though, I have a feeling you would not consider it petty or vindictive. You would consider it justice."

"Well. I guess so."

"Now. Enough talking. Let's dance."

He extended his hand, and Stevie took hold of it, and he pulled her up against him. He had left the cane leaning up against the wall, and he was counting on his body to hold itself together so that he could lead his future bride across the dance floor.

"You are...much steadier than when last we tried this."

"I ought to be. I've had time."

Time to heal. Was that what this had been? What a strange thing to call this period of time where everything had shifted, where he had gone to Montana to chase Stevie down, brought her back, convinced her to marry him.

And now she was in his arms, soft and in a gown, rather than in her snow gear.

She looked up at him, and he felt something in his chest catch fire. And rather than indulging it, he reached into his pocket and began to play music over the system in the room, and swept her into a waltz.

His leg hurt, and he did his best to ignore it. He wanted nothing more than to remain in control. He needed nothing more than to remain in control.

And so he would.

Every step was a testament to that. Every beat of the music that he hit with precision.

Stevie followed his lead naturally, and he didn't think about how extraordinarily she fit into his arms.

It was for the country. It wasn't for him. And it certainly had nothing to do with the pounding desire that was beginning to heat his blood, as he allowed her softness to sink right into him.

When the song finished, they stood there, breathing hard, and Stevie's eyes went glassy. She stretched up on her toes, and he knew that she was going to kiss him. He took a step away.

"We must focus on what matters," he said. "You have to complete your princess training. We don't want to cloud your mind with sex."

Stevie looked as if he had struck her.

"You don't… Cloud my… How dare you? How dare you suggest that… I was the one who… And why are you acting like I'm the only one that's attracted here? You feel it too."

"I never said I didn't. But the simple truth is, we must remain focused in this moment. I cannot allow for there to be a distraction, and neither can you. It wouldn't be beneficial to either of us to introduce emotion into it either."

"Do you feel emotion with sex? Because it doesn't seem like you do. If you did, you would be affected by the first time we were together, but you aren't, are you? What you are is just... You're just a man. And I ticked all these boxes for you, and you like having sex with me well enough. And are you even actually going to offer me fidelity? Or was that just to placate me?"

"Marriage is long," he said. "You don't even know what you'll want in ten years."

"Yes I do. Because I know who I am. And I know what matters to me. What's special to me, and what isn't. You don't get to... You don't get to make all the decrees. And you definitely don't get to act like I'm somehow the one that's more invested here than you are. That isn't fair. And I don't deserve that."

"You're the one making a very small thing into a very big thing. I am simply suggesting that your focus must lie elsewhere."

"Great. Well, how about this, you don't just get to demand sex when you want it, then. Because I'm not here for the sole purpose of being ordered around by you. You might be the Prince, but I'll be the Princess. I refuse to be treated like I'm small, or gauche, or inexperienced or less. Because I'm common. Because I was a virgin. If you wanted that, then you should have married somebody different. Someone who didn't know their own mind. And somebody who doesn't possess the capacity to be vengeful and petty. You identified that yourself. Why you decided to put yourself in the situation is beyond me."

His body felt like it had been brushed with fire.

He felt scalded. Because she had so thoroughly undone

the nonsense that he had spoken. Of course he wanted her. That was the problem.

But as much as he had chosen Stevie, and as much as it was for her personality, she was not going to run roughshod over him. And she was not going to make the decisions, or the proclamations now.

"Perhaps we should take a break, Stevie," he said.

"Perhaps," she said.

She pulled away from him, and stormed from the room. And he knew without a shadow of a doubt that he had made a mistake. He just wasn't entirely certain if it was a mistake his father would've made, or one his mother would've made. He also didn't know if, mistake though it was in her eyes, it was still for the best.

Because he had to be a king. And that meant he had to be stronger than simply a man.

But the tough part would be deciding which form that strength had to take.

CHAPTER ELEVEN

STEVIE DIDN'T KNOW why she had reacted so strongly to that. She wished that it hadn't hurt her. She wished that she didn't care. What she was doing was for her own benefit. The benefit of her family. She shouldn't be emotional about it.

But…she was signing up to marry this man. To be with him. Forever. And that just felt… It all felt like too much. It felt like too much, and it felt terrible. And she was at the end of her tether over it. She marched out of the ballroom, and stopped. She looked down a long corridor, and saw movement on the other side of a glass door that led out to a terrace that overlooked the ocean.

She walked toward it, unable to stop herself from being curious. She opened the doors, and saw her sisters. They were sitting on the floor of the terrace laughing, the breeze tangling in their hair.

There was a platter of cheese and fruit out in front of them, and they were laughing and chatting with each other. More carefree than she had ever seen them.

"Do you like your rooms?" she asked.

Opal looked up at her. "Yes," she said, looking rapturous. "Like a dream, Stevie."

"It really is," said Topaz.

She had never seen her sisters looking quite… Quite like

that. But it was Daisy whose expression she wanted most to see. Her more skeptical, practical sister.

She looked up at Stevie.

"This is wonderful," she said. "But I feel like… Let's talk for a second," said Daisy.

She took Stevie's arm and led her inside. "I don't want to say anything in front of them. I don't want to embarrass you. You're agreeing to marry him. And that's not a business deal. I feel like everybody else is acting like you took a different job. They're young. They don't really get it. But… Stevie, I read all of the articles about it. And the way that they say something happened between the two of you. If you tell me that it's not true. That it was made up…"

"It's true," said Stevie. She blushed heavily. She couldn't help herself. Admitting that she was quite that human was… embarrassing. How could it not be because what had happened between herself and Adonis didn't have anything to do with emotion. It had nothing to do with something soft or romantic that she might be able to dress it up in. She had thought he was attractive. And she had been afraid they were going to die. It had been base and life-affirming. It had been sexual. And saying as much to her younger sister felt…wrong.

"You love him?" Daisy asked.

Stevie winced. "Daisy, I barely know him. I… I would never recommend that you do what I did. It was… It was a morally questionable decision. I played it very dangerous with my… My health and my future. But we were trapped, and we didn't know we were going to survive and…"

Daisy put her hand on Stevie's arm. "Stevie. I'm not a child. I can see the man. I understand why it happened. You don't have to pretend that he isn't attractive, or that you didn't do what any of us would be tempted to do."

Stevie scowled. "Well. Well… You're happy here?"

"Yes," said Daisy. "Who wouldn't be? But I'm not the one that has to marry a virtual stranger in exchange for all of this. So please don't let us color your decision-making."

Stevie closed her eyes. "But that isn't realistic, Daisy. Of course it's going to color my decision-making. You're my responsibility."

"We aren't your responsibility. We are your sisters. We love you."

"I don't mean it like that. But I love you. You matter to me more than I can say. And… The truth is…"

She didn't know what to say. Because the truth was more complicated than she wanted it to be. Because the truth was going to seem unfair. Because she was actually too afraid to dig for the deepest truth of all.

"Don't worry about me. That's the truth. Because I made my decision. And it was as much for me as it was for you. And yes, it's a little bit more complicated than I wanted to admit. But that's my decision."

"Well, I can accept that. I can accept… If this is for you."

She felt raw and wounded. She didn't feel like it was for her. She felt like her sisters were enjoying their beautiful new life in a palace by the sea, and who could ever ask them to go back to a small house on a frozen mountaintop?

But if she was honest. If she was very, very honest, she also didn't think that she could ask herself to go back to a life before he was in it.

A life where he wasn't essential. Where he wasn't part of it or her.

Because this was the problem. She had spent her life being a certain kind of sheltered. And that night on the mountaintop, she had learned something about herself she hadn't known before.

That she was sexual. That she…had desires and needs and she had been neglecting them. That she wasn't just a vessel; she was more than that.

More than just self-sacrifice. It was easy right now to tell herself that what she was doing was for everybody else. But Daisy had given her an out. And sure, she would've felt guilty about it. But her sisters did love her.

And she…liked being warm.

She liked the soft bed. She liked having someone to draw her a bath. And she liked seeing Adonis's beautiful, infuriating face every day.

She couldn't say that she had feelings for him. Well, perhaps she could. But it was a stretch, she thought, to say that.

But it was also a stretch to say that she felt nothing for him. Or that it was only sex.

Yes. That felt like a stretch too.

And she felt like she was stretching. Every which way.

But if she didn't feel something, she wouldn't have been so upset, so offended by what he had said earlier.

By the way he had made her feel when he had rejected her kiss.

Because she had been caught up in the moment. In a romance that apparently hadn't existed.

She had been caught up in feelings that didn't… Didn't really exist.

She had felt silly and small.

And really, poorly. Very poorly.

Because he had been her first kiss, her first lover, and when he hadn't gotten in touch with her again afterward he had felt like her first rejection. But this really was a rejection. He hadn't been caught up in his feelings. He hadn't been unable to resist.

Tears stung her eyes. But she chose not to let them fall. She had a lot of practice with that.

"Don't worry about me, Daisy. Really. I made my choice. I'm going to be Adonis's wife. And I'm… Happy about that."

Adonis was pacing and scowling. *I'm going to be Adonis's wife, and I'm very happy about that.*

He didn't want to hear her say that. With that sadness in her voice.

But he had overheard all of it. Her telling her sister that something had happened between them. He could also tell that she was upset. And that she was putting on a brave face for her sister.

He had upset her. He had done badly, and she…

In spite of himself, he wondered. He wondered why she was staying.

And this was exactly why he should stay away from her.

Because he couldn't afford to be distracted by her. It was madness. A madness he didn't need.

And yet he was consumed by it. Filled with it.

Was this how it began? The slow stripping away of your power?

He refused to call it love. He didn't believe sexual obsession was anything like love, and yet people liked calling it that to make themselves feel better. He had engaged in any number of physical-only affairs. And no one had ever gotten their hooks into him quite like this. It was because she was different. It had to be because she had saved his life. Perhaps because she had been a virgin.

It was easy to develop this strange savior complex. Where he believed he had introduced her to the desires of her body. In this feeling of protectiveness, because she was precious in some ways. Coming from a life that he couldn't even imagine. And she had been brought into his, which made him feel like he owed her his life the way that she had saved his.

And suddenly, all became clear to him. He reasoned that while he wanted to ensure that he maintained control over his emotions, the way that he was handling things now did not demonstrate control.

If he could not manage to treat her as his princess, then what was the point of control at all?

It was not real control, it was simply avoidance. And if there was one thing that Adonis had never done, it was avoid something. Not conflict, not pleasure, not hardship. He was a man who faced all things head-on. Including plane crashes. And most definitely including his fiancée and her feelings.

That was how he found himself following the same path she had just taken to her room. He did not knock. It was his palace, after all.

Stevie was standing at the window, and she turned abruptly, her breath sharp as she did so.

"Stevie, what can I give you?" he said.

Stevie only stared at him in silence, and then screwed up her face, staring hard at him.

"What?" he asked.

"Is this your way of apologizing to me?"

"What... What gives you that impression?"

He was utterly taken aback.

"Why do you want to know what you can do for me if you don't feel sorry for what you did earlier?"

He scowled. "If I had wanted to apologize to you I simply would have."

"I don't think so. I think you feel bad."

He gritted his teeth. Because of course he did. It was why he had come.

"Do you want a gift, or not?"

She wrinkled her nose. "I would like a gift. Who wouldn't?"

"Then tell me what you desire."

"A tiger."

"I will find one."

She rolled her eyes. "I'm kidding. I don't want a tiger. But you don't know me."

"Then allow me the opportunity to know you. By telling me what you want, instead of lying like a little weasel."

"Why would a weasel ask for a tiger, Adonis? That doesn't make any sense. It would be eaten."

"I know you're just being deliberately difficult."

"Maybe. But I've been known to be. I've spent the last six years playing the part of mother to six sisters. You learn to be a little bit difficult as a matter of necessity."

"I'm quite certain you do."

"I'm not easily manipulated. So if this is an effort to do that—"

"It isn't," he said. "You're right. I am... Sorry." The word felt unfamiliar in his mouth.

"Oh. That sounded like it was difficult."

"Nothing is difficult for me."

"Of course not," she said. "Nothing."

"I am trying to get to know you. Why can't you take it as a gesture of goodwill?"

"I don't know, something about you makes me think that you're prone to weaponizing your knowledge."

"That's unflattering."

"I don't know that I trust you."

"Why not?"

"Why... Why didn't you tell me? Who you were. Why didn't you tell me who you were when we were up there together? You let me believe that it was somebody else's wedding. And you didn't tell me who you were at all. Why?"

"Because," he said. And he could feel the truth of it rising up in the back of his throat, making the back of his jaw ache. He didn't want to say it. And yet, he had already begun. He was trying to give her something, so he might as well give her the truth. He wasn't…ashamed of it necessarily, but he had also never spoken it aloud to anyone before. "Because there were unintended consequences for the way that I chose to handle my mother. She wasn't the only one who witnessed my behavior and formed an opinion. No. The whole world did. And with you, this woman who had no idea who I was, and what I thought might be the last days of my life, I wanted to be the person that I was there. No baggage, no presuppositions, no titles."

He didn't know whether or not he was shocked or gratified to see her expression soften. Perhaps both.

"I understand. My name doesn't carry any… Any weight at all. So it didn't cost me anything to tell you who I was. But you didn't know everything about me. You didn't know that I have never slept with anybody. You had never seen me in my little house. You didn't… You let me be me. In a way that I hadn't been for a very long time, so I guess… That's another way we're more alike than different. We keep finding strange ways."

"Yes," he said, the word coming out rougher than he intended them to.

"I don't know what kind of present to ask for. You're a prince and the kinds of things that you might be offering me are beyond my scope."

"What do you like?"

"I like…so many things. I like to knit. I like to garden. I like books."

"Books," he said. "I can give you books. There's a library in the palace. And it is always stocked with new books."

"Really? Not just…musty classics? Which don't get me wrong, I like, but I like a little bit of popular fiction."

"Yes. We have a book buyer for the palace."

"That's…amazing."

"Yes. And you can go use the library. Anytime you wish. You could sit in there all day. Until you have official duties, there's nothing else for you to do. You could be a lady of leisure."

"I don't even know how I would begin being one of those," she said.

"By being leisurely."

"It sounds nice…"

He extended his hand. "Come with me."

She looked at him for a moment, her expression skeptical. But then, she took his hand. And he led her from the room and down the great hall.

They went up a curved flight of stairs that opened into a massive room. There were bookshelves from floor to ceiling, ladders all around that slid on rails so that you could reach the heights.

And he watched her expression transform to one of wonder.

He wished he could make her look like that all the time. He wished he gave her more…than he took.

Funny because he would have said he had. Because she was a peasant and he was…him.

His feelings on the matter had changed.

There were places to sit all over the grand room. A chaise lounge by the fireplace.

"Should you wish to use this room, and have amenities brought to you, all you have to do is ask."

"So if I wanted to… I could ask for a cheese platter and the blankets and some hot chocolate?"

"Yes. And then another. And another. Being a princess is not only about the work you can do, or about etiquette. It can be about this too."

He felt something in him soften. "This is not just for your sisters."

She nodded slowly. "Thank you."

"Of course."

Except there was no *of course*, because he hadn't made sure that she knew about this before.

But he was in control of himself now. He had recognized where he had failed her, and he wasn't going to do it again.

That was what mattered.

He had dominion over these rogue feelings for her. And if the library could make her happy while he continued to withhold the physical, then all the better.

He had fixed it. And now it was done.

CHAPTER TWELVE

SHE FELT A little bit guilty. But it was noon the next day after he had shown her the library, and she was in her pajamas lying on the chaise by the lit fire. She had a pillow, a blanket, and she'd had a basket of pastries and some coffee, and was now enjoying cheese and hot chocolate. She had read three books so far. She couldn't remember the last time she had been this relaxed.

And yes, she was still engaged to a man who had hurt her feelings yesterday. Yes, her father was still dying. And yes, her future was still uncertain.

But she felt like there was at least some happiness to be carved out here. Not just for the sake of her sisters, but for herself. This at least was a slice of happiness.

She snuggled deeper into the blanket, and heard footsteps on the stairwell. She thought it might be Miriam coming to check on her. But her heart gave a great jump when the figure came into view.

It was Adonis.

He was wearing a white cable-knit sweater, and a pair of dark jeans. He looked…incredibly sexy. And it made her ache.

Because the romance in the books was tame compared with what she had experienced with him. Except that was physical, wasn't it? Emotionally, he was proving to be elusive, slippery.

But she thought about what he had said yesterday. About how he had talked about his own identity, and the way the world owned a piece of it. How he had hidden his name from her because he wanted to be…himself.

And that made her wonder how much of himself he kept hidden.

Had she even truly gotten to see the depths of him? She suspected not. The whole world thought that he was a shallow playboy. But was that even the truth?

"Hi," she said.

"Hello."

It was so funny. Him greeting her like he wasn't a prince. Like they weren't getting married. Like he hadn't seen her naked. Like he hadn't taken her to heaven in a way no other man ever had, and then…

Here they were.

And whatever this was.

This pounding, painful feeling at the center of her chest. That was there too.

"I expect you had a good day?"

She nodded slowly.

She found she didn't want to recline when he was in there.

She rose up from the chaise lounge slowly, a little bit dizzy, because she had been lying down for so long.

"It's been a lovely afternoon. Thank you for suggesting this."

"I'm glad. I'm not a monster."

"I know. Though, I don't think you're entirely what you appear to be either."

"You think?"

"Yes."

He looked at her for a long moment, and the tension between them seemed to grow.

She looked away, because she refused to be humiliated again like she was yesterday.

She heard footsteps, and looked up, and then he was there. He put his finger beneath her chin, and tilted upward, forcing her eyes to meet his. "I owe you an apology," he said.

"You gave me one of those yesterday."

"So I did. And perhaps it is not an apology that I owe you."

And suddenly his lips were on hers. It was fierce and intense, and utterly unexpected. But it was also… Everything.

She couldn't have denied him even if she wanted to. And she found she didn't want to.

She wrapped her arms around his neck; how glorious to kiss him when he was standing up. When they weren't freezing cold. When she wasn't afraid of dying. When she wasn't afraid she would make him bleed to death.

All things that most people didn't usually have to worry about when they made love, she assumed.

Novice though she was.

He moved his hands up her back, and she sighed, his hold so large and strong it filled her with boundless need.

He held her close, deepening the kiss. She felt a yawning, relentless need widening up inside of her. Oh, how she wanted him.

She did.

Because he was everything.

And she wrapped her arms around his neck, no longer afraid that he was going to pull away. His hold was strong. And she rejoiced in the vitality.

Also in the fact that she still wanted him. That it hadn't simply been about survival, or this strange, driving need to affirm life. She had wanted him.

They never would've met. They never would have met if

he hadn't been in that airport. And nothing ever would've happened between them if they hadn't crashed the plane. That day had changed the course of her life irrevocably. And the idea that she might never have met him suddenly filled her with a sense of panic. It was such an odd thing. Because this whole time she hadn't even been certain if she wanted this. But she couldn't imagine living without it or him either.

She simply couldn't.

So she held him, and kissed him. Let the slick friction of his tongue against hers drive her to absolute madness.

She wanted to weep with it.

God in heaven, but she did.

He pushed her back against one of the bookshelves, and her hand went up, knocking against two of the books and sending them down to the floor. Collateral damage. What could be done? He pressed his palm against hers, lacing his fingers through her fingers, holding her hand fast against the spines of the books still in the shelves, kissing her hard and deep.

It was incredible. Wonderful.

Her heart was pounding so hard, and for a moment she knew just a little bit of fear. Because what if she was hurt even worse after this? What if the feelings that were chiming through her now only got more intense? She didn't want to love him.

She really didn't.

And yet her heart was about to burst, and her stomach was tight with need.

So much need.

His firm, rough hands began to strip her clothing away from her body. It was so different from the time they had been together in the plane. When they'd had to keep their bodies covered by sleeping bags. When he had been stuck lying on his back. He wasn't stuck now.

His movements were dominant, rough. And she exulted in them. She had spent years handling everything in her life. Trying to control everything. And she had surrendered some of that control the moment that she met him, she had agreed to marry him, and he had swept her off to this place, and none of it had been what she was used to. But this felt like the ultimate expression of it. The ultimate in practicing that surrender. If lying on the chaise all day and reading books had felt like a vacation, this felt like a new life.

A new self.

One where she wasn't carrying everything. One where he was carrying her.

She was wearing pajamas; they weren't even sexy. He didn't seem to care. He stripped her top off, her pants, her bra and her underwear. She was naked, pressed against the bookshelves, and he was fully clothed.

"I want to see you," she panted.

He met her gaze, those blue cold eyes, and yet they weren't cold. They were aflame.

He put his hand between her legs, testing her slickness. And she was slick. Slick and ready. He pressed a finger inside of her, his gaze never leaving hers. "You want to see me? I want to see you come. Come for me, Stevie." He smoothed his thumb over that sensitized bundle of nerves there at the center of her thighs, and she felt herself beginning to unravel. Felt herself surrender. He pushed another finger inside of her, and she shattered. He kissed her hard, swallowing her cries of pleasure, and then, only then did he move away from her, divesting himself of his clothes, and revealing his spectacular body to her. She had gotten a glimpse of it when they had been together the first time, but only a glimpse. His bare chest was magnificent, covered in just the right amount of hair. His chest was sculpted and defined, his abs glorious and chiseled. Then he moved his hands to his belt, took his pants off, and she could see the full extent of his glorious masculinity. He was hard for her, and she had a hard time believing anything that big had ever fit as neatly inside of her as he had done then. But it had to work. It had then. It had hurt at first, but then it had been glorious. And she trusted that it would be now too.

He moved to her, one hand palming her ass, as he moved his hand down to lift her thigh, opening her to him as he thrust deep within her.

She gasped. The bookshelf dug into her back, but he filled her incredibly well. And she found herself gripping his shoulders, her fingernails digging into his skin as she cried out his name.

He growled hers.

The mutual need drove them both. It was a glory unlike anything she had ever experienced. And she didn't know if she could handle experiencing it again. And again and again, and yet, she knew that she would. That she must. Because they were getting married. But it wasn't just physical. She felt it. Felt herself begin to fracture inside. Felt herself begin to crumble. All that resolved. All that she had told herself about not falling in love. Because she was supposedly too smart. Armed with the knowledge of what it could cost to love somebody that you might lose. But this was even worse. It was uncharted territory. Because she had never thought she might love someone who simply didn't love her. Who was there, but didn't feel the feelings. And yet. And yet.

He surged inside of her one last time, and she shattered again, clinging to him, shuttering as he captured her cries of need on her lips.

"Adonis," she whispered.

And then he went over. Pulsing inside of her, his body drawn tight like a bow as he spilled his seed within her.

And when the storm ended, he looked at her with the expression of a haunted man.

And then he gathered his clothes, and walked away from her. He dressed in silence, and she didn't know what to say. She didn't know how to react, or what to do. And when he left her there, it was worse than when they had been rescued in the snow. Worse than when she had found out he was supposed to marry somebody else.

It was worse than just about anything.

But this time, she decided she was going to follow him.

He cursed himself as a fool. Because he was not supposed to do that. He wasn't supposed to touch her. After all, he had made a vow. He was not going to let himself be controlled by his desire for her. No. That was for another man. That was foolishness for someone who didn't have control over themselves.

And he was not a fool.

At least, he would've said that he wasn't. He had played the part of one with her just now.

He was, perhaps, more his mother's son than he wanted to admit.

He had genuinely gone up to check on her, and he had been overwhelmed by his need. The need that he had been trying to suppress. The need he had been trying to hold back.

He had been at the end of his restraint.

So he had claimed her. With no thought.

This was the path to madness.

The door to his room opened, no knock.

"What are you doing?" he asked when he turned and saw Stevie standing there.

"You came into my room yesterday without knocking. I thought it was fair. Plus, you just…banged me against a bookcase. I don't think we need to stand on ceremony."

"This is my palace."

"If I'm going to be your wife, then it's going to be my palace too, and you can't act like this. You can't behave like an unpredictable child. I don't deserve this. I deserve some communication. I deserve something a little bit better, don't you think?"

"I can't speak to that."

"Well, then, I guess we shouldn't speak at all. And maybe we should forget this. Entirely."

"I've no intention of forgetting this."

"Then we need to talk. Why are you so… Why are you so bothered by this?"

"Because I refuse to have feelings for you that I cannot control. It would be disastrous. Not just for you, not just for me, but for the entire kingdom."

She didn't know what to do with that. This admission that he might be in danger of having feelings for her. It was such a… Such a very strange thing.

Though it was also a terrible thing to know he thought that feeling something for her was such a terrible, terrible fate.

As if caring for him would be better.

No. It wouldn't be. He was selfish and capricious and loving him would be an awful thing.

It could be devastating.

She didn't feel especially…special. She never had. But if he was afraid of developing feelings for her, did that mean that… That at least in her own way, she was? That she was something at the very least, something more than just a good pick to be his princess. Something more than just a woman that he felt some sexual attraction to—because he must.

She crossed the room and looked at him. "I don't want to get hurt. Not any more than you do."

His lips curved upward. Into sort of an incredulous smile. "I'm not worried about being hurt. What worries me is becoming a shell of myself. Becoming a leader who cannot lead in the way that he should. That is what concerns me. Because I know what is important. And I must keep my eyes on that."

The little bubble of hope that had just existed inside of her burst. As if it had never been there.

It wasn't really about her. It was a strange wariness. Something that had to do with his father. And his mother, because he had immediately connected her to his mother because of her desire to continue doing her job even as a princess. It had less to do with her specialness, and more to do with his lack of trust.

"I don't think that I have the power to make you a shell," she said. "There's no need to worry about that."

He reached out and grabbed hold of her wrist. "But I can't control myself when I'm around you."

She realized that coming from him, that was a compliment. Or at least, he thought it was.

"I can't... I can't keep my hands off of you. You were a virgin, Stevie, none of that makes sense."

"Wow. So you're insulting me on top of everything."

"My aim is not to insult you. My aim is to tell you that you have reached inside of me into a place no one ever has before. Do you realize, I have never actually had to contend with a woman after I've had sex with her?"

She gritted her teeth. "None of that is especially flattering."

"I don't know how to flatter you."

"That's a lie. You're a renowned playboy, surely you must know how to flatter a woman."

"But that's just it. You aren't like any other woman. Whether that makes sense or not, it is true. You are not like other women, and I don't know how to manage this thing that roars to life inside of me whenever you're near. And it has never been more important that I have control. Never. You were supposed to bring balance to my life, you were not supposed to upend it."

"Honestly," she said, feeling very flat. "I cannot deal with your issues while trying to… I have been uprooted from my home. From everything that I've ever known. You're the first man that I've ever slept with. And we can't even figure out how to work things out between us like we would if… If we were two normal people. What if we had been two normal people who had sex up there on the mountain? Wasn't that what you wanted? To just be normal."

"Of course it's what I wanted. But that doesn't mean that it's what I get. What I get is to be king. What you get, is to be the Princess. And that is what we have."

"And us?"

"We have to learn to fit us around our responsibilities. It is something my mother couldn't do. It is the thing…" He shook his head. "My father couldn't do it either. Regardless of his intentions, and I believe that they were good. He wanted to show our country that he was stable, but he lost an important piece of who he was."

"And you don't want to lose yourself."

"No," he said. "Because I have not even begun to find myself as a leader."

Seeing him look uncertain, even for a moment, was an out-of-body experience. She had seen him lying in a pool of his own blood, very nearly lost to the world, and it still hadn't been this.

And she realized that she wasn't going to be able to… reach him here. This way.

She was more interested in exploring the relationship between them than she was in royal etiquette. And he was going to insist that royal duty be the thing that drove them.

It wasn't really fair of her. He had asked her to be his princess, and by default that made her his wife, but that had not been the thing he was primarily interested in. That much was clear.

She let out a long sigh. "What does that mean for us, though?"

"We will be married. As we planned."

"I don't…" She realized right then, she had a choice. She could let him continue to flounder separate from her, she could continue trying to protect herself or she could dive right in.

It was terrifying. Because he wasn't offering her any reassurance that her emotion would be met with emotion. In fact, he was basically promising the opposite. But she didn't know if she was in love with him, or if she was just entranced by the heat between them. She didn't know anything but…that she wanted him. That she was unhappy when they were separate. Happier when they were together.

She loved to talk to him. To dance with him. To touch him. She loved being near him, even when it was fraught.

So she took a chance, and she closed the distance between them. She stretched up on her toes, and she kissed his mouth.

He went stiff for a moment, and then, he surrendered.

But it was her who found herself on the receiving end of demands next. He captured the back of her head, deepening the kiss. And she was dizzy with it. Completely consumed by her need for him.

"I can't give you any more than this," he growled.

"I didn't ask for anything more." That was the promise that she made herself, and her heart.

He was giving her all of this. And she wanted to feel physically close to him. She wasn't going to trick herself into believing that for him that meant love. And she wasn't going to let herself believe that it was anything quite so simple either.

But she was desperate to feel close.

And she was committing to taking him at face value. Because the truth was…she had been so lost in her own pain, and her desire to feel special, and she hadn't given any thought to his.

His mother's abandonment was clearly what drove him.

And it mattered to him. It mattered to him so much that he didn't repeat the same mistakes his father did, but also, she suspected, it mattered to him that he didn't care again only to be abandoned. So she poured commitment into that kiss. Everything she had, everything she was. And impossibly, she found herself aroused again. But it was different. This time, it wasn't just about sex, wasn't just about physical desire. It was about making a promise to him with her body.

They hadn't known each other long. And sometimes she thought they didn't know each other well, but she knew the essence of who he was. She knew the man he pretended to be, and she knew the one he was as he lay there injured. When he got to be Clem, and not a prince.

And very few other people knew that. She had met him simply as himself. Not with all of this pomp and circumstance. All the authority that he had been carrying then had simply come from within, not from a title bestowed upon him by men and a bloodline that stretched past generations.

She had seen him. In a way that likely few other people ever got to.

And this time, he picked her up and carried her to the bed, laying her down in the center of the soft mattress. This felt like a wedding night.

Her heart felt tender, sore. She looked up at him, and she knew.

She knew what she felt. She'd been trying to tell herself it wasn't love. She'd been trying to tell herself that it wasn't anything half so dramatic.

But it was. Because she was. She was utterly and completely undone by this, and by him. By the certainty that she knew him. They had nearly died together. And now they could choose to live together. But they were going to have to choose it. He was still afraid, she was too. She didn't know what that meant. As far as where they could get to, how far they could go, she didn't have a clue.

But she wanted to try. She didn't want to close herself off out of fear. It would be like…never flying again because of what happened. It would be like sitting down in a chair and fading away into nothing.

Her heart nearly broke. Because she loved her father more than anything, but she also knew that when it came right down to it, not chasing after this with Adonis was doing what her father had done, if only prematurely. And she never would. That was her vow.

She wanted to live. Right now, she felt like she wanted to live a life with Adonis. But she couldn't control him. She couldn't control what he did, she couldn't control what he felt. She didn't have that kind of power.

But she had strength. She had to trust that. Had to trust herself.

To be strong, even if she had to go through a heartbreak.

To try, even if there was no guarantee of success.

Maybe, all along, she didn't have to wait to be wanted enough, or for somebody to prove to her she was special. Maybe she simply needed to believe that she was.

She took her clothes off again, in as big of a hurry as she had been the first time. And he removed his. Having her body pressed to his as they lay in the bed was…luxury.

Being held by him was a luxury.

She had never known a man like him. She had never known anyone like him. His kisses consumed her, and she consumed him right back.

His hands traced magic over her skin, and she maneuvered herself so that she was on top of him. She kissed his neck, his chest, moved down and examined that full, glorious masculinity of his. Then she leaned in, tasting him, testing him with her mouth.

He groaned, his hand going to her hair. She felt strong, powerful, even in the subservient position. Because he wanted her, and that was her power. It was her strength.

She could keep him with her. Could keep him interested. As long as they had this.

She moved her tongue over him, relishing the salty, masculine flavor. Then she took him into her mouth, her whole body alight with need for him.

She moved over the top of him as he was coming to the end of his control, and captured his lips. He gripped her hips, and positioned her over his arousal. She impaled herself on him, no longer the shy, tentative virgin she had been the first time she had ridden astride him.

She rode him as the storm consumed them both. As his hold tightened on her, and release began to build at her core.

And then when they found it together, they cried out in unison, united at least in this. And she knew that she could never let him withdraw from their physical pleasure. Because even if she had trouble reaching him through conversation, through romance, she knew she could always find him here.

She lay over his chest, breathing hard. She loved him.

He was going to be her husband. And that mattered so much more than the fact that she was going to be princess.

Finally, Stevie felt like she had found herself in the middle of the storm. And she was very, very grateful to discover that it turned out she was strong, special and complete all on her own.

CHAPTER THIRTEEN

A COUPLE OF days after their torrential coming together in the library, and their following encounter in his room, it was time to announce their engagement to the world.

They were having an announcement at the palace, followed by a procession through the streets.

And all he could think about was how beautiful his future wife was.

He was distracted by her, in spite of his decision not to be.

And she was… She was glorious, as ever. She had been sharing her bed with him, and there had been no more talk of feelings.

He had been hollowed out since that day.

He supposed he should be grateful.

Stevie had been very apparently pretty since the first moment he had met her. But dressed like a princess, she was resplendent. A great beauty in much the way his mother was.

It was surprising. Because he had imagined she would bring a different image entirely.

And yet…

He pushed that aside. "Are you ready?" he asked as they stood in the antechamber of the palace, waiting to go outside and face the cameras.

She nodded. "I am. Especially because I don't really have to say anything."

"Just a couple of lines you were given."

"What if they don't like me? Are you going to throw me over for somebody else? Somebody who can give the people what they want?"

She wasn't being entirely serious, he could see that. But all the same, his stomach tightened with fierce protectiveness. "You are my choice."

It was that simple to him.

He saw a flash of pleasure on her cheeks, and he wished that he could make her look like that more often.

They were compatible in the bedroom. But he could feel difficulty between them when they weren't kissing. When they weren't naked.

Her sisters and her father were also dressed in their finery. They would be following them in the procession afterward.

Stevie had finally met his father last night. It had surprised him how warm his father had been, all things considered. He was often difficult. Stiff. Then he didn't know how he would react to Stevie, who was so utterly different from any other woman his father would've interacted with.

But thankfully, he had taken to her with ease, and would be joining them in the courtyard for the press conference.

His father joined them then, looking severe. As he always did.

He really noticed, though, how much older he was looking.

"Are you ready, Father?"

"Of course I am. These are my people."

Adonis nodded once.

Then they stepped out the doors and into the spotlight. His father stepped forward. "Greetings," he said. "I know you have all been waiting for this moment. As you know, my son, Prince Adonis, was meant to marry an American heiress. But fate intervened in an unlikely way on his way to the wedding. He very nearly lost his life, but he was saved. I know that all of the media reports have already suggested this, but his pilot, Stevie Parker, was his savior. And that act changed his very future."

It was Adonis's turn.

He took the lead position. "When it comes to the choice of who I am to marry, I know that it is of the utmost importance that I choose someone who is perfect not just for me, but for Olympus. For she will not only preside over my home, but over all of you. I have never met anyone like Stevie. She is selfless. Brave. Utterly and completely lacking in pretense. My time with her gave me a window into an experience that I had never had before. And I knew that there could be no other perfect person to rule alongside me as Queen when the time comes."

And then it was Stevie's turn. "I'm Stevie. From Montana, in the USA. And I am honored to marry Prince Adonis. And to be a princess." That was the end of her script. But she took a breath, and continued on. "I'm in love with him. And I intend to express that love by giving back to all of you in the way that he does. By loving this country the way that he does. Because he is simply the most amazing man I've ever met. And… I just think it's important to say that."

He looked around, at all of the cameras, all of the people in front of them. They were speechless. What she had said had been so artless and informal, and he could see as the moments went on that they were…captivated by her.

They moved away from the balcony, to resounding applause.

"Very well done," he said.

He personally didn't react to what she had said, because

it had simply been an expedient thing to say, he was certain. But their audience had loved it.

He had liked it more than he would have expected.

Wished it were…

No. There was no point thinking that way.

They were bundled into a car, and then taken to the end of a road lined with well-wishers. They got out and began to walk down the line of people. Waving, stopping to talk.

Stevie got down at eye level with the children. At some point, he saw her engaged in a very serious discussion with a man about wages, and then with a woman about the cost of food. Stevie didn't just listen, she engaged. She shared her own experiences. She could do more than sympathize, she could empathize. Because she had also had worries about feeding her family. About budgets. It made him feel…unequal to the task before him. Because the person who truly understood it was the one the world would look at and say wasn't born into the position. And yet, he felt he was the imposter. Not her.

She was caring and forthright. She was real. More real than he had ever been.

And he wondered if living with him… He worried, if it would suffocate her.

When they finished with the parade, he watched her family interact at dinner. His father sat at the head of the table, clearly baffled by this turn of events. This noisy palace when for years it had been so quiet.

Stevie smiled, and it did something to him.

"May I speak to you?" his father asked.

"Yes."

He turned to Stevie. "I'll see you after dinner."

Her cheeks turned pink.

"What is it?" he asked his father once they were outside the dining room.

"You've chosen well. She is definitely what the people want. The reaction to her has been overwhelmingly positive. Your instincts proved to be better than mine in this instance."

His father's words fortified him. "I'm pleased," he said.

"You will have to be careful with her, though. Because she is…vivacious."

"You think I haven't noticed that?"

"I have concerns."

"Of course you do," he said. "But Stevie will never go back on what she has promised to do."

As soon as he said that, he realized it was true. Stevie would honor every promise that she had ever made. It was who she was.

She would stay with him even if she was miserable. Abjectly and completely.

That was the truth of it. Because she had promised. And she was not his mother. She would never abandon their children. She would never go off seeking her own fortune. No. She would sublimate her own wants and needs just like she had done in her own family.

The realization flummoxed him.

He didn't have to worry about her leaving him. What he had to worry about was that he would crush her. His mother had been a bird in a cage, but she had been more than willing to make her own escape. But that wasn't how Stevie lived. When she made a vow, she kept it.

He had seen her do so with her family. Even though the responsibility of it all had been crushing. And with this… She would do it to. She would stay. She would stay and she would make herself ill with unhappiness. If he let her.

I love him...

But that couldn't be true. It couldn't be.

"I'm proud of you."

His father clapped him on the shoulder, and as he walked down the corridor, he was overcome with a sense of disquiet. He walked into his bedroom, and found that Stevie was there waiting for him.

"Hello," he said.

"Hi."

"My father approves of you."

"Well. I'm very glad to hear that."

"I would have married you anyway," he said.

He began to take his clothes off, and made his way toward the bed.

Stevie let the covers fall away, and revealed her shapely figure. How he wanted her. It surpassed anything. He had been honest with her when he said he didn't typically know the women that he had sexual relationships with. And, of course, it was in all that was always inevitable that he would know his wife in that way. But he had never imagined... He had never imagined his wife being somebody that he wanted. He had always thought that duty would be the main driver. And yet. With her, the possibility for something more existed.

And yet. And yet he wondered if he could give her what she needed.

Or if he was simply consigning her to an incomplete life.

She looked up at him, her expression luminous. How was it that only weeks ago he had not known this woman?

He could not fathom it.

His life had changed, and he had changed. Perhaps it was the near-death experience. Perhaps it was just the experience. Or maybe it was her.

And one thing he did know, was that he needed to change. Maybe he needed to let himself be changed by her. Though the very idea…made him feel like he was standing on the edge of a cliff. Because hadn't his father been changed by his mother, and to what effect?

Hadn't he been changed by his mother?

He sat down on the edge of the bed. "What you did today was extraordinary."

"I don't know that I feel it was extraordinary. I just listened to people."

"They don't teach you how to do that."

"In prince school?"

He laughed, and let his knuckles drift over one of her breasts. "No. They don't. I was taught a great many things. I told you. I had my nanny. Who was quite firm with me. I didn't learn to listen, though, I learned to give people what they wanted. On the surface. I was quite expert at that. I wondered sometimes if I would've known how to do that before my mother left if she would've stayed."

"Your mother didn't leave because of you."

He nodded slowly. "It isn't important."

"Why do you think it's not important? It comes up all the time. It is your reason for so many things."

He frowned. She wasn't wrong. But he didn't like it being trotted out before him like that.

"It's the whole reason for your image. For all of your incorrigible behavior. You know that. You do. Why, then, are you afraid to admit it?"

"Because I don't want to be affected by anything. But I recognize that I am. After all, I did cultivate this whole persona to get all eyes on me. I don't suppose I ever learned how to be much more than a persona. Maybe that's the real reason I didn't tell you my name. Maybe it wasn't so much that I wanted to see you treat me as a real person. I wanted to feel like a real person. One who wasn't performing. One who wasn't on notice."

"I know what it's like," she said. "You have your life decided for you. Yours was decided by birth, mine was decided by tragedy. It makes it hard to know who you are."

"I know who I am," he said.

"Do you?"

The words were cutting, concerning. Closer to the bone than he would've liked.

"It doesn't matter, does it? The philosophy of the purpose of man is for men who don't have purpose. And there are many rich men who don't. I do. It is to serve this country."

"Now that your purpose isn't throwing yourself in your mother's face at every opportunity?"

"Indeed."

"But don't you think there's something in there? Something that you need to…dissect?"

His lip curled. "No. I don't. At least, nothing of any value or virtue."

"Virtue probably isn't your strong point."

He growled, and pushed her so she was lying on her back, and then he was over the top of her. "What did you see in me, Stevie? That night that you let me make love to you. When you had no idea who I was."

"Well. You were very sexy."

"You wanted me for my body?"

"Your body didn't hurt. I knew that you were a powerful man," she said. "There was something about you. I was drawn to you. I saw you first when you were sitting in the back of the bar. And, of course, I thought you were stunningly handsome."

"You didn't recognize me," he said, and he felt something

like desperation clawing at his chest. "So who did you think I was? Really. The heart of me. If I were to go out and meet my citizens for the first time, what would I show them?"

She frowned. "You showed them you today. You were…"

"I was a cardboard cutout. A stand-in. My name, my reputation, all of those things precede me. You met them fresh. You met them where they were, and I don't know how to do that because I don't know where I am." He shook his head. "It's that I want to build something. Something real. For my people. It is important."

He realized that it was perhaps absurd, having her pinned to the mattress, her breasts bare, as he demanded answers to the difficult question of *who he was*.

But he wanted to know whom she saw. When she had decided to call him Clem. When she had seen him unconscious, bleeding, and had saved his life. When she had kissed him that last night. When they had danced together. When they'd had nothing, and somehow it had become everything. He had no power there. And yet there had been a peace… A peace that he didn't feel outside of that place, and he wanted to figure out why.

"Adonis," she said softly, reaching up and touching his face. "You were powerful and strong, and yet I felt safe with you. You were incapacitated, and yet you made me feel cared for. And yes, there's something… Something that I can't even explain. A magical feeling of just being drawn to you. Montana was home all my life, but I saw you, and suddenly something fit into place that wasn't there before. And it was like you became home. When I said that I loved you today, I wasn't simply spouting a line for the benefit of the press. I really meant it. I really mean it. I love you. I love you because of everything. And it's hard to make a list. It's hard to quantify. It's hard to say why. Except that I didn't think that I would ever find this. I didn't even know that I wanted it. Because my father made love look like pain. So I didn't think that I… It hasn't been pain with you."

God. He felt…undone. She had said that she didn't want love, and now she was really professing hers to him? She had said that love had always looked like pain, and she was trusting him to make it not painful, when he didn't even know where to begin. He didn't know where to begin.

He felt wrecked by that. Utterly and completely.

Worse than the plane.

Worse than anything.

She would stay. She would stay unhappy and miserable. She would stay.

And yet, he had just introduced her to his people. He had just trotted around his next princess. She had to stay. He needed her. He needed her to show him who he was. To show him the way. Without her, what would he do?

"You can't love me," he said.

"But I do," she said. "I just do. Trust me. I'm a pilot."

He laughed. In spite of himself. Because it was such an absurd thing to say, and Stevie was rarely absurd. "Why does that make you an expert in this?"

"I'm very good in high-pressure situations. Also in navigating. Also… You just have to trust me."

"But how?"

It was a question about everything. How he could trust her, how she could love him.

How. When his own mother didn't even.

"Maybe we have to chalk it up to being one of life's mysteries."

"I don't want to be a mystery," he said, knowing that he sounded slightly petulant. "I have… I have seen and done so many things. I slept with more women than I can count."

"I really don't like it when you say things like that."

"You have to understand. Why I find it frustrating. I've traveled the world, had an enormous amount of sex. I am very famous."

"Yes, yes," she said. "And yet, I didn't recognize you."

"I didn't recognize you either," he said.

And somehow when he said it, it took on a whole different meaning.

"Yes, I know. Because there was no reason for you to."

He growled.

"You're in a very bad mood," she said.

"I'm not. I simply want to understand."

He didn't know what was driving him. He didn't know why he was so desperate. All he knew was that if you didn't understand, he wouldn't be able to…trust it. Not it or anything. That was simply how it was.

"You know, I don't know how other people make these decisions. But I know that I lived through something with you that very few people have ever experienced. And when I didn't have you, when it had been two weeks and I hadn't heard from you at all, when I thought you were going to marry somebody else, I was miserable. I miss you. So maybe I can't say why. And maybe I can't make you understand. But maybe… Maybe, with all the sex that you had, and all the traveling you've done, you have to accept that there are just some mysteries out there that you can't quantify. Because if you could have, you would have. Right?"

"No," he growled. "That can't be true."

"Adonis, I love you."

He felt soothed. And yet… And yet.

But he could do nothing but kiss her. Nothing but stop the conversation. Nothing but strip the covers away and decide to make love to her. Because he wanted her. Because he wanted this to go on. Because he didn't want it to end. Because he was utterly and completely obsessed with her. And obsessed with the fact that she loved him.

He wanted to hoard it. Like a greedy dragon. Hold it in his talons and keep it for himself. He wanted to offer nothing in return, because it made him feel secure. Because it made him feel like he had all the power.

Because it made him feel like he did when he knew he had created a scandal that would be in the headlines worldwide and his mother would have to see it. Yes. It gave him power in the face of love. And all love ever asked of you is that you be weak for it. He refused.

So he kissed her. Made love to her. Until she was crying out his name.

And he decided that everything else could wait. Because tonight he had her. Tonight he had her love. Tonight, he had won.

CHAPTER FOURTEEN

ADONIS WAS ALWAYS a demanding lover, but last night he had kept her up the entire night.

She decided to convalesce in the library, feeling sore and a bit raw. But really, that wasn't about the sex. It was about the fact that she had told him that she loved him, and he had said nothing at all in return.

It was very lowering.

She was trying to give to him. She was trying to understand him.

But it was difficult. He had been petulant last night, almost. Like a moody child.

But she could see that his desperation to unlock the mystery of her love was very real.

She frowned, as she looked down into her tea. Did he really not understand why somebody might love him? Had his life really been that lonely? That…barren? Perhaps it had been. Perhaps he had never really been…cared for.

His father was…distant. She found that she quite liked him. But she wondered if he had been not the most loving father. At least outwardly. She understood that. Her own father had done his best, but he had been lost in his grief.

At midday, she decided to stop feeling sorry for herself, and she wandered around the palace. Her sisters were in various rooms, reading, watching movies, playing games.

She looked into one of the sitting rooms and saw her father, sitting with the King.

She paused in the doorway. They were talking with each other. Her heart squeezed tight.

Both of those men had been very hurt by love and loss. Even if in different ways.

And they had passed that pain down to their children, even though they hadn't meant to. It didn't mean she didn't love her father. She did. But he had stopped functioning when her mother had died. And now, even with the best of intentions…

He was dying. His own behavior had sent him to his deathbed. That was a difficult pill to swallow.

Very difficult indeed.

She knew that it was probably the same for Adonis. He clearly respected his father greatly, or he wouldn't wish so badly to make him proud, to rule the kingdom in a way that would do his legacy proud. But, there was also a lot of anger surrounding his mother, and he couldn't fully believe that his mother had been entirely at fault. Adonis was too smart. He had been sent off to the nanny because he had been unruly…

He had definitely been lacking in meaningful connections. That much was so abundantly clear.

She wanted to protect him. The boy that he'd been.

The man he was now.

She felt all the complexity inside of her, the strange affection for the men in front of her, along with her disappointment that they hadn't been able to do better by their children.

It was such a strange thing, that she and this Prince had been born a world apart, so many layers of wealth apart. Many years apart, and yet, they had been through so many of the same things.

She moved away from the door, her heart pounding.

She went into the dining room, and found that a table with a lunch spread had been set out, made for any of them to grab their own plates, and so she began to make herself sandwiches, and then went and sat at the foot of the table.

She was chewing rather contemplatively when Adonis came in.

"There you are," he said. "I had to ask around with the staff to ascertain your whereabouts."

"I've been having a bit of a lazy day."

"Good. Does that make you happy?"

"Yes. Thank you. And also, my sisters being so well cared for. Our fathers sitting and having a conversation."

He raised a brow. "Are they really?"

"Yes. You know, I was thinking about our discussion last night. And I think the thing that you're discounting is fate. Because what were the odds? What were the odds that you and I met at that airport? That you hadn't managed to snap your princely fingers and come up with an even better alternative to getting to your wedding than using my plane. I think that's an impossibility. And it's the thing that you can't reason."

"I don't believe in fate."

"Why not?"

He shook his head. "Because it takes the choice out of it."

"I don't think that accepting that fate can have a hand in something takes the choice out of everything. If you take fate out of the equation, then you take out magic."

"Maybe I don't believe in magic."

"Okay. You, the Prince do not believe in magic. You have a literal castle, and have, so I've heard, had an endless number of lovers, and also been many places. Which I suspect feels quite a lot like magic."

"Was it fate, then, for my mother to abandon me?"

"We need to contend with that," she said. "What are you going to do about your mother's abandonment?"

"Excuse me?"

"You need to do something about it, Adonis. Either have a confrontation with her or let it go. What are you going to do? Create scandal after scandal for the rest of your life? After the sensation of our wedding fades, then what? Am I going to have to look forward to you doing something abominable in order to get back in the headlines when you're feeling unwell about it?"

"Have I done anything of the kind since we met?"

"No. But you… Yes, when I met you my first impression of you was that you were a very powerful man. And you are. But you're also a walking raw wound. And I think that I might be the same. I understand that. I hid mine underneath layers of practicality. Under an inability to let people get close to me, to show any vulnerability. But I'm letting myself feel it now. Some of the anger. My father didn't do the right thing by me. And I love him. I can acknowledge the complication of that. It's difficult. It's okay to be hurt, and still love somebody."

"Yes. I have already acknowledged that tension with my mother, thank you."

"Have you spoken to her?"

"Of course not. Why would I speak to the person who abandoned me?"

"Because. Because you either have to let her go completely, or you have to deal with it, because if you don't it's going to eat you alive."

"Maybe I want to be eaten alive. Maybe I want the reminder."

"But it's why you can't love me. And I had to start dealing with the reason that I couldn't love you."

"Maybe I just don't love you."

His gaze was cruel then, and it hurt, but she knew that it wasn't because what he had said was true. That was how he was handling his own pain. She let out a long, slow breath.

"I don't think that's true. Because you were very worried about catching feelings for me, so I don't actually think that you actually don't have feelings at all."

"You know, we have a country to run, and these are small, petty things."

"It isn't petty. I don't want to just be the Princess, I want to be your wife. And I was trying to accept the fact that it couldn't be that way, but now I question why. Because I was a regular girl who met a prince. And that's miraculous in and of itself. But you know what else is miraculous? The two of us meeting. The two of us finding each other. It's an extremely unlikely twist of events. And maybe you don't want to call it fate, but dammit all, make a choice with this gift that's been given to us."

He looked like he wanted to say something, but then he didn't. Instead, he turned and walked from the room, and left her there with her sandwich.

He was his father. The hard, harsh realization of that was like a gut punch.

He was his father. He was consigning her to a miserable life where she couldn't get what she needed. And she would stay. That had been bearable before he had known that she loved him. But realizing that he was imprisoning her, separating her from the feelings that she wanted, that was what made it untenable.

Sending her away would hurt her. And he hated that. Keeping her here would destroy her, it would quite literally clip her wings. And that was the thing he could not endure.

Yes, he had promised her to his people. But she had saved his life. And he owed her.

He didn't believe in fate. But he believed that people could make terrible choices that resulted in collateral damage.

His mother had done it, his father had done it. He wasn't absolving his mother by acknowledging that his father had been a bad match for her, but... He didn't want to create the same situation. To repeat the same cycle. He couldn't bear it.

Or perhaps you're afraid...

No. He wasn't afraid.

He was simply... He was trying to protect her. That was all. He was trying to do the right thing.

But he would... He would make sure that she was taken care of. He was not holding luxury hostage. He would never do that. He would make sure that her sisters were always cared for. That she had a soft life. That she had a library. But she would be free to find another man. To have a garden. To fly a plane. She could be Stevie, as he had met her, but better, instead of Stevie, squeezing to fit into a box that she never asked to be in, in the first place, and loving a man who couldn't give her what she wanted in return. Maybe she was right. Maybe it would be better for him if he could forgive his mother, let her go, have a confrontation with her, but he didn't want to change. Because the way that he was, the things that he was, kept him...safe.

She had saved his life. He owed her nothing less in return.

She'd caused him pain, dressing his wound. Sometimes pain was a kindness. As it saved you from greater catastrophe. It would be so with this.

But when he walked into the library and found her there, and she looked up at him with a glowing expression on her face, he faltered. He didn't want to be the one to take that glow away.

But he would be. Over years. As she tried and tried to fit into a life that wasn't for her.

A life that he knew didn't expand to fit those who were in it.

"Stevie, I must speak with you."

"Okay, it's a good start, because you're talking."

"I've been thinking. And I do not come to this conclusion with any great relish. But I think… I think I made a mistake. In asking you to be my princess."

He was right. The expression on her face was like being shot. He would go down in a plane one hundred times, have his leg cut clean through, to avoid experiencing this ever again. That meant he was doing the right thing, though. It had to. Because it was self-sacrificial. Because it was so painful. It had to be. It had to be.

"What are you talking about?"

"This isn't the life for you. You do well with the people, but the rest of it… It will not work. This is how it was with my mother, and in the end, it only caused pain. For all involved. I have realized that I am more my father than I initially thought, and I do not think—"

"I don't believe you. I think you're pushing me away because you need to protect yourself. Because you don't like that I said I loved you. Because you are bound and determined to turn that into an insurmountable hill. One you can't climb."

"This is exactly why it won't work. You cannot even listen to me when I speak."

"Because you lied. To yourself as much as anybody. You lie. I know what we have together. How can you say all of these things?"

"Because… Because it is true. Because maybe if we were just two people who were in a plane crash together, who met on the side of a mountain, this would be different, but it's not, and neither are we. We are nothing more or less than what we were born to be. You're a pilot. A good one. You're a caregiver. And astonishingly worthy one. I am a prince. And the role that my princess will play is a prescriptive one. Ask my mother, who felt hampered by it for those years. It is not an easy life to ask someone to live."

"Maybe not. Maybe not, but isn't… Isn't it reasonable to think that if you have enough love it will become easier? Because I've lived a life that couldn't be described as easy. But I had my family. I had love. And that's why I do it. That's why I do any of it."

"But someone should do something for you."

"This isn't for me, Adonis. You're doing it for you. I told you that you needed to figure out how to heal, but you would rather wound yourself all over again. It's like if you continued to stick a log into that cut in your leg. How are you supposed to heal? You won't let it. It does a disservice to you. To me. To us."

"All right, then. Maybe that's it. Maybe it's as simple as that. You need someone who will heal. And I don't know how. And so, this cannot be. It cannot. Don't worry, I have purchased a house for your family…"

"We have a house," she said. "We were never charity cases, we were never asking to be."

"Let me," he said. "Let me, please. Because this is… Because I want to fix it. Because I don't want to have given your sisters a taste of this life and then take it away. That's not what I'm trying to do."

"You want to be the hero of the story," she said. "Heroes are brave, Adonis. And you are a coward. It's as simple as that. You cannot redeem it. Not when you're so patently making the wrong choice."

"You think that I have the capability to love. Perhaps I don't. In the same way that I don't have the capability to heal. Did it ever occur to you?"

"No. Because the man I met on the hill, Clem, I was pretty sure that man could survive anything. Once you were here, once you had all this baggage, once you had to be you, that's when I saw your difficulty. But it's all hiding. Out of habit. I don't hide. So maybe you're right. Maybe this can't be. Maybe we can't be.

"But I love you all the same, and I want to make sure you know that. Because you haven't had enough people in your life tell you that they love you, at least I don't think so. Because I'm not even sure you know what it is. So if you are lying in bed at night, with one of your many, many lovers, years after I'm gone, and you wish that you knew what it felt like to be loved, I want you to remember that once you did. But you weren't brave enough to let yourself have it."

It was Stevie who stormed out. She did not have to be thrown out. And he was the one who felt small and fractured. And yet resolute all the same.

She thought that there was another way.

There wasn't.

She was only a pilot. And he was a prince. Eventually, she would understand. Eventually, she would thank him.

CHAPTER FIFTEEN

STEVIE FELT HALF-DEAD. The house that he had bought for them in Montana was gorgeous. Her sisters and her father were happy enough with it, even if they were all baffled by the sudden change. But everybody was tiptoeing around her, refusing to question it. She knew why. They felt like if it had been her choice nobody could express disappointment that they'd had to move back to icy, snowy Montana rather than remain in Olympus.

Everyone was concerned about her.

She was annoyed about it. Because she wanted to rant and rave about her broken heart, but she also didn't want her family to feel guilty.

It was Daisy who finally came and found her one afternoon while she was brooding at the kitchen table and drinking tea, looking out at the vast, glorious mountain view below.

It really was a beautiful house.

"Are you ever going to talk about what happened?"

"There isn't any point."

"Isn't there? It's something that happened to you."

"But... I don't want any of you to be upset."

"But you're upset. Don't you understand that matters? Don't you understand that your feelings are important?"

She scowled. "No. I have to take care of everybody."

"No you don't. And for a while, he took care of you. And it really is terrible that you lost that."

She felt her heart began to crack. She felt tears begin to spill down her cheeks. She laid her head down on the table. "I loved him, Daisy. I still do."

"Why did you leave?"

"It was him. He sent us away. He... He doesn't want to love me. He's afraid to. But I think he does. And I'm afraid... Just saying that out loud sounds silly. Like I'm full of myself. Like he had to send me away because his love for me would be too powerful and he couldn't control it. It sounds ridiculous."

"No, Stevie. It doesn't." Daisy sat down at the table and put her hand over Stevie's arm. "It doesn't sound ridiculous. Because you are that amazing. Can't you accept it? You have that prince running scared because he's never felt anything like it, because he's never met anything like you."

She blinked. She had wanted to feel special. Maybe not like this. But suddenly, she did. Because she, Stevie Parker, of Bozeman, Montana, had been too much for that playboy prince, with all his lovers, and all his travel, to handle.

She was special. She was.

Tears spilled down her cheek, and she huffed out a laugh. "Well. I'll be damned."

"Look what you did, Stevie." Daisy looked around them. "You saved us."

"Maybe I did." She let a sense of pride fill her chest, alongside the pain. "Maybe I did."

Prince Adonis could take an awful lot from her. But he could never take this.

Adonis was jet-lagged and angry by the time he landed in Los Angeles. He didn't know what he was doing here. He blamed Stevie.

But it had been weeks, and he was miserable. Stevie had

sent a message through Miriam that she was not pregnant. Miriam had looked at him like he was the very villain of the tale. He was beginning to feel like he was.

Every time he took a breath, it was like he was being stabbed with a dagger, and would a hero hurt quite so much over his own decisions? He had no way of knowing.

But without even really thinking it through, he ended up making a plan to go to Los Angeles and find his mother.

It wasn't difficult, of course. It was a matter of having the right people liaise with one another and make a meeting spot that was agreeable to both parties.

His mother had insisted it be high-profile. He found it irritating, and yet… It was the relationship he had cultivated with her. Revenge through headlines. So perhaps he deserved it. But now they would be meeting, and it would create buzz for her.

He had never wanted buzz less.

But still, he found himself walking out onto the terrace of a well-known restaurant that overlooked the ocean. And there she was, seated at the table, wearing a large, wide-brimmed hat, sunglasses on her face. As if she didn't want to be recognized, but was screaming it so loudly everyone was certain to look and make their best attempt to do so.

"Adonis," she said. "It has been a very long time."

"Yes. I believe I was a child."

He sat down at the table, feeling tense. Feeling…no connection to the woman sitting across from him. Why was he here?

"Yes. You were."

She took her sunglasses off. Her blue eyes matched his, and they were unreadable. Did she feel anything looking at him?

"I came to tell you that I am angry with you."

"Did you?"

She took a sip of her water.

"Yes. You abandoned me. When I was a child."

"I did," she said. And for a moment, he thought he saw a sheen of tears in her eyes. But just like that, they were gone. "Adonis, I made a decision. And whether you believe it or not, there's no negotiating custody with royalty. I decided to make a different life. But the life had to be separate. It was a decision that I made."

"Do you ever regret it?"

"It doesn't matter," she said. "All we have is the life we chose to live. Regrets don't solve anything, do they?"

Except, they did. Because he had them. Because he hurt. And he wanted her to hurt alongside him.

Because he… He wanted to know that everything he had done over these last years had made an impact on her. Had made some kind of difference. And he realized that was…a truly pointless sentiment to carry around inside of him. To wish pain on somebody because they had made him feel wounded. Maybe it was fair, maybe it was even understand-able. But… Why?

"Are you saying my father wouldn't allow you to see me?"

"Adonis, do you want your relationship with your father to change?"

"He's *dying*," Adonis said. "That will change things any-way."

"And all you will have is your memories. What's the point of damaging them?"

"The point is, that I would know the truth."

"Of course he wanted you to have the ability. That was how he presented it. And he didn't want to see me. I hurt him. But the end result was our total estrangement. But I accepted it. And because of that, I have to own the pain that it caused. I suppose."

"We can make a decision about whether or not we see each other now," Adonis said.

"Of course. You never seemed as if you wanted to."

"I didn't. I wanted to hurt you. The way that you hurt me."

"Adonis," she said, looking down, and then back up. "You never hurt me. You were a child. And you were caught in the middle of something complicated. Seeing you in the headlines, I hoped that you were having a happy life. I enjoyed seeing pictures of you. And I liked to think that perhaps you had a little bit of fun because of me. I know you didn't get it from your father."

That rocked him. Took a knife and twisted it in his chest. His mother had made up a story that made her feel better, about what he was doing. He had been acting out because of her.

But not for the reason she thought. And he didn't feel any triumph over any of it. He didn't want to have hurt her, actually. Because what he was staring at was the impossibility of two people who hadn't been able to deal with themselves on a deep enough level to stop their actions from hurting their child. From hurting themselves. His father had been sadder for having lost his mother. His mother had been... sadder for having lost him.

And Adonis found he didn't have the stomach to try and make anything more painful. Suddenly, he felt like a burden was being lifted from within him. He didn't look at his mother and see somebody shallow. He saw a beautiful, fragile woman who had done her very best to construct a new life with the tools she had been left.

Wasn't that what they all were doing?

Him. His father. Stevie. Weren't they all just trying their hardest with what they had been given?

Except... He had chosen fear. And that was very like his father. When he could've opened things up, changed them, to make his wife happy, to make there be a two-way relationship, he hadn't done it. Because he hadn't been able to get past his own pain, and hadn't Adonis just done the same to Stevie?

"I'm getting married," he said. "And I want you to be there."

His mother looked shocked. "I thought your engagement was off."

"Not if I have anything to say about it. My next stop is going to be her. But... If she says yes, I want you to come."

"Your father won't be happy."

"Then he'll have to be unhappy. I think everyone has been far too unhappy for too long. Something has to change. And somebody has to take the first step. It wasn't going to be me. But Stevie... Stevie told me that I needed to fix this. Because I have let it decide who I am for far too long. She was right."

"Adonis... Go and get her. So that I can be at your wedding."

"I will. And... Mother, I hope to see you there."

Stevie was planting flowers in a pot. No, she wouldn't be able to put them outside yet, but it felt like a defiant thing to do. To plant new life in the face of all this icy cold. In the face of the dead, stagnant feelings in her heart. She would not be crushed. Of that she was certain.

She was so committed to her endeavor that she didn't hear the door open. But there he was then, standing there like an apparition. Like a flower in the snow.

"Adonis…"

"Stevie, I came to tell you that I did what you said. I went and saw my mother."

The rush of dizziness and relief that she felt was inexplicable. Because he hadn't said anything about the two of them. And yet. She knew it was connected. She did.

"Oh."

"It was in the media, but I'm certain that you didn't see it, because you don't care about that. And you never did."

"I didn't," she said. "I only ever cared about…" She felt her heart begin to fracture. "I only ever cared about you."

"I know," he said, kneeling down where she was, putting his hand over hers, over the potting soil. "I know. And I cared about you, but I didn't know what to do. I chose the fearful thing. What felt like the easier thing? And I told myself that because it hurt it was the right thing. I think I inherited a streak of martyrdom from my father. I regret embracing that. I thought that because I lived a seemingly indulgent life I was not like my father. But I am. Inflexible, self-protective. Though, perhaps even more truthfully, I've taken pieces from my mother and my father, and fashioned them into a wholly unique, dysfunctional human being who doesn't know how to give or receive love. But I want to. Because I do love you. I didn't know how to accept that you loved me. I didn't know how to show it. But it matters. It matters so much. Because I can't live without you. And I don't want to. I don't want to continue on this legacy of isolation. I want you to marry me. And I swear to you, I'm not going back on my word, not again."

Stevie believed him. Because now it was easy. Because now she knew. Her own power, the power of what was between them. Because somehow, she felt stronger for having had to face the loss of them. It hadn't destroyed her. It had hurt. But she had come out with even more love for herself, and because of that, it made it easy to accept what he offered now.

"Yes," she said. "I want that. I don't care about being your princess. I want to be your wife. Because I love you."

"I love you too. It is as gloriously simple as that."

"And yet very, very complicated," she said.

"Yes. But you know, I think we can handle it. Because for all that we are very different, we are also the same. The same heart."

"Yeah," she said. "We are."

"Do you think that you…could fly us to the wedding?"

She tilted her head back and laughed. "I mean, are you sure about that? You don't think we might end up on a mountainside again?"

"If we did, I'd marry you there. In fact, I think maybe I should."

EPILOGUE

ADONIS ANDREADIS HAD always thought his wedding would be extravagantly beautiful. But he hadn't imagined it on the side of a snowy mountain in the middle of the wilderness, with only spare few people in attendance, and his mother sitting proudly at the front, watching as he pledged his life to the woman of his dreams.

Their fathers were there also, seated together, best friends now against all odds, and defying the prognosis their doctors had given.

They were both determined to live to see their grandchildren.

This was his life. This was his wedding.

His entire life had changed the day that he had met Stevie Parker in a frozen airport.

And he was grateful for it.

Because he had always been a prince, powerful, wealthy. He had traveled the world, he had had many lovers, Stevie liked to remind him of that, as a form of punishment for the number of times he had mentioned it to her previously.

But he had never truly learned anything, had never really changed, until he had met her.

And she had changed the course of everything.

It was, he realized, fate.

But the thing about fate was you did still have to make a choice. You had to take hold of it.

And so when the minister said it was time to kiss the bride, he did just that. He wrapped his arms around her, and kissed her with all the love inside of him.

"What are you thinking?" she whispered.

"I'm giving thanks. To the mountain that brought us together, and to the woman who saved my life."

"You saved mine too."

"But you saved mine in more ways than one."

"That is true," she said smiling. "I did."

* * * * *

If you just couldn't get enough of
His Highness's Diamond Decree,
then be sure to check out
these other passion-fueled stories
by Millie Adams!

The Forbidden Bride He Stole
Greek's Forbidden Temptation
Her Impossible Boss's Baby
Italian's Christmas Acquisition
Billionaire's Bride Bargain

Available now!

Turn the page for a preview of
Millie Adams's latest story
for Mills & Boon Modern

Billionaire's Bride Bargain

CHAPTER ONE

The Pitbull is on board.

SHE SENT THE text off quickly.

Woof.

That was the response from Irinka, which was *liked* by the rest of the chat.

Auggie, short for Augusta, looked down at her phone and allowed her lips to twitch, just slightly. Then she looked up at her boss and his current companion of choice.

Auggie didn't judge women for associating with Matias.

A light shone upon him.

He was the single most beautiful man Auggie had ever seen. Tall and broad-shouldered, with hair black as a raven's wing, and eyes like the night sky. They were different sorts of black, she had always thought.

The raven's wing spoke to the glossy, sleek nature of his hair.

The night sky spoke to the perils of space and the inevitable destruction a woman might face if she were to be pulled into his orbit.

Still, though, she couldn't blame the woman.

Matias was responsible for his own appalling behavior.

Though the media enabled him, in her humble opinion.

Glorious Golden Retriever Matias Balcazar
Seen Out and About With New Woman!

Golden retriever, her well-rounded behind.

The man was a pitbull.

He would eat your children.

It was how he'd gotten his nickname in the group text, which was appropriately named Work Wives.

Because Irinka, Lynna and Maude were her work wives. And best friends. They'd started Your Girl Friday five years earlier with nothing but a dream, fantastic organizational skills and determination, and it was thriving now.

They were freelance assistants who operated with the utmost discretion. They assisted the richest of the rich with their lives, from managing their personal affairs—Irinka's specialty—to providing culinary brilliance—Lynna—to the rehabilitation and management of the elaborate grounds of ancient estates—Maude.

Auggie was not as specialized as her friends. She was a wrangler, of sorts. An assistant of all kinds. Currently, for Matias, she was his air stewardess. But he spent all his time jet setting around the world in a private plane, and that meant she functioned as a traveling secretary too.

And whether he knew it or not, she did her best to keep his secrets.

She was—happily—coming to the end of her contract with him. Your Girl Friday wasn't designed to ensnare them into full-time employment for one person. So when a job was all-encompassing it had a hard limit. Six months. But her contract with Matias was only for three.

Praise be.

She could tell the exact moment he perceived her. One of

her greatest assets was her ability to function as wallpaper in whichever surroundings she currently occupied.

She was a chameleon.

One who had been spotted by the Pitbull.

She ignored the way that it affected her. The way that her stomach went tight when his dark eyes met hers. For heaven's sake, he had *a woman on his arm*. He was her boss—even if for a set period of time. And she... Well, she knew him. She might well be the only person on the planet who did. The image that they painted of him in the media was laughable.

Matias Javier Hernandez Balcazar, beloved by all, was the son of Javier Balcazar, the most ruthless Spanish billionaire in recent times. A man wholly uninterested in ethics, in kindness, in basic human decency. A conquistador of the modern era, and on and on.

There were really only a couple of things a person needed to know about Matias to know him.

The first was that he could not be told. He did whatever he wanted, whenever he wanted, as befitted his position as a billionaire. The second was that he hated his father. And from those two pieces of information flowed the truth.

The media spun a story of his life that just didn't make sense, not when you had met the real Matias.

Somehow, they saw his entry into his own father's industry as him taking what he had learned and building something with it. Not what it actually was. A cold-eyed attempt at taking over his family business and crushing it. She was certain that was what he was up to.

Of course, everyone imagined that he stood to inherit his father's wealth.

Auggie thought that the truth was perhaps slightly more complicated. Though she didn't have all the details, she knew that the truth of the matter was, Matias was anything but what he seemed.

"Augusta," he said, his accent rolling over the syllables of her name in a way that made her want to purr. "Could you get myself and Charmaine a drink?"

"Of course," she said, smiling like the decorative femme bot she was supposed to be and moving to the bar, anticipating exactly what he would have, and what the lady would be having. It was easy enough. She smiled as she poured his whiskey, and then mixed up an overly sweet drink with cherries in it for Charmaine.

Then she melted away into the background again, while standing quite in plain sight.

She picked up her phone again.

If I see another headline about what a glorious himbo this man is I will punch the next starry-eyed reporter I see.

Oh, come on, don't spoil the public's fascination with him.

This came from Lynna.

I won't, because I signed an NDA, as you know. But I'm just saying, I don't think I have ever met anyone whose public persona is as big of a lie as his.

Maude chimed in.

That can't be true. Billionaires are notorious liars. They're also usually okay with being the glorious bastards they are in full view of the public.

Is he awful?

That was Irinka asking.

No. But he's not what he seems.

At that point, Charmaine and Matias abandoned their drinks and disappeared into the bedroom at the back of the private plane. The really fun part was when Auggie had to accompany the women back to whatever city they had come from, if Matias had long-term work in the city they were landing in. That didn't happen every time, often transfer would be arranged in a different way, or the woman would stay over in the city, but never long-term with Matias. It really was an amazing trip. He managed to be a shameless womanizer who was loved by all. Even the women that he had finished with.

Nobody could hate him.

It made Auggie even more suspicious of him, frankly. Because that was some black magic. Different than the black of his hair. Different than his eyes. A kind of sorcery that she couldn't quite access.

That was the problem with him. He was *interesting*.

When she had taken the job with him she had been so certain that he would be dull. He was the world's favorite boyfriend, as Irinka had pointed out. He had a reputation for being polite, a generous employer, a man who gave extravagant tips to anyone who served him. He was quick with a smile.

But that smile never reached his eyes.

She put her headphones in because she didn't need to hear anything happening in the adjacent room. No, she did not.

She managed communications for Matias while they were

in the air, and then did some finessing of his schedule. And once the time was appropriate, she put her ear to the bedroom door. And then she opened it slowly. They were both asleep, in bed. She had become very good at simply not looking at the man. Half-dressed, enjoying the aftermath of his liaison. It wasn't her business. He was allowed to conduct himself in whatever way he chose. But she had something she needed to do.

She snagged the woman's phone off of the nightstand and turned it so that it was held up to her face. Then she flinched, swiping up the screen on the unlocked phone, and going to the photos. There were none taken. Thank God. She had deleted pictures of Matias sleeping from multiple women's phones.

There were no photos, but she could see an email banner pop up with some text.

Once you finish with him, I need you to…

And then it cut off.

She sat there and looked at it. And she felt a vague sense of disquiet. Granted, Charmaine could be getting that email about anyone. In any context.

She might not have told anyone she was having a dirty weekend with a hot billionaire.

Auggie hovered her thumb over the email app. She had lines, and boundaries. She didn't invade people's privacy. She didn't go through texts, she didn't surf through all the photos, the only thing she tried to do—historically—was keep Matias's penis off the internet.

This went outside the boundaries of that.

Whatever it is, it isn't your business.

She let out a breath, and placed the phone back, gingerly.

There were no pictures. That was all that mattered. The rest wasn't her problem and couldn't be.

She snuck back out of the room, and not for the first time, gave thanks that she was nearly at the end of all this.

Matias was so much more work than any man she'd ever contracted for. Usually she found her job a delightful challenge. She liked the freshness of having a new client every few months. Typically, what she was doing was giving extra and specialized help while someone increased workload for a new project, or needed help with some image maintenance during a challenging time.

She wasn't PR. But she often worked alongside a PR person to help with the flow of work, so that the subject of her help would look good, efficient, less stressed, etc.

Working with Matias just made her stressed half the time. And strung out on his beauty, which was a complication she'd never experienced before.

When the plane landed in Barcelona, both Matias and Charmaine tumbled out of the bedroom. Looking disheveled, but lovely, both of them.

She wondered if Matias would ever settle down, or if he was destined to remain unattached. He seemed to exist in the eternal now, but she knew that wasn't true. Because a man didn't accidentally become as successful as he was. Not even if he came from a rich family. Because he had not used his father's money to get where he was.

There was just more to him. It constantly surprised her how the world was willing to take his enigmatic smile as the truth. To assume that he was simplistic, because he was happy to let them believe so. To trip through life as a man winning at the lowest difficulty setting. Which more than one person had said about him, and he seemed completely happy to take that on the chin. He was… Pleased to let people think he was a fool.

And that, to her, was the most suspicious thing of all.

"Charmaine will be staying in Barcelona for a couple of days, she wishes to see the offices."

"Oh," Auggie said. "So I won't be making a return trip, then."

That hit her strangely, and she knew it was because of the email.

When you're finished with him...

What had the email said? She was so mad she hadn't read it.

"Are you sure she wants to see your offices?" Auggie asked.

"Yes," he said, looking at her like she was a fool.

Charmaine's eyes clashed with Auggie's, and Auggie knew a moment of deep disquiet. She didn't like the look in the other woman's eyes.

Auggie was a girl's girl. Auggie was all about the freedom and power women had to shag Matias to their heart's content without judgment.

Being a girl's girl, though, meant when she didn't trust a woman, there was a reason.

This was nothing more than a gut feeling, but it was a strong one.

"Matias, can I speak to you for a moment?" she asked.

"No," he said smoothly. "Enjoy the city. I shouldn't need you for a couple of days."

She lifted her brows. "Really."

She didn't like this at all.

"Yes. You only worked for me for three months. I find that I can function just as well without you."

"Indeed." She hesitated. "Matias, I wonder if I should just go to the offices with you?"

"No, that won't be necessary."

Maybe he was a dumb, gorgeous idiot.

She swore Charmaine gave her a small smile before they turned away and began to get off the plane and Auggie was stewing.

She didn't know what Charmaine could do being at Matias's offices, but she just felt…she felt *something* about it.

And it had nothing to do with the fact that every day, every week, Matias got more and more attractive to her.

He was like a beautiful object in an art gallery.

Nice for some, but Auggie couldn't afford him. So she would look, but she would never touch.

She packed up her things and watched as Matias got into a waiting limousine with Charmaine. Auggie was ushered into a town car. She was totally happy with that. Happy with the quiet, and the luxury that surrounded her. She was not happy to be told that she wasn't needed, mostly because she didn't believe it.

The Pitbull is disconcerting.

Why is that? Lynna asked.

Because he has brought a woman to the offices, and he said he doesn't need me.

Well, maybe he is a himbo. Only thinking with the Pitbull downstairs. Perhaps he wants to have her on his desk, Irinka said.

He is most assuredly only thinking with his downstairs brain, but he isn't stupid.

She got to the hotel room that had been reserved for her and set up her computer, and all her peripherals. She opened up Matias's schedule, and her calendar. Then she initiated a video call with the work wives.

"I'm in Barcelona."

"You look fantastic," said Irinka, who was always gorgeous in the most immaculate way.

"Glowing," Maude said. Maude, for her part, had mud

on her cheek. She was wearing dungarees, and was standing out in a field.

"Irritated," said Lynna, who was standing in a large, commercial looking kitchen.

"I am irritated. Because he has deviated from the script, and I don't like it. I'm only glad that this is my last outing with him."

"Your next contract is at least for a shorter amount of time," Lynna said. "And with a slightly less infamous man."

"We need more female clients," Auggie said, feeling full of woe.

"I would be happy to have more female clients," Irinka said, "it's only that men see our pictures and want to hire us. Also, women are happy to break up with their partners on their own. Men are the ones who typically need my services."

Irinka was a dark horse. She always had been. She acted publicly as His Girl Friday's secretary, and their avenue for connection to the rich and elite. But in reality she was a breakup artist for hire, and master of disguise. Her services required discretion, and backdoor connections, and she was an expert at both.

Auggie herself wasn't built for subterfuge. She was too honest. Keeping her opinions to herself when her clients were being ridiculous was hard enough—and also why she spent so much time in their group text.

Lynna was the best chef in the world, in Auggie's opinion. To taste her food was to taste magic. Some women could make a man long for them forever after a night. Lynna did it after a meal.

Maude was a fae thing, more at home in nature than in the city. She had once rescued a mouse from the science lab when they were at uni and had brought it to live in their dorms. Even now, her affinity for nature was her specialty.

Auggie, Lynna and Maude had all been friends since university, even though they were all from very different backgrounds.

Irinka was the illegitimate daughter of a duke, and a rumored Russian spy, and Irinka had inherited wealth, connections and a penchant for mystery. Maude had been an odd girl out, by virtue of her otherworldliness, and Auggie had related to her, because even though it was in a different fashion, Auggie felt like she was from a different world.

The American in the group.

Lynna was from Wales, but raised in Greece, with a wealthy family, who had lost everything while poor Lynna was at university. Her father had died during the horrific aftermath, and all the friends had rallied around Lynna to make sure she could still complete her studies. To make sure she could still have her life.

They'd stayed together after university too—starting His Girl Friday. With their powers combined, like they were Voltron, from the old cartoon. Individually, they were great. Together they were a powerful force. They'd overcome their past adversity and they'd turned it into something successful. Amazing.

Though she wasn't feeling all-powerful at the moment.

Worry nagged at the back of her brain.

"What?" Maude asked.

"I'm just… I don't trust this situation. And I am not his PR person, so this isn't my problem." She thought back to the number of times she had deleted pictures of his body off of women's phones. She had always squinted when she hadn't looked at those photos. Careful not to see more than she should. Also careful to make sure that he didn't end up plastered all over newspapers as naked as the day he was born.

So no, she wasn't his PR person, and he wasn't an *idiot*,

but he did make questionable decisions where women were concerned.

"You don't have to take care of him," Lynna said. "It isn't your job. You're supposed to *assist* him. This isn't... Caregiving."

She said it kindly, but it lodged itself firmly in Auggie's chest all the same.

"I know that."

"You have that look about you. That paranoid look, that says you're attaching life or death stakes to this situation, and he is not..."

"I know he isn't my mother," she said. "Also, he isn't my problem after this. But you know, if he gets into a serious situation while I'm working for him, it is not going to help our business."

"What do you think is going to happen?" Maude asked.

"I don't know. I have a bad feeling about that woman. I have a bad feeling about this situation." She just did. Even if she couldn't say why. And Augusta Fremont had learned years ago to trust her intuition.

She was in Barcelona. And he wasn't her responsibility, her friends were right. She wasn't his babysitter. So she was going to go out, and she was going to have paella. She was going to let Matias sort out his own issues.

Don't miss
Billionaire's Bride Bargain,
*available wherever Mills & Boon Modern books
and ebooks are sold.*

MILLS & BOON®

Coming next month

ROYAL BRIDE DEMAND
LaQuette

'Reigna.' He called her name with quiet strength that let her know he was in control of this conversation. 'I am Jasiri Issa Nguvu of the royal house of Adébísí, son of King Omari Jasiri Sahel of the royal house of Adébísí, crown prince and heir apparent to the throne of Nyeusi.'

Her jaw dropped as her eyes searched for any hint that he was joking. Unfortunately, the straight set of his jaw and his level gaze didn't say, 'Girl, you know I'm just playing with you.' Nope, that was a 'No lies detected' face staring back at her.

'You're…you're a…prince?'

'Not a prince, *the* prince. As the heir to the throne, I stand above all other princes in the royal line.'

She peeled her hand away from the armrest and pointed to herself. 'And that makes me…?'

He continued smoothly as if they were having a normal everyday conversation and not one that was literally life-changing. 'As my wife, you are now Princess Reigna of the royal house of Adébísí, consort to the heir and future queen of Nyeusi.'

Continue reading

ROYAL BRIDE DEMAND
LaQuette

Available next month
millsandboon.co.uk

COMING SOON!

We really hope you enjoyed reading this book.
If you're looking for more romance
be sure to head to the shops when
new books are available on

Thursday 24th
April

To see which titles are coming soon, please visit
millsandboon.co.uk/nextmonth

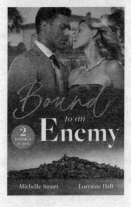
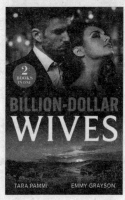

afterglow BOOKS

Afterglow Books is a trend-led, trope-filled list of books with diverse, authentic and relatable characters, a wide array of voices and representations, plus real world trials and tribulations. Featuring all the tropes you could possibly want (think small-town settings, fake relationships, grumpy vs sunshine, enemies to lovers) and all with a generous dose of spice in every story.

♪ @millsandboonuk

⌾ @millsandboonuk

afterglowbooks.co.uk

#AfterglowBooks

For all the latest book news, exclusive content and giveaways scan the QR code below to sign up to the Afterglow newsletter:

SCAN ME

afterglow BOOKS

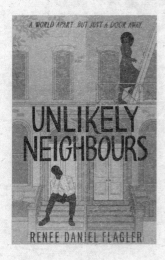

A WORLD APART, BUT JUST A DOOR AWAY

UNLIKELY NEIGHBOURS

RENEE DANIEL FLAGLER

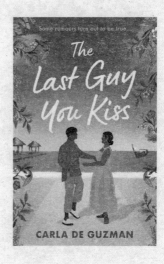

Some rumours turn out to be true...

The Last Guy You Kiss

CARLA DE GUZMAN

- Forced proximity
- Workplace romance
- One night

- International
- Slow burn
- Spicy

OUT NOW

LET'S TALK

Romance

For exclusive extracts, competitions
and special offers, find us online:

[f] MillsandBoon

[X] @MillsandBoon

[○] @MillsandBoonUK

[♪] @MillsandBoonUK

Get in touch on 01413 063 232

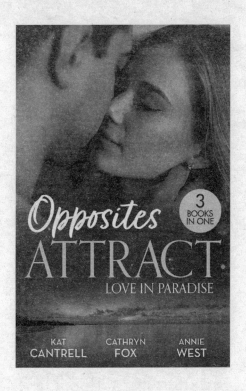

OUT NOW!

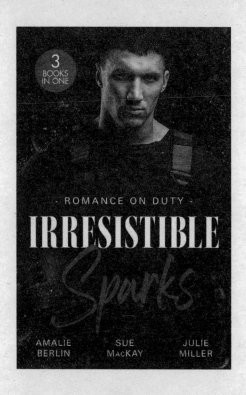

3 BOOKS IN ONE

— ROMANCE ON DUTY —

IRRESISTIBLE
Sparks

AMALIE BERLIN   SUE MacKAY   JULIE MILLER

Available at
millsandboon.co.uk